MARK BILLINGHAM

THE BONES BENEATH

sphere

SPHERE

First published in Great Britain in 2014 by Little, Brown
This paperback edition published in 2015 by Sphere

1 3 5 7 9 10 8 6 4 2

A CIP catalogue record for this book
is available from the British Library.

ISBN 978-0-7515-5220-1

Typeset in Plantin by M Rules
Printed and bound in Great Britain by
Clays Ltd, St Ives plc

Papers used by Sphere are from well-managed forests
and other responsible sources.

MIX
Paper from
responsible sources
FSC
www.fsc.org   FSC® C104740

Sphere
An imprint of
Little, Brown Book Group
100 Victoria Embankment
London EC4Y 0DY

An Hachette UK Company
www.hachette.co.uk

www.littlebrown.co.uk

No.1 bestseller Mark Billingham has twice won the Theakston's Old Peculier Award for Best Crime Novel, and has also won a Sherlock Award for the Best Detective created by a British writer. Each of the novels featuring Detective Inspector Tom Thorne has been a *Sunday Times* bestseller, and *Sleepyhead* and *Scaredy Cat* were made into a hit TV series on Sky 1 starring David Morrissey as Thorne. Mark lives in North London with his wife and two children.

Visit the author's website at: www.markbillingham.com

Praise for the DI Tom Thorne series:

'Billingham is different, and enthralling.
I defy any reader not to be hooked'
Daily Mirror

'Tom Thorne is the most interesting cop in British crime fiction at present' *The Times*

'If you haven't come across DI Thorne, treat yourself.
You won't be disappointed' *Sunday Express*

'With each of his books, Mark Billingham gets better and better. These are stories and characters you don't want to leave' Michael Connelly

'DI Thorne ████████████████████ Slaughter

Also by Mark Billingham

The DI Tom Thorne series
Sleepyhead
Scaredy Cat
Lazybones
The Burning Girl
Lifeless
Buried
Death Message
Bloodline
From the Dead
Good as Dead
The Dying Hours

Other fiction
In the Dark
Rush of Blood

For the little girl who grew up
seeing a lighthouse winking at her across
Cardigan Bay, and never forgot it.

PROLOGUE

WHAT AM I DOING HERE?

He'd thought they were burglars.

Reasonable enough assumption, all things considered. His eyes snapping open at the terrible melody of breaking glass, the creeping downstairs in his dressing gown, the two dark figures so out of place in his tiny white kitchen.

Something about the stillness of them not quite right though, thinking back. The absence of anything even close to panic and the hands thrust deep into pockets, like nobody was in any rush. The way they seemed to be waiting for him.

All so bloody obvious, in hindsight.

He'd thought he could tell what they were looking for. He'd glimpsed something in their flat, wide eyes and guessed that maybe they knew how he earned his living, that they thought there might be stuff lying around the place.

'If it's drugs you're after, you're being stupid,' he'd shouted. 'I don't keep anything like that at *home*.' He'd taken a step towards them, moved into the dim, greenish light to make sure they got a good look at him.

The digital clock on the pristine chrome cooker said 02:37.

'Come on, just piss off and I'll go back to bed and we'll pretend this never happened, fair enough?'

He'd seen the hint of a smile then, the pale face of the

taller one framed by the dark hood. Caught the glance and the nod from the shorter of the two and been shocked to see the tight, sharp features of a girl. A slash of cheekbone and full lips and something glinting on the side of her nose.

They were just a couple of junkies, for Christ's sake.

Chancers.

He'd decided he could take them, could give it a damn good go at any rate, so he'd yelled and rushed, trying to take them by surprise, to get one or both of them off balance. His pricey Japanese knives in their smooth wooden block were too far away, so, lunging, he reached for the wine bottle he'd emptied only a few hours before. A hand fastened hard around his wrist. The boy leaned forward and pulled him close, training shoes squeaking against the floor tiles as weight was adjusted and purchase gained. There was warm breath on his face and he struggled to turn his head, just in time to see the girl's hand emerging from the pocket of her hoodie; small white fingers wrapped around a handle.

Chipped, black fingernails.

Not a knife, something else . . .

Her arm stretched – arcing almost lazily towards him – and he braced himself for the punch, the slap, the scratch. Instead he felt the crack of voltage and the kick of it that dropped him hard on to the floor. Above the sound of his own screaming he heard one of them say, 'Behave yourself and we're not going to hurt you.'

His muscles were still cramping from the shock as the

hand pressed the damp rag hard across his face and there was no choice but to suck in the darkness.

And what was that, twenty-four hours ago? Thirty-six?

There's no way to keep an accurate track of time in a room without any windows. He's slept, but he's been given sedatives of some kind, so it's impossible to say how long for. It's no better than guesswork really, based on how often they bring food or the rise and fall in pitch of distant traffic hum. How many times one of them brandishes the Taser while the other unlocks the handcuffs so he can piss into a plastic bucket.

It's a basement room of some kind, he's pretty sure about that. There's a damp smell rising up from the grubby carpet and the walls are grey painted brick. There are a couple of ratty chairs and a chest of drawers in one corner but most of the space is taken up by the single bed he's spreadeagled on top of; Flexi-cuffs fastening wrists and ankles to the metal rails at either end.

He's been on his own most of the time. He's not even sure that there's a lock of any kind on the door. Not that it matters, because it's not like he's going anywhere and one or other of them sticks a head into the room every so often. He's not quite sure what they're checking on, but he's grateful for it all the same.

It seems important to them that he's not actually dead or anything.

There was gaffer tape across his mouth to begin with, but the boy took it off and now whenever they bring in the

5

fish and chips or the tea and toast or whatever it is, he tries talking to them.

What am I doing here?

Listen, you've got the wrong bloke, I swear.

Who the hell do you think I am . . . ?

Neither of them says anything, except once when the boy shook his head like he was getting sick of it and told him to shut up. Actually, *asked* him to shut up and didn't put the tape back either, which he certainly could have done.

They've never been less than polite.

It's usually one or other that pops in, except when there are trays or buckets to carry, so he can tell that something's up when they come waltzing in together and sit side by side in the ratty chairs for a while.

'What's going on?' he asks.

The boy's fingers are drumming against his knees. He stares at the girl, but even though she's very much aware she's being stared at, it takes a while before she looks back at him. The boy widens his eyes, nods and eventually the girl takes her hand from the pocket of her hoodie.

He raises his head from the bed, straining to see, and this time there's no mistaking what she's holding in her small white fingers.

He knows perfectly well what a scalpel looks like.

The girl stands up and swallows. She takes a breath. It's as though she's trying *really* hard to look serious. To be taken seriously.

'*Now*,' she says. 'Now, we're going to hurt you . . .'

THE FIRST DAY

WITH A WORD,
WITH A LOOK

ONE

You want the good news or the bad news?

That's what Detective Chief Inspector Russell Brigstocke had said to him back then. Eating his biscuits and trying his patience. Sitting cheerfully on the edge of his bed in that hospital as though they were just old mates chewing the fat. Like Thorne hadn't almost bled to death a few days earlier, like what he laughably called his career wasn't hanging in the balance.

Delivering the verdict.

Good news. Bad news . . .

Now, six weeks on, Tom Thorne glanced at his rear-view mirror and saw the huge metal doors sliding shut behind him as he drove into the prison's vehicle compound. Pulling into the parking space that had been reserved for them, he glanced across at Dave Holland in the passenger seat. He saw the apprehension on the sergeant's face. He knew it was etched there on his own too, because he could feel it twisting in his gut, sharper suddenly than the lingering pain from the gunshot wound, which had all but faded into the background.

Like a scream rising above a long, low moan.

Wasn't it usually some kind of a joke? That whole good news/bad news routine?

The good news: You're going to be famous!

The bad news: They're naming a disease after you.

Whichever way round, it was *normally* a joke . . .

The bad news: They found your blood all over the crime scene!

The good news: Your cholesterol's down.

Thorne killed the engine of the seven-seat Ford Galaxy and looked up at the prison. Walls and wire and a sky the colour of wet pavement. This place was certainly nothing to laugh about at stupid o'clock on a Monday morning in the first week of November. There was nothing even remotely funny about the reason they were here.

'He wants you to take him,' Brigstocke had said.

Back in that hospital room, six weeks earlier. The pain a damn sight fresher then. A hot blade in Thorne's side when he'd sat up straight in his wheelchair.

'Me?'

'Yeah, it has to be you. That's one of his conditions.'

'He's got conditions?'

Brigstocke had jammed what was left of a biscuit into

10

his mouth, spat crumbs on to the blanket when he'd answered. 'It's ... complicated.'

A few minutes before that, Brigstocke had announced that, despite conduct during an investigation that could easily have seen Thorne removed from the Job altogether, if not facing prosecution, he was being recalled to the Murder Squad. Miraculously, his demotion to uniform was being overturned and, after four miserable months working in south London, he would be heading back to God's side of the river again. He would remain an inspector, but once again it would be preceded by the one-word job description he had been struggling to live without.

Detective.

'I'm *guessing* that's the good news,' Thorne said.

A nod from Brigstocke and a nice long pause and the DCI could not quite maintain eye contact as he began to outline the reason for this unexpectedly positive outcome. As soon as the man's name was mentioned, Thorne tried to interrupt, but Brigstocke held up a hand. He raised his voice and insisted that Thorne allow him to get at least a sentence or two out before voicing his understandable objections.

'It's a game,' Thorne said, the moment Brigstocke had paused for breath. 'Same as it always is with him.'

'It checks out. The timings, the location.'

'I don't care what checks out, he's up to something.' Wishing more than anything that he was still wired up to the morphine pump, Thorne wheeled his chair a few feet forward, then back again. 'Come on, Russell, you know what he's like. What the hell are you all thinking?'

'We're thinking that he's got us over a barrel,' Brigstocke said.

Thorne listened as Brigstocke continued to explain how the man they were talking about – a convicted murderer currently serving multiple life sentences with no possibility of parole – had established contact six months earlier with the mother of a fifteen-year-old boy who had gone missing twenty-five years before. He claimed that he had once known the boy, that they had both been residents at an experimental retreat for troubled teenagers. After several months of communication, he confessed to the woman in a letter that he had in fact murdered her son and buried the boy's body.

'That much I can believe,' Thorne said. 'So far, that's the only bit that makes any sense.'

Brigstocke ignored him and ploughed on. He described the series of desperate visits and phone calls during which the woman had begged the murderer to reveal the whereabouts of her son's grave. How she had contacted the press and written to her local MP, urging him to get involved, until eventually, after a concerted campaign, the prisoner had agreed to co-operate. He would, he had promised, show the police where the teenager had been buried.

Then, Brigstocke had made eye contact, but only for a moment. 'And he wants you to escort him ...'

It had gone back and forth between them for a while

after that: Brigstocke urging Thorne to shut up and listen; Thorne doing a lot more shouting than listening; Brigstocke telling him that he'd burst his stitches if he didn't calm down.

'So, what the hell are we supposed to do?' Brigstocke had finished the biscuits. He screwed up the empty packet and attempted to toss it into the metal wastepaper basket in the corner of the room. 'You tell me, Tom. The chief constable's got this MP on her case. The papers are all over it. This woman needs to know about her son, to get ... closure or whatever and as far as I can see there's no good reason we shouldn't be doing this.'

'*Him*,' Thorne said. 'He's the reason why not.'

'Like I said, we've checked dates and records and it looks like he's telling the truth.' Brigstocke walked to the corner, picked up the packet and dropped it into the bin. 'He was definitely there when he says he was and that was the last time anybody saw this missing boy.'

Thorne pushed himself back towards the bed. 'He never does a single thing that he doesn't want to do. That he doesn't have a very good reason to do.' He eased himself gingerly out of the chair and on to the bed, waving away Brigstocke's offer of help and staring at him, hard.

'*Never* ...'

'So, what do you reckon?' Holland asked now. He unfastened his seatbelt, turned and reached into the row of seats behind for his overcoat and gloves. 'A couple of days?'

13

'Yeah,' Thorne said. A couple of days until they found the body or it became clear they were being taken for idiots. He reached back for his own coat, for the case containing all the paperwork. 'With a bit of luck.'

'Nice to get out of London,' Holland said.

'I suppose.'

'I mean, obviously I wish we were doing something a bit less ... you know.'

You want the good news or the bad news?

In Brigstocke's office at Becke House, the day after Thorne had been discharged from hospital. The arrangements already being made, the permissions and protocols put in place.

The argument continuing.

'Let's go over these "conditions" again, shall we?' Thorne had thrown his leather jacket across a chair and sat leaning back against the wall. 'Just to make sure I'm totally clear on all this. You know, why *he's* the one making the rules.'

Brigstocke stood, walked around his desk. 'How many times?'

'I know,' Thorne said. 'The MP, the grieving mother, the barrel he's got us across.' He shook his head. 'Anything else he wants? A particular make and model of car? Something special on his sandwiches?'

'Nothing's changed.'

'So, come on then. The stipulations ...'

'Well, *you*, obviously.'

'Yeah. Me.' Thorne puffed out his cheeks. 'You got any thoughts on that?' He looked up at Brigstocke, wide-eyed and mock-curious. 'I'm just wondering.'

'You're the one who caught him,' Brigstocke said. 'He's got some weird kind of respect for you or something. Maybe he trusts you.'

'He wants to mess with me,' Thorne said. 'It's what he does.'

'You're taking him out there, you're finding this body then you're bringing him back.' Brigstocke leaned against the desk. 'That's all this is.'

Thorne studied the carpet and fingered the straight scar beneath his chin for a few seconds. He said, 'What's his problem with the press?'

'He doesn't want any around, simple as that.'

'Never seemed to bother him before,' Thorne said. 'Happy enough with the books and the bloody documentaries. Got a nice collection of his press cuttings pasted up in his cell by all accounts.'

Brigstocke shrugged. 'Look, he knows they've been on to this ever since the boy's mother went to the papers. He doesn't fancy helicopters everywhere, that's all, like when they took Brady back to the moors.'

Thorne grunted.

'We've let the press know it's on, which should keep them off our backs, but obviously they don't know exactly when or where.' Brigstocke began to work carefully at a torn fingernail with his teeth. 'Shouldn't be a problem as long as some friendly press officer gives them everything they want once it's done and dusted.'

'Tell me about his friend.'

Brigstocke spat out the sliver of nail. 'Well, he's *saying* he'll feel a lot safer if he can bring another prisoner with him. That he's less likely to have any sort of "accident". Reckons there are too many of us who won't have forgotten Sarah McEvoy.'

'That's bollocks.'

'That's what he's saying.'

Thorne had certainly not forgotten the police officer who had been killed during the arrest of the man whose demands they were now discussing. He remembered blood spreading across asphalt. He remembered the look of elation on the man's face, just before Thorne had forcibly wiped it off. 'So, what, then? This bloke his boyfriend, maybe?'

'Possible,' Brigstocke said.

'Well, whatever the reason is for bringing him along, I'll want everything we can find on him.'

'Obviously—' Brigstocke's phone chirruped in his pocket. He took the handset out, dropped the call then replaced it. Either the conversation could wait, or it was one he did not want Thorne to overhear. 'Look, Tom, nothing about this is run of the mill, I know that. Normal procedures will be going out of the window to a large extent. This stupid place you'll be taking him back to, for a kick-off. It's already throwing up certain ... logistical nightmares, so I'm just saying you might have to do a fair amount of thinking on your feet.'

Thorne nodded slowly and reached around for his jacket. 'I've got a few conditions of my own,' he said.

Brigstocke waited.

'I get to pick the rest of the team,' Thorne said, standing up. 'Not you and not the chief superintendent. And the *moment* me or anybody else starts to think that there's no body to be found and that he's just getting off on taking us all for mugs, I'll have him and his boyfriend banged up again before his feet have touched the ground. Fair enough?' Brigstocke opened his mouth, but Thorne hadn't finished. He was already on his way to the door. 'And I don't want to hear about how much grief the chief constable's getting from the *Sun* or the *Daily Mail*. I don't care about MPs, I don't even care about grieving mothers and I really couldn't give a toss about that sodding barrel ...'

'Jesus, it's cold,' Holland said, now. He slapped his gloved hands together as he trudged around to the front of the car. He hunched his shoulders and nodded towards the prison entrance. 'I hope somebody's got the kettle on in there.'

Thorne hummed agreement. He might even have said something about hoping so too, but in truth he could think of little beyond the reason he had risen so early after a sleepless night and watched the sun come up driving a hundred miles to Long Lartin prison. Little beyond the man who had brought him here.

They walked towards the first of many gates, footsteps ringing against the tarmac and breath pluming from mouths and noses.

The man who would be patiently waiting on the other side of that wall.

They reached for warrant cards simultaneously.

The man who put that twist in Thorne's gut.

'Here we go then,' Holland said.

Stuart Nicklin was the bad news.

TWO

There *was* tea and there were also biscuits in a fancy tin, which were gratefully accepted despite being offered without too much in the way of goodwill. Holland tried smiling, then felt rather stupid and grimaced at Thorne as he turned away. He carried his tea across to the small sofa at one end of the long, thin office, leaving Thorne at the desk to deal with the red tape and the woman dispensing it.

Thorne looked no happier about the situation than she did.

The demeanour and attitude of Long Lartin's deputy governor could most generously be described as businesslike, but Thorne felt sure that both prisoners and prison officers had a different word for it. On top of the fact that she was not what anyone would call 'touchy-feely', it quickly became apparent that Theresa Colquhoun was in no hurry. She had been tasked by the governor with completing the formalities necessary for a prisoner handover. This meant a good many forms to fill in. It meant risk assessment statements to be completed and 'handover protocol' guidance notes to be distributed and carefully read through. She had reservations about what had been agreed on this occasion between the Met and Her Majesty's Prison Service and had told Thorne exactly what she thought while she'd poured the tea. Nonetheless, she was determined to carry out the job with a rigour which, to Thorne's eye, bordered on compulsion.

'This business is iffy enough as it is,' she said. She tapped a manicured fingernail against the photograph of Stuart Nicklin clipped to the top of a file. 'We don't want to make a mistake before we've even started, do we?'

Colquhoun was somewhere at the fag-end of her fifties. She was tall and angular and had seemingly done her best to avoid anything that might have softened her appearance. Her greying hair was fastened tightly back and her make-up was severe. Only her voice was at odds with the impression she wanted – or thought she *ought* – to create. There was almost no colour in it, and she spoke so quietly Thorne had twice needed to ask her to repeat herself.

Not that the conversation was exactly sparkling.

The completion of each set of forms – one for each of the prisoners – was celebrated with a short break for chit-chat. Specifically, one inane enquiry after another about the journey Thorne and Holland had made from London that morning. The route, the weight of traffic, the weather conditions at various stages.

Then back to the task in hand.

She said, 'Even when these prisoners have been handed into your care and are off the grounds of Long Lartin, they will still *be* prisoners and as such will remain my legal responsibility. I don't need to tell you I'd rather they were returned here at the end of each day, but as the geography would seem to make that impossible, they will need to be escorted to a designated facility.'

'You don't need to tell me, but you did,' Thorne said.

'As I said, best to get things clear at the outset.'

'We'll look after them.'

Colquhoun had just begun talking about procedures in the event of a prisoner being taken ill, when the message alert sounded on Holland's phone. She stared at him, like an irritated librarian.

Holland checked his message. Said, 'Back-up car's here.'

'Tell them we shouldn't be long,' Thorne said, eyes on the deputy governor.

Though he was hardly making it difficult for her, Colquhoun could sense Thorne's growing impatience, his desire to get on his way. 'My officers are busy getting the prisoners prepared,' she said. She smiled, showing no teeth, and began straightening papers. 'For obvious reasons, we only informed them that the handover was taking place today at the very last minute.'

'Right,' Thorne said.

'Obviously, it would be lovely if they were all prepped and ready for you in advance, but that would rather compromise security, don't you think?'

'Obviously . . .'

What Thorne had *actually* been thinking for several weeks now was that security protocols such as this one were little more than a challenge for the likes of Stuart Nicklin. It made sense of course that prisoners should not be given the chance to pass on details of the time they would be spending outside prison to anyone else. But it was not a foolproof system at the best of times and Nicklin was no ordinary prisoner. Over the years he had spent inside, he had demonstrated an alarming ability to gather information. To foster any number of sources on whom he could call when the moment was right.

The last time Thorne had seen him, five years before, Nicklin had gleefully advised him to shop around for his utilities and to keep an eye on his overdraft. He'd told him that he might want to think about cutting down on takeaways.

'I think I know you pretty well now,' he had said.

Getting some low-life to go through a rubbish bin was hardly rocket science, but Nicklin had also shown himself able to procure phone numbers, addresses, personal details; to monitor the movements of anyone he chose to take an interest in.

With all that in mind, it was hard to have too much confidence in the advance security as far as this operation went. There would be plenty of people in the prison administration who had been aware of the details for days already and who would have known exactly when Thorne was turning up to collect Stuart Nicklin. Officers in every force whose jurisdiction they would be passing through had already been informed and issued with descriptions and up-to-date photographs of the prisoners.

There were plenty of ... sources.

Thankfully, it only took a few minutes more to complete the paperwork and when it was done, Colquhoun called down and spoke to one of her senior officers. She told Thorne that the prisoners would be brought out to the vehicles shortly, then stood up, walked slowly round the desk and shook his hand. It felt a little odd, as though she were wishing him luck. As though she thought he would need it.

Holland was walking back towards the desk. He thanked Colquhoun for the tea, and for the 'special biscuits'.

She turned and reached for the tin, proffered it. 'Take them with you for the car,' she said.

Holland hesitated for a second or two, as surprised by the unexpected act of generosity as anything else, then took the tin. 'Cheers.'

'What's it going to be, three or four hours?'

'Could be closer to five,' Thorne said. 'Depending.'

'Plenty of time for everyone to get acquainted with one another.' She looked at Thorne. A well-practised expression of compassion that could not disguise a degree of naked curiosity. 'Though I gather you and Nicklin ...'

'Yeah,' Thorne said.

I think I know you pretty well.

'So, these just for us then?' Smiling, Holland waved the tin of biscuits at Thorne. 'Or do we have to share them?'

'Well, I'm sure my officers aren't going to say no.' The deputy governor walked back around her desk and sat down. She adjusted the position of a framed photograph whose subject Thorne could not quite make out from where he was standing. 'But the prisoners will obviously be cuffed, so it's up to you.' She looked up at Dave Holland with the first proper smile she'd managed all morning. 'Do you really want to be hand-feeding Stuart Nicklin custard creams?'

THREE

Jeffrey Batchelor raised his forearm, buried his face in the material of the thick, brown crew-neck sweater and sniffed. Fully dressed again, he looked at himself in a small mirror on the back of the door, then across at the senior prison officer who had only finished strip-searching him five minutes before.

'Just feels odd,' he said.

'Bound to,' Alan Jenks said. 'First time back in your own clothes since you came in, right?'

Batchelor nodded. 'I suppose that's right.'

First time in eight months. In two hundred and thirty-six days. He pointed at Jenks, managed a dry laugh.

'First time I've seen you out of uniform.'

Jenks checked himself out in the mirror. He was wearing jeans, same as Batchelor, with a black sweater over a denim shirt. 'Yeah, well, they don't want what's going on to be too obvious,' Jenks said. 'They want it all *low-key*.' He used his fingers to put quotation marks round the last words, then nodded towards the door and another room on the far side of Reception where two of his colleagues were prepping the other prisoner. '*He* does, anyway. He's the one calling the shots, you ask me.' He nodded, conspiratorial. 'Don't you reckon?'

Batchelor shrugged, as though any opinion he might have was hardly worth considering. He certainly had one, but he knew that where Stuart Nicklin was concerned, it was usually best to say nothing.

He'd learned that before he'd even met the man.

'I mean, you're his mate,' Jenks said.

'Not really.'

'Or whatever it is.'

'I'm not,' Batchelor said.

'Doesn't matter to me either way.'

'It's not like that.'

Jenks stared at the prisoner for a couple of seconds, then smiled like he wasn't convinced and turned away. He reached up into an open metal cupboard on the wall for the D-cuffs. Turned back and dangled them. 'Yeah well, not easy to be too low-key when you're walking about wearing these buggers.'

'I suppose not.'

Jenks stepped across, workmanlike. 'Hardly going to look like we're sightseeing, is it?'

Batchelor closed his eyes and held out his arms.

On the wing the evening before, he had looked up to see Nicklin in the doorway of his cell. A small wave like there was no need for concern, like he was just passing. He had laid down the book he was reading, got to his feet.

'All set?'

He had nodded, his mouth too dry suddenly to spit out an answer quickly.

'Not having second thoughts, are we?'

'Just a bit nervous,' he had said, eventually.

Nicklin had laughed, hoarse and high-pitched, then stepped across the threshold. 'You should be excited, Jeffrey,' he'd said. He had lowered his voice to a whisper. 'We're going on holiday . . .'

Batchelor winced and sucked in a breath as the cuffs were double locked, the snap catching the skin.

'Sorry,' Jenks said.

'No problem, Mr Jenks,' Batchelor said. 'Not your fault.'

First time back in cuffs since he'd climbed out of that van, two hundred and thirty-six days before.

Thorne stood by the side of the back-up vehicle – a Ford Galaxy identical to the one he and Holland were in – talking through the half-open window to DS Samir Karim, who would be driving, and to the woman in the passenger seat. Once they had reached their destination, Karim would be working as exhibits officer, while Wendy Markham was on board as civilian crime scene manager.

This was assuming that any crime scene was actually found, that there *were* any exhibits.

'Your guess is as good as mine,' Thorne said.

'Exhibit A . . . bugger all,' Karim said, grinning.

Thorne glanced at Markham, who seemed happy enough. Maybe, like Holland, she was just looking forward to getting out of the city. Thorne could not think of anywhere much further out.

Karim was chuckling now. 'Actually, better make that Exhibit Sweet *F*A!' With no discernible quality control when it came to his jokes, Karim was every bit as indiscriminate about gambling. He regularly took bets on time of death or length of sentence, but was equally happy to run books on the grisliest of murder case minutiae. Since being brought into the team, he had been predictably keen to discuss the odds on finding the body they were going to look for, the number of hours they might have to spend digging.

For now, Thorne was happier talking about the route.

While other areas of security were causing him a degree of concern, he could be confident that this part of the operation at least had stayed under wraps. Their progress would be monitored, the two vehicles tracked by satellite in real time, but only he and Karim actually knew which way they were going.

They went over it one more time.

'Don't worry, it's sorted,' Karim said. He tapped the side of his head to suggest that the information had been memorised. As though he had no need of the sat nav and would have happily swallowed the map Thorne had supplied were it not for the fact that it was laminated.

Thorne looked at his watch. 'If we ever get going.' They had been at the prison almost an hour and a half already. He had wanted to be long gone by now. 'Don't know why we bothered to get up so early.'

'Maybe we can make up some time on the road,' Karim said.

'Not going to happen,' Thorne said. The cars would stay in touch by radio, but it was important that they maintained visual contact too. 'Inside lane on the motorways wherever possible, Sam, all right? Nice and steady and don't be playing silly buggers and trying to overtake.' He looked at his watch again. 'It'll take as long as it takes.'

'No worries,' Karim said. 'All goes a lot quicker when you've got company, doesn't it?'

'If you say so.' Thinking about who he and Holland would be sharing the journey with, Thorne decided that they were definitely getting the shitty end of the deal. Just before turning away towards his own car, he caught Wendy Markham's eye. He read the expression and decided that he could be doing worse after all. Four or five hours stuck in the car with Sam Karim, the crime scene manager might well be creating a crime scene of her own.

Climbing into the driver's seat, he was glad that Holland had left the engine running. He pulled his gloves off, leaned across and tossed them into the glove compartment.

'Almost like that's what it was designed for,' Holland said. He had already started on the biscuits and offered the tin to Thorne.

Thorne shook his head. He had been up for more than four hours, but despite having had no more than a cup of tea – creeping round the flat so as not to wake Helen and Alfie – he was still not hungry. Catching movement on the far side of the compound, he looked up and saw an officer walking the perimeter, doing his best to control a fearsome-looking German Shepherd. He watched dog and handler walk past two more officers on their way towards the purpose-built staff coffee shop, a Portakabin that had been tarted up and pithily christened The Long Latté.

Holland leaned forward to turn the radio down. They had been listening to news and sport on 5 Live on the drive up from London and now there was a phone-in debating whether the royal family were value for money. They brought in a lot of tourists, according to John from Ascot, so were consequently worth every penny. Frank in Halifax said they were bone-idle parasites, and as if that wasn't bad enough, they were bone-idle *German* parasites.

'We need to talk about music,' Holland said.

'Do we?' Thorne asked.

'A four-hour journey?'

'Maybe five.'

'Right. So the choice of music's pretty crucial, I'd say.'

'I suppose.'

'Nothing about it in the operational notes.'

'That was an oversight.'

'Three pages on risk assessment ... page and a half on "comfort break" procedure, for God's sake, but not a single word about what we might be listening to.'

'I'm not sure there's going to be much chance. It's not a pleasure trip.'

'Surely we need to know the protocol, just in case.'

'I'll probably just connect my phone.'

'What, *your* music?'

'I've got plenty of Johnny Cash and Willie Nelson,' Thorne said. 'I've got a Hank Williams playlist that'll get us to Wales, easy.'

Holland sat back, shaking his head. 'Jesus, I know we're talking about people who've done some awful things, but these prisoners do have basic human rights, you know?'

'You're hilarious,' Thorne said. He was stony-faced, but in truth he was enjoying the back and forth. What might be their last chance to laugh for a while.

Holland helped himself to a last biscuit. He put the lid back on the tin and set it down in the footwell. He looked at Thorne.

'So, why you?' he asked.

It was the same question Thorne had asked Brigstocke, that Helen had asked Thorne as soon as he'd told her what was happening. The same question Thorne had been asking himself for the last six weeks. Before he had the

31

chance to tell Holland that he couldn't think of a single reason that didn't scare the hell out of him, the gate opened and the only man who knew the answer appeared.

That twist in his gut.

Jeffrey Batchelor was walking in front, a prison officer in plain clothes keeping pace alongside him. He stared at the sky, at the trees beyond the gates, as if mildly surprised to see that they were still there. Nicklin was a step or two behind, the hand of the officer with him reaching out to usher gently, almost but not quite touching the prisoner's shoulder.

Thorne and Holland got out of the car.

Nicklin smiled when he saw Thorne, and nodded. *Sorry I'm a bit late, you know how it goes.* If anything, he picked up his pace as he drew closer, the smile broadening until it became a grin. Were it not for the handcuffs, it looked as though he wanted nothing in the world so much as to throw his arms wide, good and ready for a much-anticipated hug.

FOUR

It would be more than twenty-five miles before they hit the
first of several motorways. Until then they would be travelling on winding, narrow roads, their progress subject to
drivers in no particular hurry. They would be at the mercy
of lumbering agricultural vehicles and unable to make use
of blues and twos except in the case of genuine emergency.
Not that Thorne had been looking forward to *any* of it, but
this stretch of the journey was the one he had been most
nervous about.

This was where they were exposed.

His eyes flicked to the wing mirror, the second Galaxy
behind.

Over the last few days, *nights*, he had entertained dark
fantasies of tractors appearing from nowhere and rolling
across their path, lorries emerging from unseen lanes
behind them, men appearing with shotguns. The car's

blood-soaked interior and the leering face of a scarecrow as the prisoners were spirited away. They were, after all, unlikely to run into anything similar in a built-up area or at sixty miles an hour on the M54. No, this was where it would happen. The middle of bloody nowhere, close to the prison and then again later on as they got near to their destination; miles from the nearest CCTV camera, on quiet country lanes that were not overlooked. Of course, Thorne knew perfectly well that it would *not* happen. He was allowing his imagination to run riot. Still, however unlikely, it remained the worst case scenario.

Where Stuart Nicklin was concerned, the worst case scenario would always be the first that came to mind.

Thorne glanced at the rear-view.

Nicklin was sitting on the driver's side, in the row of three seats directly behind him, an empty seat separating him from Principal Prison Officer Chris Fletcher. Batchelor and Senior Prison Officer Alan Jenks sat close together on the pair of seats behind that. Seatbelts fastened for them, hands in laps, the prisoners remained cuffed. Those provided by the prison had been exchanged for rigid speed cuffs: a solid piece of metal linking the two bracelets and fastened in such a way that the prisoners' wrists were fixed one above the other. That way it was impossible for arms to be thrown around the neck of anyone in front and the cuffs used to throttle.

Twenty minutes after leaving Long Lartin, they were still snaking through open Worcestershire countryside.

Outside it was cold, but cloudless. Fields that remained frost-spattered stretched to the horizon on either side, beyond drystone wall and tall hedges dusted with silver.

Twenty minutes during which nobody had said a word, the silence finally broken when Nicklin leaned forward so suddenly as to make each of the car's other occupants start. He leaned forward and craned his head, pushing it as far as he could into the gap between the two front seats.

Said, 'This is nice.'

Stuart Anthony Nicklin, who was now forty-two years old, had been expelled from school at the age of sixteen. His expulsion, together with a boy named Martin Palmer, had been for an incident of semi-sexual violence involving a fellow pupil, though it later emerged that at around the same time he had murdered a fifteen-year-old girl. This was shortly before he ran away from home and vanished for more than fifteen years.

'The countryside,' Nicklin said. 'The scenery.' He looked at Fletcher, turned around to look at Batchelor and Jenks. 'All of it.'

Nicklin had reappeared in his early thirties as a completely different person; a man with a new name and a new face, virtually unrecognisable, even to Martin Palmer, with whom he established contact once again. Despite the years that had passed, Nicklin had lost none of his power over his former partner-in-crime. He skilfully manipulated Palmer, terrifying him into acting out his own twisted fantasies in a three-month killing spree. They murdered at

35

least six people between them; men and women stabbed, shot, strangled, bludgeoned to death. Though Nicklin might not always have had his hand on the gun or the knife, it became apparent to anyone following the case that all of those deaths were down to him.

And he was more than happy to claim credit for them.

It ended in a school playground on a cold February afternoon. The man who had been scared into killing and a female police officer, both dead. Four months later, after one of the biggest trials in recent memory, Nicklin began yet another life, this time as one of the UK prison population's most notorious serial killers.

'This is what you miss.' Nicklin nodded out at the view. 'Ordinary, gorgeous things. Trees and big skies and the black ribbon of road stretching out ahead of you, like this.' He sat back and laughed, raised cuffed hands to scratch at his nose. 'Even the smell of cow-shit . . .'

It emerged during the investigation that, for almost ten years before he and Palmer had begun killing, Nicklin had been happily married. That he had been holding down a regular job. What he had been doing for those earlier 'lost' years, however, had never been altogether clear. Later, it was discovered that immediately after running away, he had spent some time working as a rent boy in London's West End. It was during this period – still in his teens and yet to reinvent himself – that, following his umpteenth conviction for soliciting, he was sent to a retreat for troubled teenagers on a small island off the north-west coast of Wales.

Tides House was an experiment that failed.

It was neither a young offenders' institution nor a children's home, but something in between; something *different*, with the day-to-day emphasis on spiritual awakening and reflection. Somewhere a kid whose future looked bleak might grow and change. Doomed to constant sniping from reactionary quarters of press and Parliament, Tides House closed its doors only three years after opening them, leaving little to show for the efforts of those behind it but ruined careers and crumbling buildings. It was while Nicklin was there, twenty-five years before, that he had met Simon Milner, a fifteen-year-old-boy with a history of repeated car theft behind him.

The boy whose body they were on their way to look for.

'It's going to get a lot better as well,' Nicklin said. 'Trust me. You want scenery, you just wait until we get there.'

Thorne looked at the rear-view again. Nicklin seemed to have shifted as far as he was able to his left, so as to place himself directly in Thorne's line of sight. So that their eyes would meet.

'We're not going for the scenery,' Thorne said.

Nicklin grunted and shrugged. 'What, you'd rather be searching on a council estate, would you, Tom? Dodging the dog turds while you're digging up some chav's back garden. You'd rather be draining a quarry?'

Thorne's fingers tightened a little around the steering wheel and he knew that it was unlikely to be the last time.

He exchanged a look with Holland, reminded himself that they were still only twenty minutes into it.

His mobile sounded, a message alert.

He reached down to the central cup-holder for the phone, keyed in his pass code and read the text from DI Yvonne Kitson.

how's it going? on my way to talk to the ex-wife

He looked at the mirror again when he heard tutting from behind him.

'Don't you think you should keep your eyes on the road, Tom?' Nicklin shook his head and turned to Fletcher. 'What do *you* think?' The prison officer said nothing. 'You look down at your phone for that all-important message from whoever it might be, next thing a tractor appears from nowhere, rolls across our path . . . '

Thorne's fingers started to tighten again and, in an effort to relax a little, he conjured a memory that immediately did the trick. A vivid and wonderful image that eased the tension in his neck and shoulders. One that allowed his jaw to slacken and the corners of his mouth to widen just a fraction . . .

He remembered a cold February afternoon. The echo of a gunshot still ringing and the look of surprise on a ruined face. Those frozen, perfect moments just after Thorne had smashed the butt of a revolver into Nicklin's mouth. Shattered teeth splitting the gums and full, flapping lips that burst like rotten fruit.

38

Eyes wide and strings of blood running through his fingers.

'I mean, for heaven's sake,' Nicklin said, leaning forward again. 'Let's get there in one piece, shall we?'

Thorne's eyes stayed on the road, the half-smile still in place.

He said, 'I'll do my best.'

FIVE

It was a sign of the times perhaps, but even as a respectably dressed woman in her forties, it felt uncomfortable to be hanging around outside a primary school. Was it best to wait in one place or move around a little? Which looked less like lurking? Yvonne Kitson guessed that she was not arousing as much suspicion as a man might and certainly a damn sight less than a seventies' DJ or children's TV personality.

Still, it made her feel decidedly uneasy.

She had been there fifteen minutes or so already and been on the receiving end of hard looks from a middle-aged couple, a woman walking past with a pushchair and a male teacher who had stood for half a minute and stared through the fence at her from the far side of the playground. Kitson had stared right back. She had been hugely tempted to march through the gate, push her warrant card into his fat face and shout, 'On top of which, I'm a mum of three kids, you twisted little tosspot . . . '

Tempting, but ultimately stupid and unjustified.

Stupid, because it would almost certainly have scuppered the meeting she was here for. Besides which, she knew that the teacher was doing his job. Those who preyed on children came in all shapes and sizes and were not all as conveniently recognisable as Jimmy Savile.

Or should that be *un*recognisable.

It was horribly ironic, Kitson thought, that the man who for decades got away with being one of the most active predatory paedophiles in the country's history had actually looked like most people's idea of one.

After another few minutes, the woman Kitson assumed to be the one she was waiting for walked out of the school and across the playground towards her. She stopped just for a few seconds outside the gate, long enough to produce cigarettes from a pocket and nod towards a small park on the other side of the road. To say quietly, as though to herself, 'Over there.'

Kitson waited half a minute, then followed and sat down at one end of a bench as the woman at the other was lighting her cigarette. She looked a little older than the thirty-nine Kitson knew her to be. She had brown hair past her shoulders and glasses with heavy black frames. Like Kitson, she wore a dark skirt and jacket.

They could both have been teachers. Or police officers.

'Waiting long?'

'Quarter of an hour or something,' Kitson said.

The woman showed no inclination to apologise for having kept Kitson waiting. She just smoked for half a minute. Said, 'Paedo patrol check you out? Short teacher with a fat face?'

'Yeah,' Kitson said, laughing.

'You want one of these?' The woman proffered her cigarette.

Kitson shook her head. 'Thanks for doing this, by the way. Agreeing to talk to me.'

'I don't have a lot of choice, do I? I need to keep you lot sweet.' She flashed Kitson a look and took a long drag. 'Only takes one stupid copper gabbing in the pub, one mention of the wrong name and the whole lot falls apart.'

'I suppose so,' Kitson said.

'It's taken ten years to build this.'

Kitson nodded back towards the school. 'Where do they think you've gone?'

She waved her cigarette. 'They think I've come out to do this, same as usual. Which means I've got about five minutes, which is fine because I don't want to talk to you for longer than five minutes.' She put the cigarette to her lips then lowered it again. 'I don't want to talk about *him* for five seconds.'

'It's nice round here,' Kitson said. The school was on the outskirts of Huntingdon, in Cambridgeshire, seventy miles or so from London. Far enough away. 'Leafy.'

The woman nodded, smoked.

42

'Kids nice?'

Another nod. She said, 'I was lucky,' then snorted at the absurdity of it.

The woman who had once been Caroline Cookson was still doing the same job she had been doing ten years before, when her life had changed beyond all recognition. Everything else about her was different though. Her name, her accent, the colour and style of her hair. She had been relocated and given a new identity once the full horror of what her husband had done became clear. A man who had called himself Cookson back then, but whose real name was Stuart Nicklin.

'I don't know what to call you,' Kitson said.

'Claire Richardson. My name's Claire Richardson.'

The officers monitoring Caroline Cookson's witness protection had given Kitson a name and phone number, the address of the school where 'Claire Richardson' worked. Beyond that though, Kitson knew nothing about her. Had she remarried? Did she have children?

Kitson asked her.

'No kids,' Claire said. 'I've had a boyfriend for a couple of years.'

'That's good.'

'Yeah, well he hasn't killed anyone yet, so you know ... that's a plus.' She took a last drag on her cigarette, dropped the nub and ground it beneath her boot. 'Mind you, I didn't know any of that was happening *last* time, did I?'

Kitson laughed, because she thought she ought to.

Claire looked at her. She was already reaching for her cigarettes again. 'I didn't, you know. Some of the papers made out that I knew, but I didn't. I still feel physically sick just thinking about what he did.'

Kitson said she believed her, because she thought she ought to.

Watching the woman light another cigarette, trying not to stare at what might have been the smallest of tremors in her fingers, Kitson told her what she had come to talk about. She explained about the prisoner escort operation that was currently taking place and why she had needed to wait until it was happening before having this and several other conversations. 'Trying to minimise the risk of word getting out,' she said.

'So what do you want from me?'

'Why's he doing it?'

Claire turned and stared, shook her head. 'Seriously? Why the hell do you think *I'd* know?'

'We thought you might have an idea, that's all,' Kitson said. 'Because he writes to you. The prison told us about the letters he writes, so we wondered if he'd said something.'

'I don't see the letters,' Claire said. 'I've got an arrangement with the witness protection team and they're intercepted. Destroyed.' She opened the side of her mouth, allowed a wisp of smoke to escape. 'Well, they *say* they destroy them. Maybe they're reading them for a laugh. Maybe they're making a few extra quid putting them on eBay. I don't give a toss, tell you the truth. I don't care about anything he might have to say.'

'What do you think's in them?'

'I told you, I don't care.'

'You're not even curious?'

'Not remotely.' She turned to look at Kitson again. 'I only went to see him once. Five or six years ago. Some journalist was writing a book and I knew they were going to come looking. I wanted to make sure that didn't happen and I knew he was the only one who could make it stop, that he'd have some ... leverage or whatever. That was the only time.' She swallowed, took a deep drag. 'The only time.'

'What did he say?' Kitson asked.

'He tried to tell me that he still loved me.' Claire leaned slowly forward and pulled her feet beneath the bench. She looked disgusted. 'That he *missed* me. Oh yes, and just before I left he told me how much better the sex with me had been right after he'd killed someone. How thinking about what he'd done, all those lovely details, made him harder when we'd been doing it, and how he was telling me all this now because he thought I'd like to know, because he thought it would turn me on. Because it was turning him on, right there in the visitors' room.' She dropped her cigarette, still only half smoked, and stood up. 'So, no. Not curious.' She turned and watched Kitson get to her feet. She said, 'Sorry you wasted your time.'

'Not to worry,' Kitson said. 'I think I've got a day of it.

Fact is, I'm really just doing a favour ... *several* favours for the copper who's been lumbered with taking your former husband back there to look for this body. Same copper that caught him, matter of fact.'

'Thorne,' Claire said.

Kitson was surprised for a moment, until she realised that obviously this woman would have known who Tom Thorne was. 'That's right,' she said.

'I only met him properly once. It was another officer who questioned me after the arrest, but then he came in afterwards, asked if I was all right.' She began to walk back towards the road. 'Then I saw him at the trial, of course.'

Kitson followed. 'Can't have been easy,' she said. 'Sitting through that.'

'Easier for me than for some.'

Kitson knew what she meant. Someone had mentioned that they'd needed to lay on extra seating in the court-room. Enough to make room for the families of all the victims.

'For ages I didn't know what to think about him,' Claire said. 'About Thorne, I mean. It was strange, because he saved me in a way, I suppose, but at the same time he ruined my life. Does that sound weird?'

'Not really.'

'I wasn't sure if I should love him or hate him.'

'A lot of people feel like that,' Kitson said.

46

SIX

The cars turned on to the M5 just before eleven o'clock, a short and less than picturesque stretch that took them through the Black Country. They passed West Bromwich and Dudley, Walsall and Wolverhampton, before the motorway curved around to the west and became the M54. Twenty-five miles further on, the Midlands would give way to Shropshire, three lanes would become one, and things would inevitably slow up again. It was the main reason that the journey was likely to take so long, that it had required such a degree of thought and planning. Of the two hundred or so miles the convoy needed to travel, less than fifty were on motorways.

Conversation up to this point had been a little stilted. The prisoners had been busy taking in the views, spectacular or otherwise, while Thorne was wary of getting into anything too drawn out with Holland for fear of missing something important being said behind him. Thus far, those with easily the most to say for themselves had been the two prison officers. Thorne guessed that Jenks and Fletcher were good friends. The conversation between the pair seemed relaxed and uninhibited, more so perhaps than it might have been back in prison, where the surroundings made it unwise to give away too much in the way of personal information.

Where shivs and sharpened toothbrushes were not the only weapons.

Both men were in their mid-to-late thirties; Jenks clean-shaven and with a dirty-blond mullet, in contrast to Fletcher's closely cropped scalp and neatly trimmed goatee. Both were well built, useful-looking, though Fletcher, the senior of the two, was shorter and wider, with a physique that did not so much suggest steroids as scream them. He had a flat Brummie accent, while the softer-spoken Jenks was pure Estuary; Kent, Thorne guessed, or north Essex.

Both were good talkers.

So far, Thorne had learned about Mrs Fletcher's minor operation the previous month and the problems Jenks was having with his car. He had discovered that Fletcher was an Aston Villa fan and that Jenks had bought tickets to see a well-known comedian just before Christmas. Now everyone in the car was finding out where each of them was planning to take their family on holiday the following year. The Jenkses were heading to Orlando – 'for the kids, obviously' – while Fletcher had settled on Barcelona, because he fancied visiting the Nou Camp stadium and his wife had some 'stupid thing about old churches'.

Thorne switched his attention to the radio, when a message came through from the back-up car. In the relatively short time they had been on the road, Karim had already radioed in once to report that there were no problems with the vehicle and that all was well with him and his 'co-pilot'. Now, Holland picked up the radio and listened, rolling his eyes at Thorne, while Karim checked in a second time to report that, essentially, there was nothing to report.

Holland put the radio back. 'He *really* needs to get out of the office a bit more.'

Thorne smiled, wondering how Wendy Markham was coping.

Nicklin leaned forward and said, 'So, who *is* that behind us?'

Thorne saw no reason not to tell him.

'They'll be the ones getting busy with the bones then?'

'Busy making sure the bones end up where they're supposed to,' Thorne said. 'We'll be meeting a forensic archaeologist up there.'

'Obviously.'

Thorne looked at Nicklin in the mirror. 'This is all providing we've got some bones to begin with.'

'Oh, there's plenty of bones where we're going.'

Thorne had done the reading. 'That's just a myth.'

'Got to be some truth to it,' Nicklin said. 'There's

49

human odds and sods turn up there all the time. Various bits and pieces knocking around on the beach or on the side of the mountain. Some poor old woman with a spade, trying to dig up her carrots or whatever ... *oh look, it's somebody's foot!*' He barked out a laugh and sat back. 'Anyway, I really wouldn't worry about having a wasted trip, because I can promise you *I* left some there.' He turned to the window. 'Not that they were bones when I left ...'

The conversation had gone as far as Thorne cared for it to go. He turned to Holland. 'You thought about holidays yet, Dave?'

'Not anywhere specific,' Holland said.

'Somewhere hot?'

'Oh yeah, and it'll have to be somewhere with a kids' club for the Pushy Princess. Or at least plenty of other kids around she can play with.'

Nicklin leaned forward again. 'How old's your daughter, sergeant?'

Holland turned around to look at him, but said nothing. This conversation had ended too.

They drove for another forty minutes in silence, maintaining steady progress in heavy motorway traffic. Drizzle had begun to spatter the windscreen. Just after they had passed a sign for the Telford turn-off, Nicklin turned to Fletcher.

'I reckon we're about due to stop for a bit. There's services in three miles.'

Fletcher leaned towards Thorne. 'You hear that?'

'We should push on,' Thorne said.

'We're entitled to a comfort break,' Nicklin said. 'We've also got a right to a minimum of one hour's exercise every day, isn't that so, Mr Fletcher?'

Fletcher caught Thorne's eye in the rear-view and nodded.

'One hour,' Nicklin said. 'And I'm only talking about stopping for ten minutes for a quick piss and a fag. Chance to stretch our legs.'

Galling though it was, Thorne remembered what Colquhoun had said and knew it meant granting the prisoners the same basic privileges that they would have back at Long Lartin. Thinking ahead, he did not want any trial based on what they might find to be jeopardised by a failure to follow the correct and lawful procedure now. As things stood, Nicklin seemed happy enough to co-operate, but it would be just like him to become awkward down the line, and complain that his human rights had been denied.

'Yeah, fair enough,' Thorne said.

Five minutes later, the two cars were pulling up and parking next to one another outside the Telford services. Leaving Markham on her own, Karim walked across to Thorne's vehicle and waited. It had already been decided that they would work on a ratio of three to one and that each prisoner would be taken inside one at a time. There was no good reason they should not kick things off with the headline act. So, while Holland waited with Batchelor and Jenks in the car, Thorne, Fletcher and Karim walked Nicklin into the services.

'Do you prefer Jeff or Jeffrey?' Holland asked. He waited, then turned back to face front. 'Suit yourself.'

'It doesn't matter,' Batchelor said. 'Either.'

They were the first words Batchelor had spoken since they'd left Long Lartin.

Holland turned back to him, nodded. 'So, enjoying yourself then?'

Batchelor shrugged. 'Better than sitting in a cell, I suppose.'

Holland studied the man in the handcuffs. He was tall and skinny, long-limbed. His light-brown hair was thin and wispy, and behind delicate glasses with thin metal frames his eyes closed tightly when he blinked, as though he was surprised each time it happened.

Delicate. *He* looked delicate. He looked, Holland decided, like a history lecturer at a sixth-form college, which is exactly what he was.

What he had been.

'So, why are you here, Jeff?' Holland asked. 'Or, why do you *think* you're here?' He gave it a few seconds. He glanced at Jenks, but the prison officer was sitting with his head back and his eyes closed, appearing to be thoroughly uninterested. 'I mean, I presume it wasn't your idea.'

'Nicklin doesn't think he's well liked,' Batchelor said.

Holland laughed. 'Oh, you reckon?'

'Liked now, I mean. By police officers. I gather an officer died when he was arrested.'

'Her name was Sarah McEvoy,' Holland said. 'She was a good officer.'

The truth was that Sarah McEvoy had been a very troubled young woman, with a serious drug dependency that had made her anything but a good officer. It was the reason she had been in that playground to begin with. The weapon Stuart Nicklin had used against her.

And she and Dave Holland had been lovers.

'So, what then? He just wants someone along as a witness, does he?'

Batchelor blinked, eyes shut tight. 'I suppose so.'

'And you were the lucky winner. Or did you get the short straw?'

'Like I said, better than sitting in a cell.'

They said nothing for a while. The rain grew a little heavier outside, noisy suddenly against the glass. Holland wondered if Jenks might actually be asleep.

'Listen,' Holland said. 'I've got a daughter, you probably heard me say that. Not as old as yours was. Not as old as ... Jodi was.' Batchelor was staring back at him now, unblinking. 'I just wanted to say that I understand what you did. I don't condone it, not for a second, course I don't. But I understand why you did it.'

SEVEN

There had been some debate about when and where to remove the handcuffs and in the end they had decided to do so in the car. To allow Nicklin to walk in and out of the service station without them. The intention was still to avoid unwanted scrutiny wherever possible and though this was one of Nicklin's 'conditions', it suited Thorne well enough. He did not want media attention any more than Nicklin did.

Blurry pictures and speculation. Manufactured outrage.

All of them were probably worrying unduly. Chances were that leaving the cuffs on as Nicklin walked in would not have caused any major problems. Thorne could not see too many people open-mouthed and scrabbling for their phones to alert the red-tops. There might be some rubbernecking, why wouldn't there be, but nobody would guess what, or more importantly *who*, they were seeing.

Watching him, as he was shepherded towards the Gents, Thorne doubted that even those who had followed the case closely, back when he was on every front page in the country, would recognise Stuart Nicklin now.

Five years ago, when Thorne had last been into Long Lartin to see him, the change had been drastic enough. Now, Nicklin looked even less like the man whose face, in one endlessly reproduced photograph, had once been so familiar. The expression of contentment that had come to be seen as defiance, eyes wide but most often described as 'blazing'. A simple holiday snap, contextualised below a thousand prurient headlines and a name that was still a convenient byword for evil.

A 'monster', who was finally beginning to look genuinely monstrous.

Five years ago, Thorne had been shocked at Nicklin's appearance, flabby and jaundiced. Now, it looked as though he had gained a lot more weight, lost even more colour, so that in places his skin appeared more blue than white; almost translucent. His eyes had sunk further into his face. His nose and the corners of his mouth were dotted with whiteheads and his teeth – many of them false, thanks to Thorne – were discoloured in places and had begun to look too big for his mouth. He was wearing a black beanie hat, but Thorne knew that beneath it, his head was bald and pitted. Thorne remembered a series of irregular, purplish lesions, like wine stains on the scalp.

As they approached the entrance to the toilets, Nicklin

stopped, and turned. 'It's only a slash, lads,' he announced. 'So I won't be keeping you too long. You should be thankful it wasn't the chicken curry for dinner last night.'

Nicklin's physical appearance was easily explained of course. Poor diet, far too many cigarettes, a lack of exercise; a life spent without fresh air. Thorne could not shake the idea though that these changes were in some strange way deliberate. He had radically altered his appearance before when it had suited him and now it felt somehow as though he were revelling in his ability to do so again. Displaying his refusal to be the man *or* the monster that anyone expected.

Fletcher and Karim waited outside with Nicklin, while Thorne gave the toilets the once-over. He ignored the looks from those going about their business as he checked unlocked cubicles and banged on the doors of those that were occupied. Once the facilities were empty, Fletcher brought Nicklin in. Karim waited outside, flashing his warrant card to prevent anyone else entering.

Thorne and Fletcher stood and watched Nicklin at the urinal.

'First piss in a while where I'm not worrying about getting shanked,' he said.

'Rubbish,' Fletcher said. He rolled his head round on his thick neck. 'Since when did you have to worry about anything like that?'

'Fair point, I suppose, boss.'

'It's everyone else does the worrying.'

Thorne knew what Fletcher was talking about. With his reputation as the prison's 'top nutter' and an unmatched capacity for instilling fear, Nicklin pretty much ran things in Long Lartin. These days there would be plenty to do the messy work for him, should it become necessary. Thorne guessed though that he was still capable of dishing it out himself, should the fancy take him. He remembered a prisoner in Belmarsh to whom Nicklin had taken a dislike while still on remand; a man left brain dead after a sharpened spoon had been calmly but forcefully inserted into his ear.

'I was just making a general point,' Nicklin said. He shook himself off and turned from the urinal, looking at Thorne while he zipped himself up. 'It feels nice, that's all I'm saying. Certainly doesn't smell quite as bad.' He walked towards the sink, taking in the surroundings as though it were the swankiest of hotel rooms. He chuckled and said, 'I don't suppose either of you feels like lending me a couple of quid for the condom machine?'

He washed and rinsed his hands twice. He took his time at the automatic dryer.

On the way out, Nicklin slowed and cast a longing glance towards the shop. 'Chocolate would be nice.'

'Would it?' Thorne said.

Nicklin smiled. He and Thorne both knew that chocolate was his weakness. DNA found on a discarded chocolate wrapper had been used in evidence at his trial. 'Go on,' he said. 'You telling me you haven't got a sweetie budget?'

Thorne looked to Fletcher. The shrug suggested that the officer had no opinion either way or that perhaps Nicklin was not alone in fancying a Mars bar. As it happened, Thorne was suddenly more than a little peckish himself. He gave Karim five pounds and sent him into WHSmith to grab a selection of chocolate bars, while he and Fletcher led Nicklin out.

'Thanks,' Nicklin said. They stopped just outside the main doors, sheltered from the drizzle. Nearby, a man sat looking miserable at a small concession stand selling AA membership. Nicklin looked at Thorne to check he had permission, then, having been given the nod, he removed a tin of pre-rolled cigarettes from the pocket of his anorak. 'Nice to see you're not going to be an arsehole about all this.'

'What about you?' Thorne said.

A few minutes later, while Nicklin was being cuffed and belted back into the car, Thorne called Yvonne Kitson.

'She never gets his letters,' Kitson told him. 'She's got no more idea than anyone else what all this is about.'

'Thanks, Yvonne.'

'It was worth a try.'

'Yeah.'

'I'm on my way to see Sonia Batchelor now. Then I'll grab some food and cut back down to visit the mother . . .'

Once the call had ended, Holland got out of the car and walked across to join him.

'Anything from Batchelor?' Thorne asked.

'Same story we've heard already,' Holland said. 'The stuff about what happened to McEvoy. Nicklin being worried he's going to "fall down some stairs" or whatever.'

'It's all rubbish.' Thorne checked to see he had not missed any messages then put his phone away. 'We know that.'

'Maybe Batchelor doesn't know why he's here any more than we do. Maybe he's just doing what he's told.'

'We'll see if Yvonne can find out something,' Thorne said.

'Mind you,' Holland said. 'That look on his face, when he asked me about Chloe. How old she was.' They both turned towards the car. Nicklin was watching them through the side window, contentedly clutching the chocolate bar that Fletcher had unwrapped for him. 'Right now, I could happily throw the fucker down a flight of stairs myself.'

EIGHT

'Have you worked with Thorne before?' Karim asked.

'Only the once,' Markham said. 'For about half an hour, but I wasn't even a CSM then.'

'Well, you must have impressed him.'

'Really?'

'Oh yeah.' Karim nodded, knowing. 'Hand-picked we were, all of us. We're the bloody A-Team!'

It was an hour or so since they'd left the services. They'd skirted Shrewsbury, crossed the river Severn and now they were no more than a few miles from the Welsh border. Wendy Markham stared out of her window at the north Shropshire countryside, bleak and beautiful. The occasional small village, gone before she could take in any more than a pub sign or the steeple of a church: Knockin, Morton, Osbaston.

She'd done a fair amount of staring since they'd set off,

in an effort to avoid too many meandering conversations with Samir Karim. He seemed a decent enough bloke, keen to talk about his wife and kids at any opportunity, but he wasn't nearly as entertaining as he thought he was. She wondered why on earth Thorne had hand-picked *him*. An exhibits officer needed to be thoughtful and meticulous, well organised. Glancing at him now, humming to himself and tapping fat fingers on the steering wheel, she found it hard to believe that Karim could organise himself out of bed in the morning.

Come to think of it, why had Thorne picked *her*? She'd only been promoted to CSM a few weeks earlier.

Six months or so before that, Markham had been a SOCO at a crime scene in Hackney, the location of what turned out to be the murder by administered overdose of a young man named Peter Allen. In a desperate hurry for information, Thorne had shamelessly played Markham off against another forensic officer; a wager as to which of them could get much-needed results back to him the quickest. He had promised her a case of Merlot and dinner if she won. She had very much enjoyed the wine, but the promised meal had failed to materialise.

She'd done a spot of checking up later on and it had been a forgivable oversight, all things considered. Bearing in mind that shortly after their paths had crossed professionally Thorne had been struggling with the debacle of a siege gone very wrong, dealing with his demotion to uniform.

It was understandable that dinner had slipped his mind.

Yes, she was damn sure she *had* impressed him. He'd remembered her, hadn't he? She couldn't help wondering though, if it was just about the work. Of course, she hoped Thorne's choice had been based on her qualifications for the job, on an unbiased assessment of her considerable ability. That said, an instinct told her there was something else going on and she would not have been wholly outraged to discover that some small degree of physical attraction had been a contributory factor. Or, to put it in terms that didn't sound like she was in court giving bloody evidence:

Wouldn't hurt if he fancied her a bit, would it?

'What?' Karim said.

'Sorry?'

'Just wondered what you were smiling about, that's all.'

Unlike Sam Karim, Tom Thorne hadn't talked about his domestic set-up at all . . .

'Nothing,' Markham said. 'Just remembering something.'

'Looks like it was something nice!'

'So, how much longer d'you think?'

Karim glanced at the clock on the dash. 'A couple of hours, maybe.' He nodded, smacked his palms against the wheel. 'Going to be an interesting one this, I reckon. Oh yes, I can feel it in my water.'

Markham doubted that Karim could piss in a straight line, never mind predict the future with it, but she could not disagree with him. Even allowing for the brief time she had been a qualified crime scene manager, she knew that this operation was out of the ordinary. The place they were going for a start. It was certainly a long way to travel without knowing if there would be any crime scene to manage at the end of it. On top of which, she would normally have been free to select her own CSIs, rather than having them foisted on her at the other end.

It wasn't a major problem. She would show Thorne that she could work with whatever, whoever was thrown at her. If she could handle four hours in the car with Sam Karim ...

'So, your wife's OK with you being away for a few days?' she asked.

Karim laughed. 'Are you kidding? She can't wait to get rid of me. She'll have her feet up by now, dirty great box of Black Magic on the go.' He laughed again.

Markham laughed right along with him, then said, 'What about Thorne's wife?'

In the rear-view, Thorne could see that Nicklin was asleep, his head lolling to one side, jaw slack. Aside from issues of self-preservation or personal pleasure, Thorne knew that there was not too much that would keep a man like Nicklin awake at night. All the same, it was disconcerting to see just how easily he drifted away. How untroubled he appeared by the stuff inside his own head.

Thorne adjusted the mirror slightly and saw that Jeffrey

Batchelor was very much awake. The side of his head was pressed against the window, eyes wide and fixed forward.

He was the one who looked troubled.

A murderer, yes, but not one like Stuart Nicklin. Not a man whose crime itself would obviously have drawn Nicklin to him. Not someone Thorne could easily imagine Nicklin being attracted to sexually either, even if – as Phil Hendricks never tired of telling him – he was hardly an expert.

So, what was he doing here?

Perhaps Holland had been right and even Batchelor himself did not fully understand why he was in that car with the rest of them. It made a degree of sense. Over the years, Nicklin had not only proved himself extremely adept at persuading people to do what he wanted, but also at keeping the reasons for it to himself, until he was good and ready.

What had he threatened Batchelor with? What had he promised?

Thorne could only hope that, in an effort to get explanations, Yvonne Kitson would be luckier with Batchelor's wife than she had been with Nicklin's ex.

He glanced across at Holland and felt the warm, familiar blush of guilt.

Holland and Kitson . . .

Just two months before, in uniformed banishment south of the river, Thorne had asked for their help in investigating a series of suicides he believed to be connected. They had gone out on a limb for him, worked under the radar on his behalf, placed their own careers in jeopardy. Thorne felt that blush heat up a little more. He knew there was little point in not being honest with himself. *He* had put their careers in jeopardy and for all he knew they still were.

Nicklin's insistence about who should escort him in the search for Simon Milner's body had seemingly allowed Thorne to wriggle off the latest hook he had hung himself on. Picking Holland and Kitson to be part of his team had granted them a reprieve too, but Thorne had a horrible suspicion that it might only be temporary. Any disciplinary investigation that had been put on hold might well swing right back into action once the bones had been found and Nicklin was returned to prison. Worst of all, as far as Thorne was aware, Holland and Kitson had no idea about any of this. They presumably believed that, like Thorne, they had got away with it.

It was not mentioned, save for the very occasional loaded comment.

A fortnight before, Thorne had asked Kitson if she could take care of some interviews while he and Holland were on the road with Nicklin.

Kitson had smiled, the picture of innocence. Said, 'This one on the books then, is it?'

'Sophie used to come up here as a kid,' Holland said, now. 'To Wales, I mean.'

Thorne turned to look at him. 'Really?'

Holland nodded. 'Yeah. Youth hostelling trips and all that, with her school. Llangollen, the Brecon Beacons.'

Sophie. Holland's long-term girlfriend, his daughter's mother. A woman who was not exactly Tom Thorne's biggest fan.

'She thinks we should come here with Chloe ...'

Holland turned round. He relaxed a little when he saw that Nicklin was asleep, but still kept his voice low. 'You know, a few days where the world isn't on some screen or other.'

'Sounds like a good idea,' Thorne said. He knew exactly what Holland meant. Alfie was a good deal younger than Chloe, but already the TV or Helen's laptop or even the screen on a mobile phone seemed to exert an almost hypnotic influence over him.

A mile or two further on, Thorne said, 'Just a tip, Dave.' He nodded at the rear-view. 'Don't let him wind you up, OK? It's exactly what he wants. He's always looking for cracks ...'

Nicklin was not asleep.

It wasn't as though he was pretending to be. He wasn't smacking his lips or letting out fake snores, nothing like that. He had just closed his eyes against the sunshine strobing through the trees, that was all. He'd let his face relax. He wasn't expecting to hear anything eye-opening or top secret.

He'd started doing it in his cell. It was probably just basic meditation, which was ironic, considering that was the kind of thing they'd encouraged the kids to do all those years ago at Tides House. He didn't think about it in those terms. It was just a question of relaxing, of lying there on his bunk and listening. He'd discovered that just by doing that, he could somehow get in sync with the rhythm of the prison. Tap into it, use it . . .

So, not eavesdropping, but he'd enjoyed what Thorne had said anyway.

It was spot on too, no question about it. Not that he was surprised. Thorne knew him almost as well as he knew Thorne.

There were cracks already and plenty more to come. Hairlines now, but they would soon be good and ready to gape. Cracks he was very much looking forward to opening up, when the time was right.

With a word, with a look, with a finger.

NINE

Kitson glanced up at the well-weathered FOR SALE sign and, when she looked back towards the front door, she saw that it was open and that Sonia Batchelor was waving from the step. She had begun talking before Kitson had reached the front door, and continued as she showed her through to a neatly arranged sitting room.

'We need to downsize,' Sonia said. 'Rachel and me. Well, I mean, obviously we do. For seven years, at least.'

Kitson nodded.

Rachel: the younger daughter. Seven years: the minimum term.

The woman sat down on an artfully distressed leather armchair and waved Kitson towards a matching sofa. She was forty-three, if Kitson remembered correctly; skinny, with grey roots showing through a dye-job and long, thin fingers that moved almost constantly against the arm of her chair. She had worked full-time for the local council up until just over a year before, something in social services. The job had been the most insignificant of her losses.

'Only silly offers so far,' Sonia said. 'Just because people know we're desperate to sell, I suppose. They know the address from the news or whatever, so they're trying to grab a bargain.' She looked around the room, nodded. 'I'm not going to let anyone take advantage of us though.'

The house was a four-bedroom semi, a mile or so from the centre of Northampton. A nice, quiet road. Neighbourhood Watch and carefully trimmed front hedges. Just over a year before there had been a family of four living here, but now there were only two. Sonia Batchelor had lived here with her college lecturer husband and two children. Today, there was only one child and Sonia Batchelor was the wife of a convicted murderer.

'I'd offer you tea,' she said. 'Truth is though I've been jumpy as hell ever since you called and I'm desperate to know what this is about.'

'Sorry,' Kitson said. 'I did tell you Jeff was all right.'

'Yes, you said that—'

'That it wasn't really Jeff I wanted to talk to you about.'

'Right, but whatever it is, it obviously involves him, doesn't it?'

'Yes.'

'So . . . ?'

'It's about your husband's relationship with Stuart Nicklin.'

Sonia narrowed her eyes. 'Relationship?'

'You do know who Stuart Nicklin is?' Kitson asked.

Sonia nodded quickly. 'Yes, well, I bet there wasn't any problem selling *his* house, was there? I mean, there's always sickos and ghouls willing to splash out on properties with those kind of associations, aren't there? Way over the asking price sometimes, if the body count's high enough. Mind you, the council knock them down more often than not, don't they? Or is that only if the killings actually happened at the house? You know, the "house of horror" kind of thing. Like Nilsen or whoever. Actually, I always get the Nilsens mixed up, Donald and Dennis. I know the surnames are spelled differently and that one was the Black Panther and the other one killed young men and cut them up and only got caught because his drains started to smell.' She blinked slowly, let out a sigh. Said, 'For Christ's sake, Sonia, shut *up.*' She looked at Kitson. 'Sorry, I can't stop talking . . .'

'Why don't I go and make us some tea?' Kitson said.

Sonia showed Kitson where the kitchen was, then stepped into the back garden and smoked, signalling through the window to let Kitson know where the teabags were, that she didn't take sugar.

Back in the sitting room a few minutes later, she said 'sorry' again. The cigarette seemed to have calmed her down. Kitson gave her another minute, drank her tea and looked around. There were family pictures in polished frames arranged on top of a large pine trunk beneath the window.

The usual.

Mum and dad and two smiling kids. Assorted combinations of the four. In the park with a dog, pulling stupid faces at the dinner table, on a boat somewhere.

Jeffrey Batchelor and his elder daughter, Jodi.

Sonia saw Kitson looking and said, 'Sometimes ... even now, it's like it didn't really happen. Like it was just a bad dream. If the phone goes in the evening, I'll think it's her ringing from the station. I'll still be expecting Jeff to go and collect her, stomping out into the hall and moaning about being nothing but a bloody taxi service.' She almost laughed. 'You got kids?'

Kitson nodded. 'Oh yeah, I know exactly what that's like.'

They both looked at the photograph for a few seconds more. Jodi's hair was a little darker than in the only picture Kitson had seen previously. The one in the file.

Just a bad dream.

The November before last, Jodi Batchelor, aged seventeen, had hanged herself in her bedroom after being dumped by her boyfriend via text message. Her father had found her body. The following day, Jeffrey Batchelor had confronted his daughter's boyfriend – nineteen-year-old Nathan Wilson – at a bus stop near his house and, following a heated exchange, had attacked him in front of several onlookers. In what those witnesses had described as a 'frenzied assault', Batchelor had kicked and punched Wilson, giving him no opportunity to defend himself. He

71

had repeatedly smashed the boy's head against a kerb-stone, and, according to the witnesses, had continued to do so long after the boy was dead.

'Stuart Nicklin is currently under police escort,' Kitson said. 'He's being taken to a location in Wales, where he claims to have buried a body twenty-five years ago. And he's taken Jeff with him.'

Sonia stared for a few seconds. 'I don't understand. I only saw Jeff last week. He would have said.'

'He wouldn't have known it was happening,' Kitson said. 'Not exactly when, anyway. That's not allowed for security reasons.'

'Still, he would have said something, surely.'

'He would have been told not to.'

'By Nicklin?'

'Possibly,' Kitson said. 'But certainly by the prison authorities.'

Sonia sat back, shaking her head as though trying to make sense of what she had been told. 'So, what is it that you want?'

'We want to know what you think about their relation-ship. Nicklin and your husband.'

'What are you implying?'

'I'm not implying anything.' Kitson leaned forward. 'Listen, Sonia, we have no bloody idea why your husband is currently keeping Stuart Nicklin company, but we do know that Mr Nicklin does nothing without a very good reason. So, right now we're scrabbling around trying to find anything that might help us. You knew that the two of them had become close?'

Sonia nodded.

'How did you feel about that?'

She grunted. 'Well, obviously I wasn't thrilled. My husband's a good man, despite what happened. He's a man with *faith*.' She held Kitson's eyes for a few moments, as though keen for what she had said to sink in. 'I'm not a believer, none of the rest of the family are, but he is. He's not a nutcase about it, nothing like that . . . doesn't force it on anybody else, but he's kind and compassionate and he's got a conscience. He's everything Stuart Nicklin isn't. So, I felt sick, if you want to know the truth. But the fact remains that Nicklin . . . *helped* Jeff in there.' She leaned forward to pick up a mug of tea, which was probably no more than lukewarm by now. 'Jeff was finding it really hard. A few weeks after he first went in, he had some sort of . . . breakdown. They had him on suicide watch for a couple of days. He was in a real state, to be honest . . .'

Kitson had read the file. She knew that Batchelor had handed himself in to the police immediately after the attack on Nathan Wilson. He had pleaded guilty to murder and continually refused to allow any consideration of diminished responsibility. He had accepted his punishment. There was no doubt that prison would have come as a shock to a man like Jeffrey Batchelor, but now his wife was hinting that something serious had happened, over and above the necessary adjustment.

'Was he attacked?' Kitson asked.

'I don't think so.'

'Maybe he was threatened.'

'I really don't know,' Sonia said. She clicked her fingers. 'But suddenly everything had changed and when I went to see him he wasn't the same person he had been the week before. There was just a blackness. There was this ... despair I couldn't shake him out of.'

'But Nicklin could?'

Sonia shook her head. 'Trust me, I know how ridiculous it sounds. I spoke to one of the chaplains in there a bit later, someone Jeff had been talking to a lot ever since he'd been inside. He couldn't explain it either, but he'd certainly noticed the difference. Jeff and Nicklin started spending time together and things changed. Next time I went in, he was calmer. More like his old self. He was talking about the future, courses he wanted to do in prison, that sort of thing.' She took a mouthful of tea, pulled a face. 'I've no idea how he did it, let alone why, but somehow Nicklin managed to talk my husband round. Thank God he did ...'

Kitson looked across at the photographs again. 'That's the sixty-four-thousand-dollar question though, isn't it?' she said.

'What?'

'*Why*. Why would Nicklin want to take Jeff under his wing like that.'

Sonia put her mug down. She sat back and folded her

arms. 'Listen, I've got no bloody idea what's in this for Nicklin,' she said. 'But I think I know what Jeff gets out of it. I think Nicklin makes him realise that what he did wasn't so terrible.' She shook her head. 'I mean, yes it *was* terrible, course it was and nothing's going to bring Nathan back or make his parents feel any better. I just mean . . . compared to what Nicklin did. Someone like Nicklin helps Jeff remember that he's just a good man who snapped, that's all. An ordinary man, who's *nothing* like the Nicklins of this world.' She looked away for a few seconds, grimacing as though she were about to cry out or spit. When she turned her eyes back to Kitson, she said, 'Maybe you've got this the wrong way round and it was all Jeff's idea to go.'

'You really think so?' Kitson asked.

'I think my husband needs Stuart Nicklin there to remind him who he is.'

TEN

They cut north for a while, the single-lane B-road running almost parallel with the Welsh border, just a mile or so away across the fields. Though they were still in England, the small towns and villages they passed through had decidedly Celtic-sounding names: Gronwen, Gobowen, Morda. 'You sure we haven't taken a detour into Middle Earth?' Holland said, clocking a road sign.

Jenks, who looked like he was no stranger to the world of fantasy fiction, laughed from the back seat. Said, 'I'll keep a lookout for Orcs.'

Once across the border, Thorne turned west and they made good progress through the Dee Valley, the Holyhead road almost precisely following the path of the river as it wound through Llangollen. To the left, the landscape was soon densely wooded with conifers, while hills rose steeply away on the other side of them, mist shrouding the higher peaks. Holland pointed out the ruins of an abbey, said that Sophie had mentioned it.

'You wait until we get where we're going,' Nicklin said. 'There's remains way older than that.'

'Nice to know,' Thorne said.

'Shame there won't be time to enjoy the sights.'

'We find the remains of that boy, I'm happy.'

'You should try and come back,' Nicklin said. 'Bring your other half.'

Driving through the small town of Corwen, they passed a statue of a warrior on horseback brandishing a sword, a couple posing for photographs in front. Jenks wanted to know who the soldier was, but no answer was forthcoming. A mile or so down the road, Batchelor said, 'It's Owen Glendower. The statue.'

'Who's he when he's at home?' Jenks asked.

'Last proper Prince of Wales,' Batchelor said. 'Last one who was actually Welsh, anyway. He led a rebellion against the English at the start of the fifteenth century. Very much the father of Welsh nationalism.'

Thorne nodded. 'One of those groups in the seventies and eighties who tried to burn the English out, weren't they called the Sons of Glendower or something?'

'That's right,' Batchelor said. 'A bit like the Free Wales Army.'

'Maybe there should be a statue of him setting fire to a holiday cottage instead,' Holland said.

Nicklin laughed. 'He loves his ancient history, Jeffrey

does. Can't get enough of it, still keeping his hand in. Always got his nose buried in some book, haven't you, Jeff?'

'I wish I knew a bit more, if I'm honest,' Thorne said. He slowed for a set of temporary traffic lights, waited for the oncoming traffic. To his right, the hillside looked almost black, dotted with drifting, white clumps of grazing sheep. 'All we got taught at school were dates, basically. Battle of Hastings, Wars of the Roses, whatever. I can still remember the dates, but I couldn't tell you who was fighting or what they were fighting about.'

'I can recommend a couple of books if you want,' Batchelor said.

'Wish I had time to read them,' Thorne said.

'Not so fond of *recent* history though, are you, Jeff?' Nicklin turned in his seat to look at his fellow prisoner. 'A few too many dead teenagers for his liking, isn't that right?'

Batchelor blinked at him.

Fletcher laid a hand on Nicklin's shoulder and gently eased him round again. 'I think that's enough now, Stuart.'

'Just making conversation, Mr Fletcher,' Nicklin said.

The lights changed and Thorne pulled away. Checking the rear-view as he put his foot down, Thorne could see how very pleased with himself Nicklin looked. As though he had just been congratulated for a remark that was hugely funny or clever as opposed to being pulled up for saying something nakedly malicious. It was clear to Thorne that the casual cruelty had not been about trying to make Batchelor feel bad. That had simply been the inevitable result.

It had all been a question of where the interest was.

Nicklin had been completely unable to tolerate someone else being the centre of attention, even if it was someone to whom he was supposedly close, even for just those few minutes of trivial conversation.

It had become necessary to adjust the focus.

Thorne remembered something he had been told many years earlier by a senior officer, when he had first joined a Murder Squad. There were, so he learned, two basic types when it came to murderers. There were those who would run from the scene of their crime as fast and as far as possible, and those who would hang around and offer to help the police with their enquiries.

There was little doubt as to which type Stuart Nicklin was.

Thorne was happy that Nicklin had been caught, happier still that he had been the one to catch him. Sometimes though, he regretted the part he had played in giving so much attention to a man who could bear almost anything except being ignored. In many ways, that man was still the child who had been expelled from school. The boy who had rescued Martin Palmer from the bullies, only to dominate and control him in unimaginable and perverse ways. Someone who had discovered, at an absurdly early age, how good it felt to hurt people and how much fun it was to make others do it for you.

Suddenly, Nicklin leaned forward, sighing heavily. He spoke in a theatrically whiny voice. 'Are we nearly there yet?'

'God, you sound like one of my kids,' Fletcher said.

Thorne had to admit, it was a very good impression of a bratty teenager. It hadn't struck him so forcibly before that Nicklin was such a skilled mimic. It made sense, he supposed, when you had spent so much of your life pretending to be someone you were not.

Nicklin was clearly enjoying Fletcher's reaction. 'Are we? Are we nearly there?'

Thorne looked at the sat nav. There was less than sixty miles to go, but according to the timings on the screen, they were still an hour and a half away. 'No,' he said.

'Only difference is I can't threaten you with taking your PlayStation away,' Fletcher said. 'Or no more trips to McDonald's.'

Nicklin turned to the prison officer and now his face was completely expressionless; eyes flat and unblinking. 'Not very much anyone can threaten me with, Mr Fletcher ...'

All but the last few miles of their journey took them across Snowdonia National Park: eight hundred square miles of mountains, forest and agricultural land, the majority of which remained privately owned. They drove west towards the coast for a while, the road twisting just beneath Blaenau Ffestiniog, the 'hole' in the middle of the park where the heritage railway and the once thriving slate mines drew thousands of tourists every year. As they skirted the edge of the huge, man-made reservoir at Trawsfynydd, Holland pointed out a pair of hulking concrete towers, stark against the mountains on the far side.

'Looks like a Bond villain's hideout,' he said.

This time it was Nicklin who enthusiastically seized the chance to provide the required information. These were, he told them, the twin reactors of a now decommissioned nuclear power station; a place to which he and the other boys from Tides House had been brought on an educational visit a quarter of a century earlier.

'They took us up to that steam railway at Ffestiniog too. Chuff, chuff, pennies on the line, all that. Then someone had the bright idea of teaching us all about nice, clean nuclear power.' He stared across the water. 'It was a bloody disaster though. There were a *lot* of dead fish in there and apparently animals had been dying all over the place ... bit of a scandal at the time. I swear that when we left they waved Geiger counters all over us.'

Fletcher said, 'Bloody hell.'

'We were all fine,' Nicklin said. 'Assuming the Geiger counters were working properly. Mind you, this stuff can take years to affect you, can't it? Maybe, if I'd ever had kids, they'd have been born with two heads or webbed feet or whatever.'

Thorne was thinking that Nicklin's absence from the gene pool was no great loss. Glancing across and catching Holland's eye, he could see that he was thinking much the same thing.

'I remember that Simon was with us that day,' Nicklin said. 'You know, Simon, who we're going to be looking for?'

'Simon, the kid you murdered,' Thorne said.

'That's the one,' Nicklin said, cheerfully. 'I remember that he was getting really wound up. Scared to death, he was. Silly bugger spent every day for weeks afterwards banging on about how he was going to get cancer.'

'I bet you had nothing at all to do with winding him up,' Thorne said.

'Oh, I had everything to do with it.' Nicklin sat back in his seat. The power station was lost to view behind tall trees. 'You've no idea how boring it was on that island, Tom. Well, you'll see when we get there. I needed a hobby ...'

The last stretch took them through Porthmadog, slowing beside the miniature railway running along the Cobb, then out into open country again, the darkening fields flooded on their right and above a streak of blue sky narrowing to grey and then a dusty pink at the horizon. A few miles further on, the vista became almost absurdly melodramatic as the sea came suddenly into view.

'Needs music,' Holland muttered. 'Like a film ...'

Twenty minutes later, driving into the village of Abersoch, the sat nav announced that their destination was ahead.

Thorne outlined the itinerary for the remainder of the day. By now everyone understood that they would not be

82

travelling to the island until the following morning. It was already after two thirty and would be starting to get dark in an hour or so. 'We need to make a start bright and early,' Thorne said. 'Give ourselves a full day. Though I'm hoping it won't take that long.'

'I'll see what I can do,' Nicklin said.

Jenks leaned forward to tap Fletcher on the arm. 'Not that we'll be complaining about the overtime, mind . . .'

'So, what's the plan for tonight?' Nicklin asked the question casually, as if they were just a gang of mates on the town and it was a toss-up between a nightclub and a quiet dinner somewhere.

'Not got one yet,' Thorne said. 'For now, we need to see what we can do about getting you and Mr Batchelor a nice uncomfortable bed for the night.'

ELEVEN

There was quite a welcoming committee.

Over and above the staff who would be required to monitor the prisoners, there was a healthy number of North Wales police officers gathered when Thorne walked into the custody suite at Abersoch police station. It was not the warmest of welcomes. Thorne was greeted with terse nods and a cursory handshake or two from a custody sergeant, three PCs, the regional chief superintendent in best dress uniform and a plain-clothes inspector from local CID. The detective – a scruffy sod who was wearing half his breakfast on his jacket – feigned a lack of interest, but was clearly there for no other reason than to gawp at their infamous overnight guest.

'You might have been better off going to Bangor,' the custody sergeant said. 'Caernarfon maybe.'

'Why's that?' Thorne asked.

'Well, for a start we're only up and running here three days a week, see.'

'Cutbacks or crime rate?'

'Those other stations wouldn't have had to open up specially, like. That's all I'm getting at.'

Bangor was another hour's drive away and Caernarfon almost as far. Doing his best to sound good-natured, Thorne explained that he wanted to base himself and his team as close as possible to where they would be leaving from the following morning. 'So we can get an early start.'

'Just saying—'

'Yeah, I've got it.'

'They'd have been a bit more geared up for all this than we are.'

Thorne said, 'You've got cells, haven't you?'

Perhaps sensing that their visitor was running low on patience, the chief superintendent stepped forward and led Thorne to one side. He introduced himself as Robin Duggan. Tall and rail-thin, with wire-rimmed glasses and acne scars, he was somewhat less dour than the sergeant and his accent was certainly nowhere near as thick.

'It's both, by the way,' he said.

'Sorry?'

'Cutbacks *and* crime rate. That's why we've had four stations in the region close completely, had twice that many relocated and got a bunch more like this with limited opening times to the public.' He balled his hand into a fist and held it up. 'We're definitely getting a bit squeezed.

But ... a town like this one, we'll rarely get more than fifty or sixty reported crimes a month. That's across the board. You probably get that many every five minutes in your neck of the woods.'

'I enjoy the excitement,' Thorne said.

If, contained within Thorne's simple statement, Duggan detected the slightest suggestion that his own job was less than exciting, he chose to ignore it. Instead the chief superintendent straightened his cuffs and ploughed on, seemingly keen to impress on Thorne that he was highly experienced when it came to cross-border and cross-boundary co-operation. That things at his end of this operation were under control. 'I've been liaising with an opposite number at the Met,' he said. 'And I think we're very much on the same page on this.'

'That's good,' Thorne said. He wondered who the opposite number might be and if talking in senior management clichés was compulsory once there were a certain number of pips on your shoulder.

'There is one slight glitch,' Duggan said. 'Which is that nobody's awfully clear who's paying for all this. The manpower, the facilities, what have you.'

'I wouldn't know about any of that.'

'Of course you wouldn't.' Duggan smiled. 'Your job's just getting him to the island and back safe and sound, correct?'

'Spot on,' Thorne said.

'Talking of which ... I'm still in two minds, but I may head on over there with you in the morning.'

'Right.'

'I'll confirm with you later on.'

Thorne nodded and tried not to look too horrified. This was not an operation he had asked for, but now that it was his, the last thing he needed was a senior officer from another force looking over his shoulder. Least of all one for whom a sheep wandering on to the A499 was probably as exciting as the job got.

'I mean obviously this has all been put together at your end,' Duggan said. 'And I know we're talking about a crime that was committed a long time ago, but if evidence of a murder *is* found, that's going to be our jurisdiction.'

'Bang go your nice cosy crime figures.'

Duggan shrugged. 'Well yes, and it's going to be complicated, I can see that. Divvying it up to everyone's satisfaction. Still, I'm sure we'll get it sorted out.'

'Let's hope so,' Thorne said. Bearing in mind that Duggan and his opposite number could not even get on the same page when it came to divvying up the bill for Nicklin's accommodation, he thought that the Welshman's confidence was probably misplaced. He looked across at the other officers milling around in the otherwise empty custody suite. He saw now that their surliness was no more than nerves.

They could not be blamed for that.

'Let's get him in then, shall we?'

Ten minutes later, the cars stood empty in the station courtyard and the prisoners were being booked in. Thorne and

Holland stood close behind them at the booking desk. Fletcher and Jenks were sitting with cups of tea next to Karim and Wendy Markham. Batchelor kept his head down, as quiet as he had been for the majority of the journey, while Nicklin seemed content to chat away to the custody sergeant while all the necessary paperwork was completed.

'I saw a sign for Portmeirion on the way here,' Nicklin said.

'That's nice.'

'It's where they filmed *The Prisoner*, isn't it?'

'If you say so,' the sergeant said.

'You know, the village? The penny farthings?' Getting no joy from the custody sergeant, Nicklin turned to Thorne. 'You know what I'm talking about, don't you, Tom?'

Thorne nodded. He'd seen it. 'Never really understood it, though.'

'"I am not a number!"' Nicklin said, good and loud. He turned round and said it again for the benefit of Fletcher and the others, then turned back to look at Thorne. 'That's the thing though, isn't it? For the last ten years, that's *exactly* what I've been. Stuart Anthony Nicklin, prisoner number 5677832.' He laughed, shook his head. 'Between you and me, Tom, I never understood it either. That stupid white balloon bouncing along the beach . . . '

The sergeant glanced up from his paperwork. 'Can you take the cuffs off now, please? The prisoners need to turn out their pockets.'

Jenks and Fletcher got up, moved to stand close to Thorne and Holland while the handcuffs were removed. Nicklin handed over his tobacco tin and wristwatch. Batchelor, just a watch.

'Right, do we need to strip-search them?' the sergeant asked.

Duggan stepped forward, nodding. 'We should follow the standard procedure.'

'They were searched at Long Lartin,' Thorne said. He looked at Fletcher, who nodded to confirm it. 'Neither of them has been out of our sight since we left.'

'Comfort breaks?' Duggan asked.

'One each, in full view at all times.'

Duggan looked at the sergeant. The sergeant shrugged.

'Look,' Nicklin said. 'It sounds like you lot *really* want to get your rubber gloves on and procedure's there for a very good reason.' He looked at Duggan, then at Batchelor. 'We don't want to get anyone into trouble, do we, Jeff?'

'We can leave it,' Thorne said.

Duggan nodded at the sergeant, who said, 'Whatever.'

'Shame.' Nicklin looked across at the pair of young PCs waiting anxiously nearby. Both reddened. 'Sorry, boys. Mind you, you'd only have made Mr Jenks and Mr Fletcher jealous.'

'Shut it now, Stuart,' Fletcher said.

Once Nicklin and Batchelor had signed to confirm the short inventory of their possessions, the PCs stepped across to escort them to the cells. Jenks and Fletcher followed as the prisoners were led away and both police officers kept their hands on their telescopic batons. Just before disappearing from view around a corner, Nicklin shouted back over his shoulder.

'You should all get an early night,' he said. 'And try not to eat anything iffy. You'll need strong stomachs tomorrow.'

Holland looked at Thorne. Said, 'That's a point, I need to get seasickness tablets.'

Nicklin had already rounded the corner, but there was no mistaking the amusement in his voice. 'I'm talking about after we get there . . .'

Thorne ran through the pick-up arrangements for the following morning, quickly shutting the custody sergeant up when the man tried once again to suggest that a different station might have made his own life a little easier. He said goodbye to Duggan who promised to call him later and let him know if he would be tagging along the next day. Then, Thorne and Holland walked out into the station courtyard, Karim and Markham a few steps behind.

'So, what *is* the plan for tonight?' Holland asked.

Markham said she didn't think they would have a great many options and Karim laughed. He said this was probably the kind of place where they still pointed at planes.

'I need a hot shower and a cold beer,' Thorne said. 'In that order.'

TWELVE

Kitson looked up from the game of Candy Crush on her BlackBerry. She returned the smile of an old man who was working at a large jigsaw and figured out that by the time she got home later on, she would have driven the best part of two hundred miles for these three interviews. North London to Huntingdon, then across to Northampton and back down, finally, to Watford. Unless the woman she had left until the end had something useful to tell her, her day's work would have generated nothing but a claim for travel expenses.

One of the care workers stopped at the table to set down a cup of tea and a plate of digestives.

Kitson thanked her.

'She won't be long,' the care worker said. 'Just doing her hair and getting some slap on. Mrs Nicklin always likes to look her best.'

Kitson stared at her, confused. She had come to see someone who – like the teacher Kitson had spoken to that morning – had been given a brand new identity. A woman whose name was not the one she had lived with up until ten years before.

The care worker shrugged, said, 'No big mystery. She tells everyone . . .'

When Annie Nicklin finally emerged through a door at the far end of the communal living room, she was being escorted by a second care worker. She walked slowly, but surely, what little weight she had supported on two sticks. Her eyes on Yvonne Kitson every step from the door to the chair.

The care worker brought a cup of tea across for her. Annie leaned her sticks against the chair then turned to study Kitson with an expression that showed no hint of animosity or suspicion. 'Right,' she said. 'Go on, love.' She spoke slowly, but her voice was oddly high and light. The London accent was still strong.

Kitson reached for her bag. 'Do you not want to see my ID?'

Annie waved the suggestion away. 'Well, you're either a copper or a journalist, aren't you? Either way, you've got questions of some sort.' Her white hair was thin in places, the pink scalp visible beneath. The liver-spotted hands were clawed against the arms of the chair. Kitson knew that she was eighty-five, but she looked even older.

'I don't understand why you're using your own name,' Kitson said.

'It's my name.'

'You were given witness protection.'

'I didn't want it,' Annie said. 'All that nonsense was their idea. Didn't want to deal with the aggravation of people trying to hurt me, I suppose.' She shrugged. 'So I took their daft name, but I was never very good at keeping my real one a secret and I told them I wouldn't move far from home.' She glanced up at an old woman shuffling past the table and lowered her voice. 'So, you know ... there were a few broken windows, dog mess through the letterbox.'

'That's why you're supposed to keep it secret.'

Annie smiled, girlish suddenly, as though she'd been gently scolded for doing something foolish and completely trivial. 'Well, it didn't really matter where I was living in the end, because I couldn't go out. I already had bad diabetes, arthritis and all the rest of it. I was falling to pieces basically, had to have one of those warden-controlled flats, so they could keep an eye on me. Then suddenly I got scared to open the front door, agoraphobia or whatever it is. By that time I hadn't got any friends left anyway.' She leaned towards Kitson. 'Funny that ... how they all drift away once your son turns out to be a serial killer.'

Kitson laughed, reached for a biscuit.

'So, in the end I hadn't got a lot of choice and moved in here.' Annie looked around. 'These are my friends now.

Most of them are too bloody gaga to know or care about Stuart.'

Kitson could see the slightest of tremors now, the woman's head shaking though her eyes stayed fixed on the same point. Thorne had told Kitson about talking to Annie Nicklin ten years earlier, back when he was still hunting for her son. She had been thoroughly cantankerous, he had said. Uncooperative and stubbornly protective of her son, even though Thorne was sure she had known perfectly well what he had done. Ten years on, she seemed a very different woman to the one Thorne had described.

One who had come to terms with the past, perhaps. Her own and her son's. One more at peace with everything.

'You mentioned journalists,' Kitson said. 'Have they been to see you?'

'One or two.'

'Recently?'

'I lose track of time, love.'

'It doesn't matter.'

'They always have the same questions,' Annie said. 'That's the funny thing. Did Stuart start fires when he was little? No. Did he used to hurt animals? Not as far as I know. Do you still love him?' She looked away for a few moments. 'Bloody stupid question, that is.'

Stupid or not, Kitson was suddenly desperate to know the answer, though Annie Nicklin's expression made it clear that was not going to happen.

'Course, they're all desperate to ask the one *big* question,' Annie said. 'Not that they do, but you can see they're thinking it.'

'Which is?'

'Did I *do* something to him?'

'What would you tell them if they did ask?'

The old woman shrugged. 'Well, I must have, mustn't I?'

Kitson, with no idea how to respond, brushed crumbs from her lap.

'You still haven't said what you want . . .'

Kitson told her about the trip to look for Simon Milner's remains and her son's insistence on being escorted by the detective who had caught him ten years ago. She said, 'We were wondering about Stuart's letters.'

'One every week,' Annie said. She sounded almost proud. 'Every single week since he's been inside, regular as clockwork. But I stopped reading them a long time ago.'

Kitson nodded. Another wasted journey. She began to wonder if she could beat the rush hour back, what she had in the house for dinner.

'They all used to say the same thing though. The letters from prison.'

'What?'

'That it wasn't my fault. None of it.' Her voice was a little less sure, suddenly, the tremor a little more pronounced. 'That I mustn't blame myself. It was the same as when I first went to see him after he was sent down. He

95

told me not to come any more, simple as that. He said I shouldn't have to go through it, that it wasn't fair. Because what happened wasn't my fault.'

Kitson stared at the smile that would not stay in place and suddenly understood exactly what Stuart Nicklin had done to his mother. What he had succeeded in doing over a prolonged period of time. He had systematically ground her down. Gradually, his real intention masked by fake concern for her well-being, he had worn away any resistance to the deep-seated conviction that she was actually to blame for *everything* he had done. That she had made him what he was. It was clear that Nicklin despised her and that making her suffer was every bit as important, as sustaining to him, as the suffering he had inflicted on his victims and their families.

Perhaps more so.

Annie Nicklin told everyone who she really was because she thought she deserved to be hated.

'So, he killed another one, did he?' Annie asked. 'This boy on the island, you said.'

'He claims he did.'

'Well, he tends not to lie about that kind of thing.'

'He's left it a long time though, don't you think?'

'He'll have his reasons.'

'That's what we're trying to find out,' Kitson said. Later, Kitson would remember that at no point did it occur to Nicklin's own mother that it might have been because he was sorry.

Annie was looking around, waving to attract the attention of one of the care workers, who came over and asked if everything was all right. Annie looked at Kitson. Said, 'I get very tired, love. Have to sleep a lot during the day.'

'It's time for your tablets anyway,' the care worker said.

Annie reached for her sticks. 'It's a wonder I don't bleedin' rattle when I walk.'

Kitson started to gather up her things. In the last look before the old woman turned away and began the slow walk back to her bedroom, Kitson saw a snapshot of someone for whom the pain of arthritis or whatever else she needed tablets for was negligible in comparison to what her own son had done to her. Was still doing to her.

Thin lips stretched across discoloured teeth. Light going in the eyes.

No, definitely not peace, Kitson thought.

After a trip to the toilet, Kitson was on her way to the front door when the care worker came hurrying towards her carrying a small box. 'Annie wants you to have this.'

Kitson took the box and turned back one of the cardboard flaps. She saw the bundles of letters, batches of sealed and faded envelopes bound together with elastic bands. 'Is she sure?'

'That's what I asked her,' the woman said. 'I mean, I know what's in there. She told me that she'd heard some of her friends crying in the night.'

'Sorry?'

'Sometimes a few of the residents can get distressed

during the night. It's quite common.' The care worker took half a step away, nodded back at the box in Kitson's arms. 'Annie said getting these out of the building might stop them having nightmares.'

THIRTEEN

The owner/manager of the Black Horse in Abersoch was clearly thrilled at having four of his rooms occupied in the depths of the off-season. Seeing his reaction, Thorne tried to imagine how excited the man might have been with *six* rooms taken, but Fletcher and Jenks had booked themselves into a rival establishment at the other end of the village. Sitting in his cubbyhole at Reception, the manager had taken the news well. He had smiled as he shrugged and muttered, 'More fool them.'

Welcoming the new arrivals like long-lost relatives, that smile had stayed plastered to Elwyn Pritchard's round, red face as he gleefully handed over keys on oversized wooden fobs, scribbled down the Wi-Fi password and escorted each of his guests to their rooms in turn. The unalloyed joy was there in his voice as he ran through checkout times the following day, made sure they knew about regulated parking hours in the street outside and explained that the boiler was playing up, while assuring them that there should be plenty of hot water for everyone provided they 'didn't go mad'.

'We'll try not to,' Thorne said.

Within a few minutes of shutting the hotel room door behind him, Thorne had taken his shower – unable, as it turned out, to go *too* mad beneath the lukewarm dribble – then crashed out on the lumpy bed for the best part of an hour and a half. When he woke, it was dark outside. He could not clearly recall what he had been dreaming about, but the thin sheets were clinging to him.

He turned the temperature of the shower right down and climbed back in.

He called Yvonne Kitson while he was getting dressed. She had not been back at home more than half an hour, she said, and was busy getting wine down her neck while she struggled to get her kids' tea organised. She gave Thorne the highlights of her conversation with Sonia Batchelor.

'So, you know … maybe Sonia's right and it's not *all* about Nicklin,' Kitson said. 'Sounds like Batchelor's getting something out of being with him.'

Thorne sat down on the edge of the bed. 'It was Nicklin that insisted on this.' He turned the phone's speaker on, tossed it on to the pillow, then lay back and pulled on his jeans. 'It was one of his conditions.'

'Just doing Batchelor a favour, maybe?'

'Maybe.'

'Worried about leaving him on his own?'

'Remember who we're talking about here, Yvonne. It's not like he's the prison chaplain.'

Kitson laughed. Thorne heard another mouthful of wine going down.

'What happened at the care home?'

She told him what Annie Nicklin had given her. At that moment the box was still sitting in the boot of her car.

'I need you to have a look at them, Yvonne.'

'Can I feed my kids first?'

'Yeah, sorry.' He sat up, walked across to collect the shirt he'd dragged from his overnight bag and draped across a chair. 'Look, I know it's a long shot, but he might have said something in one of those letters, given some hint as to what he's up to. God knows, a letter to his mother might be the one time he's honest with someone.'

'Based on what she told me, I seriously doubt it,' Kitson said.

'Well just have a look,' Thorne said. 'Obviously we're only really interested in the most recent ones. Unless you've got nothing better to do than sit and read all of them.' He watched himself in the full-length mirror on the wardrobe door as he buttoned up the shirt. When he was done, he tucked the shirt into his jeans. He ran a hand across his gut and pulled the shirt out again.

'I think I might take my wine out to the car with me,' Kitson said. 'Sit and read the letters in there.'

'Whatever lights your candle,' Thorne said.

She told him what Annie Nicklin had said to the care worker, the residents having nightmares. She said, 'I'm not really sure I want them in the house.'

Thorne closed the wardrobe door, looked around for his shoes.

His hair was still a little wet, so he put the shudder down to a trickle of water creeping between his shoulder blades.

When Thorne, Holland, Karim and Markham wandered down from their rooms and into the lounge, Elwyn Pritchard was installed behind the bar. If anybody had been playing a piano, chances are they would have stopped as Thorne and the others walked in. While the fruit machine tweeted and buzzed in the corner, they exchanged nods with a gaggle of flinty-looking drinkers who were clearly regular customers and gave the impression of having been in the bar a good while already.

Thorne took his wallet out and ordered the drinks.

'I'm guessing you're starving,' Pritchard said.

'I could eat a horse,' Karim said. 'But I'm trying to give up beef.'

It took Pritchard a few seconds to get the joke, then he laughed as though it were the funniest thing he'd ever heard; two explosive belly-laughs followed by a series of staccato hisses. When he'd recovered – though still grinning like an idiot and shaking his head – he said, 'Now, I've taken the liberty of assuming that you won't want to risk food poisoning at either of the iffy takeaways in town.'

'Won't we?' Thorne asked. He had clocked a Chinese place on the way into the village and had been thinking about hot and sour soup and Singapore noodles ever since.

'A lot of local cats go missing,' Pritchard said. 'You take my meaning.'

'Right.' Thorne glanced at Holland, who shrugged.

'I'm only messing with you, boys. Actually it's the seagulls you want to worry about. They catch them on the roof, pass it off as chicken.' As Pritchard set three pints and a gin and tonic down on the bar, he explained that he'd decided to think ahead and that he'd used his initiative. 'I opened the kitchen for you, special,' he said.

Thorne took a mouthful of Guinness. Said, 'Thanks.'

'Yeah, I thought: Sod it.' Pritchard nodded, wiping the bar. 'I'll splash out and bring the kitchen staff in for the night, because they've had a bloody long drive and they'll be wanting something decent inside of them when they get here.' He looked at Thorne. 'Sounds like you've got a big day lined up tomorrow.'

Thorne put his glass back on the bar; leaned against it. 'How do you know *what* we're doing tomorrow, Elwyn?'

Pritchard looked a little thrown. 'Well ... I know a couple of the lads at the station pretty well and one of them said something about a trip out to the island, that's all.' He pointed to one of the regulars, a skinny man with a shaved head. 'Plus, Eddie over there ... his cousin's the boatman who's taking you across in the morning, so, you know ... there you are.'

'That's it?'

'That's it.'

'The lads at the station didn't happen to say anything about who we might be taking to the island?'

Pritchard shook his head, stared down at the bar as he wiped at it a little harder. 'No, I don't know nothing about that. One of the lads just mentioned something about going to the island, that was all.'

Thorne looked at Holland, got another shrug.

He stared along the bar at Eddie, who stared right back, mouth full of crisps.

Pritchard turned and took a sip from a pint of his own. He fiddled with one of the optics for half a minute, then turned back and flipped the damp bar towel across his shoulder. 'Why don't you take a seat and I'll send one of the girls over to take your order?'

As they moved slowly away from the bar into the dining area, Holland began talking to Markham, something about a TV show they had both watched. Karim leaned close to Thorne and nodded.

He said, 'I think we should risk the chinky ...'

They sat at a table within sight of the bar, set somewhat snugly for four. It was one of several that had been laid, though there seemed little chance of anyone else having booked for dinner or popping in on a whim. Thorne wondered if they had actually just been left that way since August or whatever. The tablecloths dusted and the cutlery and glasses given a quick wipe every couple of weeks.

They studied their menus. Gammon and egg, gammon, egg and pineapple, fish and chips . . .

'Fish should be all right, shouldn't it?' Holland asked.

Markham shook her head. 'It'll all be frozen out of season, doesn't matter how close the sea is.' In fact, the sea was no more than a couple of hundred feet away from them, beyond a high wall and a line of dilapidated beach huts. Save for the light of a far-distant boat, it was pitch black outside the floor-to-ceiling dining-room windows, but they could hear the roar and shush of the water as it churned against the shore.

Holland stared into the blackness. 'Reminds me,' he said. 'I wasn't kidding about those seasickness tablets . . .'

A waitress who could not have been much older than fifteen came across and took their order. Fish and chips for Holland and Thorne, leek and potato soup for Markham and a casserole made with local sausage, which Karim decided to gamble on. They took the opportunity to get a fresh round of drinks in.

At the bar, the conversation in Welsh grew suddenly animated. Karim leaned towards the others. 'Listen to that,' he said. 'Only language in the world where it sounds like you've got something stuck in your throat.' He made a noise like a cat trying to get rid of a fur ball.

Holland laughed. 'Don't know whether I should be listening or trying to perform the Heimlich manoeuvre.'

Thorne noticed Eddie and a couple of the other lads at the bar turning to stare across at them. 'I think you might want to keep it down,' he said.

'What?' Karim sat up straight to look.

Markham spoke quietly to Karim, as if she were speaking to a child. 'You can't speak Welsh, but you need to remember they can speak English.'

Holland looked across and raised a glass to Eddie, who sniffed and turned slowly back to his friends. 'At least they know we're coppers,' he said, grinning. 'It might be the only thing that stops us getting beaten up.'

'Or it might be exactly why we *do* get beaten up,' Thorne said.

The food arrived quickly and only Karim seemed unhappy with it, his gamble having clearly failed to pay off. It didn't stop him tucking in though.

'So you think it's a problem?' Holland asked. 'The boys at the station shooting their mouths off?'

Thorne shrugged, mouth full. He swallowed, said, 'I'd be a bit more worried, but this place is so bloody isolated. It's not like anyone who fancies it can just nip over and have a look at what we're doing.' He speared a chip, angrily. 'Don't get me wrong though, I'll still be having serious words in the morning when we pick Nicklin up. Gobby sods …'

The child waitress came over and asked if everything was OK. They all made rather more enthusiastic noises than the food merited.

'He's not what I expected,' Markham said. 'Nicklin.' She looked at Thorne. Her brown hair was freshly washed and perfectly blow-dried and she had clearly taken the opportunity to reapply dark red lipstick, and mascara which highlighted eyes that were green enough to begin with. 'I mean, I knew who he was, obviously, did some reading.'

'He's changed a lot in ten years,' Thorne said.

'I don't mean physically.'

'So what were you expecting?'

'I'm not sure, just someone a bit less ... childlike. Or maybe I mean childish. In the station, when we dropped him off, that stuff about being strip-searched? It was like he was showing off.'

'He likes an audience,' Holland said.

'So why all this business about making sure the press are kept away?'

'He's not stupid,' Thorne said. 'He knows the press are going to get hold of it eventually. It's more about enjoying the fact that he can get us to do what he wants. Yeah, he likes an audience, but not as much as he likes making people jump through hoops for him.'

Karim jabbed a dripping fork in Thorne's direction. 'Making *you* jump through hoops, you mean. That's basically what he wants. At the end of the day, you're the only audience he's really bothered about.'

Thorne put down his knife and fork, picked up his glass. He'd had enough to eat anyway.

'Got a bit of a thing, has he?' Markham asked. She leaned towards him, curling strands of hair around her jaw with the backs of her fingers.

Thorne remembered the look on Nicklin's face back in that darkening playground, triumphant somehow despite the blood and broken teeth. He remembered the look on his face earlier that day, when he'd turned from the urinal to tuck his cock away. His eyes, whenever Thorne had caught them in the rear-view, as though Nicklin had been staring at it, waiting.

Thorne drained his glass. 'Yeah. A thing.'

When the waitress came to clear the table, nobody sounded interested in coffee, but Karim and Holland both seemed keen on at least one more drink before bed. Thorne pushed his chair back, announced that he was heading up. Wendy Markham finished what was left of her drink and said that she was ready to do the same.

Karim looked at his watch. 'It's not even ten.'

'Listen, I'm not your dad,' Thorne said. 'But I will be seriously pissed off if either of you isn't up to it in the morning, all right?' He pointed at Holland, nodded at Karim. 'He's a nutcase, but you should know better, Dave.'

'Just a quick half, honest,' Holland said.

Karim nodded, solemn. 'Maybe a couple of brandies.'

Thorne and Markham said 'Goodnight' to Pritchard and his friends as they left the bar, then walked in silence past Reception and up the two flights of stairs to the floor where all four of them were staying.

Markham's room was along the corridor to the left, while Thorne's was half a dozen paces in the other direction. They stood together on the landing and exchanged a look. Just an awkward moment or two of politeness before separating, a second or two too long.

'Right then ...'

'Fancy a nightcap in my room?' Markham asked.

Thorne swayed, his weight shifting from one foot to the other. He could feel the colour flooding his face and saw that the same was happening to Markham's. She was about to say something else when he managed to stammer, 'I'm really knackered, Wendy. It was a ridiculously early start this morning. Well, for *both* of us ...'

'I know,' she said, nodding. 'Stupid idea.'

'Stupid time, that's all,' he said.

They both looked elsewhere for as long as it took to let a breath out, then turned towards their rooms at the same time. They separated quickly, the floorboards groaning beneath the cheap carpet as they walked, as they fished for the oversized wooden fobs in their jacket pockets.

Casually, desperately.

Thorne pushed his key towards the lock, fumbled it and tried again.

He took care to keep his eye firmly fixed on the door that was no more than a few inches in front of his face, well aware that, fifteen feet to his left, Wendy Markham was doing exactly the same.

FOURTEEN

The writing was tiny and precise, but the way it was laid out, the words crushed against one another, meant that it took Kitson two or three attempts before she was able to read through any of the letters quickly.

It was impossible to tell if Nicklin had *written* them quickly. Had it all come out in a rush or had he taken his time? Were his descriptions and diatribes spontaneous or had he thought carefully through every phrase, perfected each image? She could not understand a need for haste, not from someone with so much time on his hands, but sometimes there was an unmistakable energy to the words. A strange urgency about them. Or was that simply down to the layout, the way the words had been crammed on to every page?

She sorted out the batches of rubber-band-wrapped envelopes before she started, laying them along the back seat of the car. She turned around to retrieve a fresh batch when she was ready and tossed the ones she had finished with back into the box, which was nestling in the footwell.

MUM,
Woken by a loud scream earlier on and found out that
someone had been ~~attacked~~ stabbed on the wing. Try not
to worry too much because I know how much you DO!
These things happen – he was all right in the end
anyway – everyone in a bit of a flap that's all.
ACTUALLY noise is the hardest thing to get used to in
here – not having any silence I mean. Outside you get
used to having those times when you can just sit and
think and it's hard when there is always a bloody
racket – bangs and shouts and screams and crying or
whatever. You just have to learn to tune it OUT until
it's just something in the background then you can
concentrate a bit better. While I was doing just that
earlier on I had a ~~strange~~ interesting thought. I was
wondering if you keep the things that were written
about me from the newspapers – you know my press
cuttings HA HA HA – not that you would want to
show them off to your friends NECESSARILY but just
wondered. It's not every mum whose son gets his name
in the papers is it and certainly not in letters that BIG!

Kitson had done as Thorne had suggested and read the most recent letters first. The whole thing felt weird enough anyway, but it was never stranger than when she was beyond the point where Annie had stopped. When she was opening envelopes. Now she was the only reader, looking at words that she was the first to see, other than Nicklin himself of course. She lifted each off-white, rectangular envelope and opened it fast, the tearing of the paper masking the sound of her breath catching every time.

In here if you know what 2+2 is and you can write your name you might as well be a PROFESSOR. Other prisoners will ask you to read letters from home or for help with legal stuff. Just because I was a teacher I get a lot of requests like that and it's fine because I quite enjoy helping out if I can – time passing keeping busy etc etc. But I also get very DIFFERENT reactions because of ~~what I did~~ why I'm in here – something like respect or even fear which was strange to begin with but can be quite useful if I'm honest. Some people found out about what happened in BELMARSH with the infamous spoon and a reputation like that can do you favours – it can keep you safe in a place like this so that's one more reason for you not to worry about me. OK? Turns out I'm the one to come to if you need a form filling in or a letter from your lawyer checking over BUT I'm also the scary one who you should avoid looking at when you're queuing up for your dinner. I'm the MAD professor! Made me think though – did I ever scare YOU??

The odd one had been opened and read by prison officers before it had been sent out. Kitson knew they did that. They would have checked all his incoming mail of course, but only dipped randomly into the letters that were going the other way. She had no idea who he might have been writing to other than Annie and his ex-wife. Did he correspond with his 'fans', of whom there were plenty? Did he reply to the marriage proposals from the crackpot bitches all desperate to snag themselves a killer as a husband? The desperate souls convinced that Mr Right would be someone with at least a couple of killings to his name.

Did you watch that tv documentary/drama the other evening about the things MARTIN and I did? Thought it was very good actually – not too sensationalist or graphic and was hugely flattered by the portrayal. Very HANDSOME actor playing my part. Not sure who they would get to play me the way I look these days – probably someone from one of those agencies supplying freaks and UGLIES for horror films. Just out of interest what do I look like when you try to picture me? IF you try to picture me. How I was just before I came in here or as a little boy?

She stopped after an hour for a cigarette, got out of the car and smoked it in the garage. She didn't smoke as often as she once had, but kept a packet in the glove compartment for the difficult days or nights. She would sneak out now and again, when everybody else was asleep, and the pack would usually last her a month or so. Her other half knew but pretended he didn't, and her eldest son had caught her once. He'd smelled it on her and gone ballistic. He'd called her a hypocrite when she'd tried to lecture him after he'd got drunk and thrown up on the landing outside his bedroom. It was hard to argue with.

I think I settled in quite fast compared to some and it's easy to forget how hard it can be for others – the panic and the sadness at missing your FAMILY. Making that ADJUSTMENT can be very difficult especially if you're in here for life. Made a new friend I think. JEFF was/is a teacher like me so there's a common bond straight away. He's finding it very tough coping in here at the moment – plenty of dark thoughts – so we talk about things a lot. Good to have PROPER conversations and it's nice being a shoulder to cry on – something I never really had but no point ~~dwelling~~ thinking about things that could not be helped, is there?

More than once, a single dried strand of rolling tobacco had fallen out into her lap as she'd unfolded one of the letters. She brushed it quickly away, hoping it was not one that Nicklin himself had plucked, sticky from his lips.

Looks like I'll be seeing DEFECTIVE inspector TOM THORNE again quite soon – going on a trip together

114

which I'm very much looking forward to. Will also be
taking the friend I mentioned before which has got me
thinking how important friendship is – especially in a
place like this – having somebody you can count on I
mean. THORNE is definitely someone who is very
loyal to his friends. Yes he probably loves the new
woman in his life and the child he's been lumbered with
but I think he understands that loyalty to friends is
definitely the most important quality anyone can have –
that friendship is not just SKIN DEEP. Let's face it
we're stuck with family for good or ill – you must know
that better than ANYONE. Luckily we get the chance to
choose our FRIENDS though. As for our ENEMIES
that's a whole different question!!!

After two and a half hours, Kitson had read as much as
she was willing to for one night. She had got through all
the letters from the previous few months and a good many
of those from much earlier. A hundred or so altogether.
She wondered how Thorne would feel about being talked
about, and not just in the most recent letters. She tried to
imagine how she would feel if she was the one Nicklin was
thinking about like that and couldn't. She put the cardboard box back into the boot of the car and tossed an old
dog blanket across it.

She smoked one more cigarette then went inside to
email Thorne.

FIFTEEN

Helen was laughing . . .

'. . . and the bloke who runs the place is like this cartoon Welshman,' Thorne said. 'With a big red face and looking like he's always just about to burst into song.' They both laughed. 'Honestly, he's like a dog with two dicks because he's got some actual guests, but he's a bit over-friendly for my liking.' He sat on the edge of the bed, moved the phone from one ear to the other and leaned down to untie his shoelaces. 'I think there's every chance we'll be murdered in our beds.'

'It all sounds lovely,' Helen said.

Thorne looked around the room, wondering what else he could find to tell her about. 'Oh and the remote control for the TV is attached to the wall . . . on a curly wire. I swear, it's actually *attached*, so people can't nick it. Does anybody bother to steal remote controls?'

'Some people'll take anything, you give them the chance.'

'Yeah, I suppose.' Thorne could hear Alfie shouting in the background. Helen's son, just a few months away from his second birthday. Helen tried and failed to shush him. 'How's he doing?'

'Well, he's not asleep.'

'Because I'm not there to read him a story,' Thorne said.

'Oh, is that it?'

'Seriously, I've got the knack of getting him off now.'

'He does miss you,' Helen said. 'His mood's different.'

'Really?'

'I've told you.'

Thorne glanced up at the mirror on the wardrobe door, saw that he was grinning.

'So everything's going OK, then, is it?' Helen asked. 'How you getting on with your new CSM?'

Thorne sat up straight. Why on earth would she ask that? Had she heard something in his voice? How could there be *anything* in his voice?

'Yeah, she's OK,' Thorne said. 'I've hardly spoken to her, tell you the truth. She was stuck in the back-up car with Sam Karim.'

'Right . . . '

Thorne could still see the look on Wendy Markham's face when she'd asked him back to her room. The intention had been obvious enough. I mean, nightcap? Had she brought a bottle of wine or something with her? Obviously, there was no bottle of anything. It was a pretty straightforward proposition. Thorne felt good about turning her down, he felt . . . noble.

And yet . . .

She was seriously fanciable, no question about it and being propositioned by anyone was nice, was a buzz. She was older than Helen, he guessed, probably early forties, but still a fair few years younger than he was. When he'd asked for her to join the operation as crime scene manager, Thorne had remembered exactly who she was and what she looked like and that he'd flirted with her a little when they'd first met. No point pretending he hadn't. Something about the way she'd spoken to him on the landing had suggested there would be no strings attached, no awkwardness afterwards.

Just a bit of fun while they were away.

'I called Phil,' Thorne said. The change of subject sounded jarring, even to him.

Phil Hendricks. Thorne's closest friend. A man whose shaved head, tattoos and body piercings made him look more like the lead singer in a death-metal band than the skilled and respected pathologist he was. Someone who remained fiercely loyal to Thorne, though that loyalty had been regularly tested, and who was usually first with a joke, despite his sadness at an unfulfilled desire to be a father.

'When?'

'Just before I called you. He wasn't answering, so I left a message.'

'Oh, I think I know why he was busy,' Helen said.

The truth was, Thorne had called Hendricks because he'd wanted to tell him about what had happened with Wendy Markham. Brag a little. They'd have laughed about it, joked about what might have been and Hendricks would have pretended to be shocked that Thorne had passed up a golden opportunity. Ultimately though, his friend would have been pleased, impressed that Thorne had done the right thing. Having grown close to one another in recent months, Helen was now Hendricks' friend too.

Thorne was pleased about it, even if that triangle had proved to be a tricky one in the past. In a previous relationship, his best friend and his then-girlfriend had regularly taken great delight in ganging up on him.

The silence between them growing dangerously long, Thorne asked himself why he wasn't telling Helen about the business with Wendy Markham. Would it not have earned him an inestimable number of Brownie points? Wouldn't it be proof positive that he was not the kind to play away when the chance presented itself? It was frustrating, but the fact was that he and Helen had not even been together six months and he could not be sure *how* she would react. She might well have been delighted, at his honesty and of course at the decision he had made. She would probably have laughed and made some crack about Markham being 'blind' or 'desperate' but would she then be spending the next few days imagining the worst? Would it actually do more harm than good in the long run?

Thorne could not see any point in chancing it.

'What did you mean, about Phil being busy?'

'I think he's got a new boyfriend,' Helen said.

'Really?'

'I called him a few hours ago and some bloke answered.'

'Bloody hell, he can't keep it in his pants, can he?'

'Told me Phil was in the shower. Said it like he was about to go and join him. He sounded a bit giggly, you know, like he was pissed.'

'Yeah, well he'd have to be to get off with that ugly bastard.'

Helen laughed. 'You ask me, there's a new tattoo on the cards.'

Though he was rapidly running out of space, Hendricks liked to commemorate each new sexual conquest with a trip to the tattoo parlour.

'Oh well, good for him,' Thorne said, thinking: Well, at least somebody's getting his leg over. It made him even more determined to tell Hendricks about the shag that got away. 'So how was your day?'

'It was fine,' Helen said.

It was code, a game they played. Helen Weeks was a DS on a Child Abuse Investigation Team and, as such, dealt with more horror and suffering every day than the average hard-as-nails Murder Squad copper saw in a month. Most of the time she chose to keep it to herself, to keep it from anyone close to her. Every so often though, the day would come when she would need to offload some of it and then

Thorne's job was simply to be there and to listen while she poured it all out.

Desperate half-lives and broken bones no bigger than a bird's.

'Fine' just meant 'not now', that was all. 'Not yet . . .'

Instead, the laugh came back into Helen's voice as she told him about a 999 call that had been doing the rounds: a tinny recording downloaded on to the phone of almost every copper she'd run into that day. A man had called the emergency services and announced that he'd been stabbed. When the operator had asked him how many times he'd been stabbed, the man said, 'This is my first time.'

Thorne was naked and staring at himself in the rust-spotted bathroom mirror by the time they said goodnight.

Helen said, 'Keep an eye on Nicklin tomorrow, all right?'

'I'll not be taking my eyes off him,' Thorne said.

He walked back into the bedroom, set an alarm on his phone and turned on the TV. He slipped beneath the thin duvet and flicked through the channels with the remote that was attached to the wall. He was tired, but watched a few minutes of some film he could not make head or tail of until he could barely keep his eyes open. He turned the TV off and leaned over to switch off the bedside light.

Within a few moments he was wide awake again.

He turned the light back on and reached for a paperback thriller that Helen's father had sent, thinking he might like it. A few pages were more than enough. Religious conspiracies and clues in paintings or symphonies or whatever. They had yet to meet, so it was understandable that Helen's father might make a mistake about the kind of thing his daughter's boyfriend liked to read. Or perhaps it was just that Thorne's mind was suddenly racing too fast for anything to settle, to gain purchase.

He got out of bed to fetch the small, laminated photograph from the inside pocket of his jacket. It had been part of the background material Brigstocke had passed on to him when the operation was being put together; a faded photo from a quarter of a century before, taken in the place he would be travelling to in the morning.

Thorne lay down again and studied the picture.

A dozen or so boys, the majority looking surly or plain awkward. The members of staff not looking an awful lot happier, save for the woman at the heart of the gathering. A shawl around her shoulders, heavy-framed glasses and a smile of satisfaction, of pride in the men and boys around her.

He took a last look at the two boys standing together at the far end of the back row, then put the picture down.

He thought about two dead teenagers and Jeffrey Batchelor waking to it every day of his life. A third, who was the only one smiling in a faded photograph. He thought about a boy who was now only bones and a mother desperate to lay her son to rest; praying that the man who had killed him was telling the truth.

Got a bit of a thing, has he?

He remembered what Helen had said to him about Nicklin, her insistence that he stayed careful. He thought about her trying to get Alfie to sleep then climbing into bed wearing one of his old Johnny Cash T-shirts.

The smell of body butter on it afterwards.

He lay awake and thought about Helen, but when he finally turned off the light and his hand crept down beneath the duvet, Thorne was thinking about Wendy Markham.

SIXTEEN

Jeffrey Batchelor spoke to his daughter every night.

In a tender rush and jumble of words that were sometimes spoken out loud he told her about his day, such as it
had been. The humour if he had managed to find any, the
small moments of triumph. He told her how very much he
and her mother and her younger sister missed her. How
sorry he was that he had got things so wrong, that he had
made it all a thousand times worse. Every night, last thing of
all, lying there in the dark as the prison settled around him,
he made sure Jodi knew how much she had been loved.

Tonight, for all the obvious reasons, the words were that bit
harder to come by. It was painfully frustrating when, for those
very same reasons, he needed to talk to her more than ever.

He pulled his knees up to his chest and wrapped his
arms around them.

The tiled wall of the cell cold against his back, head

bowed, filled with images of blood-spattered stones and white noise, he felt suddenly more lost and more alone than he had been in a long time.

He felt like he had on his first night behind bars.

Back then, whenever Batchelor closed his eyes, Nathan Wilson's would be staring right back at him. Wide and terrified, until the light in them began to die, fading slowly to a pinprick like an old-fashioned TV turning off. Blank now, but they were still zooming in and out of focus, coming up towards Batchelor's own face then falling away again, the head crashing down and down and down on to the edge of the kerb. His hands tangled tight in the boy's hair, the spatter of blood soft against them and each dull, wet crack vibrating up his arm.

Those same pictures – the sense-memories vivid and undimmed – came back now as he recalled that first night in Long Lartin. It was almost certainly the fact that he was *not* there tonight, the change in location and of atmosphere, that was making things so difficult; that was throwing him so very much off kilter.

Fear as well, of course.

Batchelor was anything but stupid, so he was as afraid as he had ever been.

He tried and failed to talk to his daughter again, so settled instead for a few simple prayers. One for Jodi, of course, and for Sonia and Rachel. One for the soul of Nathan Wilson whom he had murdered and one for Nathan Wilson's suffering family . . .

The lights went out automatically.

He lay on his side, his knees still pulled up, and waited for sleep.

The prayers had definitely helped and now, instead of thinking about the past, he tried to imagine what the next day was going to bring. The island was the perfect place for all this in many ways.

The history and the holiness.

It was tailor-made for him, Nicklin had said that.

'It's ideal, Jeff,' he had said. Lying back on his bunk, a bar of chocolate in hand and Batchelor dry-mouthed and stiff in the doorway. 'Now, trust me, I'm not a big believer in fate, but sometimes you just have to believe things have happened for a reason. That little so-and-so sending his text to your daughter and her stringing herself up. You winding up in here, on the same wing, the same corridor as me, for heaven's sake. The place I was sent twenty-five years ago that – I swear to God – could not be more spot on for you. It's all got to mean something, hasn't it? You know me, Jeff, I think about things a *lot*, but I couldn't have planned this more perfectly if I'd tried ...'

Now, Batchelor lay in the cell at Abersoch police station, and as the heating pipes grumbled above him and a group of lads began singing tunelessly somewhere nearby, his body tensed then heaved and the first sob exploded in his throat.

It was disconcerting, a cell that was this spartan. One that so singularly failed to reflect the personality of any one of its doubtless hundreds of inhabitants. Nicklin liked to think that his cell back at Long Lartin said a good deal about the man he was. There were books and magazines. There were things on the walls. There were news stories and articles and there were pictures, some of which he had painted himself and not by numbers either, like the majority of the wannabe Francis Bacons.

This was just a box; blank, utilitarian. A raised sleeping platform with a blue plastic mattress and a metal toilet bowl in the corner. Yes, there was the obscenity gouged into one of the tiles by a guest who had not been searched properly, but nothing that made him feel as though any human being held within its dull white walls might ever have had a single intelligent thought.

Still, it was only for one night.

Perhaps two . . .

The silence was a bonus though. Were it not for the occasional sound of heavy footsteps somewhere in the custody suite above, he might almost have been able to convince himself that he was quite alone. That he had been left to his own devices. The sensation was heady, gorgeous . . . until a minute or two after the lights went out, when the weeping started in the cell next door.

He gave it a minute, but it quickly became apparent that this was more than just a few tears before bedtime.

'Come on now, Jeff,' he shouted. 'There's no need for this.'

Need clearly had little to do with it, though the gasps

and racking sobs were certainly bordering on the self-indulgent.

'You need to try and cheer up. Think about tomorrow. Think about the good things . . .'

There was no let-up from his neighbour.

Nicklin waited a little while longer, then started to sing. 'The thigh bone's connected to the leg bone . . . the leg bone's connected to the ankle bone.' He was grinning, moving his head and tapping his fingers against the mattress. 'The ankle bone's connected to the foot bone . . . Dem bones, dem bones, dem dry bones . . .'

He carried on for a minute or two longer, ad-libbing nonsensical connections; knees to buttocks, toes to skulls. He listened, was pleased. The volume from the adjoining cell had definitely come down a little.

He said, 'You can't afford to lose your sense of humour, Jeff. None of us can. We're all buggered without that.'

It struck him that Tom Thorne was certainly someone who was able to see the funny side of things when necessary. He remembered one or two of the looks they'd exchanged on the journey, some of the remarks. It was very important, a sense of humour.

He lay back, thinking, humming.

Thorne was going to need it.

THE SECOND DAY

ISLAND
OF TIDES

It has been a day and a half – perhaps two days – since he's last seen or heard anything of the young couple who took him from his flat and he's spent most of that time handcuffed to the bed, feverish, shirtless and splayed out flat on his belly. It's been necessary to stay off his back of course, impossible to do anything else after what the girl had done to him. Some time the following day he had asked for the hastily applied wad of bandage to be removed, and the new bloke, the one who was now feeding him painkillers like they were Smarties, seemed happy enough to oblige.

'Air needs to get to the wound,' he had told him. 'Please. It'll heal quicker.'

His new guard, whose face he had still not seen up to that point, hadn't bothered saying anything. He'd just sauntered across and torn the bandage away, left the room before the screaming had stopped.

The air had felt icy against his flesh, painful for those first few minutes.

He's sitting up now, perched on the edge of the bed, one hand still cuffed to the metal bedstead. The wound is throbbing and the constant supply of painkillers means that his head feels like it could spin round, detach itself from his neck and fly off into the ceiling at any time. He eats with his free hand, lunch or dinner or whatever it is. A sandwich removed from its wrapping and a bag of crisps that has been opened for him. He eats, though he is not particularly hungry. He drinks from the water bottle he's been given, though he hates having to piss in the bucket. He stares at the young man who is sitting in a chair on the other side of the room, flicking through a newspaper and waiting for him to finish.

'What's happened to the other two?'

The man glances up for a moment, then goes back to his *Daily Mirror*. He is early twenties, a little on the pudgy side with wire-rimmed glasses. Pale with long, greasy hair tied back into a ponytail, a dark T-shirt and jeans. Not quite as uber-goth as the couple had been, but someone who could probably do with spending a bit more time outdoors.

'So, have they gone for good then?' He waits. 'Is it just you now?' He finishes what's left of his sandwich, then nudges the tray closer to the edge of the bed, until it finally falls, clattering to the floor.

The man in the chair looks up, startled for a second, then annoyed.

'Come on, at least the other two talked to me. What harm is there in talking, for God's sake?'

The man in the chair thinks about it, then carefully closes his paper and leans down to lay it on the floor. He sits back and laces thick fingers together across his belly. He says, 'All right then.'

'I'll need antibiotics.'

'Oh, is that right?'

'As well as painkillers. I'm grateful for the painkillers, don't get me wrong, but I'll need antibiotics to stop it getting infected.'

The man in the chair shakes his head. 'That's not going to happen.' The voice is light and girlish, there's a slight lisp. There is no accent to speak of.

'Why not?'

'Because that's not one of the things I'm here to do, is it? Going out to the chemist's or anything like that.' He nods towards the door. 'I've got plenty of food out there and painkillers when you need them, that's about it.' He reaches into the pocket of a denim jacket that is hanging on the back of the chair, pulls out the Taser. 'And this, obviously, to make everything a bit easier.'

'What, anything else above your pay grade, is it?'

The man in the chair shrugs, puts the Taser back. He reaches lazily down towards the newspaper.

'It doesn't make sense.'

The man sighs, sits up again. 'What?'

'You're feeding me, right?' He sits as far forward as he can manage, his arm at full stretch behind him. 'You're giving me painkillers, which suggests that you've got *some* interest in my well-being. That whatever's going on here, whatever the hell this is all about, you want to keep me alive and well. I mean obviously I'm not counting what that mad bitch did to me with her scalpel. That's obviously important for some reason, but beyond that, now it's been done, you're here to look after me, right? It's not five-star luxury or anything and these handcuffs hurt like a bastard, but basically you're here to look after me. Yeah? I'm right, aren't I?'

The man in the chair says nothing.

'So, letting this thing get infected is really stupid. You got any idea how serious that could be? How dangerous? Just takes a few hours for infection to set in and then all this has gone tits up, your whole plan, whatever. You need to think about that.'

He looks for a reaction, but the man just seems bored. He watches as the man bends again to pick up his paper, folds it and drags himself grunting to his feet.

'No, wait.'

The man turns and walks slowly towards the door.

'For *fuck's* sake . . .'

As the door closes with no more than a quiet *snick*, he is already lashing out with his foot to send the tray flying, the plate careering across the dirty carpet into the skirting board on the far side of the room. He yanks fruitlessly at the plastic cuffs, which only cut deeper into his wrist, then falls back with a roar of frustration. He has forgotten for a moment what has been done to him, until the instant he makes contact with the bare mattress and the pain is scalding, stabbing, exploding across his back.

Then there is nothing to do but scream.

SEVENTEEN

Thorne was up, showered and getting dressed before seven. He did not need to open the curtains to know that the weather was bad. He had to turn up the TV to hear it above the noise of the rain chucking itself against the windows. He stuffed his dirty clothes down into his overnight bag then checked his phone. There was a text from Phil Hendricks.

plenty 2 tell u 2!

In addition to a slew of junk emails there was one from Yvonne Kitson. She told him she had read through the most recent of the letters given her by Annie Nicklin. There was no important information relating specifically to the trip Thorne was on, to Tides House or the murder of Simon Milner. There *were* one or two things she thought Thorne would be interested in reading, however, and she had sent him a number of extracts.

Thorne downloaded the attachment and finished packing his things.

Before leaving the room, he sat on the bed and watched a local news bulletin. He wanted to make sure that the hotel manager had been the only person anyone from the police station had been mouthing off to. The last thing he needed to see this morning was the local newscaster cheerily announcing that a notorious serial murderer was visiting the area. He was relieved that a stolen skip-lorry in Pwllheli and some offensive graffiti at a bus stop on the Caernarfon road was as sensational as it got.

He was the last one down to breakfast.

Karim was already tucking enthusiastically into an enormous fry-up and Wendy Markham was eating poached eggs. Holland appeared to be sticking to coffee and toast and was looking warily out of the window. The sun was almost fully up and now, beyond an empty car park and a sliver of beach, the sea was – unfortunately – all too visible. It lashed relentlessly against the shingle, wind-whipped, the colour of strong tea.

Thorne took the empty seat next to Markham, who shifted slightly to make more room and smiled at him. 'Sleep well?' she asked.

'Yeah, fine,' Thorne said. 'You?'

A nod, another smile.

'I wonder if they've got any seasickness pills here?' Holland said. 'Maybe I should ask . . .'

Thorne waved until he caught the attention of the teenage girl who had served them the night before. He asked for builders' tea and a bacon sandwich. The girl solemnly informed him that the sandwich wasn't *actually* on the menu, picking one up to prove it, but as they definitely had both bacon and bread she'd see what they could rustle up. He told her he was very grateful.

Karim looked up from his plate and cheered and Thorne turned to see Fletcher and Jenks sloping in. They dumped their overnight bags near the door and dropped on to chairs at an adjoining table. Their grunted greetings and less-than-chirpy demeanours suggested they might have had a somewhat later night than was advisable. Thorne suggested they should get some coffee and, as if on cue, the manager appeared, instructing the waitress to bring a pot of coffee across for the two extra guests. Pritchard hung around, ostensibly to make sure that everyone was enjoying their breakfast, though it quickly became clear that he was keen to quiz Fletcher and Jenks on the night they had spent at the rival hotel.

'OK for you, was it?' he asked. 'Over there?'

Fletcher managed a 'yeah'.

'Decent rooms? I mean, I know they're a bit pricier than here, but that doesn't mean anything, does it?' Uninvited, he pulled up a chair and sat down. 'Some people think a coat of paint and a satellite dish means they can rip people off and I don't think that's on. What about the dinner, then? Up to scratch?'

Jenks told him that they'd spent most of the evening in a nearby pub and called in at the Chinese on the way back. Pritchard nodded and cast a knowing look towards Thorne and the others. Said, 'Feeling all right, are you?'

While the manager carried on interrogating the largely monosyllabic prison officers, Karim and Markham began talking about boats and Holland wandered towards Reception in search of seasickness pills.

Thorne turned away from the table and took out his phone.

He read through the extracts from Nicklin's letters that Yvonne Kitson had thought would be of interest. Scrolling through the text, it was a jolt the first time he came across his own name; seeing the casual way in which he and some of those close to him had been talked about. As though Nicklin was one of their number. Before he had finished reading, though, the shock, the anger had graduated into something else entirely. Having Nicklin's thoughts laid out before him like this – in a manner over which Nicklin himself could have no control, about which he had no knowledge – gave Thorne a welcome sense of something that was hard to name, but felt like empowerment.

Made him feel, for once, as though he had the edge.

The feeling stayed with him through breakfast and for the time it took the team to check out, load up the vehicles and drive down to the police station. It was still there somewhere, even when he was tearing a well-deserved strip off the custody sergeant and his two PCs; telling them he hoped that their 'fat, flapping mouths' had not jeopardised the security of his entire operation. Thorne could only assume that when he had finished shouting, once the shame-faced officers had scuttled away to collect Nicklin and Batchelor from the cells, his good mood had started to show through again. As the prisoners emerged, as Jenks and Fletcher moved to reapply the heavy-duty cuffs, Thorne tried to give nothing away, but his disposition was clearly obvious to one person at least.

Nicklin took one look at him and said, 'Someone's happy about something.'

They drove along the coast for fifteen minutes, passing quickly through the seemingly deserted village of Aberdaron, where – according to the owner of the Black Horse – their boatman lived. A mile or so beyond it, they began to climb steeply and then, following the set of printed instructions provided by the sergeant at Abersoch police station, they turned sharply off the narrow road on to an even narrower dirt track.

The two cars slowed to something below walking pace as they bumped heavily across deep ruts and potholes. The track twisted sharply down, with the overhanging branches of bare, black trees scraping against the car on one side and a steep drop to a water-filled ditch on the other. In places the Galaxy's wheels were no more than inches from the edge and though the rain had eased considerably, the wipers still had work to do. Thorne leaned close to the windscreen, hands tight around the wheel, and Holland braced himself against the dash.

'You sure that sergeant wasn't taking the piss?' he asked. 'You did upset him, remember?'

After a long few minutes, the track began to get wider and flatter and the sea appeared in front of them suddenly as they rounded a sharp corner; brown between grey outcrops of rock. Several vehicles were parked in a line along one side of the track, while directly ahead at the edge of a concrete slipway, their transportation was being prepared for departure. Thorne parked up carefully, sat there for a moment or two and studied it. He had been expecting something that conformed to his idea of what a ferry was, but the only vessel he could see looked a lot more like a bog-standard fishing boat. Thirty or forty feet long at a push, bright yellow where it wasn't dirty or rusting, and sitting on a trailer.

'Is that it?' Jenks asked. 'Bloody hell . . . '

Thorne watched a man climb down from the boat and trudge through the mud to a stockpile of large plastic canisters. He picked one up, carried it back to the boat and heaved it part way up the ladder from where it was collected by a second man waiting on the deck. Thorne guessed that the liquid slopping about inside was oil.

'Don't be disappointed if there isn't a cocktail lounge,' Thorne said.

As he climbed out of the Galaxy, Thorne saw two people emerge from a mud-spattered Land Rover that had probably been white to begin with. He nodded across, guessing who they were. They came over and the woman who had led the way introduced herself.

Professor Bethan Howell was a forensic archaeologist based at Bangor University, who had been assigned to the team by North Wales police. She was a little below average height and perhaps a few pounds above the average weight for it. She wore wire-rimmed glasses and a baggy, black cap and, in an accent rather more mellifluous than some he had heard the night before, she told Thorne that the job sounded interesting, that she was keen to get to work. She introduced the crime scene investigator she had brought with her, a pasty-faced individual named Andrew Barber. He shook Thorne's hand and stared out at the water. His expression suggested he had been offered the choice between this job or washing a corpse and now believed that he'd made the wrong decision. Knowing that Howell and Barber ought to get acquainted with the CSM and the exhibits officer, Thorne waved Markham and Karim across from the second Galaxy, then went to make himself known to the boatman.

He shouted up to the man on the deck, who in turn pointed to the man who was still busy ferrying the plastic containers across the sludge.

Thorne walked over and introduced himself.

Huw Morgan was somewhere in his mid-to-late thirties;

moon-faced and unshaven, with close-cropped dark hair. He wore dirty grey overalls and heavy work boots and, once he'd shaken Thorne's hand, he pointed with a thick, grubby finger to the man on the deck of the boat. 'That's my father, Bernard,' he said. 'He's the crew.' When he saw that Thorne was looking at a third man, who was hauling himself up into the seat of a small tractor, he said, 'That's Owen,' as if no further explanation were necessary.

'Right,' Thorne said.

Morgan continued loading the containers, while the tractor was driven across and positioned at the front of the trailer and Howell and the others unloaded their equipment from the back of the Land Rover: a small diesel-powered generator on wheels, several large canvas bags, two metal boxes the size of large suitcases and a pair of common-or-garden spades. Helping Howell carry one of the boxes across to the boat, Thorne expressed surprise that she hadn't brought rather more equipment. He'd certainly been on more straightforward jobs than this one where twice or three times as much gear had needed humping around.

'No point,' she said. 'I've made doubly sure there's everything we're likely to need. There *is* a larger boat, apparently ... the one they use to take livestock or heavy machinery backwards and forwards, but there's no vehicles once we get over there, just the odd tractor or whatever. There's no roads, as such.' Grunting with the effort, she pushed the box up the metal ladder and Morgan Senior

142

dragged it on to the deck. 'So, we don't really want to be taking anything we can't move around easily.'

'I had a *very* short conversation about using a helicopter,' Thorne said.

'Nobody willing to splash out?'

'No chance. Anyway, there's far too many of us.'

Overhearing them, Morgan shouted from the cabin. 'Going to be a bit of a squeeze as it is,' he said. 'I'm only supposed to carry twelve, tops, and I've got all you lot plus all that equipment.' He glanced down towards the cars; the Galaxy in which Jenks and Fletcher were still sitting with the prisoners. 'Plus whoever you've got in there.' He saw a worried look pass between Howell and Barber. 'Don't worry, we'll be fine,' he said. 'Just won't be very comfortable, that's all. It's a working boat, this.' He pulled on a grubby-looking green hat. 'She's not built for pleasure . . . '

Once everything had been loaded and as soon as everyone had changed into waterproofs and suitable footwear, Nicklin and Batchelor were brought out of the car. They remained cuffed as they were helped up the ladder. If Morgan was remotely interested in who was being brought aboard his boat, he made a great job of hiding it.

Like he had said, it was a squeeze. The prisoners and prison officers took seats on the narrow metal bench that ran along the edge of the deck, the handcuffs making it dangerous for Nicklin or Batchelor to remain standing. Howell and Barber sat on top of their equipment in the centre of the deck while everyone else found room where they could, grabbing hold of a rope or pole as soon as Morgan told them they needed to.

On Morgan's signal, the tractor pushed boat and trailer slowly down into the water. Once the boat was safely afloat, the engines grumbled into life and the tractor reversed back up the slipway, taking the trailer with it. Morgan gave the driver a wave, turned the boat around and said, 'Right then.'

For ten minutes or so, the *Benlli III* motored steadily out to sea, moving parallel with the Lleyn peninsula. The rain had thankfully stopped, but it still felt bumpy enough to Thorne. He was careful to watch his footing on the slippery deck as he moved forward to the edge of the cabin from which Morgan was steering the boat. He had to raise his voice above the rhythmic grind and thrum of the engines.

'Lucky with the weather,' he said. 'It was pissing down an hour ago.'

'You've got no idea.' Morgan spoke without turning around. 'We've not been able to run regular trips for months now. In the summer we'll sometimes do three full trips a day, showing tourists the wildlife, the old smuggling routes, what have you. This time of year, though, it's a dead loss. It was clear for a couple of days last week, managed to take a birdwatcher across, but otherwise it's been really bad.' Now he turned, nodded at Thorne. 'So yeah, bloody lucky.'

'Changes fast, does it?'

'You've got to keep an eye on it, put it that way. Like, I knew eventually it was going to clear up this morning, even if it didn't look that way first thing. That's most of the job, if I'm honest. No point taking a group across unless I know I can get them back again, is there? I mean, don't get me wrong, sometimes there's sod all I can do about it. We had one lot stuck out there for three weeks earlier in the year, but we try not to let that happen too often.'

Thorne said, 'Pleased to hear it.' His hands were freezing where he was holding tight to the edge of the cabin door. He dug into his jacket pocket for gloves.

'A good boatman won't just know what the weather's going to be like in twelve hours. He needs to know what's going to be happening in twenty four hours or thirty-six.' He nodded out across the waves. 'Especially with this stretch of water. This can be a pig . . . '

'Yeah.' Thorne had read about just how treacherous the crossing could be. 'So, what's it going to be like later, then? The weather.'

Morgan turned, grinning. 'Changeable.'

Thorne was stepping away when he heard Morgan say something else. He turned back. 'Sorry?'

'I said, it'll be nice over on the island though.'

'Really?'

'They reckon it's got its own microclimate. I've known days when it's snowing on the mainland and I've been walking around over there without a jacket on. Bloody strange, sometimes.'

145

'Not the strangest thing I've heard,' Thorne said.

'Yeah, well a lot of that's nonsense. King Arthur is *not* buried over there, for a kick-off.'

'Plenty are though.' Thorne was not thinking about Simon Milner. 'What is it, twenty thousand saints supposed to be buried there?'

'I don't know about that,' Morgan said. 'Certainly that's what all the pilgrims thought, what plenty of them still think, the number of them that come every year. Used to say that four trips to the island was the same as one visit to Rome.' He shook his head. 'God knows. I just think it's a special place, that's all. I don't know what you're up to over there and I'm not sure I want to, but you need to remember that.'

'Are you going to wait for us?' Thorne asked.

'Well, I wouldn't normally, but me and my dad need to service the lighthouse anyway, so we might as well hang around and take you back. I want to be away before dark, mind.'

'You and me both,' Thorne said.

'Gives you about seven hours, I reckon.'

'Your job to do the lighthouse, then?'

'Yeah, when I'm not being a boatman and when we're not being lobster fishermen. Need to do all sorts if you want to make an honest living these days.' He turned, flashed a smile at Thorne, showing off a chipped front tooth. 'Well, I suppose the likes of you are doing all right. Now that there's a lot more people trying to make a living *dis*honestly.'

They fell into a silence, the boat smashing through waves which were suddenly a lot higher as they drew close to the tip of the peninsula. Thorne turned to look at Holland and saw that he was deep in conversation with Wendy Markham. He had no idea if Holland had managed to get hold of any seasickness pills, but he certainly looked all right.

It was Thorne who was starting to feel his guts churning, the sweat prickling on his neck and forehead.

He hadn't said anything the day before, when Holland had been talking about trying to get tablets; hoping he would get away without showing himself up on what was, after all, only a short crossing. But he was already feeling as though he might not make it.

He had never been good on the water. He remembered holidays to Devon when he was a kid and nightmarish outings with his dad, on small boats, fishing for mackerel. He had always gone, not wanting to miss out on the time with his father, but if by some miracle he did manage to get through the trip without throwing up, the smell of the fish later on when his dad was gutting their catch would usually do the trick.

Now, he took deep breaths, kept his eyes fixed on the horizon through the dirty window of Morgan's cabin.

'You all right?'

Thorne nodded, hoped it wasn't going to be too much longer. 'I meant to say, I met your cousin last night. Eddie, is it? He was propping up the bar in the Black Horse.'

Morgan said nothing for ten, fifteen seconds. Then he muttered, 'Arsehole.'

A minute or two later, they were rounding the peninsula and Thorne got his first look at their destination.

'There you go,' Morgan said. 'Bardsey Island. Well . . . that's what the *English* call it.'

'What do you call it?'

'Ynys Enlli in Welsh. Island of Tides. Bloody tricky ones at that . . .'

Approaching as they were – from behind the mountain that dominated one side of the island – the first view was of cliffs and the snowflake specks of wheeling seabirds against the black crags. The island was shaped like a giant, hump-backed tadpole; no more than a mile from end to end and about half as wide. Thorne looked up at the cliffs, the hundred-foot drop on to the rocks, but having studied a map, he knew that where they would be coming ashore the landscape would be very different.

Morgan turned, saw Thorne looking. 'Special, like I said . . .'

Thorne became aware of shouting, a commotion on the deck behind him, and he turned to see that Nicklin was trying in vain to stand up. Fletcher had a hand firmly on his shoulder in an effort to stop him and while Batchelor just stared out at the cliffs, Jenks was leaning across him to help. Holland was already on his feet while Howell and her team had moved back, as far away as they could get from the struggle.

'What's going on?' Morgan shouted.

Nicklin tried again and was quickly pushed back down. Thorne saw something very dark flash across Nicklin's face, but when he turned to look up at Thorne, there was no sign of it.

'I just want to get a better look at it,' he said.

'Don't want you hurting yourself, do we?'

'It's been a long time ...'

Thorne considered for a few seconds, then gave Fletcher the nod. The prison officer moved his hand from Nicklin's shoulder, allowing him to get slowly and unsteadily to his feet. Jenks kept hold of one arm to prevent him falling.

'Happy memories?' Thorne asked.

'Not especially.' Nicklin stared past him towards the island, squinting into the spray. 'Just that last time I saw it, I was somebody else.'

EIGHTEEN

Tides House

The engines were switched off and, as the boat was guided gently towards the dock, they watched what looked very like a welcoming committee walking down a steep track to meet them. Once ashore, the boatman waited at the foot of the ladder to help each of his passengers down, taking their heavy rucksacks from them, though all but a couple of them waved aside the offer of a steadying hand. Just before he took his turn to jump down into the shallow water, Simon looked back at the boy he assumed to be the son of Mr Morgan, the boatman. The boy, who was probably eleven or twelve, had been staring at Simon and some of the others all the way across. Once or twice, he had ventured shyly out of the cabin and moved to within a few feet of them on the deck, only to be called gruffly back or given a job to do or just firmly warned to keep away.

'Huw. What have I told you . . . ?'

Simon waved, then jumped from the ladder.

He didn't see the boy wave back.

One of the three staff members who had travelled with them – two men and a woman – clapped their hands together, shouted for silence and began gathering the boys into a group. When the man and woman who had walked down to meet the boat reached them, there were handshakes all round. The woman who appeared to be in charge pulled a knitted shawl tight around her shoulders and said she hoped the crossing had been a smooth one. She looked at the boys and said, 'We've got something back at the house if anyone has a dodgy tummy.'

A boy next to Simon said, '*Tummy?* For fuck's sake ...'

The five staff members and eight boys began walking up the hill towards the line of buildings spread out at the foot of the mountain. Simon had no idea if there were only going to be eight of them. Perhaps there were more to come, or maybe others had arrived already.

For some reason, there were no members of staff at the back of the group as the caterpillar made slow and untidy progress uphill, so things fell apart fairly rapidly. The group stretched out and broke up until some of the boys began drifting from the path. One by one, a few dropped their rucksacks and went tearing down across the fields towards the sea; yelling and laughing like lunatics as they ran and pushed one another, sending sheep scattering in all directions. A staff member shouted, hands cupped around his mouth, then went running after them. Simon heard the woman say something about the new arrivals needing to let off steam. She stood and watched them, but she was seemingly more bothered about the wind messing her hair up, and after a minute she said that the boys were too hungry to go very far. That there wasn't very far *to* go, even if they wanted to. The man she was talking to looked unconvinced, but sure enough, all those who had broken ranks had fallen back in or been rounded up by the time they reached the farm.

It was like a toy set Simon remembered having as a kid. Even the colours were the same as they'd been on the box. A bright red door and red tiles on the roof, the white geese and that lush sweep of green pretty much wherever you looked.

There was a massive, old-fashioned farmhouse, with a walled area for ducks and chickens. There were barns and outbuildings and it smelled of pig-shit. Boys were already complaining about the smell, but the woman said that they'd soon get used to it. She told them that they would be eating as soon as everyone had been inside for a wash, but that it would be the last time anyone cooked for them. From now on, they would be taking turns to cook for one another. They'd be working out their own menus and then preparing meals using local livestock and fresh vegetables grown on the farm; that they would grow themselves.

One of the boys said something about growing herbs. The woman seemed pleased, then saw that the boy and his mates were laughing. She said, 'You can't grow *that* kind of herb, I'm afraid.'

Simon hoped that he would not be chosen to do the cooking first. He couldn't cook anything except pot noodles and toast maybe, but it wasn't his fault. How were you ever supposed to learn how to cook when the person whose job it was to teach you all that stuff was nodding out on the sofa with a needle in her arm? Shooting up red wine or vinegar or whatever because she couldn't afford proper gear. Stood to reason that you were never going to be Delia Smith while that was going on, didn't it? When all you could do was eat beans out of a can or try and nick enough money for a bag of chips.

He didn't blame her for anything else.

He'd made a mess of things all by himself.

The whole cooking thing though, that was definitely down to her . . .

In the farmyard, they were instructed to take off their boots, told that there would be special indoor footwear provided. Simon slumped down on a cold stone step to take his muddy Nikes off. He watched one of the men come out of the farmhouse with what looked like a basket of Chinese slippers or something. One of the boys said it was stupid and another aimed a kick at a passing chicken. He asked why they couldn't wear their own trainers and some of the other boys joined in. He started to get worked up and said it was an infringement of his 'basic human rights'.

A boy, who Simon had been a row or two behind in the minibus, sat down next to him. He seemed a year or two older than Simon, sixteen or seventeen maybe, though

Simon was a couple of inches taller. 'They don't get it, do they?' the boy said.

'Get what?' Simon asked.

They sat and watched as the argument continued.

'You get to wear your own trainers in a YOI, and it's like a status thing, isn't it? Kids wearing the most expensive ones, having special edition ones brought in to show that they're bad men, or whatever. This place is different though. They don't want any of that stuff going on, because they think it'll make us ... I don't know, *calmer* or something. That's why we've got to cook, why we've got to grow our own grub. It's all about *trust* and *responsibility*.'

Simon watched and listened, nodded occasionally. The boy used his fingers to make speech marks around certain words, like he was taking the piss. He turned away and stared back down the hill towards the boat, the red and white striped lighthouse beyond.

'Yeah, right,' Simon said. He pulled off a muddy boot. His socks were soaking wet. 'Trust and responsibility. I get it.'

'Don't get me wrong, they're mad as a box of frogs.' The boy turned back, grinning. 'But it's a damn sight nicer than Feltham, right? Smells better too ...'

Simon laughed and the boy seemed pleased and laughed right along with him. The boy stuck out a hand, saw it was muddy and wiped it on his jeans before offering it a second time.

'Stuart,' he said.

NINETEEN

The boat bumped gently along the thick layer of tyres that had been fixed to the wall. Showing remarkable agility for a man who must have been in his sixties, Bernard Morgan hopped from the boat on to the walkway and hurried towards a line of small metal sheds and a larger wooden boathouse on the dockside. As Huw Morgan restarted the engines and backed the boat away, Thorne watched the old man climb into a specially adapted tractor, similar to the one that Owen had driven back on the mainland, and use it to push the wheeled trailer down the slipway and into the water. Once it was safely in position on the trailer, the *Benlli III* was hauled out of the water, up on to Bardsey Island.

'*Croeso*,' Huw Morgan said.

Thorne looked at him.

'Welcome ...'

Nicklin said, 'Thank you, but actually I've been here before. A long time ago.' He smiled. 'It's nice to see you again, Huw.'

Morgan stared for a few seconds, nonplussed, then walked past Nicklin to the ladder.

By the time the passengers had disembarked and most of the equipment had been offloaded, Bernard and Huw Morgan had driven back from the lighthouse in a two-seater quad bike with a small trailer-box attached to the back. Huw hopped off the bike and moved to help unload the remainder of the gear. He nodded back at the trailer. 'Stick it all in there,' he said. 'We'll run it up.' He looked along a narrow track twisting up towards the mountain, a quarter of a mile or so away to their right. Five or six properties of various sizes were dotted along the base, in a line leading towards the cliff tops they had passed on their way in. Thorne could just make out thin ribbons of smoke drifting from a chimney or two and what looked like an enormous cross near what he guessed to be the ruins he had read about.

The convoy moved slowly.

The quad bike bumped up the track, the trailer bouncing and rattling behind it across rough ground thick with mud and stones. Howell moved alongside, keen to point out that there was delicate equipment on board and, after she had politely requested that they take things a little easier, Morgan slowed down still further to a notch above walking pace. Behind them, Thorne and Holland led the

156

way, with Nicklin, Batchelor and the two prison officers a pace or two behind and Markham, Karim and Barber the grim-faced CSI bringing up the rear.

Morgan had been spot on about the weather; the difference in temperature between the island and the mainland. They had been walking for no more than a few minutes and Thorne was already sweating. He tugged off his waterproof jacket, unzipped the fleece beneath.

'It's weird, isn't it?' Howell said, taking off a sweater and tying it around her waist. 'Should make our job a bit easier though.'

Five minutes later, Thorne watched the bike come to a halt fifty yards or so ahead of them, and a middle-aged man emerge from one of the buildings to meet them. The man exchanged a few words with Huw Morgan and his father, then strode down the track towards Thorne and the others. He was tall and distinguished-looking, with silver hair that poked from the sides of a flat cap and a walking stick that appeared to be for show as much as anything. He proffered a hand and, with no more than a trace of a Welsh accent, introduced himself as Robert Burnham.

'I'm the island warden.' He raised his stick and pointed back towards one of the cottages. 'And I also look after the Bird and Field Observatory up there.' He smiled. 'Jack of all trades, like most people around here.' He spread his arms out. 'Welcome to Bardsey.'

'Thank you,' Thorne said. To his ears, the man sounded more English than anything. Posh English.

'Right, we've got a base organised for you up there,' Burnham said. 'So it's just a question of sorting out the admin.'

Thorne blinked. 'Sorry?'

'Well, looking at what's in that trailer, it's fairly obvious you're planning on doing a bit of digging.'

'A *lot* of digging,' Howell said.

'Well, OK, but I wasn't told about any digging and as of now I haven't seen any paperwork to that effect.' He looked from Thorne to Howell and back again. 'I mean, I'm sure you've got the necessary permissions.'

Thorne said, 'I don't understand.' He was trying to sound cheerful, to appear mildly bemused at what was happening, but a heaviness was already starting to gather around his shoulders.

'Look, I'm sure it won't be a problem.' Burnham's eyes were flicking nervously towards Batchelor and Nicklin, towards their handcuffs. 'Why don't we get everyone inside, get some refreshments organised and we can sort everything out.' He turned and walked back up the track, leaving Thorne and those behind him with little choice but to follow.

'What the hell's going on?' Holland asked.

Thorne shook his head. The heaviness was growing, the irritation becoming something far stronger. The nausea on the boat had quickly put paid to the good mood he'd been in after reading the extracts from Nicklin's letters, and now there seemed little chance of it coming back.

They walked up the track, then up a short flight of weathered steps to a small stone building. The sign on the door, white letters etched on to black slate, read YSGOL.

'The school,' Burnham said.

'So how many kids are there here?' Thorne asked.

'Oh no, it's not used any more.' Burnham pushed the heavy wooden door open. 'Not been a school for sixty-odd years, but we still call it that. You should all be comfortable in here. It's as good a place as any to use as a base, I would have thought.'

One by one they walked through the outer door, turned sharply right and trooped through another into a damp-smelling hall which, even when the school had been fully functional, could not have seated more than a dozen children. The dark parquet flooring was worn and had come away in several places. There were cupboards lining a whitewashed wall, while the grimy windows in the other allowed no more than the suggestion of light in from the outside. At one end of the room, beneath a small stage area, was a piano covered in a filthy dust sheet, directly opposite a trestle table which had been set up near the door and laid with a shiny plastic tablecloth. A hotplate was connected to a gas bottle. Pump Thermos flasks of tea and coffee sat next to a large bottle of milk and a bag of sugar. There was a tray of sandwiches covered in cling-film.

'Just help yourselves,' Burnham said.

Before any of his team could take up the offer, Thorne

raised a hand. Said, 'Can we just get this permission business sorted out first.'

Burnham explained that the island was actually administered by a privately funded trust, dedicated to protecting its wildlife and archaeological heritage. 'I'm just the manager really,' he said. 'But I've not been told anything about digging and obviously that's problematic.'

'Why?' Thorne was making less effort to hide his irritation. 'Why is it *problematic*?'

'The island's an area of Special Scientific Interest. It's also a place of huge religious significance. There are rules and regulations.'

'I was told I couldn't bring cadaver dogs,' Howell said. She pulled off the cap she had been wearing to reveal ash-blonde hair cut very short. She ran fingers through it.

'That's right.' Burnham blanched a little at the word. 'There are strictly no dogs allowed on the island.' He stepped forward and laid a hand on Thorne's arm. 'Don't worry, I'm sure it's just an administrative snafu of some kind. I'm sure your boss or whoever it is will have completed the necessary paperwork.'

Thorne wasn't so sure. He had known many investigations hamstrung by the failure to fill in a form and convictions overturned because someone forgot to dot an 'I' or cross a 'T'. It was somewhat hypocritical of him to be so irritated, he knew that, because following procedure of any sort was not exactly his strong point. His strengths lay elsewhere and he left it to others to make up for his . . . failings in that department. After all, there were plenty paid to be little more than pen pushers, so Thorne believed he was justified in counting on them to push those pens in the right direction.

'What do you suggest?' he asked.

'Well, obviously in the first instance I'll need to speak to the trust director,' Burnham said. 'He's back on the mainland.'

'I'll speak to my boss, too.'

'Yes, good idea. Belt and braces is always the best approach with this kind of thing and like I said, I'm sure it's nothing that's going to hold you up for very long.' Burnham paused, seeing that Thorne was already frowning at his mobile phone. 'Ah, yes,' he said. 'That's going to be tricky.'

Thorne looked at him. Waited.

'If you're Vodafone, you're completely out of luck. O2 isn't a lot better, unless you want to go to the top of the lighthouse.'

'Seriously?' Holland said.

'It's the mountain,' Burnham said. He nodded towards the window, even though nothing could be seen through it. 'Blocks almost everything out. Orange is the best bet, but you'll still need to head along the track for a few minutes until you're past the line of the peak, then you might be lucky and pick up a signal.'

'This is ridiculous,' Thorne said. His contract was with Orange, but his phone still showed NO SERVICE.

'What were you expecting?' Burnham used his stick to push at the powdery edge of a loose parquet tile. 'We're almost completely cut off here. There's no running water or mains power. Compost toilets . . . '

'Shitting in a bucket,' Karim said.

'Basically.'

Thorne reached into his pocket and took out his Airwave radio. Holland and Karim both had them. 'What about these?'

Huw Morgan stepped forward and peered over Thorne's shoulder at the unit in his hand. 'Yeah, those should be OK,' he said. 'Not to make calls, mind, and you won't be able to reach anybody on the mainland, but should be OK for keeping in touch with each other. Switch to the main maritime frequency, you'll be all right.'

Thorne turned to look at him. He had forgotten that the boatman was still with them.

'We've got a receiver up at the lighthouse,' Morgan said. 'We can listen in on the boats doing illegal fishing. See, it's only me and my dad supposed to lay the lobster and crab pots round here, but that doesn't stop plenty of others trying to muscle in—'

Thorne had no wish to get dragged into a dispute about fishing rights. He held up a hand. Said, 'Let's get this done then.'

'I've got a satellite phone across at the observatory office,' Burnham said. He saw Thorne shaking his head. 'I don't tend to carry it around with me.'

'Well, I'd be very grateful if you kept it with you from now on,' Thorne said. 'In case anyone needs to get hold of me and I don't happen to be at the top of the lighthouse.'

'Yes,' Burnham said. 'Absolutely not a problem.'

Thorne walked towards the door, still staring at his phone. Fletcher and Jenks were already making themselves tea and Karim was ripping the clingfilm off the sandwiches.

'Like I said, if you keep walking up towards the abbey ... towards the ruins, you should hopefully start to get a signal in a few minutes ...'

After being cut off twice and perching precariously on a low drystone wall, Thorne managed to get through to Russell Brigstocke long enough to hear the DCI swearing for almost half a minute without drawing breath, then blaming it all on the detective superintendent.

Thorne wasn't surprised.

You didn't get very far up the greasy pole without learning how to pass the buck. He suspected that there was a course you were encouraged to attend as soon as you were promoted beyond inspector. A weekend of seminars in buck-passing, with refresher courses in fence-sitting and advanced arse-licking thrown in for the extra-ambitious. Brigstocke promised he would get everything sorted as soon as he was off the line.

'How's Nicklin?' he asked.

'He seems fine,' Thorne said.

'You know what I mean.'

'What?'

'How's he being with *you*?'

Thorne did not want to get into the letters that Nicklin's mother had handed over, or that moment in the toilets at the service station, or the way his guts jumped whenever Nicklin smiled at him. He did not want to talk about it or think about it any more than he had to.

'He's enjoying it,' he said.

'Yeah, I bet.'

'He likes it when we're on the back foot.'

'Well we need to get on the front foot again,' Brigstocke said. 'Get this boy's body found and get Mr Nicklin back to Long Lartin. See how much he enjoys that.'

'We're not going to find anything, Russell. Not unless we're allowed to dig.'

'I know.'

'This forensic archaeologist seems good, and I'm no expert but I reckon she's definitely going to need a shovel.'

Brigstocke began to swear again, this time as much at Thorne as anybody else. 'I'll sort it,' he said.

Back at the school, they sat around awkwardly, killing time.

Huw Morgan and his father had gone, presumably to begin work over at the lighthouse. A middle-aged woman, who Burnham introduced as his wife, came in to replenish the sandwiches, then left again without talking to anyone, her husband included. Burnham clutched his satellite phone as though his life depended on it, while cups of tea were drunk and small groups conducted muted conversations around the edges of the gloomy hall.

Holland, Markham and Karim. Howell and her CSI.

Thorne got up and walked towards the trestle table, past Nicklin and Batchelor, whose handcuffs had been removed for as long as it took them to eat a couple of sandwiches each and who were now sitting silently with Fletcher and Jenks, the four of them in a row beneath the line of grimy windows. Thorne helped himself to a couple of sandwiches, knowing he might not get a chance to eat anything else until they were on the road back to Long Lartin.

He did not hear Robert Burnham moving up behind him.

'Sorry,' the warden said.

'It's fine.'

'You must think I'm a dreadful bloody jobsworth.'

'Not dreadful,' Thorne said.

Burnham produced a weak smile. 'Look, I heard what that woman said about . . . dogs, so I know what it is you're going to be digging for.' He glanced across at Nicklin and Batchelor. 'How serious it is, I mean. But this place has all manner of rules and what have you and, as I'm the warden, I have to take them seriously.'

'Because it's special,' Thorne said. 'I know.'

'You've heard that?'

'Oh yes.'

'Well, only because it's true.'

165

Thorne bit off half the sandwich. He chewed quickly, then pushed the other half in behind it, talked with his mouth full. 'Sadly, if things go how I'm hoping, I won't be here long enough to find out.'

'You should come back,' Burnham said. 'Another time.'

Their exchange had barely risen above a whisper, but had clearly been audible to one person at least.

'Tell him about the king,' Nicklin shouted.

Thorne and Burnham turned to look.

'Tell him ...'

By now, everyone else in the hall had stopped talking and the silence was only broken by the ringing of Burnham's phone, which appeared to startle him so much that he almost dropped the handset. He answered the call. He said, 'Thank you,' and nodded a good deal and told the caller that he hoped he had not been too much of a bother, but that it was important to do things properly. He began to talk about some problem with the island's herd of Welsh Black cattle, but took a moment to look across at Thorne and give him an over-the-top thumbs-up.

'Are we on?' Howell asked.

Thorne nodded, looking at his watch. It was just after ten o'clock and they had wasted almost an hour. 'Right,' he said. 'Let's get out there and dig.'

'Thank God for that,' Nicklin announced. 'Be a shame to come all this way for nothing.'

He caught Thorne's eye and smiled.

Still enjoying it.

TWENTY

Tides House

Once the boys had eaten and done the washing-up, they were asked if they would like to gather in the communal sitting room.

'Nice being asked to do things,' Stuart said. 'Instead of told.'

Simon followed him into the room. 'What if we say no?'

'I'm sure we'll find out,' Stuart said.

The woman who appeared to be in charge told them that her name was Ruth. She said that they could call her 'Ruth' instead of 'miss' and that from now on she was going to be using their first names too. It was all about respect, she said. She introduced the other members of staff who were standing behind her. She used their first names as well, but Simon forgot them all straight away. He was rubbish with names, but he thought he was a pretty good judge of character and could tell right off which ones he ought to steer clear of. The other woman who was on the staff seemed OK. The bloke with the straggly beard was nice, while a couple of the others looked like they didn't want to be there at all and the one with the fat face and greasy hair was clearly to be avoided if at all possible.

Simon had come across plenty like him before.

Ruth definitely liked the sound of her own voice. It sounded similar to the voice of the judge Simon had been up in front of the last time he'd stolen a car. Like a newsreader or something, even though Simon thought that Ruth was trying hard *not* to sound like that. It was impossible though, to sound like you came from one sort of place when you came from another.

She made a long speech.

She told them she believed in fresh starts and second chances. That punishment alone was never going to work. She said they should count themselves lucky to have been sent to Tides House, but that she was lucky too, because she would have the privilege of seeing them change, of watching them blossom.

Stuart sat next to Simon, rolling a cigarette. He laughed when Ruth said *blossom* and handed Simon the roll-up when he'd finished it. Simon couldn't remember anyone ever giving him a cigarette before.

Fags were like money inside.

Ruth was still blathering on. She was fifty if she was a day and skinny as a stick, but it didn't stop some of the boys making comments, which she was close enough to hear. If the rude remarks bothered her, she didn't show it, though a couple of the male members of staff behind her looked like they'd be more than happy to wade in and crack a few heads.

'I'd like to make *her* blossom,' Stuart said.

Simon laughed because it was way funnier than the things those other lads were saying. It was clever and dirty at the same time. When Simon looked at Ruth he could see that she had gone red, which was strange, because some of the things the other boys had said were far worse and she had just ignored them. Stuart saw it too and he nodded at Ruth as he licked a Rizla, making another roll-up for himself.

'This is a very special place,' Ruth said. 'In lots of ways. You'll already have noticed it's a small island, so even though there'll be times when you might want to run, the simple truth is there's nowhere to go. Well, there *is*, but I don't think any of you is *that* strong a swimmer.' She waited for laughter, but there wasn't any. 'We may not call you prisoners here, but there are rules and we want you to follow them. The rules will make life better for all of us, because we're all living here together. Now I know this is not what you're used to . . .'

Simon saw one of the men behind her lean across to a colleague and whisper, 'You're telling me.'

' . . . but please don't make the mistake of thinking we're a soft touch. If you refuse to follow what rules there are here, if you persistently disrupt the community on the island in any way, you'll be on the next boat back. Simple as that. But . . . if you take this chance, if you embrace this opportunity, I promise that you'll get a great deal out of it.'

Stuart leaned towards Simon and said, 'What do you reckon, Si? Should we embrace it?'

Simon nodded. He liked being called 'Si'.

'Right, let's embrace it, then.'

'Yeah,' Simon said.

'We'll give it a bloody big cuddle.'

'Yeah . . .'

'We'll squeeze the bastard nice and tight, shall we, Si?'

'Yeah!'

Simon looked over and saw that the bloke with the fat face and the greasy hair was watching them. Simon felt uncomfortable, but Stuart just lit his cigarette and returned the bloke's stare until the bloke looked away.

Ruth asked if anyone had any questions.

A big lad with dreadlocks who was sitting at the front put his hand up and said, 'Is it true that posh bitches make more noise in bed?'

There were actually a dozen of them by the time the boat had finished coming and going. A dozen boys and six members of staff. 'They're still screws, by the way, Si,' Stuart had said. 'Even if they're not wearing uniforms. And they can call us "guests" all they like, but we all know that's bollocks.'

The boys slept four to a room, with the staff divided between five more, two of which were in a converted outbuilding. Ruth had her own room in the main house, while the other female staff member and the screw with the straggly beard turned out to be a couple, so they shared one.

The screw with the straggly beard got a lot of stick from the boys once they found out about that. Stuff about his girlfriend and what she liked. The two of them must have known that would happen, but still.

Simon had no idea how it had been decided, but he was pleased when he and Stuart ended up in the same bedroom. Once in the room, they were allowed to decide which of the four beds to make up and, without Simon having to say anything, Stuart dumped his rucksack down on the bed next to his. Simon was pleased about that too.

The lights went out at ten o'clock.

That first night, one of the boys on the other side of the room just kept laughing and saying, 'This is mental,' over and over again. Then, once he'd quietened down, the other one kicked off; moaning and groaning and slapping his belly, pretending he was playing with himself. After a few minutes, Stuart told him to shut up and even though the other boy argued about it briefly, he did shut up in the end, which was surprising because he was a fair bit bigger than Stuart, and that was what usually decided these things.

'You all right, Si?' Stuart asked.

'Yeah.' Simon had been thinking about his mum.

'Sure?'

'Yeah, I'm sure.' He was wondering what she would make of this place, assuming she was ever straight long enough to have a proper conversation about it. He thought about what it would be like when she was, and he could tell her, and they could laugh about it. He was sure she'd find it funny and take the piss out of everything. The two soppy screws who were a couple. Ruth being a bit up herself, saying 'blossom' and all that. 'It's weird, isn't it?' he said. 'Being on this island, I mean.'

'You rather be banged up somewhere?'

'No, course not.'

'Just going to take some getting used to.'

'I suppose.'

'It won't be for everybody. Nothing ever is.'

'Like she said though, it's an opportunity, isn't it?'

'Definitely.'

'I don't want to mess it up, that's all.'

'You won't mess it up,' Stuart said. 'I'll make sure.'

They lay there in the dark for a few minutes and listened to what sounded like a thousand babies crying out on the rocks. The spooky call of that special bird Ruth had mentioned going back to its burrow. A funny name that Simon had forgotten already.

'It's all right to be scared, you know, Si.' The bed creaked as Stuart turned on to his side. 'Everyone gets scared.'

Crying babies, or else like a load of Punch and Judy shows somewhere in the distance; that weird thing the Punch and Judy man puts in his mouth to make his voice go funny.

'You don't,' Simon said.

TWENTY-ONE

It was still called Tides House.

Robert Burnham told Thorne that it was a working farm again, had been for as long as he had been warden and that the house was now occupied by a young family, who were the island's only full-time residents. The couple had happily swapped high-pressure careers in London for long days tending hay and silage fields and watching over the island's population of sheep and cattle. 'They wanted a change of lifestyle,' he said. 'Thought it would be a good place to bring up their daughter.'

'Did they check that with her?' Holland asked.

'Shame,' Nicklin said. They were gathered at the main gateway to Tides House. A cat wandered across the yard in front of them and he tried to lure it with kissing noises. 'Would have been nice to go in and have a look around the place. See if it's changed much.'

'Not sure the family would be very keen.' Thorne stared at the farmhouse. It had been painted a different colour and there had been a couple of small additions built, but he still recognised it from the background of the photograph he had in his pocket. 'You banging on the door in your handcuffs, telling them you used to live here.'

Nicklin turned and looked out across the low-lying western section of the island; the large number of small fields that sloped gently away towards the sea. He pointed. 'The two of us ran down there,' he said. 'But I don't think I'm going to be much help until we get near the edge and I'm looking back this way. I think I'll be able to remember what I could see looking back at the house, if that makes sense. That's the best way for me to work out exactly where I was.' He looked at Thorne as if he were simply trying to explain where he might have dropped a wallet or a set of keys. 'Where I did the digging.'

Thorne opened the gate and the team trooped into the pasture.

There were low drystone walls running between the fields as well as more ancient dividing lines; stone-faced earth walls that ran across raised verges. It was hard to see what these boundaries were for any more, now that none of the land was privately owned and the sheep that darted in front of them as they walked seemed happy enough scrambling over the walls from one field to the next.

'Are sheep stupid or clever?' Karim asked. 'I can't work it out.'

The grass was lush and had been kept short by grazing. The weather had clearly not been as good in recent days as it was now, with the ground heavy underfoot and muddy water rising up around Thorne's walking boots as he went. It was only the second or third time he had ever worn the boots, though he'd actually bought them a couple of years before. Against his better judgement, he had allowed his former girlfriend, Louise, to talk him into a weekend's hill-walking. Country pubs and sex in a four-poster bed had sounded like a nice idea, but in the end there had been only blisters and an almighty row that had lasted most of the weekend.

After they had walked for ten minutes, Nicklin stopped and looked back towards the farmhouse. 'Yeah, we're definitely in the vicinity,' he said.

'Good.' Thorne shoved his hands into the pockets of his waterproof jacket. The temperature had dropped again and the wind was gusting, noisy against the nylon.

'I think there could have been trees between me and the house, but they might have gone now. A landscape can change a hell of a lot in twenty-five years, can't it? Plus, it was dark, of course.'

'Sounds like you're getting your excuses ready,' Thorne said.

Nicklin shook his head. Said, 'Not at all.'

A few hundred yards further on, Nicklin stopped again. He looked around then began pacing slowly, counting out his steps. Fletcher seemed happy enough to let him walk on unaccompanied, waiting next to Jenks who was standing with Batchelor at the back of the group.

Nicklin turned around on the spot. 'We're close,' he said. He nodded towards the place where the fields fell suddenly away to the sea. 'That's where I went over,' he said. 'Went into the water near one of the big caves down there.' He proudly described his escape twenty-five years before, the meticulous planning and the partner who had been waiting; who, as it turned out, had been made to wait somewhat longer than had been planned.

'That was Simon's fault,' Nicklin said.

'Selfish of him,' Thorne said.

They were twenty feet or thereabouts from the edge, though the drop was nothing like as steep as it was from the cliffs on the mountainous side of the island. It would not have been an altogether easy descent, but it would probably have taken no more than fifteen minutes to clamber down to an uninviting shoreline festooned with enormous, weed-covered rocks. No decent-sized boat could have reached the shore safely, certainly not at night, but that had not been Nicklin's plan all those years ago.

Thorne watched him now, sniffing the air like an animal, and imagined the seventeen-year-old climbing down to the sea, having just buried Simon Milner; wading into the freezing water towards the boat that was waiting in the dark, the light from an accomplice's torch.

'Here,' Nicklin said.

'Sure?'

'This feels right.'

Thorne looked across at Bethan Howell. 'On you go ...'

With fingers firmly crossed that the job would be finished before darkness fell, they had left the portable generator back at the school and carried the rest of the equipment down between them. Now, the various cases were laid down and opened up. Thorne saw straight away that the forensic team had brought along rather more than he had first imagined: hand trowels, buckets, sieves, tape measures, positioning rods, digital cameras and video recorders. A canvas bag held all the personal protection gear – scene of crime suits, nitrile gloves, elbow and knee pads, duct tape for sealing cuffs – while a smaller aluminium case that Howell had been carrying contained the ground-penetrating radar and computer equipment.

While the gear that was needed for the search phase was assembled, Howell led Thorne to one side. She kept her eyes on Nicklin, who was watching the preparations with considerable interest. 'How do you want to do this?' she asked.

Thorne looked at Nicklin too. 'As soon as you've identified an area where you think it's worth digging, I'm taking our friend back up to base. I don't want him here for that.'

Howell nodded, getting it. 'It's the bit he's going to enjoy.'

'Watching us digging in the wrong place.'

'You think he's going to dick us about?'

'Every chance,' Thorne said. 'And I'm not pandering to

him any more than we have to. If it turns out to be what we're looking for, then we don't need him any more anyway and I'm getting him off this island first chance I get. I want him back in a cell as soon as possible.'

'All makes sense,' Howell said. She looked at Batchelor. 'Why's the other one here? Is he connected to the victim we're looking for?'

'Nothing to do with any of it,' Thorne said. 'Just Nicklin pulling our strings again.'

Howell and Barber went to work with plastic rods and twine, dividing up an area roughly twenty-five feet in either direction from the spot Nicklin had indicated, laying out a grid. Once that had been done, Barber began putting the GPR kit together; assembling long metal handles, firing up a laptop.

Howell laid a large geological map of the island on the grass and weighed down the corners with stones. This was the flattest, most exposed part of the island and the wind was really starting to bite. 'We'll do what we can,' she said. 'But this isn't going to be quick.' She clocked Thorne's reaction, pulled a face of her own. 'Listen, we're doing it on the hurry-up as it is. If I had the time to do things properly I'd want to test core soil samples, but we don't have the equipment here and sending it back to the main-land is going to take forty-eight hours minimum.'

'I was hoping we could just pick a place to look,' Thorne said. 'Then dig until we find a body. I know that might sound like a bit of a simplistic approach ...'

'Simplistic is the only approach we've got,' Howell said. 'So far, this is all about what we can't do.'

'What can't we do?'

'We can't use dogs and there's no point using penetrometers.' Thorne's attempt at a confident nod of understanding was clearly less than convincing, but Howell seemed happy enough to reel off a paragraph or two of *Forensic Archaeology for Idiots*. 'OK, we need to identify the areas where soil has been disturbed, right?'

Thorne nodded again, with it so far.

'We could normally do that by measuring penetration resistance, because obviously soil is weakened when it's already been dug up for a grave. All a waste of time when you're talking about farmland.'

Thorne looked at her.

'How many times do you think this field's been ploughed in the last twenty-five years?'

'Right, yeah.'

'There's also no point using the naked eye to look for anomalies ... patches of richer vegetation, whatever. A decomposing body can release nutrients which work like fertiliser basically, so you're just keeping an eye out for grass that's lusher, darker. Again, no good to us, because this is animal pasture.' She nodded towards a muddy ewe that was eyeing them nervously. 'Because sheep-shit will do much the same thing.' She raised a hand to acknowledge the wave from Barber, who was letting her know that they were ready to go. 'So, as things stand, the GPR is probably our only option ...'

It looked like a high-tech hand trolley; a metal box at the end of twin handles, fixed onto rubber wheels. Cables ran from the main GPR unit to a small laptop mounted at the end of the handle. Thorne looked at the picture on the small screen; a series of jagged lines against a grey background.

Howell pointed to the image. 'That's the plough layer, see?'

Thorne shrugged, seeing only squiggles.

'So then there's a smoother layer beneath that and we're looking for evidence of disturbance that falls outside the expected parameters.' She smiled at him. 'Basically, we're looking for something grave-shaped.'

It was already eleven thirty by the time Howell began a systematic analysis of each quadrant using the GPR. It was painstaking and frustrating to watch, the process not made any more enjoyable for anybody by Nicklin's running commentary.

'Not exactly a spectacle this, is it?

'If you find buried treasure, do we all get to share it?

'Shame about the *cadaver* dogs.' He spoke the word with considerable relish. 'Can they actually still smell a body after all this time? Amazing creatures, dogs . . . even if they *do* spend most of their time licking other dogs' arses.'

He talked almost non-stop, his incessant jabber only highlighting the fact that Batchelor had been as good as mute since they'd boarded the boat almost four hours before. Each time a quadrant was ruled out and Howell and Barber moved into the adjacent section, Nicklin was quick to loudly express his disappointment.

'I really thought this was the one.

'I know it's ages ago, but I was sure that was it.

'I definitely remember looking back from somewhere round here, looking back at the lights in the farmhouse, just before I heaved him into the hole . . .'

They broke for sandwiches after an hour, a tray brought down to them by Robert Burnham's wife. A few minutes into the first quadrant after lunch, Howell beckoned Thorne across. He stepped carefully over the lines of twine and, as soon as he had reached her, Howell pointed to the screen. The zig-zags made no more sense than they had the first time he had looked, but Thorne could see that Howell was excited.

'Worth digging, you reckon?'

'I reckon.'

'Right . . .'

'This is exciting,' Nicklin said. He looked at Thorne. 'Are you excited, Tom? You don't look very excited.'

Thorne told Holland that he would be escorting the prisoners back up to the school and to stay in touch. Holland agreed to radio in every fifteen minutes and walked across to join Sam Karim and Wendy Markham, who had turned away from the wind, trying to stay warm. Markham had been carefully watching the forensic team at work, not least because – though it was far from riveting – focusing on the job had allowed her to short-circuit several unpromising conversations with Karim. Now, the exhibits officer shouted across at Thorne as he and the party from Long Lartin began trudging uphill towards the track.

'What do you want me to do?' Karim raised his arms. 'I'm not a lot of use until they actually find something, am I?'

Howell beat Thorne to it. 'If you're looking for something to do,' she said, 'you can grab a bloody shovel.'

TWENTY-TWO

Tides House

A week after arriving on the island, Simon was asked to go and talk to Ruth; given a fifteen-minute slot after breakfast and invited to 'come along for a chat'. He knocked on the door of the communal sitting room and was called in. The furniture had been rearranged, to make it look a bit cosier, Simon thought. There was an armchair, to which Ruth pointed, another in which she was sitting and a small sofa off to one side, where the screw with the straggly beard sat next to the one with the fat face and the greasy hair.

They didn't look too thrilled to be sitting that close together.

Ruth nodded towards the low table between them. There were tea things laid out on a tray, a plate of chocolate biscuits. She asked him if he wanted tea, but he said he was fine.

She poured tea for herself and her colleagues.

'Can I have some biscuits though?'

'Of course,' Ruth said. 'Help yourself.'

Simon did, then sat back and listened. Up close, her voice was even posher than he'd first thought, but it was a lot softer too, now that she was only talking to him and not to a room full of boys.

'You're going to be with us for the next three months,' she said. 'How do you feel about that?'

Simon shrugged. He didn't know what to say. Obviously, he wasn't happy about doing time, but this place was much better than anywhere he'd been before and because he thought it was a lot to do with her, he found himself not wanting to hurt her feelings. 'Good,' he said, eventually.

She was flicking through a sheaf of notes, which Simon guessed was details of everything he'd ever done. Everything he'd ever been caught doing, anyway. Now and again, she would scribble something in the margin and he tried to see what it was, but her writing was far too small for him to make it out.

'It's shocking,' she said, 'that you've been in and out of the system this often. You're clearly not a danger to anyone, are you?'

'No,' he said.

'It's just this obsession with cars we need to do something about.'

'Yes, miss.'

'Ruth.'

'Yes, Ruth,' he said. He felt himself blushing, shoved another chocolate biscuit into his mouth.

The governor at the last place he'd been was a fat, bald northerner whose face went red all the time. He'd sat behind a huge desk and peered over the top of a folder at Simon, who had always felt about six years old or something. Sitting there next to some scowling screw, while the red-faced governor had sighed at him. Or made some lame joke about how nice it was to see Simon again, how his usual room was waiting.

Ruth sat back and took her glasses off, then tossed the notes on to the table. 'What do you think of the island?' she asked.

'It's nice,' he said. 'Never been anywhere like it before.' The truth was he'd never really spent much time in the countryside, so he didn't have anything to compare it to, but he did like it so far. He liked the fact that they spent so much time outside, for a start, and even when they were in the house they weren't being shunted around. They could go where they liked, within reason, and as long as they didn't trespass on private property or take liberties they weren't being hassled or barked at. Food was a damn sight nicer too and he never worried that anyone was spitting in it.

'Have you made any friends yet?' Ruth asked.

'Yeah,' Simon said. 'Well, sort of a friend ... yeah, I think. We're in the same room, so ...'

Ruth picked up her notes again, turned the pages, nodded. 'Stuart Nicklin,' she said.

Simon thought he saw the fat-faced screw roll his eyes. He certainly folded his arms and let his head drop back a bit.

Ruth was still nodding. 'It's good to have friends,' she said. 'But we're also keen to encourage self-reliance. You need to be making your own decisions, OK? This is not somewhere where someone is there to tell you what to do twenty-four hours a day like some other places you've been. We want you to decide what to paint, if you're painting, what to cook when it's your turn in the kitchen. We want you to decide what to grow in your allocated patch of garden.'

'Can I grow some sunflowers?' Simon asked.

Ruth smiled, scribbled something down. 'I don't see why not. The way we look at it, if you can make these small decisions for yourself then hopefully you'll start to get the bigger decisions right. The decision to stop stealing cars, for instance.'

Simon nodded. He understood what she was saying. It made sense.

'What would you like to happen when you go home, Simon?'

'My mum's poorly,' he said. 'So I want her to get better.'

'Poorly?' The fat-faced screw chuckled and shook his head.

'I'm going to help her.'

'That's good,' Ruth said.

'I've got it all worked out.'

186

'Excellent.' Ruth scribbled again. 'Planning is something else we're very keen to see you do. I tell you what, why don't you write it all down and bring it to show me, next time. We'll be meeting like this once a week and I'd really like to see what you've got in mind.'

Simon told her that he would, and she seemed pleased, then the screw with the straggly beard stood up and Simon guessed it was time to leave. He hesitated, glancing at the table, and Ruth told him to take another biscuit if he wanted one. She said, 'Don't tell any of the other boys, though. That's the last packet and we won't be getting any more until the boat comes across again.'

Simon promised that he wouldn't tell, then turned towards the door. Walking past the fireplace he noticed a collection of small china animals, like the ones you got in fancy Christmas crackers or something, and he slowed down so he could get a good look. There were loads of them, lined up like they were all friends or in a zoo or whatever. A tortoise and a cat and an owl, all sorts of others. He wondered where they'd come from, if they were already here when Ruth and the others arrived.

He thought that his mum would like them.

Stuart was sitting outside and Simon realised that he was waiting to go in, that he was the next one on the list. That made sense, because they were next to one another alphabetically.

Milner and Nicklin.

Simon had been happy when he'd found that out. Maybe it was the reason they were put in the same room. He decided it was another sign that they were meant to be mates.

'What's all that about then?' Stuart nodded towards Ruth's door.

'It's just like a chat,' Simon said. 'There's a couple of screws in there, but it's mostly just her. She's got all your notes and all that. Wants to know what you think of the island. Who your friends are.'

'So, what did you say?'

Simon shrugged. He held out the biscuit he'd taken right at the end. 'I took this for you,' he said. 'I know you like chocolate.'

Stuart studied it for a few seconds, like he was trying to work something out. He said, 'Thanks,' and took it.

The biscuit had already started to melt and Simon suddenly began thinking about holding his hand out. Letting Stuart lick the chocolate from his palm and fingers. He felt the blood flooding his cheeks, so he quickly lowered his head and did it himself.

Stuart stood up and knocked on the door. He was still eating the biscuit, pushing in the crumbs from the corner of his mouth. He said, 'See you afterwards, yeah?'

TWENTY-THREE

Fletcher and Jenks had deposited Nicklin and Batchelor, still cuffed, on hard chairs beneath the window. Fletcher went to make himself and his colleague more tea, while Jenks explored the hall. He opened cupboards, took out grubby plastic toys and mildewed textbooks. He lifted the dust sheet and played a few horrendous-sounding chords on the out-of-tune piano.

Fletcher brought the tea across. Said, 'I don't know if this is strong enough.'

Jenks took it, grunted. 'Cheers.'

'I could do with a few more of those sandwiches, to be honest.' Fletcher scratched at his goatee. 'That greedy CSI bastard took all the decent ones.'

'Probably fancies himself because of that TV show.'

'Right, but he's basically just a dogsbody.'

On the other side of the hall, Nicklin tuned out the

officers' conversation and turned towards Batchelor. 'You didn't eat much, Jeff.' He spoke softly, barely above a murmur. 'When that nice old woman brought lunch down.'

'I wasn't hungry.'

'Did you eat breakfast?'

'I didn't feel too good this morning.'

'What about last night? Or were you too busy crying like a girl?'

Batchelor looked at him for the first time. His expression suggested that, once again, tears were not very far away. 'How can you act like this is . . . normal?'

'You need to keep your strength up, Jeff. All this charging about in the fresh air. You're not used to it.'

'I want to speak to my wife,' Batchelor said. 'I want to talk to Sonia.'

Nicklin sat back. 'Well, of course you do, and I've told you it's going to happen, but I don't think it's very likely right this minute, do you?' He nodded towards Fletcher and Jenks. 'I mean even if one of those idiots decided to lend you his phone, you heard what they were saying about signals. It's going to be tricky getting to the top of that lighthouse with those handcuffs on.'

'What about the satellite phone? I could use that.'

Nicklin glanced across to make sure that Fletcher and Jenks were still too engrossed in their own conversation to have been listening. 'You need to shut up about this now, Jeff. You need to stop whining.' He closed his eyes and thought for a few seconds. He listened to the low moan of the wind outside, the bleating of sheep like the horns of toy cars, and the distant scream of gulls. All these sounds were reassuringly familiar to him and the pictures that came into his head prompted a nice broad smile.

He leaned across. 'This is a chance to blossom, Jeff,' he said.

Batchelor's head dropped, then sank lower still as a sigh pushed the breath from him.

Nicklin lifted hands that were cuffed tightly, one above the other, and gently touched them to Batchelor's. 'You need to embrace this opportunity,' he said.

From the track, Thorne could just make out the team at work in the field far below him. The shiny white overalls of Howell and Barber, the bright red waterproof jacket Wendy Markham was wearing.

He keyed his radio and asked Holland what was happening.

'Just digging,' Holland said. 'Obviously, they have to go through the soil that's being removed, in case there's evidence.' Thorne could hear Howell shouting something, Holland responding. 'She says it's the backfill from the original gravecut.' Howell said something else, her words muffled by the wind. 'As soon as we find anything, I'll let you know ...'

Thorne looked up to see Robert Burnham wandering along the track from the direction of the observatory,

191

which was a couple of cottages along from the school. He stopped next to Thorne. He lifted his stick, gestured towards the fields.

'Been busy?'

'Oh yes.'

'Any luck?'

'Nothing yet.' As much to stop the conversation drifting into awkward areas as anything else, Thorne said, 'So, tell me about this king.'

Burnham looked blankly at him.

'Earlier on, remember? In the school hall, we were talking . . .'

'Oh yes, the man in the handcuffs.'

'Yeah, him.'

'He obviously knows a fair bit about us.'

'He was here a long time ago,' Thorne said.

The warden stared, then nodded, pleased with himself when the penny dropped. 'Ah . . . the home for young offenders. I remember Bernard Morgan telling me about that when I first came here. Bit of a disaster, by all accounts.'

'So, this king . . . ?'

'Oh well . . . long before my time, but yes, we used to have our own king. Went back to the nineteenth century, I think, when the island was privately owned. There was a decent-sized population then . . . well, over a hundred anyway and a local man would be crowned King of Bardsey. There was a crown made of tin, a ceremonial snuff box, it was all very serious.' He thought for a few

192

moments. 'Apparently, when World War One broke out, the last king offered himself and the men of the island to the war effort, but the government of the day turned him down because he was into his seventies by then. So, he thought: Stuff 'em, and declared the island to be a neutral power. Some say he actually threw in his lot with the Kaiser.' Burnham laughed. 'There's loads of stories. Hard to separate the myths from the facts when it comes to this place.' He turned to Thorne. 'What we were talking about before. The prison for young offenders that wasn't really a prison. That's almost become a myth around here.'

Thorne shrugged. 'Definitely not a myth.'

'Such an odd idea,' Burnham said. 'Don't you think? I mean, where do you stand on that kind of thing?'

'I just catch them,' Thorne said.

'Of course . . . which is exactly why your opinion should count, because you're someone who actually does the job. You spend your working life taking these people off the streets . . . people who have done some pretty awful things, I imagine. So, do you think we should try and rehabilitate wherever possible? Send them off for a bit of a holiday? Or should we just lock them up and throw away the key?'

Thorne stared out across the lattice of green. He could still see the white overalls, the red waterproof jacket. A still figure in a black beanie hat.

'Some of them,' he said.

The radio came to life in Thorne's hand and Holland's voice was tinny through the hiss and crackle.

'We've found something. You should probably get down here . . . '

'Perhaps later then.' Burnham had clearly overheard. 'We could carry on chatting, if you're going to be around for a while.'

'Doesn't look like we will be.' Thorne had already pushed through the gate and turned to close it behind him.

Burnham raised his stick in a kind of salute and turned away as Thorne broke into a gentle jog, letting the slope of the field do most of the work. For the first time since he'd boarded the *Benlli III*, he could feel the good mood returning. It would be great to get away and have Nicklin banged up again by dinner time. He could certainly think of a great many better ways to have spent the last forty-eight hours, but the thought of Simon Milner's mother finally being able to lay her son to rest would more than make up for it.

Those moments with Nicklin that would linger a while yet; eyes meeting in a rear-view mirror.

He was no more than a minute away from the group when his radio crackled again. He stopped and snatched it from his pocket, fought to regain his breath. 'I'm nearly there.'

'I know,' Holland said. 'I can see you.'

Thorne looked across and saw Holland waving. 'What?'

'You need to go back and get Nicklin. We'll have to start again.'

'I thought you'd found something.' Thorne could hear laughter in the background. Karim, Barber maybe.

'Yeah, we did.'

'What's going on, Dave?'

'Well, unless this kid we're trying to find had cloven hooves, this is looking very much like a dead sheep.'

TWENTY-FOUR

Tides House

'You were picked to come here,' Stuart said. 'Same as I was.' He explained that each of the boys staying at Tides House had been specially chosen. They did not want anyone with a history of violence, he said, so everyone was there because of their involvement in fairly petty crimes, even if some of them were repeat offenders. 'They're trying to get to us *before* we do anything violent. That's the whole point of it.' He smiled. 'Basically, it's so we can "blossom" before we knife anyone.'

Simon laughed, same as he always did when Stuart did that quote thing with his fingers.

He told Simon that, because of their remote location, the project had been unable to consider anyone whose family would otherwise regularly visit them in a traditional YOI. So, nobody with their own children. Nobody with parents who gave a shit.

Simon just nodded.

'It's a very careful selection process, Si. We're all more or less harmless and we're all more or less alone. We're naughty boys, but we're not irredeemable.'

They were sitting on a low wall and eating the packed lunches that were provided on days when they were working outside. Simon had been tending the small area of the vegetable garden he'd planted, while Stuart had been working with the beehives in one of the fields behind the farmhouse. Simon was thrilled that there were shoots coming through. Runner beans, peas and carrots. Spinach because it was his favourite and a few sunflowers just because his mum had always liked them.

He showed Stuart where they were sprouting; baby fingers of green through the black earth.

'Great,' Stuart said.

'So, what do you think about all this?' Simon asked.

'All what?'

Simon took a bite of his sandwich, squinted against the sun as he looked out across the fields. 'You know, that stuff Ruth says about this place being spiritual, making us feel differently about things.'

'I don't even know what spiritual means,' Stuart said.

'Oh, no, me neither.'

'Just a word.'

'Yeah, you're right. But . . . you know.'

'I suppose we should be grateful they're not shoving God down our throats. That's something.'

'Yeah, that's something,' Simon said. There were crosses on the walls in most of the rooms, but thankfully, five weeks since they'd arrived and there had been no mention yet of the Baby Jesus. 'I mean, I don't really understand the meditation business, but I can see what she means about contemplation, or whatever it is. She was right about this being somewhere where we can think about what we've done. What we want to do when we've finished our sentences.'

'So what do you want to do?' Stuart asked.

Simon shrugged. 'I don't know. Stay out of trouble long enough to get my mum cleaned up.'

Stuart poured what was left in the bottom of a bag of crisps into his mouth. 'She'll clean herself up if she cares about you.'

'It's hard though. She needs help.'

'What did you do? To end up here, I mean.'

'I've got this thing about fast cars,' Simon said. 'I just drive them for a bit and then leave them. I don't set fire to them, anything like that. I just like driving them.' He looked at Stuart. 'What about you?' He felt nervous asking. It was something you would never have done in Feltham or Huntercombe. It was a big no-no, but things felt different here, and besides, Stuart and him were good mates now.

Best mates.

'Nothing really.' Stuart crushed the crisp packet into his fist. 'Minor assault, bit of nicking. I'm not very good at doing what I'm supposed to and I've got a big mouth. I can't help winding people up.'

Simon nodded. It looked like that was as much as he was going to get and he certainly didn't want to push it.

'It's good though, I reckon.'

'What?'

'Having loads of space,' Simon said. He put his head back. 'Just look at all that bloody sky. Never seen so many stars at night.'

'You know most of them are dead, right?'

Simon shook his head.

'The light takes so long to reach us, we're seeing stars that aren't actually there any more. It's like seeing ghosts.'

'Where did you learn all that?' Simon asked. 'I can't get my head round stuff like that.'

'Just remember it from school.'

They sat in silence for a while, finished cartons of juice and lobbed apple cores on to the compost pile.

'Makes you feel . . . cleaner somehow, this place,' Simon said. 'Sort of like when you're a kid . . . a *little* kid, I mean. When you just feel hopeful about everything. You know, waking up every morning and being excited. It's nice to feel like that again, don't you reckon?'

'I'm always excited when I wake up,' Stuart said. 'You have to make life interesting for yourself, because it isn't going to happen on its own.'

'What are you two bummers talking about?'

They turned to see an older boy named Hunter standing above them. He nodded towards the vegetable patch, hands thrust into the pockets of the blue overalls that Tides

House 'guests' wore outdoors. 'Growing flowers for each other in your little garden, is it? Roses are red, violets are blue . . . '

'Piss off,' Stuart said.

Hunter looked taken aback. Maybe because Stuart had said it so casually, so quietly. Then he laughed, showing brown and broken teeth. 'The only reason I'm not going to mess you up right this minute is that we've all got a sweet thing going here and I don't want to spoil it. You talk to me like that though, you need to know there are going to be consequences.'

The boy stared at them both for a few seconds, then turned and marched towards the vegetable garden. After checking that none of the staff was watching, he stepped over the border of coloured stones into the bed and stomped happily back and forth across the neat rows of shoots and seedlings. The green, baby fingers. He looked back at Simon and Stuart while he went about his business, grinning as he ground his heels into the soil.

Simon stood up, hot suddenly and light-headed.

'Don't.' Stuart reached up and tugged at Simon's arm. 'Turn round and look at me.'

Simon did what Stuart had told him and stood listening to Hunter laughing behind them, staring out over the green to where that great big sky touched the water. The tears came and he made no effort to wipe them away.

'Don't let him see you cry,' Stuart said. 'Don't ever let them see you cry.'

TWENTY-FIVE

Conscious of the day getting away from them, with only an hour or so left before the light would begin to fade, Thorne decided to go to the lighthouse in search of Huw Morgan. He wanted to talk about the arrangements for returning to the mainland.

He wanted to see if he could buy a little more time.

It was a fifteen-minute walk, flat or downhill for the most part and pleasant enough. The mountain rising at his back and the sea roiling but relatively calm away to his left. Less of a breeze than there had been out in the fields. The tide was on its way out and the last few minutes of his journey took him past a growing expanse of flat, black rocks, most piled high with weed that shifted gently as the water retreated. A few hundred yards away, walking in the opposite direction, was a man with a bobble hat and rucksack, binoculars around his neck. The man, who Thorne assumed to be the birdwatcher Morgan had mentioned bringing across, raised a hand and Thorne waved back.

Approaching the lighthouse, its red and white stripes many feet thick now that he was close to it, Thorne was surprised to see that it was actually square. There was a small cottage off to one side and metal racks piled high with diesel containers. The quad bike was parked outside. He walked in through an open door. He could hear music playing somewhere above him, a radio maybe, so he called up.

It took five seconds for Huw Morgan to answer, his voice echoing slightly.

'Come on up, if you want.'

'It's all right,' Thorne shouted.

'Hell of a view.'

'Maybe another time.' Thorne had never been great with heights, but the experience of six weeks before had turned a minor anxiety into a major phobia. Being made to stand on the edge of a tower-block roof, being told to jump. Being tempted to jump.

Taking a bullet had been the softer option in the end.

He waited five minutes for Morgan to appear. He looked around a small kitchen and storage room, listening to the sound of the boatman's footsteps on a seemingly endless number of metal, then stone steps.

'Seriously, it's a great view.' Morgan finally appeared and immediately flicked the kettle on. He reached into a wonky cupboard, took three mugs down. 'You can't see back to the mainland because of the mountain, but if it's clear enough, looking the other way, you can see Dublin.'

'I need to know when you're heading back,' Thorne said.

Morgan peered out of the window and up at the sky. 'An hour, maybe a bit more.'

'No chance of staying any longer than that?'

'You're pushing your luck after dark,' Morgan said. 'That crossing's tricky enough as it is.' He could see the frustration on Thorne's face. 'Why don't you stay?'

'Can't do it,' Thorne said.

'Most of the cottages are empty.'

'I need to get my prisoners back behind bars. That's the deal.'

Morgan nodded. 'Probably a damn sight cosier for them as well. Not exactly tempting, I can see that, staying here this time of year.' He leaned down, took milk from a fridge and sniffed it. 'Plenty of people the rest of the time though. All those cottages get rented out, believe it or not.'

'Really?'

'Oh yeah, they'll be full come May–June time.'

'Takes all sorts.' Thorne could appreciate how dramatic the landscape was, even if wide open spaces had never excited him in quite the way they clearly did a great many others. Still, with no running water or mains power, he remained unconvinced about the place as a holiday destination, except for those with masochistic tendencies.

'Well, we get boatloads of twitchers for a start.'

'Yeah, I saw one,' Thorne said.

'They come for the Manx shearwater colony mainly.' Morgan looked at Thorne, smiled at the blank stare he got back. 'Not your thing?'

Thorne shrugged. 'I know what a magpie looks like, a robin. Beyond that, I haven't really got a clue. A chicken ...'

'Then we get the amateur astronomers coming out, because there's no light pollution, and loads of artists too. Writers, painters, what have you, coming over here on retreats. They like the quiet, I suppose.'

'So, how many on the island right now?'

Morgan thought for a minute, counted on his fingers. 'Well, there's the family up at Tides House ... there's the warden and his wife. They're not here all the time, like. I reckon he's only come across because he knew you lot were coming ... bit of a sticky-beak. There's the young couple who help him run the observatory, do all the scientific data and that.' He raised another finger. 'There's the birdwatcher in one of the small cottages ... no shearwaters this time of year, but still plenty of birds if you're mad keen. So, not that many. Put it this way, there's more of you than there are of us.'

Morgan made the tea. He handed Thorne a mug and shouted up to tell his father that there was one waiting for him.

'Down in a minute,' his father shouted.

'You gave us a bit of a laugh earlier on,' Morgan said.

Thorne looked at him.

'The sheep. We heard all about it. You're using the maritime frequency, remember.' He nodded towards a large radio receiver mounted on the wall. It looked almost steam-powered, housed in a wooden surround with twisted curly wires, but it clearly worked perfectly well.

Thorne could hear Bernard Morgan on his way down. 'I don't need to tell you I'd rather you didn't talk to anyone about any of this.'

'You don't need to,' Morgan said. 'No.'

'Only some people have already been shouting their mouths off.'

'Some people haven't got any lives,' Morgan said.

'Fair enough,' Thorne said.

'We know who your prisoner is, by the way. Well, who one of them is, at any rate.'

Thorne looked towards the radio.

Morgan shook his head. 'My dad worked it out, after what he said to me on the boat.'

'Right.' Thorne remembered Nicklin speaking to Huw Morgan just before he got off the boat. Something about seeing him again.

Bernard Morgan appeared in the doorway. He picked up his tea from the table. 'I can remember bringing those boys across all those years ago,' he said. His voice was deeper than his son's, hoarser, but the accent was the same, the intonations. 'There was some incident later on, wasn't there? Then two of the boys escaped. It was closed down fairly soon after that, if I remember right—'

205

Thorne's radio crackled into life. Holland saying, 'Guv ... ?'

Thorne said, 'Yes,' and began moving towards the doorway. He kept going, out towards the lighthouse entrance, even though he realised that the conversation was being simultaneously broadcast through the speaker of the ancient radio receiver.

Holland told him that Howell had seen something on the GPR screen and that they were digging again. Thorne told Holland to let him know if and when anything turned up. Was turned up.

When he walked back into the kitchen, Huw and Bernard Morgan were standing side by side, cradling their mugs of tea, watching him.

'Only one boy escaped,' Thorne said. 'Only one boy ever got off the island.'

Huw Morgan nodded his understanding. 'Sounds like you might have got lucky,' he said. 'If not now, maybe tomorrow, eh?'

Walking back, Thorne saw that the tide had drifted even further out, but that the masses of weeds that were plastered to the rocks still appeared to be moving. Looking again he saw that the movement was actually the rippling of blubber; that there were, in fact, hundreds of seals basking just below him on the rocks. There were a few lighter-coloured pups dotted among the groups of enormous adults, seven or eight feet long in a variety of blotchy greys, browns and speckled blacks. The creatures seemed largely unconcerned by his presence, even when he stepped down and climbed carefully across the rocks towards them. But they would only allow him to get within fifteen or twenty feet before lumbering away with surprising speed, barking and snarling, towards the water.

Thorne stood and watched them until Holland came through on the radio again.

'We've got a body,' he said.

'You sure?'

'There are bits of clothes.'

Thorne took a step back towards the verge, the sudden movement disturbing a huge bull seal, which dragged itself in the opposite direction, hissing at him.

'Training shoes,' Holland said.

TWENTY-SIX

Tides House

They had been told to stay inside, and those whose bedrooms were at the back of the house had seen the helicopter land in the field behind. Simon and Stuart had stared from their window, saying nothing. They had watched the paramedics run across the field into the house and emerge a few minutes later with Kevin Hunter's body on a stretcher.

Now, an hour later and with the boy believed to be responsible already in police custody, the ten 'guests' that still remained in Tides House were trooping into the sitting room, where Ruth was waiting to address them.

There was plenty of chat as they took their seats, plenty of rumour.

A few were saying that Hunter was probably dead already or that he'd been cut up so badly that he was gone well before the helicopter had even got there. Some were whispering about the boy who had done it, a softly spoken lad with a shaved head and dark eyes named Ryan Gough. Simon listened closely, but could not hear anyone talking about why Gough had attacked Kevin Hunter.

One of the screws asked for quiet. Then he asked again, rather more forcefully, until things got as quiet as they were likely to get, and Ruth stood up.

'Thank you,' she said. 'This isn't going to be easy.' She looked pale and tired. She looked like she'd taken a good kicking. 'Obviously, you know by now that a boy was seriously assaulted today. Kevin Hunter was attacked by another boy in the kitchen, just after breakfast.'

'Is he dead, miss?'

Simon craned his head, but could not see who had asked the question.

Ruth sighed. She was wringing her hands. 'We haven't heard anything since the air ambulance left,' she said. 'It goes without saying that all of us are deeply shocked and saddened by what's happened. A violent assault like this ... coming out of the blue.'

Simon could see that she looked close to tears. It was odd because some of the other screws looked anything but upset. Watching him carefully, Simon could have sworn that the fat-faced one with the greasy hair was actually smiling. He certainly looked a damn sight more relaxed than he usually did. A lot more comfortable.

Ruth carried on, saying how important it was that what had happened did not disturb anyone else, that everyone should try to carry on as normal and that the staff would do everything possible to make sure that things stayed the way they were.

'Of course,' she said, 'we're more than happy to speak to any boy who's upset and wants to talk to someone about how he's feeling ...'

She sat down then, and the fat-faced screw came forward. The smile had gone as he announced that the police were very keen to talk to any boy who had seen what had happened that morning or who had any information at all about it. The smile came back a little when he said how mysterious it was that nobody appeared to have seen anything, despite several boys having been in the kitchen at the time, helping clear up after breakfast.

Simon was aware that, next to him, Stuart was sitting eating a bar of chocolate and softly humming to himself. It might have been some kind of tune, but was probably just a hum of pleasure, because now Simon knew that Stuart loved chocolate more than anything. Knew that he would swap cigarettes for chocolate any time. *Any* time.

Listening to the fat-faced screw, Simon felt the smallest of trembles in his leg. He wouldn't say anything, of course. He wasn't sure he would know what to say even if he wanted to. The fact was, though, that without knowing how he could possibly have done it, Simon was positive that Ryan Gough had only stuck a kitchen knife into Kevin Hunter because Stuart had told him to.

Ruth was on her feet again ...

'We're not going to let what has happened destroy what we've built up here,' she said. 'What *you've* all worked so hard to build up.'

Simon looked at Stuart.

Stuart grinned and popped the last chunk of chocolate into his mouth.

Simon grinned back at him, happier than he could remember being at any time since he had arrived on the island.

Later, after lights out, the two boys on the other side of the bedroom were talking about what had happened. About how Hunter must have said something, must have been asking for it, and how there was no way they could possibly get that much blood off the stone floor.

Stuart *shushed* them gently and they didn't say anything else.

Simon waited a minute, took a deep breath, then said everything he'd been wanting to say, since they'd watched that helicopter rise into the sky and swoop away over the sea.

'I was thinking, it would be great if you and me kept in touch, you know, when we go back. Obviously you've got stuff to do, same as I have. Trying to sort my mum out and that, but afterwards we could meet up and hang out or whatever.

'I don't know if you're sorted for somewhere to stay after, but I was thinking there's room at my place. There's a spare room, I mean. Sometimes there's a stranger in there … some junky mate of my mum's dossing down in there, but that won't be happening after she's clean, so you could use it if you wanted. Not all the time or anything, but you know, if you were in the area and needed somewhere to crash.

'Just saying. The offer's there.

'I've written the address down, so make sure you hang on to it and if you want to give me an address or a phone number or something, to keep in contact. Yeah? Or maybe we can make a definite plan … like a date when we know we'll both be out so we can arrange to meet up in the West End or somewhere, go to a pub or an arcade or somewhere.

'I'm just saying, it would be a laugh to meet up if you wanted to, talk about this place and everything. All the wankers! The screws and everything. I mean … I don't even know when you're out, so I'm probably being a bit stupid.

'Just saying … '

Simon lay there for a while longer, staring at the back of Stuart's head, the shape of it in the half-light, then he turned over and looked at the sliver of moon that was visible through the cheap curtains.

The milky gleam off the big stupid cross on the far wall.

He was just drifting off to sleep when he heard Stuart say something. He turned over again. 'What?'

Stuart said, 'Sooner than you think, maybe.'

TWENTY-SEVEN

Thorne told Jenks to stay in the school hall with Batchelor, while he and Fletcher escorted Nicklin down to the site of the latest dig. Jenks seemed happy enough, having long ago abandoned any notion of a meaningful conversation with his prisoner and found a tattered and slightly damp book of crossword puzzles in one of the cupboards. Thorne told him that they would not be long, to be ready to leave as soon as they got back. Jenks nodded without looking up from his puzzle, idly winding strands of his mullet around a finger. Batchelor looked no more or less wretched than he had since Thorne had watched him emerge into the car park at Long Lartin the previous day.

He seemed like someone who was waking up every few seconds and realising to his horror where he was.

Robert Burnham was waiting on the track outside the school, talking to a man and a woman. They were young, nerdish-looking, and Thorne assumed they were the couple Morgan had mentioned, who helped out at the Bird and Field Observatory. They stopped talking and watched as Fletcher, Nicklin and Thorne walked down the steps. Thorne had given the go-ahead for Nicklin to smoke, though he had refused to even consider taking the handcuffs off. He had watched Fletcher take the tin from Nicklin's pocket, put the pre-rolled cigarette into Nicklin's mouth and light it for him.

If the young couple were shocked or disturbed by the sight of the handcuffs, they didn't show it, though they kept sneaking looks at Nicklin, as though he were a celebrity they had spotted on the other side of a restaurant.

Burnham introduced them to Thorne as Craig and Erica and confirmed that they were helping him and his wife at the observatory, collating data on nesting seabirds. They did not seem hugely keen to talk, which suited Thorne as he was keen to get down to the dig. Burnham had other ideas though.

'I was on my way to see you.' He held up the satellite phone. 'Your boss called . . . Bristow, is it?'

'Brigstocke,' Thorne said. He had passed on the number when they had spoken earlier. 'What did he want?'

'It was nothing urgent.'

'Sorry?'

'He was just checking that the digging had actually started. He gave me rather a hard time, actually, when he found out I was the one who'd been holding things up to begin with.'

Thorne said, 'Sorry,' though he wasn't.

'Oh, I didn't take offence,' Burnham said. 'Anyway, I told him that it had started ... the digging ... which I guessed you would have wanted me to do.'

'I'd rather you'd passed the call on to me straight away. Or at least given me the message.'

'I didn't know where you were.'

'I was at the lighthouse.'

'How was I to know that?'

'Well, next time, if you can't find me straight away, perhaps you could pass the call on to one of my colleagues.'

'I'll try,' Burnham said, looking put out. 'I do have other things to do.'

Thorne had one hand on the gate, ready to push on into the field, when Nicklin spoke up.

'Shame it's the wrong time of year for the shearwater,' he said.

Burnham looked a little wrong-footed by the comment, the fact that it had been made by the man in the handcuffs. He managed, 'Well, yes ...'

'I can still remember the sound of them at night, when they come back to their burrows. Spooky as hell.' He looked at Thorne. 'Something you should hear.'

'We've still got an amazing variety of species though.' Burnham looked at Craig and Erica. 'Haven't we?

215

Firecrests, snipe, the little owls, obviously. A flock of waxwings arrived the day before yesterday.'

'We need to get on,' Thorne said.

Nicklin nodded at Craig and Erica. 'I don't think he's very interested.'

'Well, obviously, you've got more important things to think about,' Burnham said. He nodded towards the field. 'It all seems to be happening down there.'

Pushing through the gate, Thorne noticed the binoculars hanging around Burnham's neck. He guessed the warden had been looking at rather more than little owls and waxwings.

Within a few minutes of leaving the track, they were leaning into the wind again, a stiff sea breeze harsh against their faces. With Fletcher a pace or two behind them, Thorne asked Nicklin the question that had been nagging at him for weeks. Since Brigstocke had sat on that hospital bed, eating Thorne's biscuits, passing on the good news and the bad.

'Why now?' he asked.

Nicklin raised his hands and rubbed awkwardly at his nose, scratching an itch. 'Because Simon's mother asked me.'

'She's been asking you for a long time.'

They walked on, sheep trundling out of their way.

'Maybe I thought I might sleep better.'

'You sleep fine,' Thorne said. 'And if you don't, it's more likely to be indigestion than remorse.'

216

Nicklin smiled. 'It's not about remorse. I won't insult you by pretending it is. It's about ... tidying up.' He shrugged. 'That's all it is. It's not complicated.'

'I'm not convinced,' Thorne said.

'I just made a decision, just thought: Why not? Like you might decide what colour shirt to put on. Like your girl-friend might decide what sandwich to get from the M&S opposite her station, when she goes in there every lunchtime.'

Thorne said nothing, determined not to give Nicklin the satisfaction of showing him anything.

'Like I might decide whether to use a knife or a gun or a cricket bat. You know me, I'm impulsive.'

Thorne knew that Nicklin had indeed used each of those things as murder weapons in the past, but there had been nothing rash or reckless about doing so. Plenty of time had been taken to carefully plan and cajole, to bully his partner-in-crime into killing alongside him. Control had been all-important back then and Thorne had every reason to believe that it remained so.

Nicklin smirked. 'Well, I'm impulsive *sometimes*.'

'So, no ulterior motive whatsoever?'

'No, but not out of the goodness of my heart either, because we both know there's not a lot of it in there.'

'A snap decision then, that's it.'

'Yeah, just something to do. A change of scenery and a couple of days out for me and Jeff.'

'Yeah,' Thorne said. 'That's the other thing.'

'You know why I brought Jeff along.'

'Right, you're afraid for your well-being.'

'Can you blame me?' Nicklin nodded ahead, towards the figures up ahead of them. 'Look, we both know how fond Sergeant Holland was of Sarah McEvoy, don't we? Who knows, even the coppers who *didn't* shag her might still be harbouring a grudge.'

'It's rubbish,' Thorne said. 'I know it, you know it.'

'There's some nasty drops off this island,' Nicklin said. 'Easy to slip and lose your footing. I might be nervous about the fact that you left Jenks back up there with Batchelor, if it wasn't for the fact there are so many witnesses around. That nosy old sod with the binoculars . . . '

By now, they were only a few minutes' walk from the dig. The light was starting to go and Thorne could see the camera flashes from what he assumed to be the gravesite.

'I'm glad we found him,' Nicklin said. 'Simon. I mean, obviously there'll be more legal nonsense, a new trial or what have you, but that's not the end of the world, is it?'

'Gets your name back in the papers as well, doesn't it?' Thorne looked at him. 'You must have missed that.'

'None of it's going to make any difference to how much time I spend inside, is it? We both know it's going to be *all* of it. That I'm going to die in there, unless we get a Home Secretary who's tired of being popular.'

'How d'you feel about that?'

Nicklin raised his hands again; rubbed at his scalp through the black beanie hat. 'You're not stupid, Tom. You know there's not very much that would be available to me on the outside that I can't get in prison. Most of the things I've always enjoyed are still there whenever I fancy them. I just need to be a little cleverer about getting them organised, that's all. The things I can't do are neither here nor there, really. I won't be losing too much sleep about missing long walks in the park, sunsets and all that. Evenings curled up by a log fire in a country cottage.' He looked around. 'Having said that, this is nice, I won't pretend it's not. A bit of outdoors.'

'Make the most of it,' Thorne said. 'You'll be back at Long Lartin by dinner time.'

'Thank God for that,' Fletcher said, behind them. It was the first time he'd spoken since they'd left the school. 'This place is doing my head in.'

As they drew closer to the freshly excavated grave, Thorne saw Barber help Howell up and out of the hole. Karim was sitting on one of the metal equipment cases scribbling in a notebook, while Markham was taking photographs of those bones that had already been removed and laid out neatly on black plastic sheeting a few feet away.

Fletcher stopped next to Holland and, without anything being said, Howell and Barber took a step or two away from the grave as Thorne and Nicklin walked up to its edge.

It was odd, almost as though they were family.

As though the men and women in the mud-spattered overalls and dirty gloves were giving them space to mourn.

Thorne looked down and saw glimpses of red, white and green through the mud. A tattered strip of what might have been a shirt. A frayed waistband, the loops for a belt. The human remains were tea-coloured where they were not caked with earth and it was shocking to see how much was left of the training shoes, in comparison to the few shreds of flesh that clung to the scattered bones. The sole and tongue, fully intact. Thick laces so much more resilient than veins, than the clotted strands of hair that were pasted here and there to the filthy skull.

Thorne looked across at Howell.

'Teenage male,' she said. 'The age is about right too. Certainly not ancient and I don't need the trainers to tell me that.'

Thorne glanced at Nicklin who was staring down, stony-faced. Had he not known him better, he might almost have believed him to be upset. Thorne nodded down at the remains. At a pair of flattened ribs, curling from the mud like speech marks. A glimpse of clawed fingers and one leg bent backwards. The hole in the skull that was clearly visible, even from where they were standing.

'To your knowledge,' Thorne said, 'is this the body of Simon Milner?'

Nicklin nodded.

'And are you responsible for disposing of his body?'

Another nod.

'A little louder.'

'Yes, I'm responsible.'

It was getting darker by the minute, and colder. Thorne thought he felt a drop or two of rain, though it might just as easily have been seawater.

'Why did you kill him, Stuart?'

TWENTY-EIGHT

Tides House

There was a head count just before lights out, but every-one knew it was a waste of time, the screws included. They used to joke about it. The one with the straggly beard said he couldn't count up to twelve anyway. The fact was, a couple of the lads would sneak out at least once a week and everybody knew it.

Drink and drugs were obviously off limits, however much they might have helped with 'contemplation'. Ruth had made that clear enough early on. Still, someone on the island must have had some. Maybe one of the painters or the poets had some weed and a bit of spare booze. Maybe they were happy to give some away or there was a pervy one getting wanked off in exchange for a couple of joints or whatever, but either way, boys were getting stuff from somewhere, then going out after dark for a drink and a smoke. Fires were lit and empty cider bottles were found in the fields or down on the beach.

Funny thing was, whenever the screws found out about it, it was always the 'environmental impact on the island' that got everyone hot under the collar. That was what the bollockings got dished out for; fires in the fields and plastic bottles not being disposed of properly. That was all there ever was: bollockings. The guilty party trying their hardest to keep a straight face, while Ruth shook her head and looked sad and talked about how many different people they were letting down, not to mention themselves.

Simon always remembered that joke about the inflatable kid with the inflatable mum and dad and inflatable school and everything. 'You've let yourself down, you've let your family down and worst of all you've let your school down ...'

Maybe they were all set to rethink the whole discipline business after what happened to Hunter, toughen things up a bit, but nothing much seemed to have changed when it came to checking on all the comings and goings.

How piss-easy it was.

Stuart only told him they were going that morning. It didn't leave much time, but maybe that was the whole point, Simon thought. Not too long to get worried about it or chicken out; to get cold feet and do something stupid.

Yeah, it made sense.

Not that Simon was about to question Stuart about anything.

He was thrilled to be asked, to be included in the first place.

All day long, he was buzzing with it. Looking at the other boys and thinking what a bunch of losers they were. Digging their veggies or making pots or writing some rubbish in their notebooks like goodbye letters to drugs or crime or whatever else Ruth had told them to do. One boy had spat and stuck his chin out and asked Simon what he was looking at and Simon had told him to go and fuck himself.

His heart was thumping and his mouth was dry for a long time after that, but it was a good feeling. He wasn't scared, because he knew he wasn't going to be there for much longer anyway and he knew this boy wasn't going to do anything, not so soon after what had happened with Hunter.

Mostly though, he wasn't scared because of Stuart.

The two of them smiled at each other all through that last dinner and afterwards, while they were washing up. Simon could feel their shared secret passing back and forth between them. He felt it like a shock whenever their shoulders brushed at the sink or one of them laid a clean, warm plate down on top of the other's.

For those last few hours in the lounge, while they were supposed to be reading, Simon was making mental lists: the first ten things he was going to eat; the first five places he was going to go; the three people he was not going to let anywhere near his mum ...

The dealer, obviously.

The dickhead boyfriend who always made sure she went back on the gear.

The 'best friend' who was more of a hopeless junkie than she was and just wanted his mum to end up the same way, so she could feel better about herself.

Simon was going to make sure they stayed well away, would hurt them if he needed to. Maybe he could nick a car and sell it for a change, get enough money together so they could move out of London to the countryside or somewhere by the sea. Maybe Stuart would help him. He'd ask him what he thought as soon as they were off the island.

They went about an hour and a half after lights out. Long enough for the staff to have gone to their own rooms. Simon had thought they might have to climb out of their bedroom window but, in the end, they just marched straight out of the front door. There was a bolt, but it was on the inside!

How stupid was that? Who the hell was going to be breaking *in*?

There was no moon, which was probably a good thing. Simon guessed that Stuart had planned it this way, checked on a calendar or whatever, so it would be harder for anyone to see them. Stuart had stolen a torch from the supply cupboard and some bottles of water and a few chocolate bars for the journey. Then he'd told Simon to steal something too.

Simon thought it was like a test, or something.

There wasn't any money left lying around, nobody was quite that trusting, so in the end he'd grabbed a few of the tiny china animals that were on the mantelpiece in the lounge. He thought it would be wrong to take them all, so he chose quickly and stuffed them into his pocket.

A cat, a bear, a dog, a monkey.

It was a warm night and the fields looked black. Stuart was good at leading them safely around the edges, using his torch, keeping it low on the ground ahead of them. There was the odd startled sheep, something scurrying in a hedge, but that was all.

Stuart had told him that they would have to wade out to the boat that was waiting, that it wouldn't be able to get close in because of the rocks. That was fine, Simon didn't mind the water. Stuart told him that his friend would have towels on the boat and maybe a bottle of whisky or something to warm them up.

It only took them about twenty minutes to get to the right place.

Stuart told Simon to wait and moved forward on his own, close to where the land fell sharply away. Simon watched Stuart raise the torch and flash it on and off, twice. When he saw a flash come back from out there in the darkness, Simon almost wet himself with excitement.

Stuart came back, asked Simon if he was ready. Simon started to take his shoes off, but Stuart told him not to be so stupid. There was no way he could make it down to the sea in bare feet without cutting them to pieces on the rocks. He would need to take them off at the last minute, Stuart said, tie the laces together and put them round his neck when they waded out.

Simon laughed, nervous. Said, 'Yeah, course . . .'

They walked towards the edge, Stuart in front and Simon's eye fixed on the small beam of light up ahead. Simon could not stop jabbering, shouting to make himself heard above the noise of the sea.

'I was thinking, what I said before about having a spare room? You staying whenever you liked, remember? Well, you could come and stay there permanently if you want. I don't think my mum would mind and it would be fun to be together a bit more, I reckon.

'Then, when she's cleaned herself up and maybe I don't need to be there all the time, you and me could find somewhere on our own, a flat or something. We'd have such a laugh, I reckon. I've been thinking about some of the things we could get up to. The terrible twosome! Oh yeah, I'd be happy to do the cooking, by the way. I can make loads of different meals now and I know you're not really bothered. I mean we'd have chips or a Chinese some of the time, obviously, but I'm just saying I wouldn't mind cooking us a few things. I could even find a couple of recipes with chocolate in them. Puddings, stuff like that.

'We could go out, we could stay in, wouldn't matter. Just talking or whatever, watching telly . . .

'Cheaper too, I reckon, two of us living together and who

cares if people might think it's a bit weird. Doesn't matter what people think, does it, and anyone who wants to say anything needs to be careful or they'll end up like Hunter.'

Simon stopped when he heard Stuart shushing.

At first he'd thought it was the sound of the water against the stones down below.

He stared into the blackness, thinking about the boat out there waiting for them, wondering how big it was. Thinking about what it would be like when he introduced Stuart to his mum and what she would say, hoping she was straight. He was pretty sure they would get on and Stuart would help him sort out the dealer and the dickhead boyfriend. Maybe they would end up like Hunter, too.

He thought the water was still whispering and then he realised that Stuart was standing behind him and saying his name. He turned and saw the shape of something in Stuart's hand.

Not a torch, not a bag.

It was like the water was angrier suddenly below them, chucking itself at the shore. It wasn't quite so warm any more and Simon could feel the spray on the back of his neck. He said, 'Stu,' as Stuart raised his hand and then Simon saw what Stuart was holding and knew he'd been really stupid.

He could not call his mum's face to mind, not clearly anyway, in those fractions of a second before the rock came down.

*

Twenty-five years on, standing in what was almost the same spot, Nicklin looked at Tom Thorne and quietly answered his question.

'Because he was needy.' He smiled, and turned from his handiwork as though he were suddenly bored with it. 'And like I said, I'm impulsive sometimes.'

Thorne watched as Professor Howell – who was now back working in the grave – plucked something from her sieve. She brushed mud away, then held it up between tightly gloved fingers. Thorne leaned down to get a closer look, before the small object was handed over to be given its place as one more piece of evidence on the plastic sheet. To be photographed and catalogued with everything else.

Left femur (human), right half of pelvic girdle (human), belt buckle . . .

'It's ceramic,' Howell said. 'My nan used to collect these things, got them with teabags or something.' She held it up towards Thorne. 'It's a dog, I think. No, a bear.'

TWENTY-NINE

There was not too much discussion about whether work was going to continue at the crime scene after dark. Barber was only too delighted to be earning the overtime and, with so much of the work done already, Howell was keen to press on, rather than leave things as they were overnight and come back again in the morning. As CSM and exhibits officer, Markham and Karim were expected to stay on. Markham seemed to have been prepared for such an eventuality and, if Karim looked less than thrilled at the prospect, he didn't say as much.

With the light fading fast, Howell and Barber went up to the school and returned with the lights and portable generator. They had it all set up within fifteen minutes. In the gathering dusk, Barber stayed behind to assemble the forensic tent, while everyone else went back to talk through the procedures for those who would be staying on after Thorne and the Long Lartin contingent had left.

Walking back across the field, Fletcher said, 'I don't really see why we need to put the tent up at all. I mean, it's not like there's anyone around, is it?'

Howell turned to him. 'It's not about whether there's anyone around. It's about respect as much as anything.'

'Just saying, it seems a bit daft.'

'It's what we do,' Howell said.

Thorne had already spoken to Robert Burnham, who was waiting for them when they got back to the school and seemed eager to run through the ad hoc arrangements. Thorne could see that he was someone who was very much at home with a clipboard, but only in the absence of a flip-chart or PowerPoint facilities. He would, Thorne decided, have made a very good chief superintendent.

'I think the Chapel House cottage would be best,' he said. 'That one sleeps six, easily. Obviously it's been shut down for the winter, so there'll have to be an element of make do and mend, I'm afraid. It'll be a bit dusty and a few mice might have come in out of the cold, but we'll do our best to make you comfortable.'

'Close to the chapel is good,' Howell said. 'We can leave the remains in there overnight when we've finished at the crime scene.' She nodded towards Sam Karim. 'Can we get some kind of a bed set up in there for our exhibits officer? An inflatable mattress or something?'

Burnham looked horrified. 'What, he'll be sleeping in there with . . . ?'

'Has to,' Thorne said.

'Can't be helped, Sam.' Holland was trying to sound serious, but failed to hide his grin from Karim, who was suddenly looking even less happy about staying on than he had before.

'All the bedding gets wrapped in plastic at the end of the summer,' Burnham said. 'So it should all be perfectly dry. As for food . . . I'm sure we can rustle you up some soup or something. We weren't expecting that any of you would be staying over.'

'Sounds great,' Howell said. 'Thanks.'

'Don't suppose you'd have a spare bottle of something?' Karim asked.

'I'll pretend I didn't hear that,' Thorne said. 'Not sure being pissed in charge of the body is a great idea.'

'Just thinking about keeping warm,' Karim said.

'We'll find you a hot water bottle.' Thorne turned to Howell. 'How long are we looking at?'

'Another five or six hours,' she said. 'With a bit of luck we'll be done down there by midnight.'

'Sorry it's worked out like this,' Thorne said. 'I sounded out the Morgans about hanging on a bit, but there's no way they'll wait until after dark.'

Howell shrugged. 'I've stayed in worse places.'

'There's nothing wrong with it,' Burnham said, a little offended. 'It just might be a little more rough and ready than you're used to. I'm sure you can make it nice and cosy ... get the lanterns lit. I think there's some books to read in there, puzzles and what have you.'

Markham looked at Thorne. 'No reason *we* can't have a bottle or two of something, is there?'

'None at all,' Thorne said. 'Almost compulsory, I would have thought.'

She smiled nicely at the warden. 'Any chance of scrounging something?'

'Wine all right?'

'God, yes,' Markham said. 'Actually, this might be quite an adventure.' She looked at Thorne. 'You don't know what you're missing.'

'You could always keep me company,' Karim said. 'Freezing my tits off in the chapel with nothing but a bag of old bones ... '

Thorne told them that, weather permitting, the boat would be returning to pick them up first thing in the morning, and that once he was back on the mainland he would make arrangements to have the body of Simon Milner transported back to London. He thanked the warden for his help and Burnham said that it was not a problem. Thorne wondered if the warden was feeling slightly guilty for the earlier delay, even if the hour he had cost them had made little difference in the end.

Burnham held up his satellite phone. 'Well, you've got my number if you think of anything else after you leave. Or if you'd like to come back some time for a break.'

Thorne told Markham and Karim that he would see them both back in London and thanked Bethan Howell for everything she'd done.

She said, 'The trial then, I suppose.'

'Sorry?'

'See you at the trial.' She nodded at Markham and Karim. 'We'll all be there, I imagine.'

'Sounds like it'll be quite a reunion,' Nicklin said. 'I'm looking forward to it already.'

They all turned to look at him.

'Maybe we should set up a Facebook event or something. I'm happy to do it all ... I mean I know you're all a lot busier than I am.'

Thorne looked at Jenks and Fletcher, but they just seemed bored. He glanced at Batchelor who was sitting next to Nicklin. Batchelor would not meet Thorne's eye and stared at his feet, like someone keen to avoid any association with an acquaintance who was doing something embarrassing.

Howell said, 'He's full of himself, isn't he?'

'I'm just happy that everything went well,' Nicklin said. 'I'm pleased that *you're* pleased, that's all.' When he saw Howell's smile, his own quickly vanished. He sat back, took a few seconds. 'For obvious reasons, I've been up close and personal with a body or two in my time. I've got nice and comfy with bones and blood and I'd be lying if I said that I didn't quite like it. As a matter of fact, there's been more than a few shrinks over the years who've listened and scribbled a bit and decided that actually I must be getting off on it. Getting some kind of sexual kick out of it.' He raised his handcuffed hands, waggled a finger at Howell. 'So what's your excuse?'

Thorne saw the colour come into Howell's face. He inched into her line of vision and shook his head.

Fletcher suppressed a yawn. Said, 'He won't be quite this cocky when he's back on the wing tonight.'

As bags were gathered and Howell, Markham and Karim prepared to head back down to the crime scene, Burnham pressed a blister pack into Thorne's hand. 'Those travel sickness pills you asked me about,' he said. 'I swear by these and they work fast.'

'Thanks.' Thorne snapped a couple out into his palm. As if on cue, a horn sounded from down by the boathouse, low and mournful. Huw Morgan letting them know that the *Benlli III* was ready to leave.

Halfway back and Thorne was relieved that the pills Burnham had given him seemed to be doing the trick. Not that it was particularly rough, but Thorne had become convinced that much of the problem was psychological; that just the sight of water was now enough to bring on that prickle of sweat, the first waves of sickness.

Helen had suggested going to see a hypnotherapist.

'What, you fancy a cruise or something?'

'I just thought if you saw someone about the heights thing, they might be able to do something about the sea-sickness at the same time.'

235

When Thorne had mentioned this to Hendricks, on the off-chance that he might be able to recommend someone, his friend had seized the opportunity to take the piss with both hands.

'I think it's a top idea,' Hendricks had said. 'Why don't you see if you can do some kind of a special deal for a job lot? See if they can change your shit taste in music while they're at it and maybe cure your tragic devotion to Spurs . . . ?'

'It's good that Simon's going home,' Nicklin said.

Thorne looked up and across at Nicklin, who was sitting with Batchelor and the two prison officers on the other side of the deck. Thorne was sitting next to Holland, their bags at their feet.

Holland said, 'What?'

'It's good that his mum's finally going to get him back.'

'You could have made that happen sooner,' Thorne said.

'I'm making it happen now.'

'It hardly makes you Mother Teresa.'

They were leaning towards one another, voices raised just enough to be heard above the engines.

'She must have cleaned herself up,' Nicklin said, nodding. 'Certainly sounds like she has, anyway. Simon always wanted that.' He looked back. They had lost sight of Bardsey by now and the sun had all but slipped beneath the horizon. 'I reckon that her being a junkie was probably why Simon got into trouble in the first place. I mean, it wasn't like she was ever really there to stop him, was it? Off her tits while he was running around nicking cars. Funny thing is, it was probably losing him that made her snap out of it.'

'So, you did her a favour, did you?'

'A favour?'

'Killing him.'

'Just saying, it's strange how things turn out.'

Thorne stood up, unable to look at him any more. 'Sorry if I've never associated you with happy endings.'

A few minutes later the boat was chugging across Aberdaron Bay and shortly after that the landing site came into view; a ragged line of lights on the shore.

Thorne checked his phone and saw that he finally had a signal again. As the boat slowed, he called Russell Brigstocke. He told him where he was, who was with him and that, all being well, they should be on the road within half an hour. Brigstocke sounded relieved and as the boat drifted in towards the slipway, Thorne took him through the chronology of the day.

'We found the body just after lunch,' he said.

He was distracted by something Nicklin was mouthing at him and missed whatever Brigstocke had said. Nicklin waved to get his attention, so Thorne took a step towards him, told Brigstocke to hold on.

'What?' he asked.

Nicklin smiled. Said, 'You found *one* of them.'

THIRTY

'It's rubbish,' Thorne said. 'He's pissing us around, same as always. We don't want to get hung up about this, Russell. I really don't think we should change our plans.'

'You need to calm down,' Brigstocke said.

'It's shit.'

'We should at least talk about it.'

Thorne was pacing up and down a short section of unlit muddy track, fifty yards from the slipway. Behind him, Huw Morgan had a hose trained on the keel of the *Benlli III* while between Thorne and the boat, Fletcher, Jenks, Holland and the two prisoners waited in the Galaxy. Thorne turned and saw Nicklin staring at him through the side window. He watched him shrug as though asking a question.

How are you getting on, Tom?

Thorne tried to control his breathing, to keep the anger from his voice as he told Brigstocke; passing on the story

Nicklin had told him as the boat was being hauled back on to the mainland.

'Well, I needed a shovel, obviously, to get rid of Simon, but rather than go back to Tides House for one, I tried one of the smaller cottages in the other direction. The ones they rented out. I just strolled into the back garden, pinched a shovel out of the shed and came back to start digging, piece of piss. Trouble was, the old bird who was staying there must have heard something and came marching down about ten minutes later. Waving a torch about and demanding to know what I was up to. It wasn't like I had a lot of choice, was it?' He'd smiled then, enjoying telling his tale, or simply enjoying the memory. 'I knew who she was. I knew she was some kind of amateur poet, because she'd been in to read some of her poems a couple of times. Usual shit that didn't rhyme. I think they brought her in to try and encourage some of us to write poetry ourselves. To share our feelings.' He'd rolled his eyes at the absurdity of the suggestion. 'Anyway, so there I am digging a grave for poor old Simon and she comes beetling along, sticking her nose in. What am I supposed to do? Not a lot I *can* do at the end of the day, is there? There's a boat waiting for me. I've not got a lot of time to decide.' He smiled at Thorne, rocking slightly as the boat was winched from the water on to the trailer.

'Think of it as a bonus . . . '

'A fucking *bonus*,' Thorne said now. 'I'm telling you, Russell, it's a wind-up.'

'That's what you thought about Simon Milner,' Brigstocke said. 'You thought he was having us over about that.'

'OK, fair enough. But this time I really think he is. Why wait until now, for God's sake?'

'Control—'

'Why wait until we're almost back?'

'*Control*, Tom. You said it yourself. Back foot, remember?'

'Yeah . . .'

'We at least have to look into this.'

'And what do we do while that's happening?'

'What difference is one more night going to make? I'll clear it with the governor at Long Lartin.'

'How exactly are we going to check this out? He doesn't have a name for this woman. He can't even remember what month it was, for God's sake.'

'How many people can have gone missing on that island?'

'It was twenty-five years ago,' Thorne said.

'Even so, it's not the Bermuda triangle, is it? Somebody will have missed her.'

'I still don't think it's going to be easy.'

'Just get him back in a cell for tonight,' Brigstocke said. 'I'll make some calls, get everything arranged.'

'What if it's just a game?' Thorne remembered Nicklin's demeanour just an hour earlier in the school hall, his irritation with Batchelor in the car on the drive up. 'What if it's all about attention? How stupid are we going to look?'

'Not as stupid as we'll look if there's another body over there that we fail to find, even when he's offered to show us where it is.'

'Well, he's still being a bit vague about that.'

'A perfect exercise in how to turn a positive result for us into a PR disaster,' Brigstocke said. 'If we get this wrong. And before you say anything, it's my job to think about crap like that.'

Thorne looked back at the car again and saw that Nicklin was still watching. He wondered what *his* job was?

Nursemaid? Straight man? Fall guy?

At that moment, it certainly didn't feel like he was much of a policeman.

Brigstocke had clearly pulled out all the stops quickly. Half an hour later, Chief Superintendent Robin Duggan was waiting at an otherwise deserted Abersoch police station to greet them, along with a handful of PCs and the same custody sergeant Thorne had been shouting at twenty-four hours earlier. The man did not look overly pleased to be renewing their acquaintance.

While Nicklin and Batchelor were being processed for a second time, Duggan led Thorne to one side.

'So not finished on Bardsey yet then?'

'Not yet.'

'It's all going OK, though?'

'You know how it is,' Thorne said. 'Sometimes these things take a lot longer than you expect.'

'It's best to be thorough.'

'Absolutely.'

'Nothing I should know, though?'

'Such as?'

'Such as a second body.'

'Right,' Thorne said, quietly. He could have done with a nice grave-shaped hole opening up to swallow him. It made perfect sense, of course, that Brigstocke would have told him; that as a senior officer on the force concerned, Duggan would be the most obvious port of call in terms of getting the story of the murdered woman checked out. Thorne's decision to keep Nicklin's latest confession to himself had made him look self-serving and duplicitous. As it was, Duggan seemed content, for the time being at least, with having made Thorne look stupid.

'A second murder's going to make things a lot more complicated,' he said. 'And I don't think anyone wants that.'

'No, sir.' Thorne guessed it was time to show a little deference.

'So, fingers crossed it's all bull.'

Thorne nodded.

'I'll see what I can do about confirming things one way or another, checking missing persons records from back then.' Duggan straightened his cap. 'Long before my time, of course, but there's still a few knocking about who might be able to help.'

'Thanks, sir.'

Duggan nodded towards Nicklin, who was being walked back to the desk from one of the rooms off the custody suite. 'Let's hope it's just mind-games, eh? You look anxious to get home.'

The custody sergeant waved a couple of PCs over to the desk then shouted across to let Duggan know that both prisoners had been searched and were ready to be escorted to the cells. Thorne asked the PCs to hold on and walked across.

'I'll come with you.' He looked at Nicklin and Batchelor. 'But let's take one at a time.' He thought about it, then pointed. 'Him first . . .'

As soon as they were on the other side of the door and in the corridor leading down to the cells, Thorne moved up close to Batchelor. He nodded to the PC to let him know it was all right to step back a little. He put a hand on Batchelor's arm.

'Anything you want to tell me, Jeff?'

'About what?'

'About this. About the latest revelation from your pal, Stuart.'

'He's not my pal.'

'Whatever. Your travelling companion. Anything at all you might be able to help us with here?'

With his handcuffs removed, Batchelor was rubbing at

his wrists. He blinked, closing his eyes for a second or more each time. 'I'd like to speak to my wife,' he said. 'Can you arrange that?'

'Well, there are plenty of phones here.' Thorne nodded. 'I can ask.'

'Thank you.'

'It shouldn't be a problem, but you'll have to help me first.'

'How?'

'This cock and bull about a second body ... all of us going back to the island tomorrow to find this woman he killed. You sure there isn't anything you can tell me about that?'

Batchelor tensed and seemed almost to shrink a little. He looked like he was in physical pain, as though his face were a smooth plaster mask that was cracking with it, and Thorne saw the face of the man who had discovered his daughter's body. He watched Batchelor's Adam's apple move in his neck as he swallowed hard.

'Is Nicklin threatening you?' Thorne looked for a reaction. 'Is that what this is about? Are you afraid he's going to hurt you?' Thorne felt the need to ask, but was well aware how stupid the question was. Anyone who knew Stuart Nicklin and was *not* afraid of him had as many screws loose as he did.

Batchelor looked away from him, shaking his head.

Thorne turned to the PC, said, 'He's all yours,' and went back to fetch Nicklin.

Halfway along the corridor, Nicklin looked at him and said, 'Nice to get the personal touch. Very much appreciated.'

Thorne did not answer. He said nothing until Nicklin had been shown to his cell. Then, just before the door was locked, Thorne stepped in after him. Nicklin looked momentarily thrown, his eyes darting to the PC by the door, as if he thought that Thorne were about to attack him. Nicklin could see by the look on the PC's face that the officer had similar concerns.

'Wouldn't be the first time, would it, Tom?'

Five years before, after Nicklin had got a little over-involved in a case Thorne was working and with people Thorne was close to, a message had been sent via one of Nicklin's fellow inmates. A message in broken glass, delivered at dinner time.

'Don't know what you're talking about,' Thorne said. He took another step into the cell. Pushed the door shut on the confused PC. 'I just wanted you to know that I've been reading the letters you wrote to your mother, OK, Stuart?' He studied Nicklin's face, looking for a reaction. 'Really interesting stuff, seriously. So, there's not very much I don't know when it comes to what's going on inside your big, bald head. I know all about your mummy issues, not that they were much of a surprise. I know what it's like for you inside ... *Professor*. So, whatever the hell this stupid game is you think you're playing now, you need to remember that I know far more about you than you do about me. I don't care what you think you know or what you think you're capable of doing with that information.'

Nicklin lowered himself carefully on to the bare, blue mattress.

'There's no way you're going to win,' Thorne said. 'You need to know that. You're wasting your time, because now I'm in *your* head.' He tapped a finger hard against the side of his head, shook it slowly. 'You're not in mine.'

THIRTY-ONE

After Fletcher and Jenks had made their preference clear, Thorne dropped them off at the same place they'd stayed the previous night; a pub with rooms above it, that looked as good as deserted. He told them he'd pick them up in the morning and that he hoped to know where they'd be going when he did. The two prison officers implied that a return trip to Bardsey would be all right by them, that like Andy Barber they were looking forward to collecting the over-time. In no doubt that they were also looking forward to a night on the beer, Thorne left them and drove on to the Black Horse, with Holland following in the support car.

Elwyn Pritchard was predictably thrilled to see even two of the previous night's guests returning. Even so, he still went through the charade of checking the reservations book to make sure he had rooms available. It was made fairly clear that this time the kitchen would not be opened specially and, once he had handed over the room keys on their reassuringly oversized fobs, he was happy enough to let Thorne and Holland carry their own bags.

As they trudged upstairs, they hastily made dinner arrangements.

'Chinese?'

'Not sure there's anything else.'

'See you back downstairs in ten minutes . . .'

It was the sort of all-purpose place that served pizza as well as prawn balls. It may have been Pritchard's warnings about the ratio of seagull to MSG in the food, or the fact that nobody working there looked like they'd be able to find China on a map, but either way, they both decided to settle for chips and walked back towards the hotel eating their dinners out of Styrofoam containers.

'So, what do you reckon, Dave?'

Holland stabbed at a chip with a wooden fork. 'Should have got some curry sauce.'

'About Nicklin.'

Holland popped the chip into his mouth and ate slowly, but the muscles continued to tense in his jaw for several seconds after he'd swallowed. 'He was right about one thing.'

'What?'

'Some of us haven't forgotten what happened in that playground.'

'None of us have,' Thorne said.

'Sarah, I mean.'

'I know ...'

'She died because of him and he never answered for it. Not the way he should have done, anyway.' Holland slowed his pace a little and glanced at Thorne. 'You knew about me and her, right?'

'Yeah, I knew.' Thorne sensed there was guilt lurking just behind the anger. He sensed too that Holland wanted to get stuff off his chest and he was not altogether sure he wanted to hear it. 'Listen, you don't need to explain anything to me.'

'Nothing to explain,' Holland said. 'I was stupid, McEvoy was stupid and who the hell knows how much more stupid the pair of us would have got if she hadn't been killed? But she died, so maybe that ... got me off the hook.' He poked at his dinner, lips pulled back across his teeth. 'I mean, look at me now, happy family man and all that. Happy as fucking Larry. So, maybe Nicklin did me a favour, you know?'

Thorne looked at him. 'You're talking shit, Dave. You do know that, don't you? People mess up.'

'I know that I can still remember what Sarah smelled like, and I think about it sometimes, when I'm in bed with Sophie. When I look at Nicklin, I feel like he knows that, like it gives him a thrill or something, and I want to rip his head off.'

They said nothing for a minute or more, walking a little quicker once they were past the terrace that backed on to the beach and provided a barrier between the street and the sea. The temperature was dropping quickly and the wind had started to pick up.

'So, what do you reckon to this latest bombshell then?' Thorne asked. 'This other body.'

Holland shrugged. 'Haven't got a clue, if I'm honest. You?'

Thorne shook his head. 'I can't read him and the problem is I don't know if that should be telling me anything or not. Sometimes terrible poker players are just as hard to play against as good ones. They don't know what the hell they're doing, so there's no way *you* can.' He shovelled some more chips into his mouth; they were soggy and tasteless, but he was hungry. 'Maybe he's just making it all up as he goes along.'

'It's all possible though, isn't it? What he's telling us.'

'Yeah, it's possible.'

'Killing that kid just because he feels like it, then killing the old woman whose shovel he nicked. It would all sound bloody ridiculous if it was anyone else. Him though . . .'

'I know,' Thorne said.

'Someone like him doesn't need a reason to do these things, so you never know if he's really got a reason for doing anything.'

Thorne grunted, chewed.

'That stuff he said to Howell before, about getting off on the bodies. Was that real, or was he just trying to wind her up?'

'Who knows?' Thorne said.

They dumped the remains of their dinners into a bin outside the Black Horse and wandered inside. As far as Thorne could tell, the same people were drinking at the bar as had been propping it up the night before. They did appear to have softened somewhat towards the newcomers though, the hostility of the previous evening having now been replaced by complete indifference.

Holland stepped towards the bar. 'Pint?'

Thorne hesitated, shaking his head. He was thinking about something Duggan had said back at the station.

'Later, maybe . . .'

While Holland ordered himself a drink and fell into conversation with Pritchard, Thorne walked across and spoke briefly to a man at the bar. When he had been given the information he was looking for, he left the hotel, climbed into one of the Galaxys and drove the dozen or so miles to Aberdaron.

THIRTY-TWO

It was what Duggan had said to him about a 'few knocking about'. The superintendent had been talking about police officers who might still be on the force, but Thorne realised there were others who might be able to help and to do so a damn sight quicker.

Others who had been there.

He rang the bell, stepped back and looked up at a house that was a long way removed from what he had been expecting. It was a modern two-up two-down, red brick with UPVC windows. A simple rectangle of grass at the front. A satellite dish.

When Huw Morgan opened the door, he looked confused to see Thorne standing there.

'Have you got five minutes?' Thorne asked.

Walking past the living room, Thorne could see Morgan's father watching TV. Some American drama, cops or lawyers, where everyone was a bit too good-looking to be taken seriously. The old man turned to look and Thorne nodded a hello. 'We've just eaten,' Morgan said, leading Thorne into the kitchen. 'But I think there might be some left.' He turned and shouted back down the hall. 'Dad, we got any of that stew left?'

'It's fine,' Thorne said. 'I had chips.'

'What about a beer then?'

'Beer would be great.'

Morgan produced three cans of supermarket lager from the fridge and they carried them to the living room. Huw handed a can to his father and said, 'Turn that down, we've got the police here.'

Bernard sighed and reached for the remote.

'So, is this police business or are you just going a bit bonkers in Abersoch?' Huw sat down, nodded Thorne towards the sofa. 'Can't say I blame you, there's not a lot going on. Mind you, it's a teeming bloody metropolis compared with what's going on here.'

'Bit of both,' Thorne said.

'What?' Bernard said.

'It's a bit of police business. Just a chat, really.' Thorne took a swig of his lager, which was surprisingly good. 'I got your address from your cousin,' he said. 'He was in the bar at the Black Horse.'

'Arsehole,' Huw said.

Bernard shook his head and glanced at Thorne. 'Long story . . .'

Thorne looked around. The inside of the house was as modern as the exterior. A big-screen TV, leather sofa and armchairs. There were black and white photos in frames on the wall; sea views and boats in the harbour, an island that Thorne guessed was Bardsey.

Huw saw Thorne looking. Said, 'What?'

'I was expecting you might live somewhere a bit more traditional.'

'What, a fisherman's cottage kind of thing?'

'Something like that.'

'Peat fires and ancient slates and a weathervane shaped like a whale?'

Bernard laughed.

'Listen, mate,' Huw said. 'After a long day out there with the lobster pots or whatever, I want to come home to central heating and Sky. Dad had somewhere a bit more traditional, didn't you? One of the old cottages up on the front.' Bernard nodded, drank. 'When my mum died a couple of years back though, we thought it was a good idea for Dad to sell up and move in with me. His place was on its last legs and I was on my own anyway ...'

Thorne waited in case there was more coming. It became clear that there wasn't and he was left watching Huw take a long drink and wondering if there had ever been a wife and kids, if the youngest Morgan had always been on his own.

When Huw finally put his can down, he said, 'So, this chat then ...?'

'It was actually your father I wanted to speak to,' Thorne said. He turned to Bernard. 'I was just wondering if I could ask you about something that happened a long time ago. See what you remember.'

'You might be in luck,' Huw said. 'He tends to have a good memory for things that happened years back, even if he can't remember what bloody day it is sometimes.'

'Cheeky beggar,' Bernard said.

Thorne said, 'Twenty-five years ago. Back when the young offenders were staying on the island.' He reached into his pocket and produced the photograph of Tides House that he was still carrying around. He stood up, stepped across and laid it down on the small table next to Bernard's chair.

The old man reached for his glasses and picked up the photograph. 'That what they were?' he said. 'Young offenders?' He stared at the picture, shaking his head. 'You wouldn't have thought it, the way they swanned around, lying about and taking drugs on the beach. You'd have thought they were on holiday.'

'It was a different approach,' Thorne said.

'Well, it didn't work, did it? That's why they shut it down.'

Thorne nodded. All the information had been there in the notes he was given before leaving London. The funding for the Tides House project had been hastily withdrawn following a violent knife attack on one of the boys and the escape – or so everyone had thought – of two others. The doors had closed within a few months and those in senior positions – most notably a woman named Ruth Livesey – had been pilloried in the press before being pressured into taking early retirement from the young offenders prison system.

Bernard held the picture out and Thorne moved to take it back. He doubted that Bernard had recognised any faces. If Thorne himself had not been told who was who, he would certainly have struggled to pick out Stuart Nicklin, though looking closely he could see that the eyes were the same; the challenge in the stare. He had been told that the tall, skinny boy standing next to Nicklin was Simon Milner. A shock of dirty-blond hair, an open-necked shirt. Thumbs held aloft . . .

Milner was the only boy smiling.

Thorne put the photograph away. Said, 'Anyway . . . around that time, do you remember anyone going missing?'

'You don't mean those boys who escaped?'

'A woman,' Thorne said. 'An elderly woman. I think she might have been a poet, or something.'

'Yeah, there's always plenty of those,' Huw said.

'Rings a bell.' Bernard was nodding. 'There was definitely some talk of a woman drowning.'

'Drowning?'

'Well, that's what everyone thought, that she'd killed herself. Let's face it, you can't really go missing on Bardsey. There's only one way off the island if you're still breathing and that's on the boat, so you're either there or you're dead, aren't you?'

'And this was definitely twenty-five years ago?'

'Well, I can't say for certain.' He nodded at Huw, thinking. 'He was only a lad, I know that much, so it was definitely around the time they closed the children's home down. Or a bit afterwards, maybe. I think she might have died earlier than that though.'

'What makes you say that?' Thorne asked.

'Well, she wouldn't have been missed straight away, would she?'

'He's got a point,' Huw said. 'A lot of the people who stay on the island just want to be left alone, see. Some of them go out there for months at a time, especially the arty types and it's not like they're phoning home every day, is it? Sending postcards.'

'If she went missing,' Bernard said, 'it might not have been noticed for quite a while. Especially as there was such a bloody hoo-hah about what was going on with Tides House. All the comings and goings when that place closed.' He downed what was left of his beer, nodded. 'I seem to remember taking another woman across afterwards,' he said. 'More than once, if I remember rightly. I think it might have been her sister. She wanted to see the last place she'd been staying. The place where she'd died. She might have had flowers ... it was a long time ago. Like I said, there was some talk about her drowning herself.' He leaned towards Thorne. 'I think she might have been the type, you know?'

257

'What, because she was a poet?' Huw said.

'Well, a lot of them do, don't they?' Bernard looked very serious. 'Poets, writers, what have you. Too bloody sensitive by half.' He waved his empty can at his son.

Huw laughed, standing and gathering the empties. 'Another one?'

Thorne thought about it, but not for very long.

When Huw returned with fresh beers, he dropped into the armchair. 'This is Mr Nicklin again then, is it?'

Thorne saw little point in evasion. 'It's what he's telling us. We've got to decide if we're taking him back to prison first thing in the morning or going back to the island to start looking for this woman.'

'He couldn't have known about her,' Bernard said.

Thorne looked at him, opened his beer.

'Well, Tides House was closed by the time anyone knew anything had happened to that woman, wasn't it? And *he'd* gone before that anyway, so he wouldn't even have known she'd ever gone missing, would he? Not unless he was responsible for it.' The old man popped the tab on his can and shrugged as though what he was saying should have been perfectly obvious.

Thorne took a swig. 'You should have been a detective, Bernard.'

'Looks like we'll be seeing you tomorrow then,' Huw said.

'Yeah . . .'

'Actually, the weather's looking a bit iffy tomorrow.'

'Great.'

'Morning should be OK though.'

Thorne tried to picture the blister pack of sickness tablets. He guessed he would have enough left to get him to the island and back.

'I couldn't do what you do,' Bernard said.

'Why's that?'

'Well, you're always dealing with people at their very worst, aren't you? At their lowest. Bastards like that bloke you've got with you now, the one we've been talking about. Even when you're dealing with normal people ... a lot of the time you're seeing them when they're in bits. When their lives have been destroyed.

'Let's face it, a lot of the time *you're* the one who has to tell them that their lives have been destroyed, then watch them fall apart in front of you.' He shook his head slowly. 'No ... I couldn't do that. I'll stick to the fishing and what have you, thank you very much.' He looked across at Thorne and raised his can in a small salute. 'Fair play to you though, mind. I mean, some poor bugger's got to do it, haven't they?'

Thorne said, 'True.' Thinking that only a couple of hours ago he'd all but forgotten what his job was.

Thinking that you could never forget for long.

'Listen to him,' Huw said. 'The bloke who thinks poets are too bloody sensitive.'

Bernard said, 'You're not too big to get a slap, you know.'

'Oh, here we go.'

'What?'

'He'll be wanting to arm-wrestle in a minute . . . '

Thorne smiled, happy enough to sit and drink with these two for a while and enjoy their bickering.

An hour later, walking from the Morgans' house to the car, Thorne was well aware that the three cans of beer he'd put away, weak as they'd been, were probably enough to have put him over the limit.

He pressed the remote on the fob and the indicators flashed.

There was probably only one patrol car within a fifty-mile radius but Sod's Law said that he'd run into it between here and the Black Horse, make some Welsh plod's week.

Make bloody headlines, probably.

He got into the car.

He could always phone Holland, see how much he'd had to drink. He could go back to the Morgans', ask for the number of a local taxi and come back to pick the Galaxy up in the morning. He could try thumbing a lift, flashing his warrant card and claiming it was an emergency.

He started the car and reached for a packet of mints in the door. Then he took out his phone and called Robert Burnham. He apologised for calling so late, and asked the warden if he would mind taking the satellite phone down to the dig and telling the exhibits officer to give him a call.

He was halfway back to the Black Horse when Karim rang back.

The forensic team were still hard at it, Karim told him. Looking forward to a well-earned drink and a good night's sleep while *some* people would be bedding down next to a body in some spooky chapel. Thorne told him about Nicklin's bombshell and asked him to let Howell and the others know that they would be doing it all again tomorrow.

'You might be spending two nights in that spooky chapel,' he said.

'You're kidding right?'

'Some poor bugger's got to do it, haven't they?' Thorne said.

THIRTY-THREE

Holland was still drinking when Thorne got back to the hotel. Proving definitively what an effective social lubricant alcohol could be, he was deep in conversation with a couple of the formerly surly locals at a table near the bar. Seeing Thorne in the doorway, they beckoned him across and demanded to know what he was drinking. Thorne told them that he was tired, that he had a stupidly early start in the morning, but they would not listen, pushing a chair towards him and insisting that he join them for a nightcap.

Holland went to get a round in and Thorne joined him at the bar. 'We've *all* got an early start,' he said. He told Holland they were going back to Bardsey and filled him in on the conversation with Bernard Morgan.

'Nicklin was telling the truth then,' Holland said.

Thorne was slowly and systematically tearing a beer mat into small pieces, laying them one on top of the other. He said, 'Best way to make a lie convincing is to chuck a bit of truth in.'

'So, what's he lying about?'

'No idea,' Thorne said. He tore the final fragment of the beer mat into two and added the pieces to the pile. 'I'm too bloody tired to think straight.'

Pritchard set the drinks down. He scribbled down the charges on a scrap of paper with Holland's room number on it, then swept the pieces of the beer mat off the bar into his hand. Holland picked up two of the glasses, drank the top from one of them.

'One more won't hurt . . . '

They carried the drinks across to the table and the two local lads immediately began urging Holland to carry on with his story. Holland looked a little embarrassed, more so as they pressed him.

'Come on, how many more did he kill, like?'

'Was he the worst one you ever had?'

'What happened when you got him into the interview room . . . ?'

They hung on Holland's every word as he described what could have been almost any interview, deliberately making the whole thing sound a lot less interesting than he might have done had Thorne not been sitting there. As he doubtless had been doing before. One of the lads nudged Thorne and said, 'You heard this one? Bloke who cut his victims' tongues out and kept each one as a souvenir in a different matchbox.'

Thorne nodded.

'In a bloody *matchbox*.'

'I know . . .'

As far as war stories went, he'd heard them all, told them all. The bare bones or a heavily embellished version, depending on his audience and the reaction he was looking for.

Kudos, when he craved it, or maybe just a free drink. Sex, occasionally.

'I'd bloody *love* your job,' one of the lads said. 'Sounds fantastic.'

Holland tried to demur, but the man would not listen.

'I got no problem with the blood and the bodies, nothing like that, and I mean, how good is it to actually have a chance to hurt some of these bastards? I know you're not supposed to, there's laws and all that, but I bet you still have the chance to get a dig in every now and again, right?' He went to take a drink, but lost interest in it before the glass reached his mouth, so fired up was he about the job of his dreams. 'It's got the lot, hasn't it?' He looked at his mate, who nodded, excitedly. 'Blood and gore and all the sick stuff, if that's what you want . . . the chance to solve crime and put people away or whatever, and I bet you're beating the birds away with a shitty stick, aren't you?' He looked at Holland, who could do no more than shrug and stare into his beer.

It was a very different assessment of the job than the one Thorne had been given half an hour before by Bernard

Morgan. While it was hard to take the opinions of two beered-up idiots seriously, Thorne could not help wishing that their ill-informed enthusiasm was in some way justified.

That the old man had been wrong.

'You all right?' Holland asked.

'Just knackered, like I said.' He pushed his chair away from the table and told Holland he'd see him in the morning. He had not taken more than a couple of sips of his beer and asked Holland's drinking companions if they fancied helping him out with it. They had divided up what was left between them before Thorne was on his feet.

Tonight, there was no boo-hooing coming from the adjacent cell and, though Nicklin guessed that Batchelor was only pretending to be asleep, he was grateful for the peace and quiet nonetheless.

He had thinking to do.

It was not the reason for doing it, not the main one at any rate, but he'd really enjoyed the reaction he'd got on the boat, when he'd casually told Thorne about the second body. He'd enjoyed the way they'd been with him ever since too. Solicitous and wary, both at the same time.

It was like telling a joke, wasn't it?

It was all about the timing, and he'd got it, bang on.

It had been so great afterwards, sitting in the car and watching Thorne on the phone to his boss, stomping about in the mud; shouting and screaming and waving his arms around like a madman. It was obvious that they hadn't got the first idea whether he was telling the truth or not. Thorne had been studying his face ever since they'd got off the boat, staring at him, looking for some hint. Why was he so *suspicious*, for heaven's sake?

He wasn't much of a copper, not if he couldn't recognise an honest-to-goodness confession when he heard one.

Nicklin guessed that, by now, the decision had been taken to go back the next day. They might not have found out who the woman was yet, but it hardly mattered. They might not have been able to confirm anything he'd told them, but the simple fact was that they couldn't afford to take the risk, could they?

That looming spectre of bad press . . .

They knew very well that Nicklin would find a way to get to the papers and tell them the same thing he'd told Thorne on the boat. This was a red-top's dream after all. A story that wrote itself:

I OFFERED TO SHOW THEM HER BODY
BUT THEY DIDN'T WANT TO KNOW!
We can reveal that the grave of a long-missing
poet will remain hidden, despite her killer
offering the police chapter and verse . . .

He got up and took the two steps across to the far wall. He leaned the side of his face against the cold brick.

'Jeff . . . what did Thorne talk to you about?'

There was no answer, but he didn't feel any need to push it. He would ask again in the morning and besides, he knew that Batchelor would not have said anything he had not been given permission to say. He walked slowly back to his bunk and lay down. His feet were sore and he could feel himself starting to stiffen, his back and his thighs. It certainly knocked you for six, being out and about all day. Marching backwards and forwards across those fields.

He thought about Thorne barging into his cell after him and shouting the odds, all fired up and full of himself. The stuff about his mum's letters, the things he knew, who was in whose head, all that.

Nicklin had felt like the straight man in a freakish double act.

God, it had been so hard to keep a straight face.

THIRTY-FOUR

Thorne was staying in the same room he'd been given the night before and, with no further guests expected, he had more than a vague suspicion that they had not bothered to change the bed. He wondered if that was why he had been allocated the same room. Perhaps Pritchard thought a customer was less likely to make a fuss if it was only himself he could catch a whiff of on the sheets.

That aside, Thorne found the rust-spotted bathroom mirror and the cracked handle on the wardrobe door as oddly comforting as the curly wire on the TV remote. He lay on the bed in his underpants and a faded Willie Nelson T-shirt. The phone was pressed to his ear. Though the sound of the television was muted, he continued to flick back and forth between the channels.

'At least it sounds like there's something in what Nicklin's telling you,' Helen said.

'Yeah. I'm sure there's something.' Thorne stopped at a channel showing some arty-looking film with subtitles. He wondered idly if there might be any dirty bits. 'It's just about trying to work out what that is.'

'Shame. We were looking forward to having you back.'

'Tomorrow,' Thorne said. 'I don't care if he tells me he's buried another twenty on that sodding island. I'm coming back tomorrow.'

'Well, I know one little lad who's going to be happy,' Helen said.

'You reckon?'

'He saw a Woodentop on the street today and pointed and said "Tom".'

'That's funny,' Thorne said. It had only been a few months since Alfie had begun to say Thorne's name, back when he was working in south London and still wearing uniform. 'He's asleep, is he?'

'Well away,' Helen said. 'I'm not far behind him, either.'

'Yeah, sorry for calling so late.'

'It's fine.'

'You going to be happy too?'

'What do you think? It's been a bit shitty at work, last couple of days, and with you not around it's just been . . . shittier.'

Thorne was happy to hear it, but knew it was not just because she missed his sunny personality or red-hot body. It was clear that there were things she needed to talk about and Thorne would have to put in some time as an emotional punchbag when he got home. 'Tell me tomor-row,' he said. He hoped he hadn't sounded dismissive, or uninterested.

'You sound a bit down,' Helen said.

'Well, it's hardly surprising, is it?'

'No, apart from the business with Nicklin, I mean. Everything OK?'

'I'm fine.' Thorne had managed to find a football match showing on one of the Eurosport channels. He watched, struggling to work out who the two teams were without any sound. He could hear Helen taking a drink of some-thing. The absence of that punchbag when it was needed often meant an extra glass or two of wine. 'I was just think-ing about my dad a bit,' he said. 'That's all.'

Helen said, 'OK . . .'

'Sitting there with those two tonight, Huw, and his dad. You should have seen the pair of them. They were like a team, you know? Taking the piss, pretending to get annoyed with each other . . . I just miss that.'

'Course you do.'

'Never really like that with me and my old man, but I miss it anyway. I was thinking about going fishing with him this morning, for God's sake. I haven't thought about that in donkey's years.'

'It's only natural.'

'I miss how it was before the Alzheimer's. No . . . I miss that too.'

'Tom—'

'He was funny with it, sometimes. When he got worked up. Swearing like a docker in the supermarket ...'

Neither of them spoke for a long few seconds. Thorne stared at the TV, struggling to get comfortable on the bed. He could hear Helen taking another drink.

'I'd better get some sleep,' he said. 'Sorry ...'

'Call me tomorrow when you're on the way back and I can get some dinner on. Or maybe we could just get a takeaway.'

'Sounds good.'

'Chinese?' Helen suggested. 'Without the added seagull ...'

It was after midnight and Thorne had an early start in the morning, but once he'd finished talking to Helen and established that Frankfurt were a goal down to Bayer Leverkusen, he still felt the need to have a shower. It was as much about the day he'd had, the company he'd been keeping, as it was about the fact that he could skip having one in the morning and give himself an extra half-hour in bed.

When he'd dried himself off, he lay down on the bed with the damp, thin towel around his waist.

Come on, how many more did he kill?

Was he the worst one you ever had?

I'd bloody love your job ...

He lay there for another few minutes, then he turned the television off and called Helen back.

'Sorry, were you in bed?'

271

'Almost,' she said.

'I can't sleep . . .'

There were a few seconds of crackle on the line, a siren somewhere and the fierce breathing of the sea outside his window.

'I'd better get another glass of wine,' Helen said.

THE THIRD DAY

DEADLY WEATHER

He's not taking the painkillers any more.

He'd begun leaving them on the tray, so the man doling them out has stopped bothering, which is fine. The pain has eased a little anyway, it's not stopping him from sleeping any longer. But the fact is that he wants it, wants whatever is left of it. Not taking the painkillers means that his head isn't fuzzy all the time, which is good, because it means he can focus.

And the pain lets him hold on to his anger.

He's got no idea what the man's name is of course, just as he had no idea what the couple's names were, so he's made one up. He calls him Adrian. It's the name of someone he works with, a weasely little tosser who gets on his nerves. It's a little bit nerdish too, which he thinks suits the man with his thick glasses and ratty ponytail and his hairless, white belly which is now on display again. Just an inch or two of it, sagging beneath the bottom of his black T-shirt.

Adrian sits on a chair in the middle of the room, reading a comic of some sort. He studies him from the edge of the bed. He sits close to the metal bedstead, so he doesn't have to stretch his arm out. He'd asked for some ointment for the welts where the cuffs had rubbed, but Adrian wasn't having any of it. He said much the same thing as when he'd been asked for the antibiotics. He wasn't a bloody chemist, something like that.

He watches Adrian read, the lips pursed in concentration. Adrian glances up for a second as he turns the page. He sees that he's being watched but it doesn't appear to bother him, and he quickly goes back to his comic.

'Is that any good?'

Adrian looks up again, says nothing.

'They've made a film of it, haven't they? You've probably seen it, but reading's always better, I reckon.' He swings his legs up and eases gently back towards the bedstead. He reaches round with his free hand and props up a pillow behind him, then leans slowly back against it. He winces, but grits his teeth until the urge to cry out has passed. It hurts like hell, but at least the grubby pillowcase isn't sticking to his wound, which means it's starting to scab over. 'I have this running argument with a mate of mine,' he says. 'He says they're comics. Gets really annoyed when I tell him they're graphic novels, try and explain how dark they are, how brilliant the artwork is. He doesn't listen. His loss though, right?'

Adrian looks up again and now he shuts what is undoubtedly just a comic with a glossy cover and lays it down gently by the side of the chair. He leans back and says, 'I don't want to be your friend. So you're wasting your time trying to crawl up my arse.'

'I wasn't.'

'Yeah,' Adrian says. 'You were.' He nods down to the comic. 'I don't give a toss what you or anyone else calls them, but I'm bloody sure you've never read one in your life.'

'Are they your friends?' he asks. 'The other two.'

'Never met them before.' Adrian says this almost proudly. 'We share an interest, that's all.'

'What about whoever's organised this? Whoever's in charge.'

'What about them?'

'Are they your friend?'

'How do you know I'm not in charge?'

'You said you were here to do certain things, so I'm guessing someone put you here. Put you together with the other two.'

'You're such a smartarse,' Adrian says.

'So people tell me.'

'Yeah, well look where it's got you.'

'I can hear you on the phone, you know.'

'Yeah?'

'Outside.'

'So?'

'I can't hear what you're saying, not really, but I recognise the tone. It's funny you should talk about crawling up arses, because that's exactly what I'm hearing when you're on the phone talking to whoever it is. Is it the boy or the girl? Looked to me like the girl was the one calling the shots.' He waits, but Adrian says nothing. 'Yeah, definitely her, I reckon. Even if she wasn't a nutter, she'd scare the crap out of you, wouldn't she? She's got tits and everything. Probably makes you feel a bit funny in your downstairs special place, doesn't it?'

Adrian gets to his feet. He walks over to the wall and leans against it. He licks his lips and plasters on a smile. 'Obviously, there's certain things I'm supposed to do,' he says. 'But now I'm the only one here, so there's nothing to stop me pissing all over your food if I feel like it. Nothing to stop me doing all sorts of things.' There's a sheen of sweat on Adrian's face and, standing there scratching his belly, he resembles nothing so much as the creepy, friendless twerp he has clearly been made to feel like too many times. But the sickly smile is still terrifying.

Adrian pushes himself away from the wall, moves towards the bed.

The pain has fed his anger as he hoped it would. It felt good to rant at Adrian and now, watching him get closer, he's feeling stronger than he has at any time since he was taken. He starts to imagine getting out of this room, thinks about what he will do to Adrian, how much damage he will inflict, as soon as he comes up with any sort of plan. The anger, if it is not keeping the fear at bay completely, is at least balancing things out a little.

'You want to be careful,' Adrian says. 'Shooting your mouth off.' He reaches behind and draws the Taser from his back pocket. 'Might be fun to see what happens if we push this up against your balls and give you a jolt.'

278

'I'll probably get a stiffy. A bit more painful than Viagra, but you might be on to something there.'

Adrian fires the Taser, watches the current arc between the electrodes for a few seconds, then puts it back in his pocket. 'I'm not talking about that though.' He nods towards the door. 'She left her scalpel behind.' He carries on nodding. 'Oh yeah, and if you keep winding me up, I might be tempted to have a crack with it. I mean how hard can it be, right?' He holds out his hand towards the bed. 'Thing is though, I'm not getting a lot of sleep, no more than you probably, and what with that and way too much coffee ... well, you can imagine.' Adrian's hand begins to shake theatrically and he stares at it, eyes wide, amused and mock-alarmed in equal measure.

From the bed, he stares at it too and just like that, the anger is gone. The rush of confidence evaporates. The part of his brain that is still managing to think sensibly is telling him that, despite what they've done so far, they obviously want to keep him alive. Reassuring him that money, or whatever else they're after, is far too important to them to risk killing him.

Suddenly though, it's the other part of his brain where the synapses are beginning to spark and spit. However much he tries to fight it, to dampen down the dread that presses him hard back into the pillow, a gallery of friends and family, of those he loves, is taking shape behind his eyes.

He begins to think about dying in this room.

THIRTY-FIVE

Jeffrey Batchelor closed his eyes and turned his face to the spray. He tried to imagine that the boat he was on would soon be pulling into Shanklin or Douglas or that he was heading home after a day's fishing off Falmouth with the girls. That it was Sonia, Rachel and Jodi sitting across from him and that it was their voices just audible beneath the crash of waves and the throb of engines, and not those of Nicklin or Fletcher.

Their laughter he could hear.

The Batchelors had always enjoyed holidays in the UK; 'stay-cations' or whatever they were called. He and Sonia had both travelled abroad as students and he had been all over Europe on research trips for work, but any attempt at anything far-flung as a family had usually ended badly. Foreign holidays had been cursed with illness and lost luggage, the stress of complex travel arrangements almost always resulting in arguments. To be fair, it had been the adult members of the family who probably deserved most of the blame. He knew that with other families it was the other way round more often than not, the kids moaning about being away from friends and TV and a decent Wi-Fi signal, but he and Sonia were the ones who got bitten or caught food poisoning. The ones who fell out and spoiled it for everyone else. The girls had been great as a rule, trudging off to the Isle of Wight or the Lake District without complaint, content to play their part as the younger half of the 'Boring Batchelors'. He knew that they had found it dull, the weather and the walking, the old-fashioned card games, especially as they had got older. He and Sonia had always known that they'd be off somewhere more interesting with their mates, first chance they had.

Jodi had always talked about travelling . . .

He opened his eyes, saw the Irish Sea rising and falling ahead of him, the edge of the boat moving in rhythm with it.

He was on his way to a very different island, and because he was not the same as the man who had brought him, because he was sensible and sensitive and reacted to things the way the vast majority of ordinary people did, he was as scared as it was possible to be at the thought of what was waiting for him. The things he was going there to do.

Nicklin had told him how perfect the island was, had talked for hours about the history of the place, the stories of those who had travelled to the place and were buried there.

'Think about that, Jeff,' he had said. 'Twenty thousand of them. They reckon you're only ever six feet from a rat in London. Where we're going, you're probably never more than that far from the bones of a saint.'

If it was true, then up to now Batchelor hadn't felt it. There was peace and quiet for sure, but nothing he would call spiritual. Maybe he was just too frightened to pick up on all that stuff.

More than anything, he wanted to talk to Sonia, and Nicklin was still telling him that it was going to happen. All a question of timing, he said. Batchelor had spent a long time now, trying to work out what he would say when the moment came, knowing that he might not have very long in which to say it. He would need to pick his words carefully.

Listen, love, it's me. You'll be hearing things, from reporters and from the police probably and I just wanted you to hear them from me first. You remember what happened a month or so after I started my sentence? To me, I mean. You remember that things were suddenly different . . .

Should he tell her the truth? That was the big question.

It was easy enough to tell her how much he loved her, that he missed her, but what about when it came to giving her reasons? Would she hate him if he did? He thought he knew his wife well enough to believe that she wouldn't, but it was still a gamble.

Was it worth risking that, just to have her understand?

Something happened, love. I'm talking about Jodi and Nathan. I found something out . . .

Having her hate him was not a price he was prepared to pay.

He hoped he would know what to say when it came to it, when he heard his wife's voice. He hoped that his faith would guide him. He hoped above all that there would be enough of it left by then. It had been such a struggle clinging on to it, plenty of times when it would have been so much easier to just let it go. The journey he had been on had been so strange and terrible that were it not for the conviction that it must all be somehow necessary, he would have stopped believing long before now.

From staring up at his daughter, her flawless features grey and bloated, to the sea that was now spitting in his face and moving beneath him, remorselessly bearing him towards an island built on bones.

From that bedroom to this boat.

He heard a laugh and looked across at Nicklin. The man who had saved him for reasons that were now obvious enough.

Nicklin smiled. Shouted, 'All right, Jeff?'

Batchelor smiled back, nodded.

Another price that was far too high.

THIRTY-SIX

Halfway up the track, Thorne turned and looked down towards the dock, watched the *Benlli III* heading back out to sea. The boat seemed even smaller than it was from this far away, this high up, the older Morgan almost indistinguishable from the younger as he moved around the deck.

Huw had said that, all being well, he would return to collect Thorne and the others before dark.

All being well.

Thorne looked at the sky. Was it starting to darken or was that his imagination? The wind certainly seemed to be picking up a little. He turned and pushed on up the track towards the school, Fletcher, Jenks and the prisoners in front of him. Holland moving purposefully, a step or two ahead of them.

Nicklin was saying something to Batchelor, leaning close, but from where he was, Thorne could not make out what was being said. It didn't much matter. Nicklin had been gabbling ever since they'd collected him from the station and Thorne assumed that the prison officers would pass on anything they thought might be of interest.

Burnham was waiting for them in the school hall, along with Bethan Howell, Barber and a tired-looking Wendy Markham. The warden was talkative and Howell was keen to know what the plan was, but Thorne only stayed long enough to grab two cups of coffee and tell everyone that he'd be back in ten minutes.

He walked down the steps on to the track and turned north towards the chapel. Trudging up the slope, he was struck again – as he had been the day before, when he was searching for a phone signal – by the mountain rising up to his right, looming above the farm and the scattering of cottages at the edge of the plain. He looked up, thinking that, at no more than four or five hundred feet, it was more a glorified hill than anything else, though the cliffs on the other side of it had certainly looked high enough when the boat had passed them half an hour before. It wasn't a steep rise and he wondered how long it would take someone to climb it.

How long it would take someone with the *inclination* to climb it.

He remembered once again that weekend spent walking with Louise, the excuse for the boots that had cost a small fortune and were still not as comfortable as he'd been assured they would be.

There had been several hills involved then.

It had not gone well.

Looking up, Thorne saw a man a few hundred feet above him on the slope. It was hard to tell if he was on his way up or down. The man had binoculars and appeared to be looking straight at him. Thorne assumed it was the birdwatcher he had spotted the previous day on the way back from the lighthouse.

The man lowered his binoculars and turned away.

Thorne carried on towards the chapel.

'Don't say I never do anything for you.'

Karim took the coffee gratefully, but his good cheer evaporated as soon as he remembered that Thorne was responsible for his having spent the night freezing his tits off in the first place.

Thorne nodded down at the lilo, the thin blanket folded across it. 'Looks cosy enough to me,' he said.

Karim grunted and walked quickly to the door. 'I'm desperate for a slash,' he said. 'It was either desert my post or piss in the font.'

'You're an example to us all,' Thorne said.

Once Karim had stepped outside, Thorne moved away from the black body bag lying on the floor at the foot of the altar and walked across to read the large wooden plaque on the wall. It said that the chapel had been built in 1875. The warden had already told him that, back then, the islanders had been given the choice of a working harbour or a chapel and had plumped for a place of worship.

It didn't make a lot of sense to Thorne, but he had as much truck with organised religion as he did with hill-walking or heavy metal.

Karim pushed back through the heavy wooden door, draining his coffee cup. 'Bloody hell, it's nasty enough having to piss in one of those compost things. Can't imagine what it's like to take a dump.' He flopped down in one of the pews. 'Not that we've had enough to eat to make that happen. Cup-a-Soup and a cheese sandwich was all we had last night.' He slapped his substantial gut. 'I'm wasting away here, mate.'

'I'll take you for a curry when we get back,' Thorne said.

Karim grinned. 'I tell you who else would like that.'

Thorne looked.

'I reckon our crime scene manager's got a bit of a thing for you.'

'Rubbish.' Thorne hoped he wasn't reddening, stared down at the edge of a pew.

'Seriously,' Karim said. 'She was asking me if you had a girlfriend or whatever. And don't think we didn't notice her following you up to bed the other night.'

'She didn't follow me to bed.'

'Well, she left at the same time.'

'And?'

'I'm just saying. She's pretty fit . . . '

Thorne turned away and walked towards the door. He said, 'We need to crack on.'

'So, am I supposed to stay here all bloody day?' Karim asked.

'Somebody needs to,' Thorne said. 'I'll see if I can get Dave to swap with you later on, but I shouldn't moan too much if I were you. At least it's warm in here. It's getting seriously nippy out there.'

Karim was lying down again, his feet up on the pew, when Thorne pulled the chapel door closed behind him.

He walked through the graveyard past the huge Celtic cross – its inscription commemorating Lord Newborough, who had owned the island in the nineteenth century – to the ruins of the ancient abbey just beyond. It was basically no more than the damaged remains of a sunken bell tower – all that was left of what had once been a two-storey structure that also served as a lookout post – but it was still many centuries older than the chapel Thorne had just left.

He stepped into it and immediately felt the temperature drop. A change in the sound, the quality of the silence.

There were large, flat stones arranged into some kind of table or low altar at one end. A modern wooden bench sat against the wall at the other. Thorne stood still between the two; hands thrust deep into pockets, listening to the wind's low note through holes in the stone, supposedly put there hundreds of years before by a Spanish man-o'-war the lookout had failed to spot. He stayed for a minute, perhaps two, before stepping out and walking quickly back to the track.

Fifty yards or so down, he walked past the birdwatcher he had spotted on the side of the mountain. He recognised the man's red woolly hat.

The man said, 'Good day for it,' and Thorne grunted.

Thinking that any day spent looking for bodies was unlikely to make his list of good ones.

A second or two before the man was past him, Thorne was suddenly struck by the idea that he had seen his face somewhere before. That it was more than just the red hat that was familiar. Convinced that he knew the man, but with no idea how, Thorne opened his mouth to speak, but closed it again once he realised that he had nothing to say and that the birdwatcher was already gone. He turned and watched the man stride away along the track.

Bethan Howell was standing outside the school. She was leaning against the wall, staring out across the plain, smoking.

'So, how was your night?' Thorne asked.

'Quite fun, actually,' she said. 'Well, the wine helped. We all sat around the fire telling scary stories. It was a bit like being on a school trip or something, except that the stories were true.' She saw Thorne looking at her cigarette and reached into her pocket. 'Want one?'

'God, yes,' Thorne said. 'But I'd better not.'

'I can see why you might need one.' She nodded back towards the school. 'Mr Nicklin's every bit as much of a charmer as I was expecting,' she said.

'Really? I thought the pair of you were starting to hit it off.'

She smiled. 'He's what got the ball rolling last night. Those scary stories I was talking about.' She took a drag. The wind took the ash away fast. 'I mean, you read about these characters in the paper, but you never know what they're going to be like, do you? I've spent plenty of time dealing with the bodies they leave behind, but this is the first time I've actually had the pleasure.'

'You're doing well,' Thorne said.

'Am I?'

'Yesterday, in there.' Now, Thorne nodded towards the school. 'He was doing everything he could to push your buttons. Talking about getting turned on by corpses, all that.'

'Oh, he pushed them all right.'

'Didn't look like it.'

'I was shaking like a leaf.'

'You did a good job of hiding it.'

'You reckon? I didn't know whether to burst into tears or kick him in the bollocks.'

'Well, I know which I'd like to have seen,' Thorne said.

A gull of some description flew by just a few feet over-head, and they watched as it wheeled away, screeching loudly before it dropped into a garden behind one of the cottages.

'So what's the story on this woman we're looking for?'

Thorne told Howell as much as he knew; went through Nicklin's story about being interrupted while he was digging Simon Milner's grave.

'So, that's twenty thousand saints, a teenage boy and an old woman,' she said. She took a drag and let the smoke out slowly to be whipped away from the side of her mouth. 'Not that the two dead people would be as important to any of these pilgrims as their precious imaginary saints.'

'Not a churchgoer then?' Thorne said.

'Weddings and funerals, same as most people,' she said. 'Too many funerals lately.' She shook her head. 'It's hard, isn't it, when you do what we do? How many coppers do you know who are full-on God-botherers?'

'Not too many.'

'Right. He gave us free will, did he?' She took a final, deep drag, then began stubbing her cigarette out against the wall. 'What, so we could use it to butcher people? Teenage boys and old women?' She looked at him. 'Sorry. Bit of a hobbyhorse.'

'Not a problem,' Thorne said. 'Actually, you sound a lot like my mate, Phil.' He realised that he still hadn't got back to Hendricks, had yet to hear the grisly details of his friend's latest conquest.

Howell dropped the nub into the pocket of her waxed jacket and nodded out across the fields. 'So she's out there somewhere, is she? Body number twenty-thousand and two.'

Thorne nodded, then walked past her towards the steps that led up to the school. He said, 'Let's go and see if our friend feels like telling us where, shall we?'

*

Inside the school, Nicklin was holding court.

Markham and Holland were whispering in the far corner of the hall, Batchelor stared into space and Fletcher and Jenks looked as though they'd heard it all before, but Burnham and Barber sat transfixed by whatever lurid prison yarn Nicklin was regaling them with.

Nicklin looked up when Thorne and Howell came through the door. He looked relaxed, one leg crossed over the other, his handcuffed wrists resting on one knee. 'He'll tell you.' He nodded at Thorne.

'Tell them what?' Thorne asked.

'Some very strange things go on inside Her Majesty's prisons.'

'Some very strange people in there.'

'Can't argue with that,' Nicklin said.

Burnham shook his head, sadly. 'I can't help wondering if we've got it all wrong,' he said.

Nicklin turned and stared at him. 'Go on.'

The warden shifted slightly in his chair. 'Look, I'm just a layman and I'm not saying we should go back to Victorian times or anything, but it seems to me that we give these people too much freedom in there. That's the one thing they're supposed to have lost, isn't it? I mean, isn't that the whole point? So then we lock them up in places where they're free to do all sorts of things. Free to take drugs and commit horrific acts of violence.' He lifted his stick a foot or so, waved it in Nicklin's direction. 'Where the likes of you are free to carry on terrorising people.'

Sitting next to Nicklin, Fletcher grunted and smiled. 'Well, you'll not be hearing any argument from me.'

'As I said, just a layman.'

Nicklin nodded, like he was weighing up what had been said. He turned his gaze on Burnham. 'How often do you get post out here?'

The warden looked nonplussed for a second or two. 'Once a week,' he said. 'It comes over on the boat, obviously. Why?'

'No reason,' Nicklin said. 'I should just be a bit careful how you open it from now on, that's all.'

Burnham blanched. 'Sorry?'

Nicklin sat back, beaming. 'Joke.'

Thorne stepped forward and laid a hand on Burnham's arm. 'I'm going to have to throw you out now, sir. There are things we need to talk about.'

Burnham stood up a little faster than he might otherwise have done. He said, 'No problem,' and walked quickly to the door without looking back.

Thorne looked hard at Nicklin, and Nicklin, a picture of innocence, said, 'What?'

'Some people might consider what you just said as threatening behaviour.'

'Oh come on, it was a joke. Can't you even make a joke these days?' He shook his head and looked mournfully at Fletcher. 'It's political correctness gone mad, I tell you.'

'We need to get on,' Thorne said.

Nicklin was looking at the door. 'People like him are full of opinions, aren't they? Didn't stop him lapping up a few horror stories, did it? Sitting there with his tongue out and his limp little dick twitching for the first time in God knows how long.'

Thorne remembered the men in the Black Horse the night before, hanging on Holland's every word. It didn't seem to matter which side of the fence the storyteller came from, people were always captivated by tales of trauma and transgression.

Deviance never ceased to be fascinating.

Talking of which . . .

'Right then.' Thorne took a chair from against the wall, dragged it across and sat as close to Nicklin as was possible. Knees almost touching, as though they were in an interview room. As though there were not an audience watching, enrapt, with tea, coffee and biscuits on a trestle table a few feet away.

'Where is she, Stuart?'

'Really?' Nicklin looked mildly disappointed. 'You really want me to make it easy for you?'

'I want you to stop pissing us all about. I'm perfectly happy to call that boat back right now, and we can all go home.'

'You might be,' Nicklin said. 'But I'm not sure how your superiors would feel.' He smiled. 'You know she's here, don't you? Course you do, because you've checked. So how would it look if you just happily sailed away and left

294

her? How would her family feel? Do you want to go back to uniform, Tom?'

'Just tell us where to look.'

'Oh, come on ... you're a suit again now, aren't you? You're one of the elite. Shouldn't you be showing us all that you deserve it?'

Bethan Howell was shaking her head and, a few feet away, Holland sat back and folded his arms. Said, 'This is so out of order.'

Nicklin showed no sign of having heard him. His eyes were on Thorne.

Thorne stared right back, fighting to keep his temper. Seeing Nicklin's pale puffy features blur, then sharpen into those of the man he'd arrested for murder ten years before.

Shattered, bloody ...

There was some comfort in the memory, an easing of the longing to do it again, witnesses or not.

'I mean, just for your own self-esteem surely,' Nicklin said. 'Don't you fancy doing a spot of detective work?'

THIRTY-SEVEN

'She's got a name,' Brigstocke said. 'She was called Eileen Bennett. She was fifty-three when she disappeared.'

'Nicklin said she was an old woman.'

'Yeah, well, she would have seemed old to Nicklin when he was seventeen, wouldn't she? My kids think I'm ancient.'

Thorne was back at the abbey ruins. He turned his face away from a raw wind coming off the sea, struggling to shake off the stiffness in his neck and shoulders and watching the signal indicator on his phone move perilously close to no bars. It had been more or less obvious since the conversation with the Morgans the previous evening, but he asked anyway.

'Are we sure about this?'

'Well, trying to get twenty-five-year-old incident reports out of North Wales police is proving tricky to say the least,'

Brigstocke said. 'But the case is certainly on record. She was reported missing by an elder sister. The woman's dead now, but she used to travel to the island every year apparently, to throw a wreath into the water.'

Thorne turned around, looked out to sea. That was what Bernard Morgan had been trying to call to mind the night before.

'So . . .'

'So, why won't he tell us where she is?'

'Obviously we're wasting our time trying to fathom him out,' Brigstocke said. 'He won't, simple as that. Or at any rate he won't *yet*. We've just got to deal with it.'

'Let me guess,' Thorne said. 'Has he got us over that barrel again?'

'Well, he's right, isn't he? Fact is, it's not going to look too clever if we just do nothing. If we refuse to search.'

'Can't we say that he was deliberately obstructing the search?'

'It's not a good idea—'

'It's the truth.' Thorne needed to raise his voice above the wind, but it wasn't an effort. 'Come on, Russell, they'd love nothing better than to slap his ugly mug all over the front page.'

'Oh, that'll be happening however this turns out,' Brigstocke said. 'But you know how it works. They'll sell a lot more papers if it's an exclusive interview with him than if they've got a few comments from the likes of you and me. He can tell them all sorts of things.'

'I warned you this would happen,' Thorne said. 'Back when you were giving me that good news, bad news shit.'

'That was when it was all about Simon Milner.' Brigstocke was starting to get defensive, a tone to his voice that Thorne knew he should take as a warning. 'We didn't know about Eileen Bennett back then.'

'It's a game, I told you that. It always is.'

'We need to find her,' Brigstocke said. 'Bottom line.'

'How do you suggest I do that?' Thorne looked back along the track and saw Howell and Holland coming towards him. He could see the smoke drifting from Howell's cigarette. 'I know that waterboarding's probably frowned upon, but I'm more than happy to give it a go.'

'What does he want?' Brigstocke asked.

'God knows.'

'I mean, is there something specific? A bigger cell? Comfier toilet seat, what?'

'I don't think it's anything physical.' Thorne told Brigstocke what Nicklin had said to him in the school hall. 'It's about me,' he said. 'We both know that's what it's always been about. Why else am I here?'

'So, do what he says.'

'*What?*'

'Do some detective work.' Brigstocke's voice dropped. Friendly again, conspiratorial, but only up to a point. 'Listen, Tom, if he's saying that, it must be because he knows you can work out where she is. There must be clues of some sort. Something. God . . . how should I know?'

'I'll do my best,' Thorne said.

Holland and Howell were only fifty feet or so away. Thorne raised a hand to them. He did not want them to hear him arguing with Brigstocke and he needed to confer with them anyway. See if either of them had any bright ideas. He wanted to get off the line, but not before he'd said, 'I still think waterboarding would be easier.'

By the time Holland and Howell reached him, Thorne was sitting on the edge of the wall that ran around the graveyard, the ancient bell tower rising up behind him. Howell heaved herself up and sat next to him, her boots bouncing against the stone.

'So, what's happening back there?' Thorne asked.

'Well, he hasn't suddenly decided to draw us a map of where she's buried,' Holland said. 'If that's what you mean.'

'He didn't say a lot after you left.' Howell dug into her pocket for her phone and, seeing that there was a signal, she began scrolling through her messages. 'Just sat there looking rather pleased with himself.'

'He's got every right to be,' Thorne said. 'He's got us where he wants us.'

Howell grunted. 'Right, he's got all the attention. The power.'

'My boss reckons he's asking me to try and work out where Eileen Bennett's body is because he thinks I should be able to.' He saw Howell looking at him. 'The woman's name.'

Howell nodded and went back to her phone, smiled at something.

'I'm glad that somebody's getting good news,' Thorne said.

'Just my daughter checking in,' Howell said. 'Well, asking for more money. She's at uni.' She looked up at Thorne. 'You're more than welcome to say I don't look old enough to have a daughter at university, by the way.'

'I was thinking it.'

'I'll settle for that.' She put her phone away. 'You two got kids?'

Holland told her that he had, but that his daughter Chloe was a long way off going to university. She told him he should start saving up now, then looked at Thorne.

'No,' he said. 'Well . . . sort of. A stepson. Sort of . . . '

The three of them stared out across the plain at the patchwork of fields stitched together by lines of earth or dry stone. Thorne could just make out two figures walking in the distance. North to south, away from the lighthouse, along the cliff path that would lead them past the island's small stretch of beach. He could see that it was a man and a woman and realised that it was Craig and Erica; the couple Burnham had introduced him to the previous day, who were helping out at the bird observatory. Thorne guessed that they had been working in one of the hides along the cliff path, checking out nesting sites or whatever it was they did.

'It had to be quick,' Holland said.

'What?'

'Nicklin. He was on his way off the island, right? From what he said, he hadn't even meant to kill Milner, it was just a spur-of-the-moment thing. So, there's a boat waiting for him, his mate's out there in the dark flashing a torch or whatever. He's already got one body to get rid of. I can't see him taking a lot of time in getting shot of another one.'

'Makes sense,' Howell said. 'He's dug a grave for the boy, then Eileen comes along, demanding to know what he's doing with her shovel. He's got to think quickly.'

'He's not going to dig another grave,' Thorne said. 'No time for that.' He watched Craig and Erica moving past an area of the field close to where they had recovered Simon Milner's body. Just beyond lay the drop down to the sea; the rocks over which Nicklin had clambered to get off the island twenty-five years before.

'Maybe he took her back to the cottage,' Holland said. 'Have we checked to see if there's any sort of cellar? What about a well? I bet there's loads of wells on the island.'

'Wouldn't the police have checked that out?' Howell asked. 'Once they knew she was missing.'

'He didn't take her back,' Thorne said. He stood up on the wall and stared out. Craig and Erica had stopped to look at something. They must have seen him, because one of them waved. 'He threw her over the edge. God, it's obvious, isn't it?'

Howell held out a hand. Thorne took it and pulled her to her feet. 'So, what, you think she was washed out to sea?'

'Maybe, but he's dropping heavy hints that she's still here somewhere.'

Holland shook his head. 'Like you said though, could all be rubbish.'

Thorne grunted a 'Maybe.' He was trying to remember something Nicklin had said the day before. Pacing around in that field, trying to locate the spot where he had buried Simon Milner. That was when he had told Thorne about his escape; the waiting boat, his route down to the sea.

That's where I went down . . . went into the water . . .

'I know where she is,' Thorne said. He jumped down on to the track, the impact pushing the breath noisily from his lungs. He straightened, moved quickly to the nearest gate and pushed through it into the field.

Holland helped Howell down from the wall and they followed; moving as quickly as they could across grass that was still damp, doing their best to catch up as Thorne jogged across the field towards the point where the land ran out.

THIRTY-EIGHT

Wendy Markham had discovered a cupboard stuffed with old magazines and was sitting on the small stage at the far end of the hall, thumbing through copies of *Woman's Weekly* and *Woman's Own* that were older than she was. Barber was hunched over a table nearby, struggling with a jigsaw he was convinced had some pieces missing, and Fletcher and Jenks sat within touching distance of the tea and biscuits, exchanging gossip about a female colleague who had allegedly got a little over-friendly with an armed robber in the prison library.

Nicklin and Batchelor sat close together on a bench underneath the window. Nicklin did not have to make any special effort to talk quietly. He had become well used to having conversations in a place where you were almost always in danger of being overheard; where a degree of concealment in word as well as deed had become second nature.

'So, what did you and Thorne talk about last night?' he asked. 'When he walked you down to your cell.'

Batchelor shook his head. 'I told him I wanted to speak to my wife, that was all.'

'What did he say?'

'He said he might be able to make that happen.'

Nicklin smiled. 'I'm guessing he wanted something from you first though, right?'

'Yes, but I couldn't give him anything, could I?'

'No you couldn't.' Nicklin looked across and saw Fletcher watching them.

'Everything all right, Stuart?'

'Couldn't be better, Mr Fletcher.'

The prison officer bit a biscuit in half and gestured with what was left of it. 'You won't get away with this for very long, you know?'

'Get away with what, Mr Fletcher?'

'Pulling DI Thorne's plonker like this. He doesn't strike me as a man with a lot of patience.'

'Come on, Mr Fletcher. It's not too bad hanging about here, is it? Isn't this better than patrolling the wing?'

'That's not the point.'

'On top of which, Barcelona's a pricey place, exchange rate on the euro and what have you. So if you want to enjoy your holiday, you'll need all the overtime you can get.'

'All right, Stuart, that's enough.'

'If you know something, you should tell him,' Jenks said.

'I'm only trying to make things a bit more interesting.'

'I'm not sure he sees it that way.'

'Come on, how would it look if I helped the police too much?' Nicklin waited, allowing the officers time to consider what was clearly an extremely serious question. 'How would that go down back at Long Lartin? I've got a reputation to protect, haven't I?'

'Oh yeah,' Jenks said. The quieter and less demonstrative of the two officers was as animated as Nicklin could remember. 'You've certainly got one of those.'

Nicklin waited until Fletcher and Jenks were whispering again. Something about the 'pair of them being at it like rabbits in the fantasy section'.

'Why did you bother asking Thorne? About ringing your wife. I told you I'd make sure that happens, didn't I?'

'Yes, but if I could have done it last night, it would have made things easier, don't you think? One less thing to worry about.'

'I'm not worried about anything, Jeff.'

'No, I don't suppose you are.'

'Are you worried?'

Batchelor pushed his boot back and forth across the floor, leaving worms of dried mud on the worn parquet.

'Look, of course you are, but it's not like you needed your arm twisting or anything, is it? That's not how I remember it.'

'No,' Batchelor said.

'You remember what you were like back then?' Nicklin

shook his head as if the memory pained him, as though it were almost too terrible to contemplate. 'After the letter?'

'Of course I do.'

'Who was it showed you a way through that?'

Batchelor dislodged some more mud on to the floor.

'Right. So, I wish you'd trust me. It's hurtful that you don't.'

'I don't mean to hurt you,' Batchelor said, quickly.

'I'll tell you much the same thing I told Thorne yesterday,' Nicklin said. 'It's not out of the goodness of my heart. I mean, you're not stupid, you know that. But ultimately it's something that suits both of us, isn't it? It works for both of us or neither of us. Which is why I need to know that you're still OK with everything.'

'I'm OK with it.'

'Good.' Nicklin leaned across until their shoulders met. 'And I won't forget about that phone call. It might not be the longest conversation you've ever had, mind you.'

'That's fine,' Batchelor said. 'I don't have very much to say.'

'Probably best.' Nicklin looked up and saw that Fletcher and Jenks were watching again. Nicklin raised his hands and gave them a clumsy, handcuffed thumbs-up. Fletcher shook his head, as though Nicklin were a persistently naughty yet charming schoolboy.

Jenks looked rather less amused. 'I mean it,' he said. 'You need to tell Thorne where this body is.'

'There's bodies everywhere on this island,' Nicklin said.

'He could start digging almost anywhere he fancied. Nine times out of ten he'll find some bones.'

'This woman's body,' Jenks said.

'Thorne's not daft, is he?' Nicklin raised his hands again. 'I wouldn't be sitting here wearing these things if he was. I'm sure he'll work it out eventually.' He turned his face towards the window, what little daylight the caked-on grime allowed through. 'Talking of which, what's the time?'

Jenks glanced at his watch. 'It's just after eleven.'

'Already?' Nicklin shook his head, looked at Batchelor. 'I don't know where the day's going, do you, Jeff?'

THIRTY-NINE

The descent was not quite as straightforward as Thorne had thought the day before. It took the three of them more than double the fifteen minutes Thorne had estimated it would take when he'd first looked down at the drop, but he guessed that a seventeen-year-old boy with a body to get rid of and a boat waiting to take him to freedom might have done it rather quicker than that.

Once they had reached the shoreline, it was hard to tell if the tide was on its way in or out. Either way the water was up over their ankles as they stepped carefully around those rocks that were too large or uneven to walk across. Howell was wearing wellingtons, but if they were going to get where they were heading, Thorne and Holland had little choice but to let the seawater fill their boots and soak the bottom of their jeans. At almost every step, curses were muttered or shouted, depending on their severity. Howell laughed, assured them that there was no need to censor themselves on her account. Within a few seconds, she had slipped on a rock and grazed her wrist trying to steady herself. She let fly a torrent of invective that stopped Thorne and Holland in their tracks.

'See?' she said. She licked at her injured wrist and started swearing again.

'Something about your accent though,' Holland said, when she'd finished. 'Makes "fuck-shit-fuckety-fuck" sound a bit more poetic than when we say it.'

Thorne pointed. Said, 'There you go ...'

They began moving again. The wind was stronger suddenly and it felt like there was rain coming. They took their time, stepping cautiously across jagged rocks that were thick with slime and wading slowly through puddles of weed, until they finally stood at the entrance to a cave. The opening was no more than five feet high and narrow.

Wide enough, Thorne thought; if you were crouching, dragging something.

'He mentioned there were caves down here and I just thought ... I don't know.' He looked at Holland. 'Brigstocke said there might be clues, so maybe he mentioned the caves for a reason.'

'Does your head in,' Holland said. 'Even trying to think about what he might be up to.'

Howell said, 'It makes sense.' She looked back along the shoreline, the way they'd come, then turned to the cave. 'He dumps her in there, throws a few rocks over the body, then wades out to meet his mate. There's no reason why anyone would ever have looked down here. There's no access from the water.'

'No reason they'd be looking in the first place,' Thorne said. 'People assumed she'd drowned, that she'd probably killed herself. So, beyond a cursory check, no reason to be looking for a body at all.'

They had been inching closer to the cave entrance as they'd talked. Now the three of them stood at the opening, peering into the blackness. Though the sky had darkened somewhat, there was still plenty of light, but little of it seemed able to reach inside. Thorne took out his mobile and turned on the Flashlight app. Holland did the same.

Thorne looked at Howell. 'You OK?'

'Not great with confined spaces, tell you the truth.' She rubbed the back of a hand across her forehead, adjusted her cap. 'Bit of a bugger bearing in mind what I do for a living.'

'Yeah, must be,' Holland said.

'I tend to pass on the cellar jobs,' she said. She shook her head. 'Costing me a small fortune, because *so* many people hide bodies in cellars.'

'Do you want to wait here?' Thorne asked.

'No, I'll be fine.' She kicked a small rock out of the way. 'If she's in there, it'll be my job to go in and bring her out, won't it? So no point putting it off.'

Holland said, 'I'm a bit of a girl when it comes to mice. Not mad keen on spiders come to that.'

'I'm fine with creepy-crawlies,' Howell said. 'God, I'd *really* be in trouble if I wasn't.'

Thorne considered telling Howell about his own issues with heights and water, but thought better of it with Holland listening. Holland was someone he trusted, broadly, but that wouldn't count for much when tongues got loose after a beer or two. These things could get around an incident room faster than pubic lice in a brothel.

He said, 'Everybody's got something, haven't they?'

Thorne led the way, with Howell sticking close behind him. Though water had gathered in small pools just outside the entrance, the cave was largely dry inside. The floor sloped upwards slightly and they crouched instinctively as they moved further away from the daylight, Thorne shining his light on to a floor of compacted sand and small rocks while Holland checked the walls in case there were any smaller hollows or fissures running off to the side. It went back no more than twenty feet before narrowing and turning sharply to the left, but it quickly became clear that the cave contained nothing beyond a small colony of crabs, dried seaweed and cracked shells.

Thorne turned around and pushed past Holland towards the entrance.

'Next one?'

'Lead on,' Howell said.

Fifteen minutes later, they emerged disappointed from the third cave within fifty feet of the spot where they had reached the bottom of the drop. Holland pointed ahead to where the shoreline curved out of sight. 'Might be some more round there,' he said.

Thorne shook his head. 'I can't see him taking her that far.' He kicked out at some weed and swore a lot less poetically than Howell. 'I was sure she'd be in one of them.'

Howell sat down on a large rock and reached for her cigarettes. 'Do you mind? I just need a quick one.'

'Help yourself,' Thorne said.

'Actually it wasn't nearly as bad as I thought it was going to be. I thought there'd be stuff ... dripping on us.'

Thorne watched her, saw the flame from her Zippo light up a sheen of sweat on her face and neck.

'It's probably a good job,' she said.

'What?'

'Well, it wouldn't have been very easy carting all our stuff down here, would it? The lights, the generator, what have you.'

'At least your CSI won't be complaining,' Holland said.

'It'll make a change.' Howell took a drag. 'Andy Barber's a moaning sod at the best of times. He wasn't my first choice for this, tell you the truth. He can be a bit lazy sometimes ... ' She froze, the cigarette halfway to her mouth.

Thorne looked. 'What?'

'Jesus, you OK?' Holland asked.

Howell looked up at Thorne, panic-stricken and paler suddenly than she had been going into that first cave. 'He was supposed to check,' she said. 'I asked him to check while I was taking the remains away. It's routine procedure, for pity's sake.'

'Check what?' Thorne asked. 'Bethan?'

Howell stood up. The wind blew the cigarette smoke into her face and she narrowed her eyes against it. 'You were right.' She glanced up, towards the edge of the land above their heads and the fields beyond. 'What you said before, when we were up there.' She looked at Thorne. 'He didn't dig another grave.'

FORTY

He'd thought they were burglars.

Yes, it was a stupid time to be doing it, not even halfway through the morning, for heaven's sake, and you'd think your average self-respecting burglar might worry about there being someone in the house. No, he hadn't heard a window breaking or anything like that, but they could just as easily have walked straight in through the back door. Nobody bothered locking all their doors and windows, certainly not during the bloody day when they were in the house. There wasn't too much crime round there beyond a spot of perfunctory vandalism and a few kids doing a bit of blow every now and again and he had bugger all worth nicking anyway.

Yes, they had known what his name was.

All the same, robbery had seemed like a reasonable assumption. His best guess. After all, what else could they possibly have been doing there?

The two of them.

Standing in his kitchen in broad daylight, dark hair, hands in pockets of dark coats. A glimpse of pale faces, tight and fierce. He pictured a pair of perching ravens or rooks, blinked the image away before he started to shout and moved down the hall towards them.

'The hell are you? What do you want . . . ?'

He'd been doing some paperwork in the living room. Sitting at their knackered old computer, getting stuff together for the tax return. Putting numbers into columns had been doing his head in and he wasn't really concentrating anyway; half listening to something on the radio, which he supposed was why he hadn't heard the back door open and close. He'd been almost done. He'd been thinking about nipping to the pub for his lunch, wondering what to do with a few free hours in the afternoon, when there was a second or two of silence on the radio and he heard someone saying his name.

He had shouted, convinced he had been hearing things, got no response.

So, he'd stepped out into the hall just to make sure and that was when he'd seen them.

'The hell are you? What do you want . . . ?'

His voice sounded a bit higher than normal, and the tremor that had started in his belly when he'd heard his name being called had spread to his arms and legs. The distance between himself and the intruders was swallowed up in seconds and he raised his hands, balling his fists

315

when he realised that they were moving every bit as quickly as he was. They were rushing towards him, grimacing or grinning, it was hard to tell which.

Hands coming out of pockets, too fast for him to see what was in them.

He grabbed at the bigger one, the one who was on him first; sensed straight away that he was stronger than his assailant and swung him round into the wall, sending pictures crashing. He swore and grunted as they struggled. He moaned and threatened, then he felt something pressed to his neck. He smelled burning and the snap-and-fizz blew the words from him, sucked the strength away in a second and then it was only the carpet and the broken glass rushing up to meet him.

If he lost consciousness, it was for no more than a few seconds and he was wide awake as they lifted him. Carried him down the hall and then up. The agony that screamed in every muscle was way beyond anything he might have felt as his head cracked against the treads or when they dropped him halfway up the stairs.

'Careful,' one said.

'Does it matter?'

'Don't make me laugh.'

The pain had eased a little by the time they laid him not very gently down on the bathroom floor. He smelled bleach and soap, piss on the mat around the toilet. The cramping in his muscles had diminished to the point where he was able to raise his head just an inch or two from the lino.

To say, 'I've got some savings. There's money in the bank. I can get it ...'

One of them said something and the other one might have replied, but anything they said after that was drowned out once the bath taps had been turned on.

Lying on the floor, he understood now what was coming, even if he still had no idea why. He was too weak suddenly to move or cry out. To stop his bladder opening. To say anything beyond a whispered 'please' that was lost beneath the rush and splash of the bath filling.

FORTY-ONE

This time, they were able to leave the vast majority of their gear behind at the school. Now they knew exactly where to look. Though they might want the lights and generator down the line, for the time being they needed nothing more sophisticated than spades and later – if Howell was proved right – they would require only the equipment necessary for the recovery of Eileen Bennett's remains.

Twenty minutes after Thorne, Howell and Holland had returned to the school and begun asking awkward questions, the entire party was walking back down across the fields, moving swiftly towards the location where Howell and her team had spent the majority of the previous day. The mood among them was rather more fractious than it had been at any time since they had set foot on the island. The professional calm had been shattered beyond repair.

Howell was still shouting at Andy Barber and he was happy to shout back.

'Look, it's not like we were working in a mass grave or anything. This isn't Bosnia, is it?'

'You didn't do what I asked you.'

'Because I didn't see any point.'

'*What?*'

'We were there to find one body and we found it.'

'It's standard practice.'

'Come on, calm down, love.'

'Don't tell me to calm down and *don't* call me love.'

'Sorry—'

'All you had to do was your job and you didn't, because you couldn't be arsed. Because it was late and you wanted your bed.'

'I said I'm sorry, all right?'

'If I'm right about this, sorry isn't going to be good enough.'

'It won't happen again.'

'Too bloody right it won't happen again. Not with me anyway, because you won't be part of any team I'm working with, simple as that.'

A few feet behind them, Markham looked at Thorne and raised an eyebrow.

'She's right to be pissed off,' Thorne said. 'I'm pissed off, but she's the one with the authority as far as that dickhead's concerned, so she gets to dish out the bollocking.'

Markham nodded, impressed. 'Remind me not to fall out with her.'

'Were you planning to?'

'I don't want to fall out with anyone,' Markham said. 'You included.'

'Why should we fall out?'

'I'm just checking we're OK, that's all.' She lowered her voice a little further. 'We never really said anything about the other night.'

'Oh.'

'Just had one glass of wine too many, that's all.'

'It happens.'

'Sorry if I put you on the spot.'

'You didn't.'

'I suppose I'm just saying you don't have to worry about me doing my job.'

'Why would I?'

'If we've got another crime scene, I mean.'

'I'm not worried,' Thorne said. He shoved his hands deeper into his pockets and stared ahead, increasing the length of his stride just enough to take him a pace or two ahead of her.

At the rear of the group, the two prisoners and their minders moved in silence. Nicklin had not said a great deal since Thorne had returned from the caves and the accusations had begun to fly, but the look on his face once it kicked off had convinced Thorne that Howell was on the money. He also realised that Nicklin had been right in suggesting that it was not that difficult to work out where Eileen Bennett's body might be.

Thorne was embarrassed, angry with himself that Bethan Howell had worked it out before he had.

Half an hour later, Barber and Holland had taken their jackets off, picked up shovels and were excavating a grave that had been carefully dug out and filled in the day before. From which the body of Simon Milner had already been exhumed. As they dug, Howell was carefully moving the spoil from the edge of the grave, should examination prove necessary later on, while the rest of the party stood in a rough semi-circle around the gradually deepening hole.

Nicklin was smoking again. Like the handcuffs weren't there, like he hadn't a care in the world.

It had begun to rain, a soft drizzle that was gathering strength, but none of those observing seemed much inclined to head back indoors, even if Thorne had given the word to do so. They appeared content to stare as the heavy, wet earth was shifted, to stand in the rain and watch for that first glimpse of bone.

It didn't take very long.

Less than an hour after starting to dig, a few inches below the level at which Simon Milner's remains had been found, a mud-crusted femur was uncovered; a tattered grey ribbon of what might have been a skirt still attached.

Nicklin turned to Thorne, said, 'Ta-daaa!' He flicked away the remains of a roll-up and nodded towards the grave, the bone dangling between Dave Holland's finger and thumb. 'See, it wasn't that hard, was it?'

Thorne said nothing, aware that Nicklin was not the only one looking at him and waiting for a reaction. He stared down at one of the discarded shovels. He thought how easy it would be to bend down and pick it up and he wondered what sound the blade would make as it bounced off Nicklin's bald head.

'Right, let's get sorted then.' Bethan Howell did not need to look at the bone twice. She was quickly into the grave and ordering Barber and Holland out of it. 'We need to get the tent up,' she said.

Barber offered to go and get it, clearly feeling the need to score some Brownie points fast. 'I'll bring the rest of the stuff down as well.'

'Hurry up, then.' Howell watched Barber walk away, then carefully laid the bone down at the edge of the grave.

With Fletcher at his shoulder, Nicklin wandered across to where Thorne and Holland were standing. Holland was putting his jacket back on. There were streaks of dirt across his cheek and forehead, plastered into place by sweat. Nicklin leaned in close. 'So, you reckon there might be the odd bit of her rotted down in there?'

'What?'

He raised his hands and pointed. 'In what's all over your face. Must be at least a few remnants of flesh and gristle mixed into the dirt. Powdered blood . . . '

Holland quickly touched a finger to his face, then turned

away and stepped across to where Wendy Markham was brandishing a fistful of tissues. He took several and stood watching the exchange between Nicklin and Thorne as he wiped his face good and hard.

'Why did you do it like that?' Thorne asked.

'Like what?'

'You could just have thrown the two bodies in together. Simon and Eileen. That would have been the quickest thing to do, surely.'

'Probably,' Nicklin said.

'But you buried Eileen first. You covered her up and then you buried Simon on top. You separated them.'

'Why wouldn't I?' Nicklin looked genuinely shocked that anyone might not understand his actions. 'They weren't family, they hadn't even *met* as far as I was aware. I had no way of knowing what they believed, what their wishes might be. To have done it any other way would have been ... disrespectful.'

Thorne barked out a dry laugh. 'So, you murder them both for no good reason and then you're worried about being disrespectful afterwards?'

'Absolutely.'

Thorne shook his head and looked across at Howell, who was climbing into a body suit, snapping on plastic gloves. 'God, listen to me. Like I'm talking to someone normal.' He looked at Fletcher. 'Why am I even surprised?'

'Some of us have to deal with this shit every day,' Fletcher said.

Nicklin said, 'It's good that I can still surprise you, Tom. It shows that our relationship isn't going stale.' He grinned, then shivered; looked up at the darkening sky. 'So, what do you think? Any chance of going back and getting inside for a while? I'm soaked, and I'm sure you are, and there's probably some fresh tea and coffee up there by now.'

'Yeah, let's get you and Mr Batchelor out of the rain, shall we?' Thorne said. 'You might not have a lot of time to dry off, mind you. Apart from Professor Howell and her team, we're about done here, so I'm going to try and get the boat back to fetch us a bit earlier. See if we can get on the road.' He looked across at Fletcher and Jenks. 'Get you all back to the prison in time for dinner.'

Fletcher said, 'Great,' though he clearly did not mean it.

'That's a shame,' Nicklin said.

'Not from where I'm standing,' Thorne said. He was enjoying the disappointment on Nicklin's face, in his body language. 'I'm very happy to get away early.'

'Can't we at least wait until the poor old dear's been taken out of there?'

'She wasn't a poor old dear,' Thorne said. 'She was fifty-three and she had a name.'

Nicklin acknowledged the perceived lack of sensitivity with a small bow of the head. 'OK, can we wait until Eileen's out of there?'

'Afraid not,' Thorne said. 'The governor's very keen to have you back as soon as possible and, seeing as you've done your bit, we can leave it to others to finish the job.' He glanced across at the grave. 'Not that you did a lot this time round.'

'I knew you'd enjoy working it out,' Nicklin said. 'That's why.' He looked at Bethan Howell and shook his head. 'I'm very surprised she beat you to it, frankly.'

But Thorne was only half listening, having spotted the warden marching purposefully down towards him from the track. Burnham was waving, with what looked like his satellite phone in his hand.

Thorne walked up to meet him.

'I was on my way to see you.' Burnham was a little breathless. 'I've just been talking to Huw Morgan.'

'Perfect timing,' Thorne said. 'Can you call him back? I need to see if he can get over here to pick us up any earlier.'

Burnham said, 'Ah,' and Thorne knew that there was a problem.

'What?'

'Well, that's why he was calling. I'm afraid that Bernard has been taken into hospital.' He mistook the expression on Thorne's face for concern. 'It's nothing serious. I think he just took a bit of a turn.'

'That's good to hear.'

'It does give you a problem though.'

'Can't Huw do it on his own?'

'It's a two-man job, I'm afraid,' Burnham said. 'You remember how the boat gets brought out of the water?'

Thorne lifted his hands and laced them through his hair.

He could feel a headache starting to gather behind his eyes. 'Can anyone else do it? There must be somebody he can ask.'

'Not that I know of,' Burnham said, 'and I'm sure he'd rather be with his father anyway. But even if there was someone to do it, you'd still be in trouble.'

'Why?'

'Because finding someone to make the trip's neither here nor there. It's the weather that's buggering everything up. Huw says it's not looking too clever.'

'Yeah, he told me it might be iffy,' Thorne said, 'but look.' He held his arms out, as though Burnham were somehow unaware of the weather conditions around them. 'It's only a bit of rain, for God's sake.'

'It's a bit of rain *here*, but it's what it's like on the other side of the mountain that Huw's worried about. He must have told you that the weather here can be totally different from what it's like over there, and right now he reckons it's too dangerous.'

'Jesus . . . '

'Huw knows what he's talking about, I'm afraid.' Burnham shook his head, stared down towards the sea. 'Bardsey Sound is treacherous at the best of times. Well, it's how the island got its name, of course . . . '

Once again, Thorne had stopped listening.

He turned round and looked back across the field at the men and women clustered around the freshly dug grave. Whatever anybody else in the group was doing, he knew that Stuart Nicklin was looking right at him. He watched him step across to Batchelor and say something.

Two murderers, one of whom would always be highly dangerous and unpredictable. Two men, who, despite the presence of well-trained prison officers, were his responsibility.

Thorne turned back in time to hear the warden saying something about food from the farm. He nodded, said, 'Right . . . '

'So, fingers crossed Huw can get back for you all first thing in the morning.'

'*Everything* crossed,' Thorne said.

'We'll be all right until then, don't you worry about that.' Burnham sounded cheery, almost excited. He was clearly someone who relished a crisis and was confident in his own ability to cope with one when it came. 'There's plenty of space and I'm sure some of those who stayed on the island last night have told you that it wasn't quite the end of the world.'

'They said it was fine, yes.' Thorne pointed to the phone in Burnham's hand. 'I need to make a call. Do you mind?'

'No, of course not.' Burnham thrust the phone at him.

Thorne took it and immediately began walking away, dialling as he went.

Behind him, Burnham said, 'Don't worry, we'll all muck in, we're used to it.' He raised his voice as Thorne got further away from him. 'Trust me, if you've got an emergency on, you really couldn't wish to be anywhere better . . . '

FORTY-TWO

'I said, didn't I?' Brigstocke had been pulled out of a meeting and something in his tone – a disconnect, a hesitance – told Thorne that he was not getting the DCI's full attention. 'Six weeks ago. I told you there might need to be a certain amount of thinking on your feet.'

'Come again?'

'A bit of improvising.'

Thorne was walking slowly round in a wide circle at the top edge of the field, his view changing every half a minute or so. Looking back at Burnham, then down towards the crowded graveside; across at the lighthouse, then straight out to sea. 'It's a nightmare,' he said.

'Come on, it's not that bad.'

'I want to get him back to Long Lartin.'

'Course you do, but one more night isn't going to hurt.'

'We're pushing our luck already.'

'Meaning . . . ?'

'Meaning I don't like to improvise when you're talking about someone like Stuart Nicklin. It's hard enough to predict how he's going to behave at the best of times. We need to do things the right way.'

'Fine, so what do you suggest?'

'What about a chopper?'

'Seriously?' Brigstocke laughed. 'I know it's a bit rough and ready over there, but do you really have to cut your own wood?'

'I'm not joking,' Thorne said.

'You might as well be, Tom, because it's not going to happen. Look, if there was any kind of danger, any threat to life and limb, then maybe. But what have you got over there? One body, another one in the process of being recovered and two prisoners being very well monitored by multiple police and prison officers. You've got no chance, mate.'

'I want to get off this island.'

'Understood, but I'm not sure what you want me to do.'

'Some support would be nice for a kick-off,' Thorne said. 'Any support, come to that.'

Brigstocke sighed. 'If it makes you happy, I'll make a call, OK? But don't hold your breath.'

Thorne began walking back across the field towards Holland, Howell and the others. He guessed that by now it would be obvious to most of them that there was a problem. The man who had dug that grave twenty-five years earlier, who stood watching the same piece of ground being opened for a third time, would certainly know.

'Listen though,' Brigstocke said. 'Well done, all right. I know you weren't very happy about that whole good news, bad news thing. I know we didn't give you a lot of choice.'

'No, and I'm really pissed off about it now.'

'Yeah, well it's good news for Eileen Bennett's family, isn't it? It's good news for Simon Milner's mum.'

'Don't do that, Russell,' Thorne said. 'Don't pull that sentimental crap because it won't work.'

'Jesus, what's it been, three days?' That edge had crept into Brigstocke's voice again, friendship giving ground to rank. 'You could have spent that time sitting outside some scrote's house or filling in paperwork for CCTV footage. Waiting for some jobsworth at a mobile phone company to return your call. At least you've achieved something.' There were voices in the background, laughter. 'I've spent the last three days in meetings, playing bullshit bingo.'

'You want me to feel sorry for you?' Thorne said. 'Sleeping in your own bed every night and not getting pissed on in the arse-end of nowhere. Not having to play nursemaid to a nutter like Stuart Nicklin. Christ, it must be awful for you.'

'I'm just saying.'

'I want him locked up again, Russell.'

'One more night, all right?' Brigstocke waited, took Thorne's silence as acceptance, grudging though it may have been. 'Oh, and don't pretend the sentimental thing doesn't work with you. I've seen you cry at cowboy music. That one where he only stops loving her because he's dead.'

'Sorry, mate, I'm not really in the mood to joke about this.'

'Listen, I've got to get back,' Brigstocke said. 'Eyes down for more bullshit bingo. Let's talk later, OK?'

'Remember to make that call,' Thorne said.

'You're breaking up . . .'

'Don't give me that.' Thorne took the phone from his ear and shouted at it. 'Get me a helicopter, Russell . . .'

He hung up, slowed his pace a little and, once he had his breath back, he dialled Helen's number. The connection seemed to take ages, though it was probably no more than fifteen or twenty seconds of clicks and ominous silences.

The call went straight to her voicemail, so he left a message.

He said, 'It's me,' and turned his face away from the wind. 'Everything's gone tits up here and it looks like I'm not going to make it back tonight, so I just wanted to let you know that.' He was trying to sound a little less miserable than he felt, but it was an effort. 'Call me later when you get a chance . . . actually, I'm only getting a signal in one place, so it's probably better if I try and call you. Not sure what time, but I'll try not to make it too late.

'Anyway . . . hope your day's not too shitty and talk to you later on.' He looked across and saw Holland waiting, his arms outstretched, asking. 'Give Alfie a squeeze . . .'

All of them except Howell and Barber who were working in and around the grave, drifted across to join Thorne as soon as he was back. As he had suspected, his agitation – in the conversation with Burnham and the phone call with Brigstocke – had been clear enough from half a field away. Everyone was understandably eager to know what was happening.

Thorne could see little point in sugaring the pill.

The weather was unlikely to change, the boatman's father had been taken into hospital and there was no chance of hearing the *whump-whump* of helicopter blades any time soon.

He said, 'We're all staying here tonight.'

Several people started talking at once; asking questions, then taking an unhelpful stab at answering those of others. Thorne raised his hand and kept it there until the last person had shut up. He told them exactly what the warden had told him.

'I don't like it any better than you do,' he said. Fletcher, Jenks and Holland certainly looked every bit as miserable as Thorne felt at the prospect of spending the night on the island. 'But there's not a fat lot we can do about the weather, is there?' Even as he said it, he realised it was much the same thing Brigstocke had said to him and he began to wonder if he'd given the DCI too tough a time on the phone. Then he saw the look on Nicklin's face and decided that he had not been nearly tough enough.

Standing between Fletcher and Jenks, Nicklin was shifting his weight slowly from foot to foot. For a few seconds he looked as concerned, as apprehensive as everyone else, until the temptation to smirk became too strong to resist.

'The best laid plans of mice and men,' he said. 'And coppers.'

FORTY-THREE

It was one of the few perks that came with knocking on a bit, with being as old as he was, at any rate. There wasn't a great deal to celebrate, what with hearing in one ear all but gone, the need to sit down to put trousers on and a tendency to forget what he'd walked into a room for. Still, there were one or two things that came in fairly useful now and again, and being able to play the 'doddery old git' card when it suited him was one of them.

It was funny really, because of the two of them he was the one with the knack for it. The one who had taken to technology almost as fast as the kids did these days.

They'd been late getting it, computers and what have you, but he'd figured out the basics quickly enough. Emails, websites, all that. When it came to using it for things he didn't fancy though, it was usually easier just to plead ignorance. To make out like it was all mumbo-jumbo, like he was far too long in the tooth to be bothering with any of that, thank you very much.

Oh no, *that* wasn't for him . . .

Course, he was happy enough being a 'silver surfer' if and when it suited him – like sending emails on the sly to that saucy old mare who ran the newsagent's – but not when something like a tax return came along. So, he'd happily left the boy to it all morning and had a few hours to himself.

Bloody lovely!

He couldn't remember the last time he'd gone fishing for pleasure, so he'd grabbed his rod and tackle box, filled up a Thermos and walked down to a spot he hadn't used in years. Those few hours had flown by and it hardly mattered that he hadn't caught much. A couple of nice whiting for the freezer was more than enough, anyway. It had just been nice to do something he loved without the pressure they were under most other days, when they were out there in all weathers trying to pay the bills and keep a roof over their heads. Sitting there with your line in the water for no other reason than the fun of it, with time to think and enjoy the day was not the same thing at all. God, no . . .

Brilliant, it was, and now, walking back to the house with those whiting heavy and swinging in a plastic bag, he almost felt bad about the subterfuge. The playing stupid. He might tell the boy tomorrow, once the tax stuff was done with. He'd shout and sulk for a bit, but they'd laugh about it later on, out on the boat where there wasn't the time or space for stupid grudges.

They'd open a few cans of beer and maybe he'd fry them up one of those whiting for their tea, once they'd been across to the island and back.

He dropped his stuff in the hall, called the boy's name out as he carried the fish through to the kitchen. He put the bag down on the draining board and picked out the knife he would use to gut them. He flicked the kettle on, took the milk from the fridge, then walked out of the kitchen and down the hall to the living room.

The computer was still humming. The screen still filled with columns of figures, the cursor flashing.

He stepped out into the hall and shouted up the stairs. 'Given up, have you, you lazy bugger?' He listened, but could hear nothing but the tick and grumble of the kettle growing louder.

He walked up the stairs, the pain in his right knee a sharp reminder of one other thing that was horrible about getting old. It was odd, he thought, how he hadn't felt any of the usual aches and pains sitting there on the beach, listening to the gulls scream over his head and sipping tea from a flask. That was the way of it, though. He could feel like a teenager out there on the boat all day, pulling in lobster pots or scrubbing the deck. Then, he'd sit at home all evening, groaning in agony like he was barely ten minutes from popping his clogs.

He stuck his head round the door of the boy's room.

He wandered into his own, though he'd no expectation of finding him in there.

Knocked it on the head and gone down the pub, he thought. Can't say as I blame him. Maybe they needed to pay someone to come in and do the bloody tax return for them. Sort all the paperwork out, come to that.

He was already loosening his belt as he nudged the bathroom door open and saw what was in the bath; moving closer until he saw the face below the water.

He cried out and buckled, tried to say his son's name.

His hands were fists, tight around his belt and, try as he might, he could not unclench them. Not when the two figures moved up quickly behind him and lifted him from the floor. Not when they took his head and held it tight, their fingers clawing at his ears, in his hair.

Not when they pushed it down towards the freezing water, then under, until he was close enough to kiss his boy's face.

FORTY-FOUR

The woman who answered the door at Tides House was a good deal skinnier and far less apple-cheeked than the stereotypical farmer's wife Thorne had imagined. The smile was more nervous than welcoming as she stood aside and asked him to come in.

'Robert told us you'd probably be coming over,' she said.

'On the scrounge, I'm afraid,' Thorne said.

'It's fine.' She closed the door and stuck out a small hand. 'I'm Caroline Black. Come on through . . .'

Thorne followed her down a long corridor before they turned sharply left and ducked under a low lintel into a large kitchen. A tall man with hair tied back into a ponytail turned from a sink of washing-up. He was wearing baggy cargo shorts and a zip-up fleece.

'This is my husband, Patrick,' Caroline said.

Patrick Black held up hands swathed in yellow rubber gloves and waved them to explain his inability to greet Thorne any more formally. 'Hi,' he said. 'Have a seat. There's coffee in the pot, if you'd like some.'

Thorne thanked him and walked across to a crowded pine table. There were several piles of paper, children's toys, the signs of a recently eaten meal – condiments, tablemats – that Caroline immediately proceeded to clear. When she'd finished, Thorne sat down and looked around. The warm and cluttered farmhouse kitchen came much closer to fulfilling his expectations than the farmer or his wife. The soothing tones of Radio 4 from a wind-up radio. The old-fashioned metal coffee pot sitting on top of a well-used range. Genuinely distressed flagstones and a scarred Welsh dresser. A child's plastic tricycle next to a partially dismantled engine on a tarpaulin in one corner.

As Caroline poured him a coffee, Thorne was surprised to see a black and white collie eyeing him from a basket near the door. 'Oh,' he said. 'A dog.'

Caroline looked at the dog and then back at Thorne.

'I thought they weren't allowed on the island.'

'Holly's a working dog,' she said.

'It's just that we weren't allowed to bring a dog.'

'Like I said, she's a working dog.'

Thorne could see there was little point in taking the conversation any further in that particular direction, so he just nodded.

'We thought you'd be gone by now,' Caroline said.

'So did we.'

'Yes, well, you're not the first to be stranded thanks to the weather and you won't be the last.' She poured herself a coffee, added milk from a carton on the table. 'There were some holidaymakers here last year who had to wait a fortnight to get off.'

'Oh, God,' Thorne said.

'Don't worry.' She carried the pot back to the stove. 'I'm sure it's not that bad.'

'Let's hope not.'

She smiled, quick and thin, standing at the end of the table drinking her coffee and watching Thorne drink his. She was wearing loose-fitting jeans and a woollen waistcoat, the T-shirt underneath a perfect match for her bright-red Crocs. 'So, what exactly is it that you're doing anyway? In the field, I mean. It's the second time you've started digging in the same place.'

Patrick turned from the sink, said, 'You can't ask him that.'

'Why not?'

'I'm sorry,' Thorne said. 'I'm afraid I can't really go into any detail.'

'Told you,' Patrick said.

Caroline shrugged and pouted for a few seconds, her chin resting on the rim of her coffee cup. 'It's not like we can't guess what's going on.' She walked across to the window and nodded out. 'We've got a pretty good view from here.'

Thorne stood up and walked across to join her. It had already begun to get dark, but there was a clear line of sight across to the lights in the distant field. To the illuminated tent, inside which Bethan Howell and her team were still hard at work.

'I mean, it's not an episode of *Time Team*, is it?' She leaned a little closer to the window; peeling grey paint on the frame and glass that had several air bubbles captured within it. 'It's just a question of who you're looking for down there and who the two men in the handcuffs are.' She looked at Thorne. 'We saw them the other day standing at the front gate. One of them, anyway. Just staring at the house.'

Patrick had moved on to the drying-up. 'She was hiding behind the net curtains,' he said, laughing. 'Watching him watching us.'

'Believe it or not, he stayed here once,' Thorne said. 'In this house.'

Caroline looked confused. 'Really?'

'A long time ago.'

Patrick turned from the sink. 'Back when this was a home for wayward kids or whatever they called it.'

'Right.' Thorne sat down again, picked up his coffee. For a moment he thought about showing them the photograph in his pocket, then decided against it.

Here's your gorgeous farmhouse the way it used to look. Just ignore the teenage serial killer and his mates . . .

Caroline turned from the window, her curiosity piqued still further. 'So, why's he back here?'

341

'You're wasting your time,' Patrick said. He looked at Thorne and shook his head. 'He can't tell you.'

Footsteps sounded suddenly on the stairs, then in the corridor outside before a girl, five or six years old, came running in. She froze as soon as she saw Thorne, stared at him for a few seconds, then moved quickly to her mother, staying close to the wall. 'When are you going to come and read?' she asked. 'You promised.'

'I'll be in soon.' Caroline ran her fingers through the girl's hair. 'I've just got something to do first, so why don't you go and get your pyjamas on and then I'll be up.'

Patrick said, 'Go on, chicken,' and the girl turned and trudged reluctantly back to the door.

'Can I take Holly?' she asked.

Her mother said that she could, so the girl called the dog across and the two of them trotted out of the kitchen. Caroline watched them go, then turned to Thorne. 'I think we've got a right to know what's happening,' she said. 'Who we're dealing with here.'

'Trust me,' Thorne said. 'If we thought there was anything you needed to know, we would have told you.'

'So, why don't you tell us when our daughter can go back out to play again?'

Thorne hoped he did a better job of keeping the edge from his voice than she had. 'There's never been any need to keep her inside the house,' he said.

'Really?'

'Really.'

'With dangerous criminals walking about? I mean, I can only presume they *are* dangerous. The handcuffs, the number of people with them.'

'We don't just let them wander around,' Thorne said. 'They're being guarded constantly. There's no risk to anyone. None at all.'

Caroline did not look convinced. She walked across and dropped her mug into the hot water.

'Having said that, obviously nobody would have wanted your little girl walking down to ... you know.' Thorne nodded to the window, the fields beyond it. 'So you were probably right to keep her indoors.' He finished his coffee. 'We'll be gone tomorrow, that's a guarantee.'

'But in the meantime, you need feeding.'

'I'm really grateful for your help,' Thorne said. 'Anything you can spare.'

She walked across to a small door, which Thorne had not noticed until now. She opened it and flicked on a switch. Thorne saw stairs heading down, bare floorboards, a naked light bulb. 'This food? Is it for you and the other officers, or is it for everyone?' She glanced at her husband then looked back to Thorne. 'For the men in handcuffs?'

Patrick dried his hands on the tea towel and draped it across the handle of the range. 'Come on, Caz, what do you think?'

'We're not allowed to starve them, I'm afraid,' Thorne said. 'Maybe they can just have leftovers.'

Caroline nodded, showing no appreciation at all of

Thorne's attempt at levity, then stooped quickly and disappeared down the stairs.

Patrick picked up a wine bottle and two glasses and joined Thorne at the table. He offered one of the glasses to Thorne.

'I'd better not,' Thorne said.

'It's good,' Patrick said. He poured one for himself. 'Home-made, but it does the trick. If you're lucky, Caroline might bring you a bottle or two up from the cellar with the rest of the stuff.'

'Great,' Thorne said. 'I'll have some later then.'

'*Iechyd da*, as they say in these parts.' Patrick held out his glass and Thorne touched his empty coffee cup to it. The farmer glanced towards the cellar. 'She's been a bit jumpy ever since you lot arrived,' he said. 'It's all about Freya, you know?' He was English, like his wife. He had a high, light voice, a trace of a Northern accent. 'I mean, it's one of the reasons we took this place on, because we thought it would be different from life back there. No need to worry about . . . certain things. A good place for her to grow up, you know?'

'And is it?'

'Oh yeah. It's great for me and Caz too, don't get me wrong. The spiritual side of it. Oh yeah, we get a lot out of that.' He nodded, swirled the wine around in his glass. 'It's bloody hard work mind you, but honestly, we wouldn't want to be anywhere else.' He downed his wine and poured himself another. 'I don't suppose you've had much chance to look around.'

'A bit,' Thorne said. 'I went over to the lighthouse. Saw the seals.' Saying it, Thorne realised that he'd actually covered a good deal of the island in the last two days, even if most of the time had been spent in the distinctly *un*-spiritual pursuit of long-dead murder victims. 'Yeah, seen a fair bit.'

'You wait,' Patrick said. 'Now you're spending the night, you'll get a look at the most incredible sky you've ever seen. Well, you will if this bloody rain eases off. We've got special "dark sky" status, did you know that?' Thorne said that he didn't. 'Because there's no light pollution. Well, no pollution of any sort, come to that.'

'Right.'

'It's a one-off, this place.'

Thorne said nothing. He wondered how much longer Caroline was going to be in the cellar. He could hear her moving around beneath them.

Patrick must have caught Thorne glancing at the cellar door. He said, 'We keep all the dried goods down there. Rice, pasta, what have you. Loads and loads of tinned stuff. Fuel for the generator.' He held up the bottle. 'Plenty of this too, like I said. I tell you what, if there's ever a nuclear attack or the world gets overrun by zombies, we're quids in.'

'How often do you get back to the mainland?'

'I haven't been back for six months,' Patrick said. 'Caroline goes over every couple of weeks, does a bit of shopping or whatever if she's feeling a bit low. Buys herself some clothes. A treat, you know? Obviously, once Freya's going to school she'll be going across every day.'

'You think you'll still be here then?'

'God, I hope so.' Patrick leaned across the table. 'Not sure I'd be able to cope in a city now.' He drank half a glass, thought for a few moments. 'Whoever you are, whatever problems you might have had before, somewhere like this forces you to make peace with yourself. Do you know what I mean?'

Thorne hadn't got a clue, but nodded anyway.

'Not that it worked for your friend in the handcuffs. The one who was here when he was a boy, I mean. I suppose some people are just more attuned to that side of things than others.' Patrick nodded, seemingly pleased with his own insight. 'The spiritual side.'

'He's definitely not one of them,' Thorne said.

'Come on then, how dangerous is he?'

'Sorry?'

'Well, it's pretty clear he's not a fraudster, anything like that.' Patrick tapped a fingernail against his glass. 'What do they call them, white-collar criminals? I mean, like Caz said, you're not down there digging for gold coins, are you?'

Thorne wasn't sure why the farmer was asking, when he had already seen similar enquiries from his wife go unanswered. Perhaps he thought that, man to man, with a bottle of wine on the table, he might be more successful than she had been. Or that information which Thorne might consider too frightening for her ears might be suitable for his.

Whatever, his reasons for wanting to know seemed anything but voyeuristic. There was none of the excitement Thorne had heard in the voices of those lads in the Black Horse; that desire for a cheap thrill that Nicklin had accused Burnham of harbouring.

All Thorne saw and heard was sadness. Resignation . . .

'I'm sorry,' he said. 'I can't.'

Patrick raised his hands. 'No, *I'm* sorry. I didn't mean to put you on the spot.'

'It's understandable,' Thorne said. 'I'd want to know, if I was sitting where you are.' He watched the man reach for the wine bottle and tried to imagine exactly that. He asked himself how he would cope if he were doing what Patrick Black did.

He doubted seriously that he would last a week.

The work was clearly strenuous and the hours ridiculous, but he told himself that he could handle that. The spartan nature of the domestic arrangements was unpleasant, but he thought that he would probably get used to them.

The problem would be his own company.

He looked across the table and wondered just how well the man sitting opposite got on with himself, day in, day out. Why, however attuned he was to all things spiritual, he was drinking a third glass of wine in less than ten minutes.

Thorne stood up when he saw Caroline Black emerge from the cellar with a couple of what looked like well-stocked plastic bags.

'This is going to have to do,' she said.

Thorne took one of the bags from her, very happy to hear bottles clinking inside. 'This is great, thank you.'

'Should be enough to get you through the night.' She passed the second bag across. 'And breakfast in the morning.'

'It's really kind of you.'

'We help each other out on Bardsey,' Patrick said. His voice was a touch deeper now, a little less precise.

Thorne said, 'Right,' and turned towards the kitchen door. 'Listen, it was really nice to meet you.'

Caroline Black was standing at her husband's shoulder. She said, 'Just a shame about the circumstances, that's all. I hope you understand when I say we'll be glad to see the back of you.'

Somewhere upstairs, Thorne heard the dog bark, the little girl telling it to be quiet. A childish impression of the tone she had clearly heard her mother use.

'I understand,' he said.

Stopping at the door, he noticed an old tobacco tin on the dresser and wondered whether one or both of them smoked. He suddenly had a clear image of the two of them sitting outside on a warm evening, enjoying their front garden and sharing a fat joint as the sun began to sink. Waiting for the stars to begin peppering that vast, amazing sky and watching their daughter chase the dog across the fields.

'His name's Stuart Nicklin,' he said.

Patrick Black clearly recognised the name. He said, 'Ah . . .'

Thorne watched the farmer reach for his wife's hand. 'And I'm truly sorry I brought him here.'

FORTY-FIVE

Sleeping arrangements had yet to be finalised, but it was decided that Chapel House would be the best location for everyone to eat dinner. Having been occupied by the forensic team the night before, the chill of winter vacancy had already been taken off the place. The plastic covers had been removed from the soft furnishings and wood brought in for the fire. A pair of Calor gas hotplates was up and running.

The emergency rations generously supplied by the Blacks turned out to be both limited and strictly vegetarian. It made the choice of recipe simple enough, but did not go down very well with certain members of the team.

Fletcher had stared, incredulous, as the ingredients were taken out of the bag. 'It's like bloody student food,' he said. A sing-song, Brummie whine.

'How would you know?' Jenks nudged his colleague aside and picked up a tin.

'For God's sake ... *beans*?' Fletcher looked thoroughly disgusted. 'It's a farm, isn't it? Don't they keep chickens or whatever?'

'Look, it's quick and it's easy and we can make plenty of it.'

Fletcher walked out of the small kitchen and sat down. 'I tell you what, the only way I could stomach living here is if they flew a Nando's takeaway in once a week ...'

If the preparation of rice with tinned tomatoes and kidney beans was straightforward, the table plan was rather more convoluted. While Jenks performed cooking duties and Holland and Fletcher sat with Nicklin and Batchelor in the living room, Thorne tried to come up with the seating arrangement that would best suit the somewhat unconventional group that was gathered for the first dinner shift. With Karim maintaining the watch over the body in the chapel and Howell, Markham and Barber still working at the crime scene, the first sitting would involve only Thorne and Holland, along with the two prisoners and prison officers.

Having wrestled with several permutations, Thorne eventually settled on an arrangement which saw Nicklin and Batchelor seated at either end of the small dining table, with a cop and a prison officer separating them, one of each on either side.

'Are we going to have those little cards with our names on?' Nicklin was watching Thorne from the living room. 'That's always a nice touch.'

Thorne ignored him.

Nicklin lifted his wrists. 'How about handcuffs as napkin rings?'

'How about you keeping your mouth shut?'

'Seriously, I reckon prison-chic could be the next big thing in designer tableware.'

Thorne went back to ignoring him.

Twenty minutes later, Jenks laid down a large saucepan of rice and another of tomatoes and beans, and the people around the table began helping themselves. There was a plastic bowl of grated cheese and some Tabasco sauce Jenks had managed to find at the back of a cupboard. There was bottled water and defrosted wholemeal bread, which Nicklin and Batchelor were quick to take pieces of, as they were both using it as a substitute for cutlery.

Nicklin pushed food against the bread with his fingers, then brought it quickly to his mouth. He chewed, shaking his head. 'It's bloody ridiculous,' he said, mouth still half-full. 'We do have a basic right to eat like human beings.' He looked from Thorne to Fletcher and back again. 'They let us have cutlery in prison, you know.'

'Plastic cutlery,' Fletcher said.

'There's a lot more officers around in prison,' Thorne said. 'With weapons.' He slowly and deliberately used his fork to gather another mouthful for himself. 'I can't take the risk, can I?'

'Not even a spoon?' Nicklin wiped the back of his hand across his mouth. 'Come on, how much damage can

352

anyone do with a spoon?' He reached for more bread and carried on eating, clearly enjoying the reaction from those who were only too well aware of exactly what damage he had done in Belmarsh a decade earlier.

'What about you, Jeff?' Holland turned to Batchelor. 'You think we're denying your basic human rights?'

Batchelor shrugged. 'Not really.'

'Because you're more than welcome to make an official complaint when we get back.' Holland glanced across at Fletcher, sensing a receptive audience. 'There's probably a form to fill in where you can describe how traumatised you were by the lack of proper condiments.'

Fletcher laughed and Holland looked pleased with himself.

'It's fine,' Batchelor said. He used a chunk of bread to push some of his food from one side of the plate to another.

'Actually, Al, this isn't too bad after all,' Fletcher said.

'See?' Jenks said.

'I mean, you're not Jamie Oliver or anything, but it's tasty enough.' He reached for another spoonful of rice, then put half back in the saucepan when Thorne reminded him there were four more people yet to be fed. 'Don't get me wrong, be even better with some meatballs or a leg of chicken in it, but beggars can't be choosers, I suppose.'

'Suffocation, I reckon,' Nicklin said.

Thorne looked at him. 'What?'

'The most effective way to kill someone if all you had to

do it with was bread.' Nicklin nodded, thinking it through. 'You fill their mouth with it, block their nose off ...'

'What the hell are you on about?' Fletcher asked.

'If you want to get rid of someone badly enough, you use what's knocking around, don't you?'

'All right,' Fletcher said. 'That's enough.'

'Of course you do.' Nicklin pushed some more food into his mouth and licked his fingers. 'And seeing as I'm not being allowed any cutlery, I'd be forced to improvise.'

Fletcher pointed, said, 'I think you need to shut the hell up, right now.'

'Bloody hell, Mr Fletcher.' Nicklin widened his eyes, as though taken aback. 'Keep your hair on. I wasn't being serious, was I?'

Thorne looked across at the prison officer, who was suddenly looking seriously rattled. It was exactly as Thorne had explained it to Nicklin a minute or so before. Normally, someone like Fletcher would have a great many more of his colleagues around him and, even then, a professional distance was always observed. There would never be this degree of ... intimacy with a prisoner, and certainly not one like Stuart Nicklin. Yes, there was a relationship of sorts, a civility that was maintained wherever possible for the good of both sides. He would do what needed doing but, at the end of the day, it was Fletcher's job to bang the likes of Nicklin up every night and walk away.

They were not supposed to be breaking bread at the same table.

354

'No, because if I was being serious,' Nicklin said, 'I'd just use *this* . . .' He held up a fork and, for a second, everyone at the table froze.

Fletcher shouted and pushed his chair back hard, jumping to his feet at the same moment that Thorne did; that Nicklin dropped the fork on to the table and raised his hands.

'You took your eye off it, didn't you, Mr Fletcher?'

Fletcher snatched the fork back, breathing heavily, relief quickly giving way to rage and the look on his face suggesting that he would like nothing more than to drive the fork straight into Nicklin's face. Nicklin stared right back at him and then turned his eyes to Thorne. They were wide and bright, as though he were happily feeding off the tension that was suddenly fizzing around the table.

'Let's get the cuffs back on,' Thorne said.

'Calm down,' Nicklin said. 'I wasn't going to do anything, obviously.'

'*Now.*'

Nicklin meekly held his arms out. 'I was just making a point.'

Thorne turned to Batchelor. 'You finished?' Batchelor nodded, but Thorne could see that his food had barely been touched. 'You sure?'

'Not hungry,' Batchelor said.

Fletcher and Jenks were fastening the handcuffs back on to their prisoners' wrists when the front door opened and Howell and Markham trooped in. As she stripped off her dirty plastic bodysuit, the archaeologist explained that Eileen Bennett's body had now joined Simon Milner's in the chapel and that Barber was still doing his penance by bringing the last of the equipment up. She tossed suit and gloves into the corner then, while Markham disposed of hers, she dropped into the seat that Thorne had vacated.

'Something smells good,' she said.

'Dig in,' Thorne said.

Jenks brought some clean plates to the table and Howell reached for a serving spoon. 'Oh and Sergeant Karim wanted me to tell you that his "stomach thinks his throat's been cut" and to ask when it's his turn to "get some effing dinner".'

Markham sat down, asking where the wine was as she reached for the water. Then, once the room was a little less crowded, Fletcher and Jenks eased Nicklin and Batchelor out of the way towards the living room.

Thorne picked up the two bulky plastic torches that he'd dug out of the cottage's supply cupboard as soon as they'd arrived. He checked that they were working then waved Holland across. He said, 'Come on, Dave. You can relieve Sam for an hour and I'll try and work out where we're all sleeping.'

As Thorne and Holland walked towards the front door, Thorne heard Nicklin shout, 'It's really very nice, but Mr Fletcher thinks it needs meatballs or a leg of chicken, don't you, Mr Fletcher?'

Thorne didn't hear Fletcher answer.

FORTY-SIX

Even with torches, the journey of a hundred yards or so to the chapel took Thorne and Holland almost ten minutes to navigate safely. The track was rutted and growing muddier with the rain, the slightly raised grass verge on one side disappeared for long stretches without warning and the edge sloped steeply away towards the fields.

It was more than just the desire to avoid a broken ankle that slowed them down. Despite the drizzle, there was remarkably little cloud and, without saying anything, they stopped several times, switched their torches off and stared skywards.

'Never seen so many stars,' Holland said.

'No light pollution,' Thorne said. 'That's why.'

'Really?'

'It's got dark sky status. That's why loads of astronomers come.' He nodded. 'Well, you can see, can't you?'

'How come you know all that?'

'I know stuff,' Thorne said. 'Don't sound so bloody surprised.'

'Can you name any of them?' Holland asked.

'What?'

'Any of the stars. The constellations.'

Thorne stared for a minute, then pointed. 'That's the one that looks like a saucepan.' He had a memory of his father pointing it out. He had probably been shown more, but that was the only one he could ever remember, or identify. The one he always looked for.

'The Plough,' Holland said. 'Because it looks like an old-fashioned plough, see? It's also called the Big Dipper.'

'Looks like a saucepan,' Thorne said.

'It's actually called Ursa Major,' Holland said. 'I used to have a poster of all of them on my wall. Weird, the crap you remember.'

'That means a big bear, right?'

Holland nodded.

'Looks bugger all like a bear.'

'I think it's only a part of the bear.'

'Only if the bear's carrying a saucepan,' Thorne said.

They stared for a little while longer, the beam from the lighthouse playing across them every thirty seconds or so, each of them turning slowly on the spot to try and take it all in.

'Amazing,' Holland said.

Thorne could not argue. 'Come on,' he said. 'Before

Karim goes ape-shit. I've seen him lose it if the queue's too long at the kebab house.'

Samir Karim was certainly delighted to see them and was eager to get out of there and on his way to the Chapel House. He could not leave quickly enough, especially once Thorne had told him that spicy chicken stew and mashed potatoes were on the menu; that beer had been opened and that Howell and the rest were already getting well stuck into the little of it they had been left.

Once Karim had gone, Holland said, 'You're evil, you know that?'

Thorne looked down at the pair of body bags lying side by side at the base of the altar. The slump in them where there was nothing but air, the light from dozens of candles flickering across the black plastic.

'It's all relative,' he said.

Having left Holland at the chapel, Thorne walked the hundred yards further on up towards the cottage suggested by the warden; the one he had recommended as providing the most suitable accommodation for the six now forced into spending the night on the island.

'Hendy,' Burnham had said. 'The Old House. Oldest on the island. You'll be fine there, I reckon.'

Now, walking from the track towards the front door, Thorne stopped and turned. Something between a scream and a song was drifting from the direction of the lighthouse. He muttered, 'Hell was that?' though there was nobody there to hear him and it took a long few seconds before he realised it was the call of the grey seals. He walked on towards the cottage, playing his torch-beam across the peeling red of the front door, thinking that he could not imagine a sound more designed to terrify someone on a pitch-black night in the middle of nowhere.

The front door was open.

The interior of the cottage was cold, smelled damp, and its layout was predictably archaic: front and rear parlours, a walk-in pantry; a small 'back' kitchen off the main one. Thorne explored the ground floor by torchlight, then retraced his steps, stopping every few minutes to light one of the small gas lamps that were dotted around on window ledges and sideboards. As more of the place was revealed, it became clearer than ever that visitors did not come to the island for its luxurious accommodation. He had no idea when the cottage had been built, but the seventies-style décor and heavy furnishings – most even shabbier than those he had seen back at the Chapel House – did little to increase its appeal.

Thorne stood in the half-light at the bottom of the stairs. He looked back at the doormat with its worn and faded CROESO and reminded himself that none of this was important.

Yes, he could have done without the chill and the shadows, and the sudden scurryings that told him Burnham had been spot on about those sheltering mice, but it was a place to spend the night, no more than that. He and everyone else would have to make the best of it.

He walked upstairs to check out the bedrooms.

Once he had lit a few more lamps and familiarised himself with the layout of the first floor, Thorne was able to hazard a guess as to why Burnham had thought the Old House would be ideal. There were four bedrooms: a double, a single and two with twin single beds. For reasons of safety and security, Thorne had already decided that certain people would be required to share rooms. It was unlikely to be a popular decision, but at least there was the necessary number of bunks.

Make do and mend was one thing, but nobody would have been happy about sharing beds.

Thorne laid a gas lamp down on the chest of drawers in one of the twin bedrooms at the back of the house and walked across to the window. He peered out into the darkness. The sky was only a fraction lighter than the charcoal blanket of fields, the stars scattered across it all the way down to the sea. He wondered if Robert Burnham had sat and drawn up a chart, if he had worked out the permutations of the bedrooms, cottage by cottage, before choosing the most suitable. Thorne made a mental note to thank him, for that and for his help in getting the food out of the Blacks . . .

Thorne froze at the sight of a torch beam darting below him in the cottage garden.

The enveloping blackness meant there was no way of seeing to whom the torch belonged, to make out so much as a shape. Nonetheless, Thorne watched the milky beam skitter through the grass for a few moments, then along the

361

base of the stone wall before it was turned upwards suddenly towards the building and passed across the window at which Thorne was standing.

Instinctively, Thorne stepped back for a second. Then, for want of anything better to do, he moved back to the window and banged on the glass. The light vanished and it was impossible to say if the person had simply moved out of sight or if the torch had been switched off.

Thorne turned and hurried for the stairs.

He could not really explain why he felt the need to get down and out into the back garden as quickly as possible. After all, a darkness as profound as this one meant that anyone out and about would need to use a torch.

It was hardly suspicious.

He told himself that circumstances were making him unnecessarily jumpy, that it was probably just that bird-watcher out in search of the bird whose name he could never remember. The one that came back to its burrow at night, with the spooky call Nicklin had mentioned.

But hadn't Burnham said it was the wrong time of year?

Maybe it was the warden himself, come to see how Thorne was settling in. Perhaps it was Caroline or Patrick Black.

By the time Thorne had forced the stiff, heavy bolts on the kitchen door and burst through into the back garden, there was no sign of anyone.

He stood still and listened.

There was only the softest kiss of the wind through the

long grass, the distant wail of a grey seal and the hiss of the drizzle against the corrugated iron roof of the outside toilet. Thorne shone his torch across the lean-to, the moss on the stone wall, the cracked wooden door.

He pushed the door open with his foot and stepped inside. It smelled musty, that was all; probably a damn sight better than it did when there were holidaymakers in residence. A plastic seat had been fixed on to a simple wooden platform. There was a large metal jug and a row of damp and crinkled toilet rolls on one side.

Thorne positioned his torch so that it shone in roughly the right direction and unzipped. He pissed quickly, his shoulders tense, and when he had finished, he picked up the jug to flush, but it was empty.

He took out his radio as he walked back out into the garden.

'Dave?'

Holland took a few seconds to answer. 'Yeah, I'm here.'

'Have you been out of the chapel?'

'No. What's the matter?'

'I thought I saw someone outside the cottage, that's all.'

'Not me.'

'OK, not to worry ...'

Thorne turned at a noise from the other side of the cottage and ran around the side of the building. The grass was even more overgrown here and whipped around his calves as he emerged at the front in time to see a torch beam playing across the gate.

He pointed his own torch and shouted, 'Who's that?'

His voice was a little higher than normal.

He watched as the stranger's beam moved, then intensified, pooling beneath a chin and lighting up a pale face; the eyes in shadow and the inside of the mouth black when it opened.

Wendy Markham said, 'It's me . . .'

FORTY-SEVEN

Earlier, from the window of the sitting room in Chapel House, Batchelor had watched the last of the day slip from view and it had felt like the darkness was being hammered into place; nailed down.

As if the light had gone for good, out there and inside him.

Now, he sat on a hard sofa next to Alan Jenks, listening to Fletcher and Nicklin talking on the other side of the room. They seemed to have been talking for hours already, an incessant jabbering. Every word, each bark of laughter, another nail . . .

The others were still eating next door. The archaeologist and her team, their conversation bleeding through the stone wall. More laughter, more *ordinariness*, and Jenks next to him with his nose in some magazine or other, like this was just a waiting room or something.

Like there was nothing terrible out there in the dark.

I just wanted to say goodnight, best girl . . .

The stupid thing is that I think you'd have quite liked this place. It's certainly not like anywhere else I've ever been, or even heard of. There's such a lot of history here and you know how much I love the fact that you inherited a passion for all that from me. Well, that's what I tell myself, anyway. All the bad stuff you got from your mum, obviously. The inability to be anywhere on time or to file things or to keep your room tidy. Your strange affection for chaos.

It's so ironic, really. Considering what I did, the journey I've been on to get here. It breaks my heart that we never got a chance to come here together. To do so many things.

He glanced to his left, saw Jenks lick the end of a finger and slowly turn a page. Fletcher was talking to Nicklin about football and Nicklin was pretending to be interested. The rise and fall of chit-chat was still drifting in from the next room.

This place would actually make the perfect prison, you know that? Like Alcatraz or somewhere. Like Robben Island, where they kept Mandela, where you talked about going, remember? I was thinking how awful it must have been, being a prisoner somewhere like that. Somewhere like this. So much space around you, such a big sky. That's so much crueller in a way than how things are now. Don't you think? I mean, I reckon I've had it fairly easy compared to that, all things considered.

Bearing in mind what I did. How wrong I got it all.

It's weird how easy I find it now, talking to you like this and yet I still haven't got a clue what I'm going to say to your mum later on. I keep going over it, trying to come up with a few lines, but everything just sounds corny and rubbish. I can be like that with you though, because I just imagine you rolling your eyes and telling me how 'sad' I am. The way you and your sister did if you saw me dancing or if I didn't know what some piece of slang meant or something.

It's what dads do, isn't it? What they've always done. We're hard-wired to embarrass you and to grumble about you coming home late and using the place like a hotel. We're on safe ground with all that stuff, aren't we? We know how we should behave.

It's the other things.

The things nobody should ever have to deal with.

When we don't know what to do because your heart is broken, and when the pain you're in is so real and so raw and we can't do anything to make it better. When we walk into your bedroom and find you ... you know? And afterwards, when your mum's making a noise that's not like anything we've ever heard before, like something's being torn out of her.

Finding out the truth about what actually happened was terrible, I can't pretend that it wasn't. Like tumbling into the pit. But there's some consolation in knowing that because I got it so wrong, you're loved up there as much as you ever were here. As cherished.

Right now, I'm cold and I'm scared, but that's a real comfort.

He looked up at a noise from across the room and understood that Nicklin was talking to him.

367

Sorry, Jode, I've got to go.

He nodded, hating him. Hating being dragged so roughly up and away from her. From a perfect, waking dream of death to a nightmare of shadows and shit and something terrible in the dark.

'You never been a football fan then, Jeff?'

Love you, baby.

'Jeff?'

Love you, love you, love you . . .

FORTY-EIGHT

'I just came to see how you were getting on,' Markham said.

Thorne nodded, but hadn't really listened. 'Were you in the back garden a few minutes ago?'

'No.' She looked confused. 'Are you . . . ?'

Thorne had already turned and was on his way back round to the rear of the property.

'Is everything OK?'

'There was someone out there,' Thorne said. 'I saw a torch.'

Markham followed a pace or two behind, pushing through the long grass at the side of the cottage. 'Maybe it was my torch reflecting off something,' she said. She emerged into the garden and noticed the generator. 'Off that, for a start.' She turned round and nodded back towards the front of the cottage. 'Could it have been the lighthouse, maybe?'

Thorne said, 'No. I don't know. Maybe . . .' He was in

much the same spot he'd been in a few minutes earlier, shining his torch around the garden, raising it to throw the beam on to the base of the mountain directly behind. Markham did the same, though neither torch was powerful enough to see much beyond the line of rocks and small bushes twenty or thirty feet up.

'So, how's it looking inside?' Markham asked.

Thorne turned and looked back at the cottage. 'Well, it's not exactly five-star,' he said. 'Probably still better than a Travelodge though.'

'You got all the beds sorted?'

Thorne shook his head. 'Just had a look around and put the lights on, basically.'

'Come on,' Markham said. 'I'll give you a hand.'

She pushed open the back door and Thorne followed her through the two kitchens into the parlour. She took one look at the fireplace and immediately began opening cupboards until she found a small cache of old newspapers and kindling, a few logs and a box of firelighters.

'Woman make fire,' she said.

'What's the point?' Thorne asked. 'Once we've brought the others over from Chapel House, we'll be going straight to bed. I'm not envisaging cocoa round the fire.'

Markham knelt and began tearing off sheets of paper, twisting them into knots and tossing them into the grate. 'Might as well,' she said. 'Even if we just keep it going for half an hour or so now, it'll take the chill off. You'll all be sleeping in your overcoats otherwise.'

'I suppose,' Thorne said.

Before he could do a great deal to help, Markham had got a decent blaze going. She stood up and admired her handiwork.

'You've done this before,' Thorne said.

She said, 'It's all fairly basic,' then looked and saw that Thorne thought it was not basic at all. 'God, you're a real city boy, aren't you?'

Before Thorne could answer her, another of the ghostly seal-calls echoed from the other side of the island. 'Can you blame me?' he said.

Markham threw another log on to the fire and wiped her hands off on the back of her jeans. 'Right,' she said. 'Let's go and have a look at these bedrooms.'

They moved from room to room, lighting the lamps; pulling pillows, sheets and duvets from protective bin-liners, turning mattresses and making up beds.

'We had a place in the country when I was a kid,' Markham said. 'Me and my brother hated it most of the time. Moaned like mad and drove my mum and dad barmy, going on about how boring it was. Still, I learned how to make a fire up, how to skin a rabbit, all that.'

Thorne looked at her.

'I'm kidding,' she said. 'This was the Cotswolds, for God's sake. You were never more than fifty feet from Waitrose or a tea shop.'

Thorne tossed a pillow on to a single bed. 'No, I'm not

the biggest fan of the countryside. My ex used to talk about getting out of London. She was Job too, so we talked about relocating every so often, but I just can't imagine being a copper and not being in a city.' He began stuffing a second pillow into its pillowcase. 'I mean, what the hell are you supposed to do all day in the countryside if you're a copper? Nick people for being pissed in charge of a muck-spreader?' Markham laughed and he enjoyed hearing it. 'Patrol the village fête and make sure there's no drug-cheats at the duck racing?'

'Trust me,' Markham said. 'I've been at plenty of seriously nasty crime scenes in places like this.'

'Really?'

'Well, not like this. You know, the countryside, but in places where there *are* actually some people around to do things to one another.'

Thorne dropped the second pillow down, straightened it. 'It's not for me,' he said. 'Too much fresh air, I get dizzy.'

'Your ex . . . ?' Markham said.

Thorne looked at her. Each was holding two corners of a duvet cover; the final one of six. They shook it out.

'Ex, because she was a copper too? I can understand how tricky that is.'

'No, there was other stuff,' Thorne said. Stuff he had no intention of talking about. That he had only recently begun talking to Helen about.

A lost baby.

A grief that had gone unexpressed until it was far too late.

He let go of the duvet cover, stood back and watched Markham wrestle a duvet into it. 'Actually, I'm with another copper now,' he said. 'So . . .'

'Helen,' Markham said.

'Right.' Thorne guessed that she had got the name from Karim. 'Yeah, she's great.'

Markham looked at him and nodded, as though she knew he had said that to try and counteract the potent fantasy that was unfolding in his head and working elsewhere. Images that had been taking shape and growing more elaborate since he and Wendy Markham had walked into that first bedroom.

To water down the guilt a little.

Once the final duvet had been laid in place, they made their way back downstairs. In the parlour, the fire had died down somewhat, but it was noticeably warmer.

'You were bang on,' Thorne said.

They stared at the flames for a few moments, the shadows moving on the wall behind them; across painted stone and watercolours of seascapes in heavy, wooden frames.

'So, who gave you that then?' Markham asked.

'Sorry?'

She lifted a finger, touched it to Thorne's chin. The short, straight scar that ran along it.

'Ah . . . that was a woman with a knife.' He nodded when he saw Markham grimace. 'Believe it or not, a woman I was actually in bed with at the time.'

373

Markham's eyes widened. 'Blimey. You must have seriously under-performed.'

'No, it wasn't that.'

Something else Thorne most certainly did not want to get into. The wound a prelude to an event that even Helen did not know about yet.

'She got stroppy,' he said, 'when I refused to sleep in the wet patch.'

A log crackled and spat and Thorne bent to grab tongs and retrieve a smouldering ember. When he straightened up, Markham was smiling and now it wasn't only his proximity to the fire that was making Thorne's face hot.

'Some women are just plain bloody selfish,' she said.

FORTY-NINE

When Thorne and Markham got back to Chapel House half an hour later, dinner was finished and Karim had returned to his less than pleasant duties at the chapel itself. Holland – relieved in every sense – was talking to Bethan Howell while Barber, having finished clearing things away, had continued the necessary arse-kissing by volunteering to wash up in freezing water.

Once Thorne was back, people began gathering in the cottage's large sitting room. Extra chairs were pulled in from the parlour and around the dining table. The fire was in need of some attention, which Markham was happy to provide and, within a minute or two, she had worked the same incendiary magic as had been conjured at the Old House a short time before.

'That's lovely,' Nicklin said. He raised cuffed wrists, as though to warm them at the fire. 'No crumpets in those plastic bags, were there?'

There were nine of them crowded into the room. Markham had been quick to get one of the bottles of wine open and pour glasses for herself, Howell and Barber. With everyone else present on duty or in handcuffs, they were the only ones drinking anything stronger than tea. Thorne was on the last of the coffee from the school, already resigned to the fact that he would not be getting a great deal of sleep.

Truthfully, Thorne was uncertain as to the best way to proceed. It was only a little after nine o'clock and, though he was not exactly comfortable with everyone sitting around as though they were all on holiday together, it was still too early to go to bed. There was an hour or so yet before he would want to move the prison party across to the Old House for the night and he was happier killing the time somewhere warm.

'We'll stay here for now,' he said. 'It's more comfortable and I'd prefer it if we all stayed together as long as possible.'

There were several murmurs of approval. Markham muttered something to Howell about 'opening that other bottle.'

Nicklin seemed keen to endorse Thorne's decision. 'Yeah, definitely better to be together,' he said. 'We should make the most of it anyway, because it's back to reality tomorrow.'

All eyes in the room were on him, but nobody said anything.

'It feels a bit unreal this place, don't you think?' Nicklin looked from face to face, seeking a response. He shrugged. 'Well, it always felt that way to me.'

Thorne grunted, made no attempt to disguise his contempt. 'So what, when you were killing Simon Milner and Eileen Bennett, that just felt like a dream or something, did it?'

'Killing always feels a bit like that to me,' Nicklin said. 'Like I'm watching someone else do it.'

Suddenly, Thorne's mouth was very dry. Something about the casual way that murder was being described, like any hobby, humdrum and unremarkable. That, and the tense being used.

Feels, not felt.

Nicklin smiled. 'I always enjoy the view, though . . . '

A shocked silence settled for a minute or so after that but, as soon as it had been broken, conversation in the room quickly splintered into assorted hushed and simultaneous exchanges: Holland asking Thorne what time he thought they'd be back in London the following day; Fletcher and Jenks talking holidays; Howell and Markham laughing as the wine continued to go down easily and they whispered about Sam Karim and Andy Barber.

In a moment of quiet, Markham said, 'Come on then, who's got a good story?' When Thorne looked across, she added, 'Last night, we sat around telling stories. It was a laugh.'

'Nothing scary,' Howell said. 'Well, not *very* scary,

because we didn't want to frighten Barber too much.' Fletcher muttered something and she looked across. 'What?'

'What are we, Girl Guides?'

Jenks laughed, said, 'Girl Guides.'

Howell stared daggers at Fletcher across the top of her glass. 'I don't think you'd have been tough enough for the Girl Guides.'

'I don't know,' Thorne said. He could easily imagine the forensic team sitting around the previous evening, putting the red wine away and swapping tales, but this was a very different line-up of potential storytellers. 'Not sure it's a good idea.'

'Why not?' Markham asked. 'It helped to pass the time.'

'Still.'

'That's all I was thinking.'

Thorne looked hard at her, in the hope that Markham might see what he was driving at. The slight shake of her head and widening of her eyes made it clear that she didn't.

'I know a fantastic story,' Nicklin said.

Thorne pointed at him. 'That's why it's not a good idea.'

'No, seriously.' Nicklin leaned forward in his chair, excited. 'This is an absolute cracker, I promise you. It's got the lot ... it's tragic, but it's also funny. There's a murder, obviously, I know you wouldn't expect anything else, but it's also got pathos, mystery ... and there's a twist at the end I guarantee you won't see coming.' He nodded. 'Best.

Story. Ever.' He looked at several of the faces now turned to his. 'Well?'

'I got no problem with it,' Fletcher said.

Nicklin turned to Thorne. Said, 'It's only a story.'

'This better not piss anybody off.' Thorne looked to Markham and Howell but saw no sign of anxiety, no inclination to object. 'If you upset anybody . . .'

'What are you going to do?' Nicklin asked. 'Send me to bed?'

Thorne was hugely irritated to see Fletcher and Jenks smile, half-expecting the latter to moronically repeat, 'Send me to bed.' He gave Nicklin the nod, stared down at his coffee.

Nicklin cleared his throat. 'Now, I should point out before I start that this isn't really my story at all.' He nodded across to where Batchelor was still sitting on one of the sofas next to Alan Jenks. 'It's Jeffrey's.' Heads turned towards Batchelor, but he continued staring at a spot on the worn carpet a few feet in front of him, as he had been doing for as long as anyone else in the room could remember. 'I promise to try and do it justice, Jeff.' Nicklin waited, shrugged when Batchelor gave no response. 'So, you all know why Jeff's sitting over there in handcuffs, do you? How a nice, mild-mannered history teacher like him ended up in Long Lartin with a bunch of murderous nut-jobs like me.'

Thorne raised a hand. 'OK, that's enough.'

'It's background,' Nicklin protested. 'It's important if the story's going to make any sense.'

Thorne glanced at the man Nicklin was talking about. If Batchelor was bothered by what was being said about him, there was no sign of it.

'Come on,' Fletcher said. 'What's the big deal? I don't think anyone here seriously thinks he's in prison for not returning library books, do they?'

'Whatever,' Thorne said.

'Right,' Nicklin said. 'Well ... the sad truth is that Jeff walked into his eldest daughter's bedroom one morning and discovered that she'd killed herself.' He spoke quietly, without colour. 'I'm sure I don't need to tell you how horrible that was. Just unthinkable, especially for those of you who've got kids.' He looked at Holland, gave a small nod. 'Now, the agony that Jeff must have felt that morning is not even something I can begin to put into words, but it turned into something else when he found out why his daughter had hanged herself. It turned into rage.

'Seems that Jodi, his daughter, had been dumped by her boyfriend.' He shook his head. 'Little scumbag she was going out with decided he wanted nothing more to do with her, and instead of telling her face to face, he'd sent her a text. That was it. Jeff's little girl woke up one morning, saw that text message and it felt like her life was over.

'So, she took the cord off her dressing gown, put it round her neck and five minutes later it was.

'Now ... bad luck usually plays a part in stories like this and it was Jeff's bad luck that he ran into Nathan, the aforementioned little scumbag, at the bus stop, the day after Jodi had killed herself.' There was more in Nicklin's voice now as he began to relish the telling, reaching a part of the story he found especially appealing.

A view he enjoyed.

'Bad luck for Nathan too, as it turned out ... because the old red mist descended, understandably, all things considered, and our Jeff, who up until that point would not have said boo to a goose, beat the little shit to death right there and then with his bare hands.' He looked at Jeff, then to his audience. 'I know ... who would have thought it?

'So, Jeff hands himself in, because he's a good, God-fearing citizen. On top of which, he's covered in this kid's blood and there's half a dozen witnesses, so there's not much point pretending he didn't do it. He's charged with murder, blah blah blah, there's a trial and he's sent down. End of story.' Nicklin paused for effect, then leaned even further forward and dropped his voice to a whisper in an attempt to heighten the drama. 'Only it isn't ... not by a long chalk. This is actually where it starts to get really interesting, because a few weeks after Jeff gets sent to prison, he receives a letter—'

'Shut up!'

Everyone turned to look at Jeffrey Batchelor, who was staring white-faced at Nicklin. The muscles were working in his jaw and his skinny chest strained against the arm that Jenks had thrown across it.

Nicklin cocked his head. 'I beg your pardon, Jeff?'

'I said, shut up ...'

Thorne watched, intrigued. Batchelor had seemed oddly disconnected from almost everyone for the majority of his time away from the prison, but on those occasions when he had interacted with Nicklin, there had always been an element of fear in the way he spoke; the manner in which he held himself. Looking at Batchelor now though, Thorne could see that it was entirely absent.

Batchelor was no longer afraid.

'This is my story,' he said. He raised his cuffed hands and pressed them against his chest. 'It's my *pain*.' His clenched fists rose and fell in his lap as he spoke; measured, the anger held in check. 'It's all mine and you can't have it . . . however much you want it, however much you feed off it. It's mine, so I'll tell it, OK?'

Nicklin did not seem unhappy. 'Fill your boots,' he said. 'I think I'd probably tell it better, but it's your funeral.'

Batchelor sat back, waited until Jenks had removed his arm, then nodded, to reassure the officer that there would be no need to replace it. 'Yes, I got a letter,' he said. 'I'd had a lot of letters . . . from Nathan's family, I'm sure you can imagine the kind of thing. Wanting me to rot in hell. The horrible stuff they wanted to happen to my wife, to our daughter.' He swallowed. 'Our other daughter.

'This one was something different though. It was a letter from Nathan's best friend, Jack. He was writing because he wanted me to know that Nathan had loved Jodi more than anything in the world and that he would never have split up with her. Jack said he knew that was true.' He shook his head, barely perceptible, as though he could still not quite believe what he was about to say. 'He knew … because it was *him* that had sent the text message.'

Thorne looked around the room, saw the stunned reactions and guessed that he was wearing much the same expression. He let out the breath he had not realised he was holding.

'In his letter, Jack told me he'd taken Nathan's phone when he wasn't looking,' Batchelor said. 'That he'd sent that text to Jodi as a joke. He wanted me to know that Nathan hadn't had anything to do with it, that I'd murdered someone who was completely innocent and was as devastated by Jodi's death as anybody. It had all just been a stupid … joke.' Batchelor blinked slowly, screwing his eyes up. 'I got that letter and I … went to pieces.'

Thorne reached for his cup and filled his dry mouth with tepid coffee.

'Jesus,' Markham said.

Nicklin grunted a laugh. 'Yeah, well not even *he* could help.' He looked around the room. 'You do know Jeff's a little bit Goddy, right?' He nodded, as though that explained something. 'Nearly lost his faith, that letter turning up like that. Understandable though, you find something like that out. That's when we got close, isn't it, Jeff?' He looked across, but Batchelor had gone back to studying that fascinating piece of worn carpet. Nicklin carried on as though he was not there at all. 'He was all over the place, back then, poor bastard. I pretty much talked him round. Saved his life, or good as.' He leaned back, pleased with himself, rolled his head around, working the stiffness from his neck. 'What did I tell you, though? One hell of a story, isn't it?'

Bethan Howell was the first to move. She stood up and lifted her jacket from the back of the chair. 'I need to get some air.'

Nicklin nodded towards the window. The rain was starting to beat more heavily against it, thrown against the glass on angry gusts. 'It's horrible out there,' he said.

Howell began to put her jacket on. She said, 'It's horrible in here.'

FIFTY

Howell was sheltering beneath the front porch. Thorne had followed her and for a minute they stood in silence. They stared out through the curtain of rain across the dark fields, the wind riffling through Howell's short blonde hair and whipping the smoke from her cigarette into Thorne's face.

'Sorry,' she said.

'It's fine,' Thorne said. 'It's nice.'

'You sure you don't want one?'

Thorne shook his head.

'It's very impressive.'

'What?'

'That degree of self-control.'

'Not about everything,' Thorne said.

Howell took a drag, sighing out the smoke like she had really needed the nicotine hit. 'Christ,' she said. 'That story.'

'I know.'

'Your daughter dies like that, you lose it and beat a kid to death, then you find out it was the wrong kid.' She looked at him. 'That it was just a bloody joke.'

Thorne nodded, shivered a little.

'I've got two kids,' Howell said. 'Eighteen and sixteen, and they're still doing stupid things like that on each other's phone. Messing with the other one's Facebook account, playing jokes, you know? Fraping, they call it.'

'Right.'

'It only takes one careless remark, doesn't it?'

They said nothing for a few moments, then Howell half-turned and nodded back at the front door. 'He loved it, though, didn't he? Nicklin. Like Batchelor said, he feeds off stuff like that.'

'I should have shut him up earlier,' Thorne said.

'It wasn't your fault.'

'Truth was, I wanted to know the end of the story.'

'We all did.'

'I was at the farm,' Thorne said. 'When I went to get the food, you know? We were talking about pollution . . . how there's no pollution here at all.'

Howell nodded. 'Yeah, the island's pretty amazing, isn't it?'

Thorne knew that it was. He had seen it walking to the lighthouse, sensed it standing at the abbey ruins. 'It *was*,' he said. 'We've ruined it.'

'You're being daft.'

'Bringing him here. That's as much pollution as any-where needs. Nicklin and the reason we brought him. It's like we caused an oil slick or something. Like we turned up and dumped shit everywhere.'

'Maybe you should come back,' Howell said.

Thorne looked at her. The lamp hanging from the porch cast just enough light to see the fine spray across her forehead, her eyes squinting against the rain and the smoke.

'Like Burnham said. You should come back another time.'

Thorne shook his head. 'There's always going to be associations, isn't there? How much peace are you ever going to get, when all you can see is his face grinning at you and bones in a plastic bag?'

Howell watched him for a while. 'I'm guessing you see his face quite often.'

'More often than I'd like,' Thorne said. 'There's been a few like that down the years, but he's the worst.' He sucked at a curl of passing smoke. 'I hope he hasn't got into your head.'

'No chance,' she said. 'Anyway, it's strictly dead people's faces for me. Most of the people I . . . find don't have faces any more, so I make them up. I don't know what Simon Milner or Eileen Bennett looked like, but I'll imagine it.' She gestured back at the front door. 'Trust me, I'll have forgotten that arsehole's face tomorrow.'

Thorne wasn't sure that he believed her, but he stood

for a few seconds in silence, thinking just how wonderful such a forgetting would be. He reached into his pockets, producing his phone from one and a torch from the other. He turned up his collar and nodded along the track. 'I need to make a quick call.'

Howell took a final drag. Said, 'You can stay here. I'm going back inside.'

Thorne explained that he had no wish to get soaked, but that the abbey ruins had so far proved to be the only place where he could get a mobile signal.

'Typical,' she said. 'Six-hundred-year-old ruins on an all-but deserted island and I can't get a decent signal in my front room in the middle of Bangor.'

'Maybe those monks knew something we didn't.'

'What, silence and celibacy? I don't think I'm interested.'

'Didn't they also make shedloads of wine?' Thorne said. 'They were probably pissed most of the time.'

'That's a fair point,' Howell said. 'Talking of which ...'

She was crushing her cigarette against the wet stone wall as Thorne turned on the torch and stepped out into the rain.

'So where's everyone sleeping?' Helen asked.

'Still not sorted it out.'

'I presume you'll be staying close to Nicklin.'

'Yeah, I'll have to be.'

'Not too close though, right?'

'Not if I can help it.'

Standing in the ruined belltower, Thorne was largely sheltered from the worst of the weather, though enough rain to piss him off still came in through the 'windows' when the wind blew in the right direction.

'What about the forensic team and what's-her-name? The CSM?'

Thorne turned his face away from the wind and water. 'Markham.'

'I can't hear you.'

He raised his voice above the growl of the surf crashing on to the rocks just ahead and below him. 'Wendy Markham.'

'Yeah, her.'

'She's staying in the same place she was last night,' Thorne said. 'With Howell and the CSI.'

'What about you and the prison lot?'

'We're in a separate cottage. Me, Dave and the four from Long Lartin.'

'Sounds cosy,' Helen said.

'Oh, it'll be lovely. I reckon we'll be keeping each other awake all night, giggling and talking about girls and foot-ball.'

'I still find it hard to believe there's only one boat. Or that there's nobody else capable of sailing the bloody thing.'

'Just the way it is.'

'It's definitely coming tomorrow, is it?'

'Don't tempt fate, for God's sake.' Thorne turned and looked towards the sea, watched the beam from the lighthouse sweep across the stretch of water in his line of vision and away. Once the darkness had returned he could just make out the lights of a large boat in the far distance. 'Don't worry,' he said. 'Any problems with the weather tomorrow, I'm swimming for it.'

For a few minutes they talked about what Helen had been doing at work. They talked around some of her ongoing cases – the banter and the bullshit and the less than serious moments – though it was clear that she still wanted to talk properly when Thorne got back.

'I know it's only Wales,' she said.

'What?'

'It feels like you're on the other side of the world, or something. Just a long way away, you know?'

'Feels like that to me too,' Thorne said. 'Something about this place. It's like going back in time.' Helen replied, but the line broke up and he couldn't catch it. 'Listen, do you know what *fraping* is?'

'Yeah, it's when kids put fake pictures or status updates or whatever on somebody else's Facebook page. Frape is Facebook rape, you get it?'

'Nice.'

'You're *so* not down with the kids.'

'I think that's probably a good thing,' Thorne said.

'You fancy going out somewhere tomorrow night?'

Thorne could not be sure exactly what time he would

390

make it home the following day, but barring disasters it would be in time for dinner. 'Sounds great,' he said.

'I'll see if I can get my dad to take Alfie.'

'What about Indian?' Thorne waited a few seconds for a response, then looked at his phone and saw that he had lost the signal. He moved from one corner to the other, held the handset at arm's length, swearing loudly enough to raise several dead saints as he tried to get the signal back. When the tell-tale bars eventually reappeared on the small screen, he called Helen again, but she was engaged.

He waited, guessing that she was trying to call him back.

He looked out into the blackness, paying particular attention to the lower slopes of the mountain rising up behind the chapel, still thinking about that torch-beam he had seen in the back garden of the Old House.

He turned and stared past the point where the land fell away, but he couldn't see the boat any longer. It was only the noise that told him the sea was there at all.

Howell and the others were sitting around a table in the parlour when Thorne returned to Chapel House. If the empty one on the floor was not evidence enough, the laughter and increased volume of conversation pointed towards a second bottle of wine having been opened. Barber was dealing from a tatty-looking pack of playing cards and each person had a pile of matches in front of them.

'All good?' Holland asked.

'Wet,' Thorne said. He looked around for something to dry his hair with, but could see nothing. With no bathroom facilities, towels were clearly the responsibility of those visitors who could bring themselves to wash at a kitchen sink in ice-cold water. He shook the water from his hair, pointing towards the closed door and the sitting room beyond. 'Everything all right in there?'

'Fine,' Holland said, picking his cards up. 'Nobody fancied listening to Nicklin any more, that's all. So we came out here.'

'He's in a talkative mood,' Howell said.

'Nobody likes a chatty psycho, do they?' Markham fanned her cards out, every inch the experienced player.

'I don't know,' Thorne said. 'It's when he's sitting there saying nothing that you want to worry. When the cogs are turning.'

Holland tossed a few of his matches into the middle of the table. 'Four,' he said.

'Call,' Markham said.

Thorne leaned down and snatched Holland's cards from him. 'Come on, Dave. I think we need to get that lot bedded down.'

'Shame,' Holland said. He pushed back his chair, then reached for the empty box at the other end of the table and began dropping his matches back in. 'I was making a killing here.'

When Thorne opened the door to the sitting room, all heads but Batchelor's turned to him. 'We should make a move,' Thorne said. He stepped inside and looked at Fletcher, then at Jenks. 'Time to get your boys to bed.'

Nicklin was the first one to his feet, Fletcher quick to follow, a little taken by surprise.

'Bagsy the top bunk,' Nicklin said.

FIFTY-ONE

'No chance,' Fletcher said. He peered into the bedroom and shook his head, as though he were no more than a dissatisfied guest at a hotel. 'Don't even think about it.'

'And there I was thinking this was your job,' Thorne said.

'Well, that's where you're wrong, isn't it?' Fletcher planted his feet and squared his shoulders. 'This is not what I'm paid for.'

'No, not normally, I understand that. But these are special circumstances.'

'I don't care.'

'Everybody else is having to adapt.'

'There's not enough money, mate. Nowhere near. Sorry, but you'll have to sort something else out.'

'Such as what?'

'*You* share a fucking room with him.'

As soon as they had arrived at the Old House, Thorne had escorted the group from room to room; allocating beds, talking through the protocols that would see everyone safely through to the following morning. Thorne had told Holland to take the first of the single rooms and Holland had not complained. Jenks had seemed fine about sharing a room with Jeffrey Batchelor once Thorne had pointed out that the prisoners would be handcuffed to their bedsteads throughout the night. Batchelor had said nothing. Nicklin had moaned briefly about human rights, but Thorne sensed that it was just for show and the protest petered out once Thorne had made it clear that there was simply no alternative.

As they had approached the second of the rooms containing two single beds, Fletcher – seeing what was coming – had begun grumbling and hanging back, like a child in fear of the dentist who has just heard the whine of the drill.

Now they stood on the landing outside the room. Cop and prison officer staring one another out.

Thorne was nominally head of the entire operation, but it gave him no formal authority over either of the officers from Long Lartin. Both had seemed content up to this point, happy to go along with everyone else while they clocked up the overtime. This, though, was a sticking point, and it was clear that Fletcher was not going to budge.

'I'm frankly rather hurt, Mr Fletcher,' Nicklin said.

Fletcher shrugged. 'I couldn't give a toss what you are.'

'I'm the one that's going to be handcuffed to the bed like a wild animal, so you'll be perfectly safe. I don't see what it is you're objecting to.'

'And *I* don't have to give you reasons.'

'Is it a personal hygiene issue?'

'It's a not wanting to share a room with a murderer issue.'

Nicklin nodded towards the other officer. 'Mr Jenks doesn't seem to have a problem.'

'It's hardly the same thing.'

'No? Jeff beat an innocent boy to death with his bare hands.'

Fletcher looked at Jenks. 'You fancy swapping, Alan?'

'I'm fine as I am,' Jenks said.

'I'll do it,' Thorne said. 'I'll share with Nicklin, OK?'

Fletcher nodded, satisfied.

'You take the other single room.' Thorne tossed his holdall into the bedroom. 'And all doors to stay open, OK?'

The arrangements hammered out, they all trooped into the room that Jenks and Batchelor would be sleeping in. While Fletcher stayed close to Nicklin, Thorne and Holland assisted in getting Jenks's prisoner into bed. It was a fairly straightforward procedure, certainly once everyone had agreed that it was cold enough to necessitate sleeping fully dressed. Batchelor's jacket and shoes were removed and as soon as he was beneath the blankets, one handcuff was unfastened and swiftly attached to the metal bedstead.

Batchelor immediately turned on to his side, face to the wall, and did his best to get comfortable. Jenks asked him if he was OK and he grunted, tugging at the blanket with his free hand.

Nicklin said, 'Sleep well, Jeff.'

Batchelor nodded and did not move again.

Thorne asked Fletcher and Holland if they would get Nicklin bedded down in the other room, while he went downstairs to make a final check on security arrangements.

'Try not to be too long,' Nicklin said.

Thorne turned for the door. 'And don't worry about being gentle with him.'

'Oh, and a glass of water would be nice . . .'

Thorne could not find any kind of key, but made sure that the heavy bolt on the front door was pulled across. He did the same with the back door, but not before he had opened it and stood for a few minutes, shining a torch into the rear garden.

Everything seemed as it should be. The wind had died down a little, but the rain looked to have settled itself in nicely. Leaning out and peering back towards the chapel, he could see light flickering behind the stained glass windows and leaking from the Chapel House just beyond it. He doubted very much that any of those inside would be going to bed any time soon. He wondered how strong the Blacks' home-made wine was and what state Bethan Howell and the rest of them would be in the following morning.

Moving back through the house, Thorne checked all the windows, before ending up in front of the fire that Markham had lit an hour or so before. It was little more than glowing embers now, the occasional flicker as a small flame licked for a few seconds from beneath a partially burned log.

Thorne blinked, saw a shaft of browned bone emerging from black earth.

I've got nice and comfy with bones and blood ...

He turned to head back upstairs and noticed a large, leather-bound notebook that he had not seen before, on a table near the door.

A visitors' book.

He opened it and slowly turned the pages, read through the comments.

Never been anywhere like this!

As magical as everyone told me it would be.

I'm no saint but I can't think of anywhere I'd rather be buried.

Thorne did not have a pen and would probably not have used it even if he had, but just for a moment or two, he imagined turning to a nice, clean page and scrawling a heartfelt 'sorry'.

Holland and Fletcher had done as they were asked and were waiting for Thorne in the bedroom. Nicklin lay in the bed nearest the door, the arm that was now handcuffed to the metal bedstead stretched out behind him, as though he were casually reaching for something.

Thorne told Holland and Fletcher to get some sleep, and reminded them to leave their doors open. 'Anything you're not happy with,' he said, 'I want to know about it.'

'There's plenty I'm not happy with,' Fletcher said.

'You know what I mean. Anything moving that isn't a mouse, you come and tell me.'

When Holland and Fletcher had gone, Thorne removed his jacket and muddy boots. He pulled off the damp fleece he had been wearing all day and replaced the T-shirt that was underneath with a fresh one from his bag. He turned his back on his room-mate while he changed, but guessed that Nicklin was watching. He lay down on the bed, exhausted suddenly, laced his fingers behind his head and stared up at the ceiling. There was wallpaper coming away in one corner and filaments of cobweb swayed around the light-fitting.

Not enough money, mate . . .

Fletcher was a moaning pain in the arse, but Thorne could hardly blame him for not fancying this.

The lantern still sputtering on a shelf near the window was not exactly bathing the bedroom in light, but Thorne decided to leave it burning nonetheless. He knew that Nicklin had been secured, but that did not mean Thorne was looking forward to spending the night just a few feet away.

He was certainly not going to do so in the dark.

'This is probably as much for me as it is for you,' Nicklin said.

Thorne turned his head, watched Nicklin make a song and dance out of rattling the handcuffs.

'To protect me from myself.'

'Go to sleep,' Thorne said.

'You in bed over there ... just a few feet away.' Nicklin puffed out his cheeks and shook his head in mock relief. 'I really don't know if I'd be able to control myself.'

Thorne turned away again and closed his eyes.

FIFTY-TWO

The man who – unbeknown to himself – had been christened 'Adrian' by the only other person in the house sat in the small kitchen watching television and eating toast. He slathered peanut butter over the latest piece and put two more slices of bread under the grill.

He checked his watch.

Another ten minutes and he'd go in to clear the prisoner's dinner things away, see if he needed the bucket. That was the bit he really disliked, all the messy stuff. Making meals and dealing with piss and shit like he was just some nurse or something. Couldn't be helped though. He had known this would be part of the job when he'd taken it on, so there was no point in complaining – even if there'd been anyone around to complain to – and the fact was he was happy enough to do the job, menial stuff included, because at the end of the day it was an honour.

The others had felt the same way, the couple he'd taken over from.

'We're lucky,' the girl had said. 'Plenty of other people would jump at the chance.'

He wasn't sure there were *plenty*, but he knew what she was getting at. He guessed there would be a good few people keen to seize an opportunity like this one. It was as close as they were likely to get to a celebrity and, if the worst happened, they might get a taste of it themselves. In newspapers and books, maybe even movies one day. That was what you called a silver lining!

So, there was cooking and there was cleaning up, but the part he liked best of all was when he spent time in the room with the prisoner. Just sitting there reading or whatever, watching him and listening to all the desperate rubbish he came out with. Those were the times when he knew he'd done the right thing, because it was a buzz he couldn't remember getting from anything else he'd ever done. Not from games, and that was probably what came closest. However many aliens or cops or hookers you were wasting, only the real saddos actually got off on it. Only the proper losers imagined they were doing it for real. He enjoyed playing, no mistake about it, but they were just games.

This was something altogether different. This was genuine power over another person. It was life and death, simple as that, and that was a rush you didn't get every day. Certainly not working in telesales.

The man, whose name was actually Damien, turned his toast over and reached for the wooden knife block next to the cooker. He drew out the biggest knife and touched a finger to its edge. Not for the first time, he wondered whose place this was. It didn't appear very lived in, that was for sure. It didn't feel like the knife he was holding had been used for a while.

He thought about what he'd told the prisoner about the scalpel, the girl leaving it behind. It wasn't true of course, he'd just wanted to scare him, but the fact was there were loads of other knives knocking around, if he chose to use them.

He smelled the burning a second too late and quickly pulled the blackened toast from beneath the grill. He tossed it on to a plate and finished the piece he was eating while he waited for it to cool.

It had done the trick, that stuff about the scalpel. It had scared him. He'd seen the colour go out of the cocky bastard's face, drain away just like that and he hadn't said a great deal since.

He sat and chewed his toast and thought about other things he could do.

If just watching him was this exciting, he wondered how it would feel to take things a step or two further . . .

He couldn't be sure how it would go down with whoever was running things, him doing anything he hadn't been specifically told to do. He would be careful, obviously. He knew that the prisoner had to be kept alive.

It would all be over soon enough anyway.

If everything went according to plan – whatever the plan was – he'd be out of the house by the end of the day. So, it couldn't really hurt if, between now and then, he used a bit of initiative, could it? Beyond the job he'd been given – to watch the prisoner, to keep him fed and watered until the time came – he didn't know any of the details, none of them did. But there was always a chance it might actually help, doing a tiny bit more damage.

Something creative.

He picked up a slice of the burned toast and used the knife to scrape away the charcoal.

Maybe he'd see how things were when he went into the bedroom to clear the stuff away. See if there were any more smartarse digs about who was in charge, about how he got on with girls, all that.

He scraped harder, watched the flakes and puffs of black dust drift into the sink, and imagined the knife working at a shin, or on the back of a hand.

Yeah, he'd see if the man on the bed had anything else to say to him, and decide then.

FIFTY-THREE

'I can't sleep.'

'I don't care.'

'I think it's because I'm too excited.'

'What the hell have you got to be excited about?'

'Well, I know this isn't exactly the lap of luxury, but it's still the first night I've spent in ten years that isn't behind bars. The first room I've slept in that doesn't have a lock on the door.'

'Make the most of it.'

'Oh, I intend to. Bed's pretty nice, actually, not too soft. What about yours?'

'Make the most of it, because it's strictly a one-night deal.'

'Oh I know. Stroke of luck and all that.'

'Not for me.'

'Any news on Huw's father, by the way?'

'Like you give a toss.'

'Just wondered if it was anything serious. You didn't say.'

'No, I didn't.'

'There's no point blaming yourself for any of this, you know.'

'I wasn't.'

'What can you do? I mean, you can't control the weather, can you? Mind you, you can see why we Brits love to talk about the bloody weather so much, can't you? I mean, it's one of the few things in the world that's still unpredictable these days, isn't it? That keeps things interesting. See, we like to think that we can control our lives, that we're on top of everything with all our technology, but it's only really the trivial things we've got any sort of handle on or say in. No amount of flashy gadgets or apps are any good when it comes to shit like the weather. You think you've got it covered, don't you? You check all the forecasts or whatever and then *bang*, it surprises you. Lets you know who's boss. Same thing with illness or accidents or what have you. Same thing with death . . .'

'You going to keep talking shit all night?'

'Take murder for a kick-off.'

'I'll gag you if I have to, you know that, right?'

'I bet you'd love to.'

'These are special circumstances. I can do whatever I want, if I think the situation merits it.'

'It's the same as the weather, that's all I'm saying, Tom.

Murder is. You know it's coming, because it always has, but you don't know what and exactly when and basically there's sod all you can do about it. *You* know better than most why most murders happen. People kill each other because they've had one glass too many or because they fancy someone they shouldn't. Because they're greedy or getting their own back or because someone looked at their other half the wrong way in the pub. They snap one day after too many years being bullied or belittled or passed over. Ordinary, dull, stupid reasons. So, you know why murders happen, but it doesn't make it any easier to stop them happening, does it? Harder, if anything. I mean, yes, it might make the killers a bit easier to catch, but those same reasons for doing it in the first place are going to be there year after year, century after century. Making more work for priests and gravediggers and people like you.'

'You've clearly got far too much time to think.'

'And whose fault is that?'

'Maybe you should be spending a bit more of it doing things. Making yourself useful.'

'What, you think I should be getting busy in the prison workshop? You think I need a hobby?'

'Why not?'

'You wouldn't let me have a spoon. You really think the Fletchers of this world want to let me loose with power tools? Now ... in terms of weather, your ordinary murderers, your drunks and jealous husbands and skint smackheads ... they're just like ... drizzle, or whatever.

They're everyday, much-as-we-expected. They're bog-standard. No challenge at all for someone like you, am I right?'

'You think it's a game?'

'Far from it. I'm just saying, not exactly taxing, is it? When the wife who's been having an affair is lying on the kitchen floor with her brains bashed in and her old man's done a runner. When the arsehole who likes to knock his girlfriend around gets a bread knife stuck in his chest while he's asleep and there's a blood-soaked nightie in the washing basket. Even a copper like that retard you've stuck in the chapel could crack cases like that, right? That's just normal weather conditions. But then there's the freak stuff that you can never see coming. The tsunamis and the tornados. The deadly weather.'

'And that's killers like you, is it? The special ones. That what you're saying?'

'I'm saying . . . not run of the mill.'

'You're every bit as ordinary. Every bit as stupid.'

'You know that's not true.'

'You're a bog-standard nutter who makes a splash and gets ideas above his station.'

'A splash?'

'A few books and TV documentaries and thinks he's way more important than he actually is.'

'Karim could never have caught me though, could he?'

'How the hell should I know?'

'Course you know. You know it's the likes of me that get

your blood jumping. Same as those idiots that get off being in the middle of hurricanes, the ones that go looking for them.'

'I need to get some sleep . . .'

'Come on, be honest, just for once. If you had a choice between solving a hundred ordinary murders . . . catching a hundred examples of drizzle on two legs, or one of me, what would you choose?'

'This is stupid.'

'Admit it, Tom, you're a storm-chaser.'

'Go to fucking sleep.'

'I told you—'

'*Try.*'

Thorne closed his eyes, but they were quickly open again. Wide and unblinking. Watching the cobwebs dance in slow motion just below the ceiling and struggling suddenly to hear the sea above the roaring of his blood.

Asking himself a question that Nicklin had already answered.

What the hell have you got to be excited about?

FIFTY-FOUR

It might have been an hour later, or perhaps it was two, and Thorne was listening to the low rattle and wheeze of Nicklin snoring, when he heard footsteps on the landing. He sat up and swung his feet to the floor just as Fletcher appeared, putting on his jacket, in the bedroom doorway.

'Batchelor needs the toilet.'

Thorne saw Jenks arrive at Fletcher's shoulder, Batchelor with his handcuffs back on, pale suddenly and haggard.

'You want to take a radio?' Thorne asked.

'He's not going to be long.' Fletcher turned to Batchelor. 'Are you, Jeff?'

Batchelor shook his head.

'Take Holland with you, if you like.'

'I think we can manage,' Fletcher said. 'This one's no trouble.'

'Long as he has no trouble doing what he needs to do.' Jenks grimaced and hunched his shoulders, fastened the top button on his jacket. 'Still pissing down out there.' He ushered Batchelor away towards the top of the stairs and Fletcher followed a few seconds later.

Thorne listened to the steps as Batchelor and the prison officers descended. Their voices muffled, then barely audible at all. The dull, distant clatter as the bolt on the back door was thrown back. Becoming aware that the snoring had stopped, Thorne turned to see that Nicklin was wide awake and watching him.

FIFTY-FIVE

Batchelor sits on a cold wooden seat and does what he was only ever supposed to be pretending to do, but which has now become something he needs more than he can ever remember. He sits and empties his bladder and bowels and listens to Fletcher and Jenks talking outside the door, the rise and fall of their exchange just audible above the clatter of the rain on the corrugated iron roof. Fletcher, who had told him 'not to make a meal of it'. Jenks, who had always treated him decently enough, who had taken one look at the spartan facilities and shuddered and said, 'Wouldn't be able to go, myself. No bloody chance. Need a few more of the home comforts, mate. Proper bog paper for a kick-off and something decent to read.'

Batchelor sits and does what he has to, a long way past caring.

Now, it's almost time and he still can't put them together in any way that sounds acceptable. The things he wants to say to his wife. He's presuming that it's all going to go the way he's been promised, that he'll get his chance. He looks at his watch. Sonia will almost certainly be in bed by now, dead to the world on all those pills she's been gulping down every night since Jodi died. It might end up being no more than a message in the end, a few stammered words after the beep.

Just as well, probably, he thinks.

Hearing her voice would only make it harder.

Make it impossible . . .

Outside the door, Jenks laughs and Fletcher says, 'Yeah, well it's what they do, isn't it? The French. Basically, they just shit in a hole in the floor. Like the bog seat hasn't been invented or they can't afford one because they've spent all their money on garlic, or whatever.'

Batchelor hears Jenks say something and laugh again. Then there are footsteps and a third voice outside the door.

A London accent, a chuckle in it.

'Bloody hell, don't tell me you're the queue.'

'No, mate,' Fletcher says. 'You'll have to jog on though.'

'Sorry?'

'We're prison officers and we're working. One of our prisoners is in there.'

'So?'

'Come on, mate, don't be a twat about it. Just use the shitter in the next cottage along, there's a good lad.'

413

Batchelor sits and sweats and pushes back tears with the heels of his hands. He knows what's coming, so after a few seconds he moves his hands from his eyes to his ears because nobody says he has to listen to it, and then, with the noise from outside deadened by the thrum of his rushing pulse, the stench and the dread yield one glorious moment of revelation and he finally realises what he needs to say to Sonia.

That there's only ever been one thing he's wanted to tell her.

Nicklin says, 'I don't see what you're so worried about, Tom.'

Thorne turns from the window. 'Sorry?'

'I think Fletcher and Jenks can handle one prisoner using the toilet.'

'I know.'

'So, what was all that about Holland going with them? Taking a radio.'

'Since when do I answer to you?'

'Just making conversation.'

'Did I miss the bit where you became a detective chief inspector?'

Nicklin laughs and shifts back on the mattress, the bedsprings groaning beneath him, until he is sitting up. The hand that is cuffed to the frame is now twisted behind his back. 'Actually, I think I'd make a pretty good copper,' he says. 'A DI at least, I reckon . . . Murder Squad, obviously.'

He looks at Thorne, scratches at his chest with his free hand. 'You know, takes one to know one and all that.'

Thorne steps back across to the window. He can see a single torch beam below in the rear garden, the small circle of light fixed against the bottom of the toilet door, as though the torch is on the ground. He can just make out shapes in the rain and the rhythm of a conversation.

'Maybe that's why you're so good at it,' Nicklin says.

Batchelor is trying not to listen, but in the end he cannot help himself and he knows the sounds, because he recognises them.

He has heard them before.

He cannot be certain of the method, though the speed of what happens coupled with the fact that there is not *that* much noise means that he can hazard a guess. Surprise is an important weapon, of course, but with one man against two, something rather more tangible was always going to be required. So, not identical, these terrible sounds on the other side of the door, but close enough.

Panic and terror, then realisation.

They were the sounds Nathan Wilson had made, his face a mask of blood by then and something that was not blood leaking from the back of his skull on to the pavement. The sounds of someone fighting for their life. Moans and gasps as Batchelor had smashed the boy's head down again and again and half-spluttered pleas that went unheeded until they became drooled and fractured mumblings.

415

The ragged fall of that last breath.

Now, a few feet away from him, there are other noises, a little more prosaic, that tell Batchelor the situation outside has changed, is moving forward. The soft thump of a body as it hits the ground, an arm flailing through long grass, and slowing. The clatter as someone slumps against the side of the outhouse and slides down.

Then nothing. Half a minute when it's just the rain and the wind and the gurgling in his gut, until he hears the heavy steps flattening the wet grass and sees the door give a little as someone leans against it.

Hears the voice, the mouth up close to the wood, the London accent with a chuckle in it.

The man outside the door says, 'Time to go, Jeff.'

Thorne bangs on the window, the glass rattling in the frame, but he sees no movement below him, no reaction of any kind. He tries to open it, but it's been painted shut and refuses to budge.

He turns and walks back to the doorway. He leans out and shouts along the corridor.

'Dave . . . '

'I don't know why you're getting so worked up,' Nicklin says. 'It's not been that long.'

Thorne shouts again.

'Maybe Jeff's having a little trouble.' Nicklin pulls a face. 'I mean, it's hardly surprising, is it? It's not as if anyone's been eating very healthily the last few days.'

416

Holland shouts back. 'Everything all right?'

'I need you.' Thorne steps back into the room and goes back to the window.

'Maybe you should go down there yourself,' Nicklin says.

'Thanks for the advice.'

'Just saying, if you're really worried.'

Holland appears, blinking in the doorway, pulling a sweater on over a T-shirt. He yawns and says, 'What?'

'I need you to go downstairs and check on Laurel and Hardy,' Thorne says. 'They took Batchelor out to use the toilet and that was about twenty minutes ago.'

'It was ten minutes, tops,' Nicklin says.

'I know how long it was.'

Nicklin looks at Holland, rolls his eyes. 'He's panicking.'

'Take your radio,' Thorne says.

'Right.'

'Where is it?'

'It's in the bedroom.'

'Well go back and get it and get down there.'

Thorne and Nicklin watch Holland turn and walk quickly back towards his bedroom. Thorne moves back into the room and resumes his position at the window.

'You can go with him if you want,' Nicklin says. He rattles his cuffs against the bedstead. 'It's not like I'm going anywhere, is it? Well, not yet anyway.'

Thorne turns from the window and looks at him. He feels a flicker of something in his gut, there for a second, then gone.

The cuffs are rattled again. 'Something tells me you'll be taking these off in a minute.'

'I don't think so,' Thorne says.

Nicklin leans back and closes his eyes. Says, 'We'll see.'

Holland sees the two bodies as soon as he pushes open the back door and sweeps the torch beam across the garden. Jenks is lying on his belly in the grass. Fletcher is sitting with his back against the toilet wall, as though it's a balmy summer's evening and he's catching forty winks. There is blood pooled between his legs and the rain has begun to take it, running in stringy rivulets and dripping off the edge of the concrete platform on which the toilet has been built.

Holland keys his radio. He squeezes hard to control the tremor in his fingers. He says, 'Fletcher and Jenks are down. Stabbed, looks like. They're both down.'

He waits, stepping towards the toilet door, which is closed.

Thorne's voice crackles back at him. 'Say again, Dave.'

'Shit . . . there's so much fucking blood.'

'Whose blood, Dave? Where's Batchelor?'

Holland yells out as he kicks the door open. It clatters against the wall and swings back again, but Holland can see that the stall is empty. 'Batchelor's gone,' he says. 'Fletcher and Jenks are down and Batchelor's gone.' He turns on the spot and swings his torch around wildly, in case Batchelor is still somewhere nearby, but there's only rain and the dark wall at the end of the garden. The mountain rising up on the other side.

'What about signs of life, Dave?' Thorne is not shouting, but his voice is raised and he is speaking slowly. 'Have you checked for signs of life?'

Holland is panting by now. He wipes the rain from his eyes, lays his torch on the grass and kneels down next to Fletcher. He grabs a wrist and presses his ear to the officer's chest. It comes away wet, and the radio is slick with blood when he brings it to his mouth.

'Nothing,' he says.

'Are you sure?'

He crawls across to where Jenks is lying and turns him over, grunting with the effort. The man's chest is sodden, the stain on his jacket black in the half-light from the open doorway behind them.

'Dave?'

He checks for a pulse. He leans close to the man's face and waits for a breath, holding his own while he listens.

'Shit.'

'Talk to me, Dave.'

'Shit . . . there's nothing,' Holland says. 'Just blood . . .'

Thorne is still at the bedroom window, the radio pressed to his ear, listening to Holland gasp and curse, when he spots the torch beam moving on the mountainside. The light skitters, perhaps five hundred yards away and fifty feet up,

419

briefly illuminating rocky outcrops and grey clumps of heather and gorse as it climbs upwards.

He keys the transmit button.

'Batchelor's on the mountain,' he says. 'Him and whoever killed Fletcher and Jenks. You need to get after him, Dave.'

'You don't think Batchelor killed them?'

'No chance,' Thorne says. 'Somebody came for him.' He looks again, but he can't see the torchlight any longer. 'Quick as you can, Dave. I'll radio Karim and get him to follow you.'

Holland tells Thorne that he's on his way.

It's still dark on the mountainside and Thorne guesses that whoever is using the torch knows very well that there's a chance he will be seen and is choosing to use it only when necessary. He looks down into the garden and sees the beam of light swing as Holland picks his own torch up.

He turns to Nicklin. 'This was never about you, was it? It was always about Batchelor escaping.'

'Well, it's an escape of a sort, I suppose,' Nicklin says.

Thorne sees Nicklin smile, waiting for the penny to drop and when it does Thorne understands what Batchelor is doing, what he's being led away to do.

'This is the perfect place for him to do it,' Nicklin says. 'Very peaceful very . . . spiritual. Besides, you'd be amazed how hard it is to get it done in prison. They've been watching him anyway, you know, since he had his wobble when he got that boy's letter. But even if they weren't, it's never very easy. Trust me, if it was, people inside would be topping themselves every day of the week.'

Suddenly Holland's voice cuts in, hoarse, urgent. 'I was wrong. Jenks is still breathing. Jesus . . . '

'You sure?'

'He's alive, but only just.' Holland sounds close to tears. 'What the hell are we going to do?'

'I'll sort it, Dave.'

'We need to get him to hospital . . . get a helicopter or something.'

'I said, I'll sort it. I can get a phone signal at the abbey ruins.' Thorne is already moving across to the bed. He drops down on to the edge and reaches for his boots. 'You get after Batchelor, all right?'

'Shouldn't I wait with Jenks?'

'Listen, if you don't get to Batchelor before he reaches the top of that mountain, there's going to be another body to worry about.'

'OK . . . '

'Be careful, all right, Dave? Whoever's up there with him is obviously dangerous. As soon as I've made the call I'll join you.'

Holland tells Thorne that he's on the move. He says, 'Don't forget to call Karim.'

Thorne ends the transmission, punches the button again and says, 'Sam, are you awake? We've got an emergency up here. Sam . . . ?' He struggles to pull his boots on, cursing as he waits for a response.

421

'I don't want you to tell Karim what's happening,' Nicklin says.

Thorne looks up. 'What?'

'Tell him to relax. Tell him there's nothing to worry about.'

Thorne freezes, fingers tight around his bootlaces.

'Yes,' Nicklin says, 'you *are* going to the abbey ruins, but I'd prefer it if you left your phone here, along with your radio.'

Thorne gets slowly to his feet. That lurching in his belly is back suddenly and it stays there, like speeding across an endless series of humpbacked bridges. 'What's going on?'

'Remember the letters?' Nicklin asks. 'The ones I wrote to my mother?'

Suddenly, Thorne cannot think straight. He shakes his head, struggling to understand. 'Yes ... what?'

Nicklin's expression makes it perfectly clear that he's enjoying Thorne's confusion, the delay before he puts him out of his misery. 'Look, I know what you think you're supposed to do, what the procedure is, and so on. The thing is, I'm not really sure you can save Alan Jenks anyway and, more to the point, aren't there other people you care about more?' Nicklin waits, cocks his head. 'People that need you?'

Thorne stares at his prisoner for no more than a second or two, but he sees a confidence borne out of craft and careful planning; of complete certainty that Nicklin is going to get what he wants, because he knows Thorne too well.

When the radio crackles into life and Samir Karim says, 'I'm here, guv. What's the problem?' Thorne raises the radio slowly to his mouth.

He says, 'Relax, Sam, it's nothing to worry about.'

Across from him, Nicklin nods his approval.

'False alarm.'

Batchelor stumbles again in his effort to keep up and cries out as his palm is scraped by the edge of a low rock.

'You all right?'

Batchelor nods, too out of breath to shout.

The man who stabbed Fletcher and Jenks is perhaps twenty feet ahead of him and has not lost his footing once. Batchelor has still not got a good look at him, but the man seems young, certainly younger than he had been expecting. Not that he had known what to expect, not really. It was just that, despite some of the events he had witnessed in prison, the people he had encountered, it still seemed strange to him that someone so young could do such things so easily.

Every couple of minutes, the man turns the torch on for a few seconds, scans the terrain up ahead, then turns it off again. He clearly knows where he's going, has already worked out the quickest route to the top and the cliffs on the other side.

Batchelor watches the man stop, waiting for him to catch up.

'Come on,' the man says. 'We haven't got all night.'

He tries to move faster, but it feels as though there are weights attached to his boots and despite the water that has soaked through his trousers, his legs feel like they're burning with the effort of lifting them.

'This is for you, you know,' the man says.

Batchelor knows that it is, but finds it hard to feel anything like gratitude when other, stronger feelings are crowding in, demanding space. He'd heard those noises and seen the blood. He had been made to step over the body lying in the grass.

'Besides which, there are other things we've got to do tonight.'

Batchelor is well aware of that, of course. The plans made for him are no more than the start of it. A distraction.

When he gets to within a few feet of his guide, Batchelor says, 'What about the phone?'

'What about it?'

'I was promised that I could make a call. I need to make a call.'

'No signal yet,' the man says.

'You get one on the mountain.' Batchelor steps closer to the man. 'That's what I was told.'

'Not until we're nearer the top.'

'How do you know? You haven't even looked.'

The man ignores him. He turns away and flicks the torch on. For a few seconds, Batchelor can see raindrops falling from the bushes and splashing on to black earth and glistening slabs of rock. Looking up through the drizzle, he can see a sky decorated with more stars than he even knew existed.

He decides that these are the things he'll try and hold on to for what's left of his climb. What's left of everything. He resolves to push away all those other images, the memories that remain washed in innocent blood, and to try and remember the good things instead.

The things for which he counts himself blessed.

Up ahead, the man turns the torch off. He says, 'Onwards and upwards.'

The instructions he has been given are all about where to look and what to look for. Nicklin has said nothing specific about timing, but Thorne knows very well that he needs to run. In daylight and good weather, it would be just a short walk back down to the chapel, but the track has grown more treacherous and even with a torch to light the ground ahead, it takes him five minutes to reach the ruins at the end of the graveyard.

He is out of breath by the time he gets to the bell tower, but it's panic as much as exhaustion. He steps inside and walks towards the arrangement of large, flat stones at the far end.

'It's not really an altar,' Nicklin had said. 'Just looks like one, but whatever it is, there's an offering waiting for you. There's a small space underneath the stones. You just need to reach inside . . .'

Thorne kneels down and does what Nicklin has asked.

His fingers close around something and he pulls out a brown, A4-sized Jiffy bag wrapped in clear plastic. He stands up and uses his torch to examine it, but there's no writing, no postmark. Nothing. Just a sealed envelope.

Thorne turns and looks across the graveyard to the chapel, huddled against the foot of the mountain, the lights burning inside. He could be there in less than a minute and briefing Sam Karim. Sending him after Holland or down to the observatory to rouse the warden and use his satellite phone to call the mainland. If Alan Jenks is not dead already, Thorne could be making an effort to save his life.

He turns the padded envelope over in his hands.

Without knowing what its contents are, Thorne knows instinctively that they leave him with no choice but to do what he's been told. He remembers the look on Nicklin's face and knows that doing anything else will cost him in ways he is trying hard not to think about.

Helen, Alfie . . .

A seal screams from the rocks down by the quay and Thorne steps out of the tower. He turns back towards the Old House and does not stop running until he is standing at the foot of the bed to which Stuart Nicklin still lies handcuffed.

'Doesn't matter how old you are, does it?' Nicklin says. 'It's always exciting when the post arrives.'

Sweating and still breathing heavily, Thorne holds out

the package, water dripping from the plastic wrapping, from his sleeve.

Nicklin lazily raises the wrist that is handcuffed to the bed-frame and waits for it to catch. 'I think you'll have to open it,' he says.

Thorne looks down at the envelope and wipes away the moisture from the wrapping. He hesitates, dry-mouthed, his guts watery.

'Any time you like,' Nicklin says.

Thorne rips away the plastic, turns the envelope and tears at the seal. He opens it and stares inside. He says, 'For Christ's sake, are you joking?' then empties four chocolate bars on to the bed.

'Those are mine,' Nicklin says, reaching eagerly for one and nodding at the envelope. 'I think there's something else in there though.'

Thorne reaches into the envelope and brings out a smaller, padded package. He quickly tears it open and removes contents which are almost weightless; something paper-thin and pressed between two sheets of kitchen towel.

Watching, Nicklin tears with his teeth at the wrapper of his chocolate bar and takes a bite.

Thorne lifts the top sheet of kitchen towel, which sticks to whatever is beneath it for a second or two and comes away stained. A few spots like old blood on a plaster. Something creamy, pus-coloured.

It takes him a moment or two to understand what he's holding.

It's a ragged square, pinkish-brown, maybe six inches by six and curling a little at the edges. A pattern of some sort . . .

'I hope it's in decent nick,' Nicklin says. 'I told them to take good care of it.'

Trying and failing to swallow, Thorne continues to stare down at the piece of human skin now lying across his palm. The bile rising into his throat is beaten only by a strangled gasp when he recognises the design. The swirling letters, the fine lines in red and blue ink.

'Right,' Nicklin says, still chewing. He raises his wrist again, but this time there is no trace of humour in his voice. 'Let's get these fucking things off, shall we?'

Immediately, Thorne reaches into his inside pocket for the key to the handcuffs, but he does not look up, does not take his eyes off the delicate slice of skin. His thumb moves gently across the edge of it, traces what there is of the familiar image, the fragment of a word.

Aren't there other people you care about more?

He had been there when the tattoo was done.

FIFTY-SIX

Batchelor had been right, and had been unable to talk to his wife on the phone. As it was, Sonia had stopped answering the phone a long time ago anyway. There had been so many abusive phone calls. Not only because of what he had done to Nathan Wilson, but from sickos who just wanted to say something cruel about Jodi. The same sort of twisted individuals who had never met or even heard of his daughter before, but who seemed to take delight in leaving messages on her Facebook page, in the days following her death.

> saddo! won't be missed
> sorry your not hanging about any more
> obvs your boyf was right to chuck a loser like u . . .

He had been enraged at first, but later the anger had given way to pity.

What on earth happened to people?

Even now, all these months later, mail was still opened carefully and calls were screened. Calling from the prison, he would wait for the beep, then say, 'It's me,' knowing she would be listening if she was there, that she would pick up. Not at this time of night though. No amount of shouting was going to wake her once those pills had kicked in.

His wife's anger had never given way to anything.

He had left a message, said what he needed to.

Up ahead, the man with the torch was waiting for him again, but this time Batchelor knew it was not because he was lagging behind. The man had not stopped to let him catch up. It was simply because there was no further he could go.

With the man training the torch to help him, Batchelor closed the distance between them as quickly as he could. He pushed through tangles of sodden heather and clambered over a series of rocks. Huge, flat stones lying one across the other, the way he used to leave plates draining beside the sink, too lazy to dry them up.

You wash, Dad, I'll dry . . .

Once upon a time, before it had all fallen apart, Jodi and he had done the washing-up together. Singing along with the radio and dancing like idiots, Rachel scowling at the pair of them from the other side of the kitchen.

Do you really have to sing that loud?

'Right,' the man with the torch said.

'Right.'

'I suppose I should leave you to it.'

Batchelor said, 'Thanks.' Without knowing what the etiquette for such situations was, he held out a hand.

The man leaned in to shake it, then stepped away again. 'OK, then. Good luck . . . '

Batchelor nodded, but luck was the one thing he did not need. Gravity would certainly get the job done. He just needed to summon one final surge of courage. He turned and watched his guide – the man with the torch, the man with the knife – walk away along the cliff edge, then turned back to face the sea and the vast emptiness above it.

It's what I want, Jode, you know that. But now I'm actually here . . . you know?

The wind had gathered strength suddenly as they'd got closer to the top. It was still no worse than heavy drizzle, but the wind was whipping the rain into his face, needle-sharp. He grimaced and tried to turn away from it, but it was impossible to avoid if he wanted to face the drop head-on.

Obviously, I hate doing this to your mum and especially to Rachel, but it feels right, and besides, I'm fairly sure their lives will be a lot better without me dragging them down. I know you're not alone, I know Nathan is with you, but I need to be with you too and the truth is I can't stand feeling this any more. I don't want to wake up every morning and have to face what I did. This feels like drawing a line under everything . . . if that makes any sense.

He laughed out loud.

Well, I'm guessing it does, because if anyone knows what that feels like it's you. Right, love?

He could hear gulls screeching nearby. He could see nothing looking up, so he wondered if they were nesting. Perhaps they felt threatened and were simply letting him know that they would fight to protect their young.

I was too late for that, wasn't I, Jode? And when I did fight, I picked the wrong target. Silly old sod . . .

He bent to pick up a stone and lobbed it into the darkness, losing sight of it well before it hit the rocks a hundred feet below. He closed his eyes and asked himself which was better. Should he lean and topple or simply step out into nothingness?

He was amazed he hadn't thought of this until now.

He suddenly found himself thinking about Wile E. Coyote chasing The Road Runner and running out of land. Those legs wheeling in fresh air for a few seconds before he drops, that lugubrious expression on his face when he realises what's about to happen. Always the same, comical sound effect.

Coming, best girl.

Batchelor stepped out, smiling.

FIFTY-SEVEN

Thorne was sitting on his bed, watching Nicklin on the bed opposite, rubbing his wrists and polishing off his second bar of chocolate, when Holland came through on the radio.

'It's no good,' Holland said. He sounded frantic, exhausted. 'I don't want to use the torch too much because they'll see me coming, but it's pitch black up here, so I've no bloody idea where I am. Unless I'm following exactly the same route they are, I've got no bloody chance. Hello ...?'

Thorne looked at Nicklin, who nodded to give his permission. 'Just keep trying, Dave.'

'I'm telling you, it's a waste of time.'

'Stick at it, OK?'

'Where's Karim? Did you send him?'

'He's not far behind you.'

'I'll call him.'

Thorne saw Nicklin shake his head. 'Don't do that, Dave. I need to keep the channels clear.' The lies came easily. 'I sent him to the Warden's to call for a helicopter. Look, as soon as I've heard something back from Sam, I'll get up there myself. We clear?'

'Nicely done,' Nicklin said, when Thorne laid the radio down. He picked up a third chocolate bar then dropped it back on to the bed. 'Best save a couple of those for later.'

Thorne looked at the patch of skin that was now lying on the small table between the two beds. 'Is he alive?' The last word caught in his throat, so he swallowed and asked again.

'I tell you something,' Nicklin said. 'It was hysterical, you barging into that cell the other night. You were so bloody cocky about my mother's letters, thinking you knew something you didn't.' He lowered his voice a little, a bad imitation of Thorne's. '"I'm in your head". Not if I don't want you to be, you're not.'

'Answer me.'

'I'd love to say there were clues in there, in the letters, but that might be stretching it a bit. I mean, not even *I'm* that good and I hadn't planned this back then, not all of it, anyway. It's weird though, isn't it, some of the things that were in there, the things that you didn't pick up on? Like I knew, but I didn't know, like maybe there was something subconscious going on when I wrote them. You see what I'm getting at? All that stuff about you and your friends,

434

how loyal you are.' He smiled. 'That line about friendship being "more than skin deep?" Classic. Something told me even then that you'd end up reading them. I knew bloody well my mother wasn't reading them.'

'*Is he alive?*'

'Well, those who are helping me have certainly been *told* to keep him alive and well.' Nicklin nodded towards the square of skin that had been cut from Phil Hendricks' back. 'Well, alive at any rate.'

'Because, if he isn't, or if anything else happens to him—'

Nicklin held up a hand. 'Yes, yes,' he said. 'Taken as read. I won't get away with it, blah blah blah, I'll be looking over my shoulder for the rest of my life. But it's really up to you, isn't it? How willing you are to go along with a few simple instructions.'

Thorne waited. He suddenly remembered what Helen had told him about speaking to a man she had assumed to be Phil's latest conquest. That had clearly been one of those helping Nicklin; someone who must also have been responsible for the text Thorne had received from Hendricks a few days earlier. It was becoming apparent that there were several of them: the man who had killed Fletcher and taken Batchelor; those who were holding Hendricks.

Accomplices, *disciples* . . .

Twisted and needy, fame-hungry. A certain type of killer attracted a certain breed of acolyte and there could be nobody better than Stuart Nicklin at cultivating a willing network of them.

Something else suddenly became terribly obvious. 'It wasn't Huw Morgan who called and spoke to Burnham, was it?'

'He's obviously a damn good mimic though, you have to admit that.'

'Are they both dead?'

'You'll need to be more specific.'

'Huw Morgan and his father.'

'Well, I can't be a hundred per cent certain,' Nicklin said. 'I gave no specific instructions either way, but one or two of my little helpers are rather eager to please, so there's a fair chance, yes.' He nodded to acknowledge Thorne's look of disgust, then raised his hands as though keen to stress the mitigating circumstances. 'Come on, I couldn't rely on the weather turning, could I? So, we had to make sure there was no way the boat could get back here. Actually, I've got no idea what the weather's really doing over there, but obviously I'm hoping it's not going to be too tricky to get a boat over. I mean, getting off the island is rather the point.'

Thorne understood now that Nicklin was planning to do exactly what he had done twenty-five years earlier, the first time he had escaped from Bardsey Island. There was a boat coming, probably piloted by whoever had made sure the Morgans were unable to come. They were probably already on their way to collect Nicklin and his accomplice on the island, the man who had taken Batchelor on to the mountain.

'How much did Batchelor know?' Thorne asked.

'No more than he needed to,' Nicklin said. 'He didn't actually want to know any more. It was just about him getting the chance to top himself the way he wanted, that was all. I mean he knew more or less what I was planning to do, course he did.'

'But he didn't know about Hendricks.'

'Oh God, no. He would never have agreed. Far too squeamish. I even offered to make sure that the kid who was really responsible for his daughter's death was made to suffer, once I'd sorted myself out, but he wasn't interested. He's very forgiving.' Nicklin glanced towards the window. 'Actually, we should probably be talking about poor old Jeff in the past tense by now.'

Thorne could not help wondering if the same thing would apply to Alan Jenks. He looked across and all too easily imagined flying at Stuart Nicklin, doing a lot more damage than he had done all those years before in that playground. But he remembered the feel of his friend's dead flesh beneath his fingers and knew that, whatever else happened, he must fight the urge to hurt the man responsible.

'So, what do we do now?'

'Well, it must be obvious to you what's at stake. Yes?'

Thorne nodded.

'I'm giving you my word that once I'm safely off this

shitty rock and back on the mainland, I'll make the necessary call and your friend will be released. You just need to make sure that I'm given adequate time to get there. Once that happens, obviously all bets are off and I understand that you and a lot of your colleagues will be out looking for me, but you need to make sure that doesn't happen before I make the call.'

'It won't.'

'That's good to hear.'

'I'll do whatever I have to.'

Nicklin nodded, looking pleased, then stood up and told Thorne to lie down. 'Quick as you can.'

Thorne did as he was told and saw Nicklin moving towards him, brandishing the handcuffs. 'Come on, there's no need for those.'

'Best to cover all the bases,' Nicklin said.

'I've told you, you'll get what you need. Why would I risk anything happening to Phil?'

'Oh, if I'm being honest I know you won't,' Nicklin said. 'This bit's just for me.' He grabbed Thorne's wrist, dragged it across and cuffed it to the bedstead. When he was finished he stood back to admire his handiwork. He raised his hands and mimed taking a photograph. 'It's an image I'll enjoy taking away with me, that's all. Just a bit of fun.'

'You know Holland will be back?' Thorne said. 'Maybe well before you get taken off the island?'

'That's a possibility.'

438

'What do I tell him?'

'Anything you like,' Nicklin said. 'You could always just tell him the truth, I'm sure he'll understand. Come to that, you'll need to think about what you're going to tell everyone else who's going to want to know what happened. You could try telling them that, while you were preoccupied with an escaped prisoner, I somehow managed to get my cuffs off and overpower you.' He moved his head from side to side, like he was weighing the story up, how well it would play. 'Or like I said, just tell them exactly what happened, that you were trying to save a life. You might want to finesse things a little, fiddle with the timings. Leaving a prison officer to die is never going to sound good, is it, however much you tart it up?'

Nicklin moved to the corner into which his jacket and boots had been tossed. He sat on a chair and began to put them on. He said, 'You shouldn't be too hard on yourself about this.'

'I'll try not to be,' Thorne said.

'Seriously. It's worked out pretty well for Simon Milner's mother, hasn't it? For Eileen Bennett's family.'

It struck Thorne that Brigstocke had said much the same thing only a few hours earlier. 'What about Jeff Batchelor's family?'

'That was his choice.'

'Fletcher and Jenks didn't have a lot of choice, did they?'

'They chose the job, same as you did. You deal with dangerous people, there's always going to be an element of risk.' Nicklin finished fastening his boots, stood and walked back across to the bed.

Thorne looked up at him and they stared at one another for a few long seconds. 'Haven't you gone yet?'

'Come on, when a plan comes together, when you get to a moment like this, you have to enjoy it a bit, don't you? Plus there's one other thing.' He took a step closer, his knees against the edge of the bed. 'Twice now, you've done a good deal of damage to my face.' He rubbed a hand across his mouth, gently dabbed at his cheeks. 'Once in person and once in a rather more cowardly fashion by getting someone else to put broken glass into my food.'

'You'd tried to hurt my friend.'

'Oh I remember.'

'And you've got your own back now, wouldn't you say?'

Nicklin said, 'That's a matter of opinion,' and bent to punch Thorne hard in the face.

Thorne cried out, tasting the blood filling his mouth, feeling for teeth which were no longer where they should be. Breathing heavily, he turned his head and looked back up at Nicklin, who was rubbing his knuckles, flexing the fingers. As soon as he had resumed eye contact, Thorne sucked in a deep breath and said, 'Again . . .'

Nicklin nodded and Thorne tensed, closing his eyes as the fist came down a second time. He felt his lip split when his front teeth burst through it and blood leaking from his nose. When he opened his eyes a few seconds later and blinked away the tears, Nicklin had gone.

There were only footsteps going down the stairs and a tune being whistled it would take Thorne until the following day to place.

'I've Got You Under My Skin'.

THREE WEEKS LATER

MARKED
ON THE INSIDE

FIFTY-EIGHT

Driving to the school after the conversation with the police officer, Sonia Batchelor did her best to keep the anger in check. She did not want Rachel to see it. Things were tough enough as it was and she did not want her daughter to think that she was not in control, not keeping on top of things.

It was hard though.

There had been that same exasperation in Kitson's voice, something else that sounded like boredom.

'Yes, me again,' Sonia had said.

'You weren't joking, were you?'

'Of course I wasn't. I told you, I won't be fobbed off.'

'Nobody's trying to fob you off, Sonia.'

'Good. So, any news?'

It had been a week since she had announced that she would be calling twice every day, morning and afternoon, and would continue doing so until someone told her when her husband's body was going to be released. When she and Rachel could bury him. Today, Kitson had sighed, then said what she had said the day before and the day before that.

'Your husband's death is closely connected to the murders of two prison officers. It's part of the same case. Until investigations have been satisfactorily completed, it can't be released. I'm sorry.'

'And when's that likely to be?'

The exasperation obvious then. 'You must know I can't possibly answer that.'

'Jeff killed himself.'

'Nothing is official though, I'm afraid. Not yet.'

The inquest into Jeffrey Batchelor's death had been convened and immediately adjourned, as per standard procedure. As yet, no date had been set for its resumption.

'I don't understand what you're all waiting for,' Sonia had said. 'What it is you still don't know.'

'I'm sorry—'

'He left me a message.'

'Look, I know it's hard, Sonia, but it's just the way things are done.'

There had not been a great deal to say after that. Once again, she had asked if it was possible to talk to the detective who had been there when it had happened. Kitson had told her that Tom Thorne wasn't in today and that, for obvious reasons, he was not directly involved in the investigation.

Sonia had seen him on the news.

It had been a big story, after all. Front page and first up on the TV news for almost a week. An escaped serial killer, two murdered prison officers, an attack on a pair of local fishermen – father and son – leaving one of them dead. Jeff's death not worthy of its own headline; a sidebar at best.

It had not been the detective's fault, that had been made very clear from the word go. Doctors, police officers, prison governors queuing up to say that the man responsible was one of the most dangerous and manipulative psychopaths they had ever encountered.

Right, and now he was running around somewhere.

After fifteen minutes trying to find a parking place, she was ready to scream. She wanted to jump from the car and punch somebody. Instead, she sat, watching the kids come out, scanning each group of girls for her daughter's face, fingers tight around the steering wheel. In truth of course, it wasn't Kitson she was angry with, or Tom Thorne or the stupid way things were done.

It was Jeff himself.

He left a message . . .

'*Sonia, love, it's me. There isn't a lot of time and there's not much of a signal where I am, so I'd best be quick. Doesn't take too long to say sorry, so I should probably be all right. There's nothing else to say that you don't both know already . . . you and Rachel. So, I'm sorry. That's it, darling. I'm so sorry . . .*'

She spotted Rachel walking out of the gate on her own,

seeing the car and raising a hand. Sonia pressed a button on the dash to open the car's boot, then turned her face away and reached into her bag for tissues.

Rachel tossed her bag into the boot and climbed into the car. She automatically leaned forward to retune the radio.

'You OK?' Sonia asked.

'Yeah, fine.'

'Did anybody say anything?'

'A couple of stupid comments, that's all.' Rachel shrugged. 'Doesn't bother me, Mum, I swear.'

Rachel was refusing to look at her, but Sonia could see the smallest tightening of skin, the tremor in her daughter's chin. She started the car and accelerated out into traffic, forcing a 4x4 to brake hard, ignoring the blare of a horn and refusing to raise a hand in apology.

Thinking: *Coward, coward, coward . . .*

Annie Nicklin had spent the evening playing gin rummy with a couple of the residents who were still awake by nine o'clock. They had all laughed a fair bit and shared a packet of custard creams, and she had won, which was gratifying, though it didn't much matter of course.

When the game had finished and the staff began ushering residents towards their beds, Annie collected a large glass of water from the kitchen and walked slowly back to her room. She said goodnight to her favourite care-worker. The young woman she shared a fag with sometimes, who popped out to get her a bottle of something every now and again. The one who talked to her without letting her eyes drift towards those of a nearby colleague she was hoping might come across and rescue her.

They stood and watched the lights flashing on the artificial Christmas tree in the corner.

'You been fleecing Betty and Frank again?' the woman asked.

'It was only rummy,' Annie said. 'And I had to keep telling them the rules.'

The woman laughed and said, 'Sleep well, Annie.'

'You too,' Annie said.

As soon as she'd closed the door to her room, she switched on the radio, the volume nice and low. Just a voice to keep her company, same as always. She liked the phone-in programmes best, especially when there were arguments. She wanted to know what was happening in the outside world. In here, it was all about soap operas and quiz shows on the television, and how long it was until the next meal.

Nothing that mattered.

She got undressed, pulled on her nightdress then dug out the postcard from the back of her underwear drawer. It had arrived nearly three weeks before. A sea view, a Pwllheli postmark. She had guessed there was no point handing it over to the police, knew very well that he would be long gone by now. A couple of coppers had called at the home, right after that business on the island, neither of them as friendly as that woman who'd been to see her just before it happened. They obviously thought there was a chance he might turn up to pay his old mum a visit. She'd set them straight, told them there was no chance, that they were wasting their time.

Not such a stupid idea, as it turned out.

She sat on the edge of the bed, turned the card over and read it again.

see you soon
  s X

She put the card back and took out the ball of clingfilm in which she'd hidden the tablets. It had been easy enough to get them: wandering into some of the other rooms at mealtimes or when there were visitors; opening bottles or slipping a blister pack into the pocket of her dressing gown. Taking the odd few here and there until she had more than enough.

She plumped up her pillows and climbed into bed.

She unwrapped the clingfilm and laid out the contents on the duvet.

All sorts of shapes and colours.

On the radio, someone was saying something about the government. She didn't really care, but his voice was nice enough and that was the main thing.

She listened for another minute or two, then said, 'Not if I see you first,' and reached for the glass of water.

FIFTY-NINE

While Thorne had made wholly reasonable assumptions about his means of escape, Nicklin had actually still been on Bardsey Island many hours after the last police officer and paramedic had left.

He met up with the 'birdwatcher' when the man came down the mountain to the pre-arranged rendezvous point. Only then did Nicklin reveal that he himself would not be going with them. That the boat was to come back for him much later on and that the birdwatcher would be the one to make the all-important phone call once they had reached the mainland.

Nicklin knew that Thorne would do as he was told, but he was less certain about Holland, or that other one they had left in the chapel. He could not afford to take the risk that the boat might be intercepted. Besides which, he would enjoy being right under their noses the whole time they were running around the island like headless chickens.

He watched the boat disappear into the darkness, then clambered back up to the plain and walked towards the abbey ruins, heading for the huge Celtic cross that marked the tomb of Lord Newborough. He climbed over the low, walled enclosure and lifted the small grating all but obscured by the long grass. The entrance to a hiding place he had discovered twenty-five years before. Over preceding decades, local children had loosened the grating and though the family had sealed off the vault itself, there was still space enough at the bottom of the steps where someone unconcerned about comfort could stay hidden.

He had spent long hours back then, sitting in the cold, stone box. Snug and quiet, eight or ten feet below the gravestones, the space not quite big enough to stand upright in.

There had been several occasions, all those years ago, when Ruth and her cohorts had convinced themselves that he had somehow managed to get off the island. They had alerted the police, only for Nicklin to stroll casually back in the following day. He could not be certain, but he liked to imagine that when he did finally escape – the same night he had killed Simon Milner and the old woman – they had thought he was just playing silly buggers again and had not bothered telling the police until it was far too late.

Until it had become clear that they were the silly buggers.

The night he left Thorne cuffed to the bed, Nicklin did

exactly as he had done so often back then, when he had been a 'guest' at Tides House. He lifted the grating, squeezed into the entrance and pulled the grille back into place. Once he had descended the half-dozen steps to the level of the vault, he settled happily into the hole.

He worked his way very slowly through his remaining bars of chocolate.

He listened to the activity above him.

He heard the helicopters come and go, ferrying in police officers, taking away the bodies of Fletcher and Jenks. He heard the swoop and buzz of aircraft on the far side of the mountain and presumed they were searching for Batchelor's body. It was not until he was back on the mainland that he knew for certain they had found it.

He waited the best part of three days, before emerging from his hiding place in the early hours of the morning, scrambling down to the water and meeting the boat. By that time, a scrap of crime scene tape fluttering from a fence post was the only hint that anything out of the ordinary had ever taken place on the island.

Three weeks on, Stuart Nicklin looked very different from the man who had climbed from the earth beneath a Celtic cross, stretching as though he'd had no more than an iffy night's sleep.

He very much doubted that even his own mother would recognise him.

Not that she would get the chance, of course. He had only sent that card to make her think that it was a possibility, but he had no intention of going to see her, of spending so much as a moment in a place that stank of piss and death and broken biscuits.

Now, it was time to get out and enjoy himself a little.

He got up and walked across the lounge. A week into December and there was tinsel wherever he looked and a plastic Santa on the wall above the bar area. He mixed himself a strong Bloody Mary and helped himself to a couple of bags of crisps.

He was genuinely pleased to see that Tom Thorne seemed to be doing all right. Last thing he would have wanted was for Thorne to lose his job, anything like that. From what Nicklin had seen, the detective inspector seemed pretty much back to his old self.

It looked like there was not even going to be a scar on his lip . . .

It was fine, because he knew very well that what happened on Bardsey had marked Thorne on the *inside*, which was far more important. That, and the enduring image of Thorne handcuffed and helpless had got Nicklin off a time or two, his hands busy beneath nice clean hotel sheets.

He checked the departures board and saw that he was being told to go to the gate. He knew there was plenty of time yet, so he settled back down with his drink. He smiled at one of his fellow travellers gathering up carry-on luggage and bags of duty-free. The man smiled right back. Everyone looked excited about escaping the pre-Christmas chaos for some much-needed winter sunshine.

He sat back and flicked through a travel magazine.

Two weeks on an almost deserted island.

The irony was not lost on him, of course, though he was hoping for rather better weather.

SIXTY

It had been late morning on the day after Stuart Nicklin's escape, and Thorne was in the A&E department of Bryn Beryl Hospital in Pwllheli, having his wounds treated by a red-headed nurse named Olga, when the call finally came through to him. This was several hours after they had traced the signal from Phil Hendricks' mobile phone, which had been turned back on an hour or so before that. Forty-five minutes since armed officers had raided a basement flat in Catford, south-east London.

'Tom?'

There had been tears from both of them and words choked back. Thorne, struggling to speak anyway, his lip badly swollen and only partially stitched back together.

'Phil . . .'

'You sound funny.'

Later, Thorne would not be able to recall clearly what else had been said. They had spoken one another's name, something about Thorne's voice, and after that it was all a bit of a blur.

'Probably the painkillers,' Helen had said.

'I suppose.'

Now there were more tears, from Helen on this occasion, as the three of them sat and ate together for the first time since it had happened.

'Don't you start,' Hendricks said.

'Shut your face.' Helen got up and began gathering the remains of the takeaway from the Bengal Lancer. Hendricks had said that while he was being held captive this was the thing he had been looking forward to the most.

'I was exaggerating, obviously,' he said later. 'Just thinking that, you know, if it made the papers, we might start getting a few free poppadoms thrown in.'

Though Thorne was still spending most of his time at Helen's place in Tulse Hill, they had decided to get together at Thorne's in Kentish Town. It was around the corner from the restaurant but, more importantly, Hendricks did not yet feel too comfortable venturing far from his own flat, which was only five minutes away, on the edge of Camden.

This was the first time he had left home other than for hospital appointments, of which there had been many.

'I spend most of the time just standing in the kitchen,' he had said, while they were still eating. 'Going over what happened that night they snatched me. Re-imagining it, you know? This time, I manage to get to the knives and I stab the pair of them. I stab them *lots*.'

Helen returned from the kitchen with cans of beer. They were opened and slowly drunk from to cover a sudden, awkward silence.

'No more from Dawson then?' Hendricks asked.

Thorne shook his head. 'Yvonne Kitson called earlier. I'm not sure there's any more to get.'

Hendricks emptied his can. 'Give me five minutes with him.'

The man Hendricks had known as 'Adrian' was actually Damien Dawson, a twenty-seven-year-old telesales operative from Essex. His fingerprints had been all over the flat in which Hendricks had been held and were on record, following a caution eighteen months earlier for stalking an actress who had spoken one line in an episode of *Doctor Who*. Since his arrest, he had told officers from the Kidnap Unit that he had been recruited via an internet chatroom by the female half of the couple he had met later on. He remained adamant that he did not know anybody else's name or how any of them had come to be involved.

Thorne guessed that this was the same couple who had been spotted in and around Aberdaron. Casually walking the streets hand in hand, in the hours leading up to the murder of Huw Morgan and the assault on his father, who was discovered trussed up, battered and bleeding, a few feet away from his son's body. The pair who had later taken the boat across to collect Nicklin and the mysterious 'birdwatcher' from Bardsey.

Mysterious, until Thorne had remembered why the face of the man in the red woolly hat had been so familiar. A face that, unlike his mentor's, had not changed a great deal in twenty-five years.

A creased and faded photograph. The figure standing on the other side of Stuart Nicklin from Simon Milner.

A boy with shaved head and dark eyes.

Having done some digging, Thorne discovered that Ryan Gough had never been charged with the attempted murder of Kevin Hunter at Tides House. With no witnesses willing to make any sort of statement, the case against the boy had never quite stacked up. Thorne had no idea what Gough had been doing with himself in the intervening years, but he had the horrible suspicion that Fletcher and Jenks were not the first people he had killed on Stuart Nicklin's say-so.

As things stood, he could not be certain they would be the last.

'They'll keep working on him,' Thorne said. 'Dawson.'

'He came into the bedroom again,' Hendricks said. 'Not long before he left. Waving a kitchen knife around and talking shit about what he was capable of doing with it and I really thought he was going to do something bad. Something worse, you know?'

'Don't think about it,' Helen said.

'When you get that scared, you realise that you'd do anything, say anything.'

'Nothing wrong with being scared,' Thorne said.

Hendricks looked from Thorne to Helen and back, tried to drink from a can that was already empty.

'You should come with me,' Thorne said, changing tack.

'Where?'

'Back to Bardsey.'

Two weeks from now, for the funeral of Huw Morgan. It was, Thorne had decided, the least he could do for Bernard, who had lost his only son in such terrible circumstances. That was worth putting up with the five hour drive, another night in the Black Horse, dosing himself up on seasickness pills for the crossing.

'Why?'

'Just a thought.'

'What, like some sort of therapy?' Hendricks smiled, but he didn't look very amused. 'Taking me to where it all happened, so I can deal with the trauma a bit better?'

'Never occurred to me,' Thorne said.

In truth, it hadn't, at least not as far as Hendricks was concerned. Thorne had wondered though if he might do himself some good, going back to the island while things were still fresh, raw.

Laying a few ghosts to rest, sooner, rather than later.

'I just thought you might like it, that's all. Birds and seals . . . stars, all that.'

'We'll see,' Hendricks said. 'Hospital appointments, you know.'

Helen got up to fetch Hendricks another beer and Thorne said that he would have another one, if she was going. While she was gone, they talked about the latest round of treatment on Hendricks' back. Skin grafts were notoriously tricky and the process would be a laborious one, but Thorne knew it was going to take his friend far longer to recover emotionally.

He also knew that the same went for him.

Sitting there at the table, picking at a piece of leftover bread, Thorne was suddenly struck by a memory of hearing Nicklin snoring, that final night on Bardsey. The irritating wheeze, just before Fletcher and Jenks had turned up and announced they were taking Batchelor outside. Having set everything up, knowing what had already been done and what was about to happen, Nicklin had actually slept.

When Helen came back with three more cans of beer, Thorne said, 'Shall we go and get this done then?'

They carried their drinks out into the small back garden, where Thorne emptied the contents of a plastic bag into a metal rubbish bin. Helen handed him the grimy bottle of lighter fluid that had been gathering dust behind the barbecue since an abortive attempt to use it the previous summer.

Thorne looked at Hendricks. 'You want to do the honours?'

'No, you go ahead, mate.'

'You sure?'

Thorne laid a hand on Hendricks' arm, caught Helen's eye. He was careful to stay well away from the shoulders, the bulge of bandage between them all too obvious beneath his friend's shirt. His apology was implicit in the gesture, likewise its acceptance in the nod from Hendricks.

Things had not gone quite as smoothly between them in those first few days. There had been a good deal of anger, of accusation. If the blame was somewhat irrational, Thorne could certainly understand where the anger was coming from.

He had told Holland and everyone else the story that Nicklin had suggested. He had said that his primary concern that night had been to save Phil Hendricks' life, that the danger to it was obvious to him and that the decisions taken had been made with that foremost in his mind.

He had not told them that he was sent to fetch that package from the abbey *after* he had learned that Alan Jenks was still alive. That he had looked down at that piece of skin and taken a decision while Jenks was bleeding to death in the garden below.

He had not told them that he had made a choice.

Again . . .

Thorne had looked up at Stuart Nicklin that night and demanded to be punched a second time, not because it would make his story any more convincing, but because he wanted it.

Because he deserved it.

'Can we hurry this up?' Hendricks asked. 'I'm freezing my tits off out here and I don't want to lose them an' all.'

It had been a week or more before Thorne had seen Phil smile, or heard that irritating, whiny laugh. Without knowing what might still be medically possible so long after the fact, Thorne had held on to the piece of Hendricks' skin. Once it became clear that nothing useful could be done with it, he had given it back to Hendricks, who had promptly announced that he would be taking it to the tattoo parlour to get the design replicated, as soon as there was new skin to work on.

Hendricks had stared down at his own ruined flesh and shaken his head. Said, 'Jesus, I always knew that being your friend was a pain in the arse, but this is ridiculous ...'

Thorne stepped forward and squirted the fluid across the mound of paper in the dustbin, scattered sheets and torn envelopes, watching the crazed handwriting blur and bleed as it was soaked. A few words catching his eye as he squeezed the bottle dry.

the MAD professor
  the things MARTIN and I did
DEFECTIVE inspector TOM THORNE

Helen handed him a large box of safety matches. It took several attempts before he got one to stay lit, but the papers caught quickly enough. They stood back, eyes narrowed against the smoke. Hendricks said 'good riddance,' and the three of them raised their bottles and watched the letters burn, scraps curling and rising slowly up through the sparks like charred butterflies.

ACKNOWLEDGEMENTS

As always, I am enormously grateful for the efforts of everyone at Little, Brown, particularly my wonderful editor David Shelley and his team. I am hugely lucky in continuing to work with Robert Manser, Tamsin Kitson, Emma Williams, Jo Wickham, Sean Garrehy and Thalia Proctor. Long may my luck hold. At Grove Atlantic in the US, Morgan Entrekin, Peter Blackstock and Deb Seager have provided much-appreciated shots of faith and enthusiasm in the books, for which I am hugely thankful.

I am deeply indebted to Colin and Ernest Evans for their immeasurable patience, advice and input, and for getting me there. There would be no book without them. I hope you're happy with how I portrayed your island . . .

Diolch o'r galon.

For help with the forensic anthropology in the book, thanks are due (along with many, many drinks) to Professor Sue Black, Director of the Centre for Anatomy and Human Identification at the University of Dundee and Professor Lorna Dawson, Principal Soil Scientist in the Environmental and Biochemical Sciences Group at the James Hutton Institute. Their generosity and expertise is matched only by a seemingly limitless capacity for answering stupid questions.

www.hutton.ac.uk

www.millionforamorgue.com

Louise Butler was helpful on matters of prison procedure (thanks, Lou), the words of Wendy Lee and Tony Fuller were wise as always and I could wish for no more sympathetic and eagle-eyed a copy editor than Deborah Adams. Sarah Lutyens rocks, and remains the agent that every author dreams about having. I am thankful every day that she's mine.

And thank you Claire, above all. For taking me to Bardsey Island and for thinking that it might be an interesting place to take Tom Thorne.

AUTHOR NOTE

Bardsey Island (Ynys Enlli) lies just two miles beyond the tip of the Lleyn peninsula. It is 1.5 miles long and just over half a mile wide. The mountain, Mynydd Enlli, rises to 167 metres. Whether the remains of King Arthur or of those twenty thousand saints are buried there or not, it is every bit as unique and magical a place as Tom Thorne comes to realise by the end of *The Bones Beneath*. Though I may have taken the occasional liberty with geography in service of the story, I have tried my utmost to capture the stark beauty and atmosphere of the island and can only hope that the curiosity of some readers has been piqued by the facts about its history, mythology and scientific significance that are scattered throughout the novel.

For anyone interested in visiting Bardsey Island, there is no better place to start than here: **www.bardsey.org/english/bardsey/welcome.asp**. This site gives details of the trust that administers the island as well as information about its arts, archaeology and natural history. It also provides prospective visitors with everything they need in terms of how to book day trips or longer visits, with pictures of all the available accommodation. I can assure anyone thinking of visiting that the journey is exhilarating, the hotels on the mainland are fantastic and that the cottages available for rent are not as spooky as the one Tom Thorne is forced to spend the night in.

www.bardsey.org/english/staying/staying_bardsey.htm

Bardsey is a National Nature Reserve and a Site of Special Scientific Interest. Further details can be found here:

www.bardsey.org/english/the_island/natural_history.htm

Those specifically interested in the island's birds can get detailed day-by-day reports from the Bird and Field Observatory, with wonderful pictures and up-to-date information about more than 175 species, here: **https://bbfo.blogspot.co.uk**.

The last King of Bardsey, Love Pritchard, died in 1926, and was buried close to the beach in Aberdaron cemetery. Find out all about him, the kings who ruled before him, and what became of the legendary crown of Bardsey here: **www.bardsey.org/english/the_island/king.htm**

Bardsey Lighthouse was built in 1821, stands a little over thirty metres high and, unlike almost all other Trinity lighthouses, is square. The top of it is also the only place on the island I was able to get so much as a glimmer of a phone signal, and I dislike heights as much as Tom Thorne.

www.trinityhouse.co.uk/lighthouses/lighthouse_list/bardsey.html

Bardsey's religious significance, its history as a place of pilgrimage and the story of those twenty thousand saints are detailed here: **www.bardsey.org/english/the_island/pilgrims.htm**

A remote and all-but-deserted island, cut off from the mainland with *no mobile phone signal* is, of course, a wonderful place to set a crime novel. In reality, however, I cannot remember spending time anywhere as peaceful as Ynys Enlli. Though not a religious person myself, I can fully understand its status as a place of pilgrimage and can see why it is so beloved of artists, writers and natural historians. If even one reader who has enjoyed *The Bones Beneath* is tempted to visit Bardsey Island – to hear the Manx shearwater at night, to watch the sun set behind those spectacular abbey ruins, to escape the stress of modern city living for a few days or simply to search for the place where Stuart Nicklin buried those bodies – then I shall be a very happy author.

Mark Billingham, London, 2013

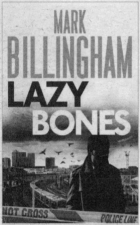

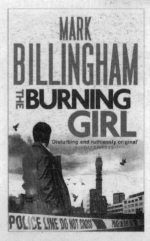

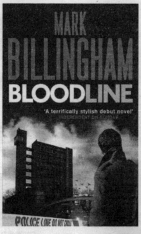

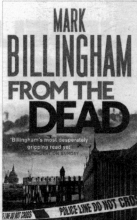